JOHN W. CAMPBELL AWARD-WINNING AUTHOR

R.A. M^{AC}AVOY
AND NANCY L. PALMER

SHIMMER

SEQUEL TO ALBATROSS

MW00810423

SHIMMER
Copyright © 2018 by R.A. MacAvoy and Nancy L. Palmer

All rights reserved. No part of this book may be reproduced or transmitted in any form or by any electronic or mechanical means, including photocopying, recording or by any information storage and retrieval system, without the express written permission of the copyright holder, except where permitted by law. This novel is a work of fiction. Names, characters, places and incidents are either the product of the author's imagination, or, if real, used fictitiously.

ISBN: 978-1-61475-556-2
Cover design by Janet McDonald
Kevin J. Anderson, Art Director
Cover artwork images by Adobe Stock
Edited by Awnna Marie Evans
Published by
WordFire Press, an imprint of
WordFire, LLC
PO Box 1840
Monument CO 80132
Kevin J. Anderson & Rebecca Moesta, Publishers
WordFire Press Hardcover and Trade Paperback Edition 2018
Printed in the USA
Join our WordFire Press Readers Group and get free books, sneak previews, updates on new projects, and other giveaways.
Sign up for free at wordfirepress.com.

❀ Created with Vellum

For Teachers and Librarians everywhere

1

Immigrant

The last thing Dr. Rob MacAulay saw before they closed the doors into the secure room at the airport was Thomas's face, with his brown eyes narrowed and his face as closed as the locked door.

It wasn't that they hadn't expected this: a pitch to take US asylum. But he had hoped for something that would begin in a more original fashion. Less boilerplate. During the years of his life, Rob had often been considered odd, but rarely stupid. Yet here was the dreary room and the dreary man attempting to seem both stern and compassionate. And doing neither so well.

"Dr. MacAulay, welcome to the United States," he said. He wore some sort of military uniform Rob did not recognize. "I'm Colonel Emmett Landers of the NSA-RC." He would have been a tall, imposing fellow had not Rob been taller than most men already, and tired of being imposed upon.

"And if you don't know the lingo, that's the Refugee Committee of the ..."

"I do know what it is, Colonel Landers," he said. "And I thank you for your welcome. However, as I am not entering the country as a refugee, I am not certain why I stand before you."

For a moment Rob was not certain whether the colonel had understood him. He knew his intonation took some getting used to, but he had been careful to be clear. Rob leaned over the desk to get nearer to the fellow, but although Rob MacAulay had come in determined to behave himself, the man retreated a few inches. So then did Rob, to be polite.

Colonel Landers replied "I know you aren't, Doctor. Not *officially* a refugee."

"Not a refugee in any sense. By my visa, I'm simply ..."

But Landers continued the procedure of two men cutting each other off. Rob thought he himself had probably started it, and now it could become an added irritation to what was bound to be irritating already.

"You enter as the husband of the man who until a few weeks ago held you against your will for some time in Scotland. I'm here to tell you there are other ways open for you to enter the United States."

The room held a desk and two chairs. The desk was closer, and Rob settled himself onto a corner of it. He took a deep breath, which exited as a sort of whistle out his nostrils. "Thomas is the man I married. Completely by my own choosing. And he is also the man who saved my life. If you know anything about my recent history, Colonel Landers, you know this."

Landers gave a sort of smile. He had begun the interview standing, and still did not sit down, so in that position they were able to look at one another eye to eye. "All I know is what I read in the newspapers, Dr. MacAulay. But I believe the United States could be of some use to you."

Here it came. There was going to be some form of dangling hook; Thomas had warned him so. "And I hope to be of some use to the United States, also. I am an experienced teacher of both Mathematics and Physics. That is, assuming I get a work permit. But now I would like to leave this room."

"We can offer you a work permit. In fact, we can offer you work. With the government. After your experience in Britain ..."

Once again Rob cut him off. It seemed it was going to be necessary. "Am I being held here—in this room—against my will right now?"

His voice, which tended to float high when under stress, was now bouncing off the windows, where frozen rain was already pattering.

"Of course not, Dr. MacAulay. Last thing we'd want to do."

As Rob was finally able to open the door, Colonel Landers held out a card to him. Rob ignored it. He strode out the door, found himself in a jumble of people going in every direction, and looked for Thomas.

"So. Was I the bad guy?" Thomas's voice was neutral and his face as still as stone. By this, Rob knew how deeply angry he was.

"Yes. That was implied. And more."

They marched together, like primitive warriors, out the doors to the cab station. "Tell me," said Thomas.

Rob considered. He looked at the huge New York airport that spread on each side of them and he sighed. "I'm not so good as you are at reading hidden messages, Thomas. Nor at faces. Nor at keeping my—my temper."

At this Thomas's stone face cracked into a grin. "You raised your voice at the man?"

"Believe I rattled the windows. Though the weather helped me there."

Thomas almost grinned, for the weather so often seemed to help Rob MacAulay. As had the natural world of the High-lands, Scotland. It was hard for him to think of Rob in a city.

Thomas found a shuttle to the car rentals and hit his fist

against the door, which had been closing. They entered the driverless van. "Can you simply tell me? I don't want to wait for the recording in your jacket. Tell me every word."

Rob did. It had not been so long a conversation.

"That's not so bad," said Thomas. "No threats, at least."

Rob shrugged. "I have no one they could threaten. And what sort of threat could they use on me? On *me?*" He laughed at the idea. "And as you are the bad guy, Landers didn't think to try that approach."

Rob MacAulay now knew how to measure that tension behind Thomas's stillness. It was a sort of heat. As the drone shuttle moved forward, he tried to cool Thomas down. "You have always said in moving to the US we were going from the frying pan to the fire. I don't think it's been so bad as all that."

"No. Considering."

"Considering what, exactly?"

They trundled on. Thomas sighed. "Considering Russia. And China."

Rob scratched his head. Fiddled his fingers in his lap. He would have put an arm around Thomas, except they both would have found that awkward in public. "At least it's not the situation in Britain," he said with an attempt at brightness.

"Rob, I hereby welcome you to a place where the situation in Britain is not of major consequence."

They curled from one row of airline stop-offs to another, and the movement pressed Rob into Thomas's side. He was looking down into the crown of waving silver hair. Thomas was still radiating heat, and he said to Rob, "Remember, we still have a few weeks to kill before the lease on the Sullivan house is expired. I ought to introduce you to my home country."

"I have been here already, you know. To at least seven major cities."

Thomas turned, his tension was gone, and his face was alive again. "Not cities. I mean the country! There are things in North America you will not believe. I still don't believe them. Beauty.

"Besides, it will keep us in the public eye."

Rob groaned. "Not that again."

But it was just that. Visibility. Thomas's idea of visibility was to stay in front of cameras while they ignored all the various attempts at an interview. Thomas was good at this sort of procession. Rob just followed him like a dog.

He had never before gone so far, so fast, in his life. Starting westward along the northern border in one of the few bullet trains in this huge country, Thomas chose their path out of his oldest, favorite memories, and to Rob it was as though he were dropped into a childhood of adventure stories. Ancient forests, wild animals, and mountain piled upon mountain. Huge lake after lake.

If only they didn't have to move so fast, it would have been heaven.

Under the bare-branched and piney shores of the Great Lakes he could imagine Hawkeye in some sort of birch-bark canoe. Thomas told him of the enormous color-scape he had missed by a few months. Thomas unfolded the virtual projection leaves of his tablet, and showed him images of the different maples in autumn, the golden oaks, the fields of squash and maize. Rob was content with the architecture of the branches against the sky.

Recently, although not in their lifetimes, the eastern lakes had been known to freeze over, so that a man might walk from the US to Canada. He looked out at the plunging water, so much like a sea, and wondered how it would feel to step over such a stretch of ice. They would have been like the humans who had marched east over the Bering Straits so long ago, except going the other way.

Thomas's enthusiasm about the geography often veered into his outrage concerning what he felt over the sins of his countrymen. The hatred of immigrants and the generations of poverty resultant from the American practice of importing people as so much product. In that outrage he sounded much like Rob's deceased wife, Janet. It seemed best not to mention that now. Rob understood the outrage, but he'd begun to feel the freedom that came with distance from a tragedy. The freedom of being a foreigner.

They passed through the prairies and into the Great Plains, where Rob had the amazing fortune to witness herds of bison standing with their heads against the wind. He was surprised how close the animals would let him get to them. He locked his fingers into the tangled hair between the black horns of one. He was surprised at its gentleness.

So was Thomas. Most surprised. He suggested Rob extricate himself. With great difficulty, he seemed to be restraining himself from saying more.

When he touched the bison, Rob felt no fear, for he hadn't known he was supposed to feel fear. But he suddenly understood why they were built as they were, with the front ends so heavy: their faces lost in all that fur. Cattle, back in Scotland, turned their hind ends to the wind. One species chose avoidance of the wind, and one chose confrontation. That was most interesting, and he discussed it with Thomas, who requested he observe at a distance.

The sky was unimaginably huge above them, and clouds were flung east as such speed it was as if the sky itself was coughing them up. One animal Thomas told him was a wolf began to follow them, but not in any predatory way. Again, Thomas remarked on the change from just a few years ago, when wolves avoided humans like the plague. Again, he suggested Rob's behavior was inappropriate for the wolf's sake, so Rob put his hands in his pockets. The animal still followed them.

Thomas lectured on about all the natural history, but also about the unending oppression of the Native Americans. Rob heard a great deal about the genocide of the Native Americans.

They took a different train through the passes of the mountains. The clouds were a solid sheet below them, and in an odd way it was like being back in the Hebrides, except that during the stops of the train, he dared not put his feet into any pools of grey "water" lest he plunge to his death, and also the height had him feeling swimmy and his ears popped repeatedly. His nose bled. So did Thomas's. They laughed about it together, and then the train plunged down toward the Pacific.

Sequoias. Redwood forests, their needles soft as butter in his fingers. The Pacific Ocean, so clean and wild. And cold. So cold. Mendocino. Santa Barbara. The Pacific Coast was a lovely, magical thing. The shore was rockier than that of the Hebrides. And the water was so cold, even in Santa Barbara, where there were palm trees.

Thomas rented a car and turned them eastward to what he called "The Big Rez" and "Four Corners." In the middle of winter, the desert was not hot, as Rob had expected, but it was beautiful beyond belief, and all seemed to be sky. Eagles, common as ravens at home, dived over them, screaming. Thomas said nothing here about inappropriate behavior, and Rob tried hard to ignore the eagles.

In an astonishment called Monument Valley, Thomas began to talk about the vicissitudes of the Diné people. Rob had rehearsed his response to this latest lecture.

"Thomas," he began gently, as they sat in a rented car, "As I speak for the latest group of oppressed people whom you have saved, might I ask you to put a lid on it?"

And Thomas did. To Rob's great surprise, Thomas didn't mention oppressed people again. It was a great relief.

Now, as they approached the east again, they began to give interviews. Thomas actually sought out interviews, particularly with small television and radio stations, where Rob spoke with great enthusiasm of the beautiful country he was seeing. How he had spent his life travelling from one University forum to another and had never before seen the country. He avoided all discussions of politics, even when the interviews were being done with Thomas and him together. He also found himself being asked about sexual matters, of all things. In Scotland that simply would not have happened. He needed instructions from Thomas on how to avoid such talk. If any behavior was inappropriate, this was.

But he was now quite familiar with the idea of becoming publicly recognized—and if he could manage it, publicly liked —because he was aware that Thomas encouraged it so that it would be hard for any one or any group to make them simply disappear. In Scotland that method had worked a treat.

Thomas was just being Thomas.

At the end of this long journey—this "honeymoon"—they had one last follow-up interview with Yvonne at Rolling Stone. This was done online and with no photos. Rob spoke entirely of the beauties he had seen in the United States. Thomas forwarded a snapshot from his own phone of Rob, dressed in no particular outfit, but with the neck entirely exposed.

The lease on Thomas's house had now expired and they were ready to move in. To go to Thomas's home. In a certain way, a new form of life was beginning for both men.

2

The Red Cardinal

Outside the huge French doors was a blanket of new snow, dropped last night onto the previous layer of white. The insulation of those sheets of triple glass was so fine that nothing streaked the glass to show the difference in temperature between the -2 degrees Celsius and the inner hall of the Sullivan house. The hand-knotted Persian rugs had been rolled up and Thomas had taken possession of his Aunt Grace's legacy in his usual manner: turning the ornate ballroom into a practice room. Elegant wood was covered over by interlocking foam blocks—all grey.

"What are you looking at, Rob? The snow again?"

Rob shook his head. "That's still a sight, but the bird there is impossible. Simply impossible. Nothing could be so red. All over. And bold as brass, looking straight at me."

"Must be a cardinal," answered Thomas. "Yep. It is. Nothing special at all."

He spoke with a swaggering pride, as a prince of some old country might describe the ruins of his ancestor's elegant castle: just a cardinal. A splotch of impossible red on impossible white.

Nothing special.

The red bird sat in the branches of the old Japanese maple, planted only eight meters from the doors. It opened its heavy amber bill, outlined by black, snapped its tail, and sassed at them, claiming the bird feeder Thomas had bought only this weekend and hung from the branches of the bare tree.

Rob MacAulay allowed Thomas his moment of arrogance, claiming the bird as his heritage, just as he had a few days ago claimed the layers of brilliant snow. Nothing special, indeed. "I'm still waiting to see the blue ones," he told Thomas.

"Blue Jays. I got you the book. Put them together with the cardinal and the snow and you have our traditional Christmas card."

They stood up. Rob found his left shoulder was twitching from effort, and, of course, Thomas noticed. He began his Chinese muscle work on the spot, which was curative, but which hurt sometimes. Like now. Rob slipped off-balance on his left knee and then his right, sinking down onto the foam flooring. Before he could fall entirely, Thomas stopped him and slapped him soundly along one side. "Come on, Rob. No field collapse until the push-ups are done."

Rob didn't mind being bullied by Thomas in play. Or rather, he didn't mind often. And it was a fine thing to see Thomas so simply happy, after all the tension of the autumn. Journalists, slavery, one bathroom to share.

Tension.

Rob took a deep breath and settled down onto this three-finger push-up position. He sank down into the proper stance —which he could never have accomplished a few months ago —and began to do his proper, authorized push-ups. Thomas, beside him, did push-ups with him—one-handed push-ups, so he could turn and look at Rob as he worked.

"So." Rob was panting.

"We're going to be all goofy again, aren't we, my ..." He stopped and didn't finish his sentence.

That was one remaining awkwardness between them. What were they to call one another? Neither man liked the idea of being two husbands. Rob, because it seemed so terribly unbalanced a wording, and Thomas—well, because he was Thomas. It occurred to Rob that what they were was simply a binary system, revolving about one another. Perhaps the center of mass was not even or constant, but what did that matter? Such objects were always eccentric.

The dull grey rings they wore on their left hands seemed enough of a symbol for Thomas. The astronomy didn't interest him. He didn't like any words of description, when human feelings were concerned.

Rob, however, wanted to be exact in the matter of language.

He was at the bottom of one careful push-up when Thomas called, "Stop. Right there."

Rob did, his nose barely touching the grey foam. He still found the position difficult to maintain.

"You look," said Thomas, "just like a grasshopper. Only backwards."

"I used to be a cockroach, if I remember correctly, Thomas."

"Grasshopper!"

Thomas bounded to his feet. "And when I was a kid, we used to pick up grasshoppers. This way." He swooped down over the taller man and grabbed him around the elbows, locking his arms in position. He thrust his own head and shoulders under Rob's extended bent arms, and plucked him off the mat, swinging Rob over his head as he rose. Rob was upside down, head to the ground and legs waving.

"Don't drop me. I've broken my head too often!" Rob felt his stocking feet touch the arched ceiling, which had seemed so high above.

"I won't drop you. Promise. Just arch over. See if you can lift me in turn. I've seen a couple guys perform this down a whole room!"

His enthusiasm was contagious, and Rob did try, but his back was long and not as strong as Thomas's, so they came down in a heap: a heap with Rob on the bottom. He wasn't hurt, for Thomas's own back *was* strong. Still Rob was flattened, ignominiously.

Thomas was full of yelping laughter, his face, for once, as red as Rob's. "It was never a matter of strength, my odd bird. It's balance, and so you *must* be destined to get it, and then we'll be able to spin each other down the room like so many Chinese …"

"Thomas!" Rob called in a different sort of voice. His head was pressed sideways, looking out the French doors again.

The red cardinal had turned into a girl in a red puffy coat with pointed hood. Around her amber face was a black smudge of hair leaking out of her coat-hood. She was staring at them in alarm, standing close outside the doors. She turned and ran, leaving a dim blue wake though the virgin snow. Thomas lifted off him in one movement.

"Who was that?" he asked Thomas, who was blank-faced. All the wild goofiness had fled. As instantaneous a reaction as two entangled electrons, thought Rob MacAulay.

"Little Red Riding Hood, I think," replied Thomas, but coldly.

━━━

IT HAD BEEN ONLY six days since they had come to rest in the house that had once belonged to Thomas's old Aunt Grace Sullivan. She had left it to Thomas, along with an amount of money that to Rob—who had long lived on an academic's salary and had thought himself fortunate—was breathtaking. Thomas had used that legacy as his foundation toward University education at various good technical schools in England. It had also been his start at the crapshoot he called day trading in New York stock markets. It had been an enormous surprise to Rob, finding he was linked to a man with so much money. It had been—it still was—embarrassing. Since Thomas had taken on Rob as a man without a name, let alone money or clothing, this financial difference ought not to matter. Not to matter to either of them. Not after the oddities of human bondage and bullets shooting.

Yet it did make for one more awkwardness. And now this.

He had looked around him at the beautiful brick house on the even more beautiful old twenty acres, walled in like something which, in Scotland, would likely have been willed to the country a few generations ago, and tried not to feel like a Jane Austen heroine.

It was obvious that, to Thomas, the wealth of the place had no meaning. The memory of Aunt Grace, however, was something powerful. And now something new seemed to be attacking that memory. And it was only a little child in a red coat. Running.

THOMAS DRESSED himself in his long coat and boots, and grabbed an old watch cap from the row of hooks by the mudroom door. He was aware of Rob dressing himself behind him and wished, for one guilty moment, that he still had the authority to tell him to stay behind. He was aware that following the girl's tracks through the snow was not what Rob would have done. He felt he was behaving like a heel. That he was behaving like a Rich Man and that the man he had married would see it as such. But he was unhappy about the invasion of the Sullivan grounds.

He had come back home as a goddamn celebrity, with an

even more famous man beside him. All they had to make a private place for themselves were these twenty acres. No drones, no public cameras. Just a house built well and solidly at the end of the nineteenth century, and enough land around it to make it seem still rural. And they had possessed it for all of six days before the goddamn intrusion.

He heard the snow crunch around his feet and analyzed the temperature as just a few degrees under zero. No—reset to home—under thirty-two. It wasn't that cold. The white frosting on every bare tree branch told him the same. If it were really cold, the snow wouldn't cling. That girl hadn't been able to lift her feet over the snow, so he might as well have been following a straight line through the clean snow-pack. Behind him he could hear Rob, walking in Thomas's own footsteps, lifting his feet high and putting them down.

"I'm not planning on shouting at the kid, Rob," he called over his shoulder. "I just have to know where they've made a breach."

Oh, even that sounded like a nasty man talking. He would have to explain when this was done.

She had come from the direction of the old pine tree. Old Grace had loved that knobby thing. So had Maria—though Thomas scarcely remembered Grace's long partner, Maria, and when she had died he was too young to have known what the woman meant to his aunt.

As he recalled, there had been talk of a housing develop-ment being built next to the Sullivan property. It was only about eight years ago that he'd heard about it. Thomas now was forced to believe that the houses had been built. That cardinal of a child probably hadn't come many miles through the snow in the early morning specifically to spy on them. It didn't matter, now, why she had come.

So what on earth did she think she had seen, to make her run like that? All sorts of bad images tried to fill Thomas's head.

TONY KAYE WAS TRYING to explain things to the neighbor-hood guards, knowing she could only get herself in trouble. Just because she had used a tree like a ladder to climb over the brick wall to the private park for most of her life, and all of the kids in the complex did so, didn't mean it was legal. And Mom would be really upset with her about this. Dad, too. Maybe Dad.

But she had seen a man attacked. So undeniably attacked: thrown to the ceiling and then pinned down again. His face had been looking at hers even as she turned to run.

Maybe he was dead. He had been looking at her and maybe he was now dead. Being in trouble with Mom was nothing. Nothing.

"And again, Miss Kaye, how did you see this?"

This was stupid. Emerson, the older guard, already knew about the tree and the kids climbing it to the private park. Everyone did. The corporations so rarely occupied the mansion, the place was almost like an extension of the gated community. Like houses built next to a state forest, or some-thing, only smaller. No one ever cared until now. "I climbed over at the turn-around, where the tree has branches that go straight up. If you're not too big, you climb it and down the one on the other side. Only that one doesn't go so far down so you—oh, please, Emerson. I think the man might be dying!"

Balderas, the younger guard, put his mitted hand on Tony's shoulder. It made a crunching sound, with the snow still on the mitt. "We don't have authority to go in there, Tony. We're not police."

"Call them!" She found she was shouting. She had promised herself she wouldn't behave like a kid in front of the guards, but this was all so stupid, stupid, stupid!

From over the five-foot wall came a voice. A measured, grown-up's voice. Full of grown-up authority.

"I don't think that will be necessary, Officers."

Tony couldn't see over the wall. She walked backwards in the snow, trying to see who was talking.

There were two men on the other side of the wall. The same two men she had seen. The one talking was the attacker —the one who had thrown the other man over his head and pinned him down. He had a dark blue wool cap over his head and a coat lined with dark fur.

The other man, who wasn't dead after all, was leaning over the wall with his head on his arms. He had no hat at all and dark hair that stood up in odd directions, and his coat was navy. He was still looking at her. He smiled.

He spoke, and he had an accent. Mom said everyone had an accent, you just didn't know from where, but this accent was one Tony hadn't heard before.

"I think the lass was alarmed to see us doing acrobatics in the work-out room. I'm new to it, you see, and had a wee accident and we fell down."

They all looked at him.

AS ROB ATTEMPTED to analyze the situation, he noticed the snow was beginning again. Huge flakes, coming slowly down at complex angles, each weaving and tacking through the air like so many boats in the water. They were landing on the little girl's black hair. On the uniform of the bulky man in earmuffs, and on Thomas's dark blue watch cap. Emotions, too, were weaving and tacking.

Thomas was protecting his boundaries. Not so much now from the child, who had retreated—sensibly, Rob thought— but from the hired neighborhood guards. Thomas would not be rude, but he might make the interaction even colder.

And the guard asked the inevitable question, "And who would you be, sir?"

And Thomas made the inevitable answer. "I might ask the same of you, as I am standing on property I own. And there are prints in the snow that make it obvious someone has been on it without authorization."

The guards perked up and together recited their one known fact as though it were the Holy Gospel. "That property is owned by the Thomas Heddiman Foundation...."

"And I am Thomas Heddiman. I've even brought my wallet, with identification, although I didn't think to need it on my own ..."

Rob sang out high and loudly, "Will you all shut up now and let me speak?".

They did shut up, as his words rang over the snow and down the turn-around and into the development of expensive houses and small yards. The little girl, who had seemed on the edge of running yet again, stopped and turned to him. Thomas also turned to him—stopped mid-word.

"Children *will* play. That's what makes them children. And we moved in to the place only six days ago, so they probably don't see the grounds behind this pretty brick wall as anything but a playground, occasionally with bothersome seminars going on. At least, when I was a lad, I would have done the same.

"Now there is a couple living in the house, as in all these houses you are paid to protect. That is the only change. The lass—the girl—thought she saw a man hurt and it was kind of her to care. I am always glad to find when someone does care about another.

"And I don't want to start our residency here with bad feelings amongst the neighbors."

He realized, hearing his voice ring in his own ears, and by the silence all around (including from Thomas), that he had been preaching, as well as singing his piece. "I'll shut myself up, now," he said, and stepped back from the wall.

But as he stepped back, the child in red ran forward along

her own snow-trail and began to climb up the low, half-stripped branches of the cypress—hemlock? Whichever sort of conifer it was that she had used to get in to the garden earlier.

"I'm sorry." She said to Rob. Face to Face. Her face was dark and warm-toned, but her lips a bit blue with the cold. "I trespassed and I knew it was wrong. My mom will freak about this, but … but …"

"You thought I was hurt," Rob replied. "And if I were your mum, I would tell you that makes up for everything."

The guards were moving back down the turn-around to where their car waited. Rob saw them moving back up along their snow tracks, and he wondered if he should have remembered their names. Had he heard their names? Thomas was standing exactly where he had stood when he had begun his defense of property, but he was looking at Rob, not at the private community guards. Looking at Rob and the cardinal girl.

"What's your name?" Rob asked her.

"Tony. It's Breton, really, but they call me—I call me—Tony."

"Your name is Breton?" said Rob. And said Thomas. Together. A perfect octave and a fifth apart.

She was grabbing the top of the wall with her mittened hands. The mittens were wet with melted snow. They were red, like her parka. Thomas approached and pointed at them. "That can't be comfortable. And you could get frostbite."

Rob reached down over the wall and took young Tony under her puffy arms and lifted her up. Thomas scraped the snow off a section of the wall and they sat her down, facing them.

"Yes, B-r-e-t-o-n. Isn't that beyond uncool?"

The grown-ups made neutral noises. Tony asked Rob two questions, so fast they trod on each other's heels.

"Where do you come from? What do you do?" And then,

thinking she had been impolite, added, "And what's your name?"

Rob replied, in sequence, "South Uist. Schoolteacher. Rob." And he put his hand on Thomas's shoulder. "And this is Thomas."

"Oh!" She kicked her booted heels against the wall. "And you live here now? Like people?"

"Exactly as if we were people," said Thomas, grinning for the first time since Tony had appeared at the French doors.

"I promise I won't climb over your wall again," she said, looking at Rob, and then, as an afterthought, at Thomas.

"But we'll still be neighbors," Rob replied, and he lifted her again, and using the advantage of his height, let her down all the way to the ground.

They walked back toward the house. It was snowing harder, but the flakes were still large and wind-borne. "I guess we could put in a gate there," said Thomas, shaking snow from his head. "I never considered it before. No one lived there."

Rob was watching the pattern around them. "They seem to be going in circles. Does your snow do that often?"

"Here, it does. I think the shape of the land and trees is—special. I always liked that about Aunt Grace's place."

⸺

THE NEXT EVENING, the seventh evening in the old Sullivan house, after deliverymen in coveralls had taken out the elegant corporate furniture that had been the contents of the house, and others had re-planted the old furniture belonging to Thomas's Aunt Grace and her companion Maria, Thomas found a package he had stored away and lost track of. Here it was, among the old furniture and knick-knacks that contained many stories Rob would have to learn.

"I can't believe it!" Thomas rolled back and forth on the

floor of an exploded room of boxes and an old chintz sofa. "I'd thought I'd lost the originals, when I went to school in England. Grace saved them for me!"

This was the same man who had stood like a warrior at the barricade against a duo of uncertain private guards and a little girl this morning. To see his face now was a delight.

Rob had rarely seen Thomas so spontaneous, so enthusiastic, so simply happy.

"Look at these, Rob. It's all of the *Absolute Sandman*, still cased!" He peered out of his own rhapsody for a moment, to look at Rob's face. "You have read comic books, haven't you, Rob?"

"I missed that part of life, somehow."

He thrust the black stack toward Rob. "Well, you have the best place to start. Right here."

As he was so clearly expected to, Rob sprawled out his legs on the Persian rug and pulled one of the massive tomes out of its casing.

"I'd start with the first," said Thomas, sitting beside him and leaning in. "Unless, of course, you're just looking to see the artist's style. And there were a number of different artists. All good, of course …"

So much was expected of him at this moment. Rob felt like a student being introduced to the works of Hawking for the first time. "I've a lot to take in," he warned Thomas, who at the moment was a head of bright silver hair, blotting all light from the book in Rob's hands. "I don't have the basic vocabulary for comic books."

"That's okay. It's okay." Evidently Thomas was an anxious sort of tutor. "The stuff will catch you.

"Or it won't. And that's okay too."

Rob sat there with the heavy black book in his hands and felt it would definitely not be okay with Thomas if the work didn't catch him up. He pushed Thomas out of the light and opened the book at random.

There were a series of colourful, impressionistic panels with simplified faces, word-balloons, and other words in black type that seemed to indicate background noise. Much like Yownie's cartoons, but in order, and it was not obvious what the order was. It was narrative, obviously, so the order was important. Were there not arrows or pointers of some kind?

"Some people," Thomas began, "say that you ought to simply start in part eight, where Dream and Death talk together while feeding the pigeons. That's where the whole thing became multi-dimensional...."

"Multi-dimensional?"

"Yes. But I started from the beginning. If you don't start from the beginning, you'll wind up having to reference back and forth until ..."

"Thomas," said Rob gently, "I think you will have to let me be alone with all this. For a while."

And Thomas did. He moved entirely out from the light of the desk lamp sitting on the floor.

Rob leaned his back against an impressive fireplace and began to attempt the world of comic books, while Thomas moved back and sat quietly, his eyes hungry for Rob to understand. To understand everything about Sandman. About the young Thomas. He sat in the shadows and watched Rob's dark, mutable eyes wander over the pages of Neil Gaiman's Sandman, and he watched him learn the art of reading comic books.

THE NEXT DAY, finished with one week at the Sullivan house, Thomas left Rob alone and drove to his teacher Kyan's studio, intending to announce that he had returned from exile, and that he felt he was worthy to be taken back. Rob had felt this moment coming all week. He didn't know the entire circumstance, nor in what manner Thomas felt himself cured of the wrongness that had sent him on pilgrimage, but he knew that in some manner it involved himself, and in some manner it did not. So he just let his binary go and spent a solitary afternoon trying not to worry.

How could a teacher not be proud of a student like Thomas? If he could have done so, he would have presented himself to the old man as a symbol of what Thomas could do to help humanity. Or at least one human.

Rob walked the circuit of the brick wall repeatedly, looking over the top at the busier world outside. Beyond was the new housing development, with young trees and young houses, and in the distance he could glimpse the development's own wrought-iron gate. There were children, as was shown by plastic tricycles and basketball hoops filled with snow, not to mention the leaves in bright colors cut out of paper and taped to window-glass, but the children must all have been at class. And where did the children play, in that carefully tended, guarded enclave? His own small, community-owned island home, though surrounded by dangerous waters, had been so much more free.

North of the development was a riding stable and a gate in the wall that led to it. There was even an old unpaved path leading from the one place to the other. Had old Grace Sullivan once been a rider?

Rob knew they were waiting for Thomas's own horse, MacBride. He would be shipped to this place and then this gate would open. Rob lifted the padlock on the metal gate in the brick wall. It was not rusted, but the keyhole was clogged with detritus.

Maybe the horse would be allowed to wander back and forth. Was that done in places like this, and with a horse so fancy? With grounds so fancy? Rob looked at the manicured landscape, almost like that of the Royal Dornoch Golf Course, and thought a horse would make quite a change. A welcome, wonderful change, like that which every delivery of old chintz overstuffed furniture from Aunt Grace had made to the house itself. MacBride was something called a Three-Day Eventer. He had seen photos of a mysterious creature—half Thomas and half horse—dressed in dramatic outfits and sailing over jumps in what he assumed was perfect form. If it was Thomas, it would have to be perfect form. In the pictures, MacBride was as white as the snow that was now melting from the branches around Rob. Rob himself had never seen a horse that white, and wondered how that had been accomplished.

Rob hoped to become as useful an object in Thomas's life as the horse. It was yet for him to discover how.

⬛

THE EVENING BEFORE THIS, behind one of those windows decorated with colored-paper maple leaves, Tony had told her parents The Story. She was clever enough to have figured out that hiding such an enormous incident forever was going to rebound against her. She was also clever enough to know when to reveal it, which was when both Mom and Dad were together and dinner was almost on the table.

"I met the new people next door today," she said, as she was laying out the table-wear on top of the paper napkins.

"What new people, Tony? Are you saying the Singhs moved out without saying anything? Or Ms. Connor and her sons? I just don't believe that." Mom was in the kitchen, her head in the oven, checking for the temperature of the free-range chicken they usually had on Tuesdays, when she got home early enough to roast a bird.

Dad was seated on a chair in the dining nook. His head had been buried in the text he used for his undergraduate intro course. As he'd also written the text, this preparation didn't absorb him too much. He looked at his daughter thoughtfully. "Whole story, Breton. Don't dangle us on a line, here."

Dad would always pull the whole thing out of Tony. She depended on this, in case Mom got upset. Dad could be relied upon to be the buffer. She let the knives, spoons, and forks clatter to the table.

"By next door, I don't mean the houses here. I mean the place behind the wall."

"You mean there's another corporate retreat, and they were doing something out in the snow? Brr!" Mom stuck her head into the room. Her dark face was damp from the oven's moisture.

Tony looked at the leaf-speckled window and not at either parent's face. "No. Now there's a real couple going to be living there. I met them."

Mom came in and sat herself down in a dining-room chair. "Someone bought the whole place? Who could afford that, these days?"

Tony took a deep breath and began as she had rehearsed. "Thomas said he owned it already. That he was moving in with his—I don't know; when it's two men, do you call them both husbands?"

"Whoa!" said Mom.

"Thomas? Do you mean Thomas Heddiman himself?" said Dad, slapping his textbook shut.

This reaction was more than Tony had expected. She had hoped her story would slide down easy. "He didn't say his last name. They're just Rob and Thomas. I like them. Especially Rob. He says he's a schoolteacher. I didn't say you teach at Harvard, Daddy. I thought that might make him feel bad."

Her father shared a glance with her mother and Tony would have given a lot to know what that glance meant. "This Rob—very tall man with an accent? Scottish accent?"

"He's not from Scotland, Dad. He says he's from … I don't remember. South someplace. And he sure does have an accent. I never heard any one like him before. And Thomas isn't so tall, but he can see over the wall."

Mom and Dad stared so hard at Tony she thought she might get away without the rest of the story at all.

"Rob picked me up and put me on the top of the wall and they talked to me. Rob said we were going to be neighbors and he hoped we would get along."

Mom stood again, drying he hands on her cooking apron. "Well, why wouldn't we get along?" And then she thought about it again, and remembered more.

"Oh! Oh! *That poor man!*"

"What do you know, 'Thena?" said Dad, shaking his head at Mom. "We're going to be moving in high circles, I guess." Then he turned a merry eye at his daughter. "I don't think you have to feel sorry about Rob MacAulay being just a schoolteacher, Breton. He's a famous scientist."

"And the man was a slave," added Mom with more force. "Like your many-times grandfather."

More conversation followed, which Tony was allowed to follow without speaking. She never had to talk about trespassing at all.

3

We Meet the Master

Rob was sitting with his back against the chintz sofa, after an evening studying the shapes of snow in the garden, taking samples of unfamiliar leaves to be categorized and hoisting himself over the Sullivan wall in various places to view the surroundings. The cold and the end of day's light had driven him back to the house and, of course, to the study of comic books. He'd been waiting for Thomas.

He came home later than Rob had expected. It had been a long dark evening in the latitude of Massachusetts. Rob heard the main gate swing open and the crunch of snow as Thomas's car approached along the winding drive. Faster than he usually came home; Thomas was ridiculously careful of the Sullivan property, and was generally a conservative snow-driver. The garage opened, and Rob sat in the expansive room —could such a room be called a parlour?—surrounded by years of Sandman comics, arranged as though they were so many mathematical works to be proofed. He waited for Thomas's approach.

Thomas came into the room like a grand candelabra, lit

and flickering on all candles. It was enthusiasm, not anxiety, that was pushing him. Rob felt his whole body warm to see it. A dozen greetings or questions formed in his mouth, but none were said. He just lit up in response to the light coming from his binary star and waited for the answers.

"Rob," he began, standing before him, next to the enormous, useless fireplace, dressed in clean grey cotton flannels and woolen socks, his body showered and dry and rumpled. "I'm so happy!"

"Saying that was actually unnecessary," Rob replied. Thomas came over and lifted Rob off the sofa by the arms and swung him around. The image of Yownie's little lad in trainers occurred to Rob, and again he wondered how that woman in Scotland had pegged Thomas Heddiman so well when she had not yet met him.

"Though I realize how very much I've lost in over two years since I left the master, it doesn't seem to matter anymore."

"The master? Thomas, you said that was a word that you, as an American, could never use!" Rob allowed himself to be tossed around the circle—there was so much room in this place—in a way he could not have permitted a year ago without falling flat. One leg forward, one leg back, never interfering with each other.

"I said you couldn't use it to me! The old man is different. Different culture. Different people entirely."

Rob thought to mention he was a different culture, but it seemed meaningless. And he didn't want to stick a spanner into Thomas's mood. "You certainly have worked out, Thomas. You're still giving off heat, and it must have been a long drive home."

Now the spinning had lost its momentum, and Rob found himself locked in a rare Thomas Heddiman body-hug. When they were on flat ground, that position meant that Rob, if he lifted his chin a bit, could rest it on Thomas's silver-bright

27

head. It smelled of cheap shampoo. He could feel his binary's heartbeat: not as fast as one might expect, but so strong. Then he was released.

"Kyan said he hadn't called me all that time because I hadn't called him. It was that simple to him!" Thomas chuckled at this. Was he chuckling at his teacher or at himself?

"It seems that simple to me also," said Rob, who reached out and stroked the top of Thomas's head. Rumpled or not, it looked much the same. "But I can't really understand the situation."

"We'll fix that!" Thomas's complete assurance took the wind from Rob's sails.

"Ah—Thomas. You've been studying with the man for thirty-three years now. I'm not sure how I will fit in."

"Thirty-one years. Remember I have been gone. Getting you here."

Getting me, full stop. That was what Rob wanted to say, but it sounded so vulgar.

It was safer to take this direction, "You weren't really gone from him, love. You spoke of him every day. All your workout, all your play. Your teaching me: it was a sort of communication to him, wasn't it?"

Thomas's brown eyebrows drew together, but the brown eyes underneath were still sparking amber in the lamps of the room. "No. I was communicating with you, Rob. In a language learned from the old man. But I'd misunderstood a whole lot."

Rob grinned in his horsey, large-toothed way, not so much because he agreed with Thomas's statement as because he'd gotten away with calling Thomas 'love.'

"He wants to meet you. Soon as we can manage."

"Oh." Now it was Rob who retreated into awkwardness. He was alone in the room, surrounded by light and by emotions that might not actually include him.

Who was the fellow Kyan Sensei wanted to meet? What had Thomas said about him?

When a man brought home a pet, especially a cartoon of random mathematical equations and subatomic particles with a comet (and birds) shooting through at the edges, there was much room for misunderstandings. And what was Rob, at the moment, without occupation or independent identity, except Thomas's pet? Possibly he was not so to Thomas, but to others? He could see himself as a bit of a disappointment. This must have been evident on his face.

"No, no, Rob." Thomas slapped him firmly on the shoulder, in a manner that made him rock from side to side. Fresh from workout, Thomas had a tendency to distort Rob's orbit. "Don't worry. Kyan doesn't rely on hearsay. He just looks at a man and sees him!"

Oh, grand.

Rob continued smiling. Thomas deserved that much, as a reward for all that anxiety, all that joy. And every newlywed had to go through 'meet the family.' It had just been delayed for Rob. Usually it came before the vows. And Rob had not yet even undergone the inspection by Jan, Thomas's sister, wherever she was.

For Thomas it had gone easier, as Rob had no family except the many people who had protected him. He had met them before Rob had even revealed them to Thomas.

And that was one more part of living with a games-master.

4

MacBride and One More

I t was in the last hours of the night they got a phone call.
Rob hadn't yet successfully opened both eyes when he
heard Thomas plunging around the bedroom. "It's
always like this, with deliveries! You wait so long and
then 'Pow!'"

For a moment Rob was confused, as no one he knew was
pregnant. He had been deeply asleep.

"I've got to be there," Thomas was calling, from the bathroom, where water was running. "I do NOT want him to land
here and find no one he knows waiting. Not after this long...."

Shower. Toothbrush.

Oh. It was the horse. MacBride. Rob slid a foot out of the
bed. Cold leaked on to the floor of this house worse than any
cold in Scotland. Or at least any that Rob could remember. He
stumbled through the dark, around the huge bed in a huge room
with parameters he had not yet memorized, drawn toward a
crack of light from the bathroom door. Thomas was already
half-dressed. He seemed surprised to see him standing there.

"Oh. Rob." Thomas blinked and shook his head, as

though breaking a train of thought. "You … don't have to do this with me."

Rob stood in the doorway, half in the white light of the bathroom, and half in the dark. "You don't want me?" That sounded so pathetic that he began again. "Is it more appropriate he sees only you, after so long?"

Thomas lowered the toilet cover and sat on it. "No, Rob. MacBride is an old guy. He's seen everything. Done everything. Everywhere. It's just that it could still be a long wait, and since he isn't your horse, and isn't your responsibility, it might not be a lot of fun."

Rob stepped entirely into the light, bowing by habit through the lintel, though he did not have to. "I think I'd like to," he said.

If he hadn't gotten to know Thomas so well, he might not have been able to tell that the man had relaxed. Rob had made a good decision.

THE PADLOCK HAD BEEN a long time unused. They stood there in the dark with snow around their boots, and Rob held a strong torch at the key insertion as Thomas emptied the detritus stuck in the hole with a can of compressed air, then lubricated the lock with a smaller can of oil. Their breath made such a cloud that Rob was not certain what was happening.

"You are always so ready for things," he noted, as Thomas put the tools back into the rucksack that Rob was wearing and inserted the key. But it still took some twisting and maneuvering, with Thomas's bison-skin gloves.

"If I were ready for this, I would have played with the lock days ago," said Thomas, tightly. It finally gave, and the padlock was jerked open. The keys were returned to the rucksack, and both men set to kicking the snow out of the way of the long, galvanized steel gate. It shrieked open.

On the other side of the Sullivan wall stood a path lined by conifers, obscuring the stables from the garden. They were not as well pruned as the trees in the garden, and they'd grown toward the center of the gate. Beyond this point the snow was trampled by other people's feet, so the going was easier.

So this was the stables. Rob had expected a place more ramshackle, and definitely smellier. But what with the temperature standing below zero, perhaps the heavier molecules of the smell fell out of the air. Rob must have been standing there woolgathering about temperature and molecules for some time, because Thomas took the torch from his hands and led the way forward.

There were huge paddocks to either side. No animals stood within them tonight, and the latest fall of snow was almost smooth. Everything man-made was of metal, and the two of them walked forwards a good distance before coming to any stables.

It must cost a good deal to keep one's horse here. Rob thought of the stocky cobs and hill ponies that had been kept back in the islands for tourist's use, and the asses—no, now he must call them donkeys—that the people themselves used. Nothing like this.

Of course, they hadn't had weather like this, either.

They walked by rows of solid stables, and Thomas took the easy way through, sliding open a door and leading them over the rubber mats that ran down the center of one. Here it was warmer and redolent with the smell of horses. Not just manure, but horses. Some of the stall tops were locked and some were open, and they were greeted by sleepy nickers. Large eyes shone in the edge of the torch's beam. Thomas was careful not to shine the thing in anyone's eyes.

"These are well-cared-for horses," whispered Rob. He

found he was speaking as he might have in some hospital, as though the horses might be sleeping through some nurse's intrusion.

"They'd better be," said Thomas, a bit protectively.

The cost must be dear indeed.

Rob knew he was smiling at the horses as they marched through. He knew this because his lips were slightly cracked, and the smile hurt. Two of the animals nodded their heads at him, and he found himself nodding back. Just to be polite. Thomas snickered at him. Not nickered. Snickered.

Each stall had a nameplate and a brass hanger with a halter on it. Down the sides of the aisle ran ropes with blankets on them. Almost elegant. They came to the other end of the building and Thomas put his weight on that particular sliding door. Unlike the gate, it made little noise. There was a similar stable, perpendicular to the one they had left, and Thomas led them towards a door in the middle of it. This door was human-sized, and he entered with a knob.

"You really know this place."

"I should," said Thomas. "Aunt Grace kept all her horses here. It was hers, back then."

This was much like the previous stables, but increased in scale. Rob had not known Thomas's aunt had kept horses, though he ought to have expected it. Thomas's interest hadn't come out of nowhere. One of these horses, with open stall-top, was white, small, and pretty. It wagged its entire neck at them. Rob refrained from wagging back, but he did turn his head and gave the mare a friendly sniff.

"They're an outgoing bunch," Thomas commented as they strode through.

"Well, ponies—horses, I mean—are so."

"Not always. Did you like being rousted out of bed tonight?" Rob could see a gleam of Thomas's teeth in the torchlight.

Rob felt no need to answer.

Outside this building stood two arenas, one of them enclosed and more soundly built than many places in which Rob had sheltered in the past few years. It was to this imposing hall they had been headed. The front door was massive, but as Rob attempted to add his own weight to Thomas's, he found it moved as smoothly as the others.

Within, Thomas reached to the right of the door and flipped a switch. The entire place lit up so brightly, Rob found he was squinting. "Well!" Rob said. And, "Oh, my!"

"Is that the well-known Scottish gift for understatement?" asked Thomas, dryly. The place was huge, lovely, and groomed like a Zen sand-garden, though not in sand.

Light bounced off a ring of clerestory windows that ringed the arena. The arched metal ceiling was also broken by skylights, but they were white with snow. "No. There is no such thing. The people of Scotland can come out with vulgarisms with the best of them! My tongue-curb is that of a schoolteacher. I inherited it from my Da. All we need is to come out with a random fuck-it-all and lose our positions. Quick as a sick dog can spew." He shot a glance at Thomas. "There. Do I sound more human to you?"

His own binary raised one brown eyebrow. "You've almost mastered the idiom perfectly, Mr. Spock." Thomas pulled off his watch cap and shook out his silver hair. Undid the toggles of his coat, which was lined, like his gloves and boots, in dark, bushy bison. Rob opened his own woolen long coat. Under it he had a knit jumper—no, he should begin to call it a sweater.

A row of plastic chairs waited by the wall, and Thomas lowered himself into one. "I wish you'd let me order you a real coat. If you're planning on staying the rest of the winter. After all, you do wear leather shoes."

Rob took the next chair over. His was blue. Thomas's chair was red. "I know. I know. I'm inconsistent."

"Actually," Thomas gave a meaningful pause. "You remind me of Jane Eyre. Being married in grey wool."

"I wish you'd use a different analogy, Thomas. I feel dependent enough, already."

Thomas snorted, shook his head, and leaned forward in his chair.

Rob folded his hands, still in mittens, on his lap. Wondering if Thomas was actually upset with him. "I know. Inconsistent, again."

Thomas mumbled something. Rob thought it was "It would just make me ... happy."

"Then I'll do it," he sang back. "Dress me in a robe of many colours. I'll dance for you on the village green!"

Thomas seemed also to be checking to see if Rob were upset. "Stoneham used to *be* a village," he said.

"I know. And you also used to burn witches in Massachusetts."

"Oof! Where'd *that* come from?" Now he was grinning broadly.

"I've been doing research. Whilst not studying the deeper meanings of Sandman, volume six. We also killed witches in Scotland. Much more recently, too. In Dornoch, of all places. We are barbarians, after all. The Romans couldn't civilize us." Rob let his long legs splay out until he leaned his knees against Thomas's.

"Well, you're living in the US now. I'll trade your barbarities, three for one."

They chattered on, about Hadrian's Wall, the Highland clearances, and the near-extermination of the 500 nations with great, distracted good will, until the sky began to lighten. They had reached the topic of energy and how it differed from what was generally called a "force," when Thomas pulled his phone from his coat pocket and checked the time. "I told you it might be hours. People think, once they reach State 93, that they must be at our gates. I only hope the Mothership can make it through."

"Mothership?"

"You'll see," said Thomas, and at that moment he raised his head.

Rob heard it too. It was the old-fashioned roar of a purely petrol engine, along with many tires crushing the snow.

They pushed open the doors together, and it was already first light out there, and the northeast end of the stables was visible, with two last buildings, one for horses, and one, slightly smaller, clearly for a human residence. Near that house was the main entrance to the stables, and it was not a ranch-gate, but a huge wrought-iron thing, old seeming, and ornate. There was an enormous horse-van outside on a small road Rob had not seen before, and it was shining in three colors from bow to stern, or whatever terms one used for a horse-van. It was attempting a three-point turn into the gate, which was opening before it.

Mothership. Of course.

A dim figure was pulling open one side of the gate. Thomas ran forward over the packed snow to help. "O'Brien!" he called as he ran. Rob stood in the snow and watched the vehicle enter.

He remembered his first thought of the morning and reflected that human deliveries were never so splendid.

The long van was nudged in the road behind the gate. The man named O'Brien called directions to the driver. O'Brien was, by his speech, Irish-born. There seemed to be an unusual number of such people around Boston.

Thomas waited at the middle of the vehicle, where the driver was sliding open a generous door.

Rob stood where he had placed himself, so as not to be in the way. O'Brien stepped up to him, huddled against the cold. He was a short man. Rob took only one pace away, for he was being re-trained by Thomas. He turned his head sideways to look at the stableman, who said, "I didn't expect Himself would be here at this hour to meet his horse."

Himself. That word was not usually meant a compliment. "So, you knew Thomas before this?"

O'Brien looked at Rob, met his eyes sideways. By the flicker in his own, maybe O'Brien felt he was being mocked. Rob gave him a grin of full teeth.

"I don't know much about all this," he admitted. "I've never been through these gates before. Only have lived in the house next door a week or so." He pulled off his right mitten. "My name is Rob."

O'Brien took his hand and gripped it. His grip was strong, but it didn't hurt Rob's healed hand. "Oh, I know who you are," said O'Brien, and Rob wanted to deny that. To tell the man that he couldn't know. But it was not the time for that, and Rob was not the important person here.

The important person was being led down the ramp, his white head hanging low and sleepy, enormous brown eyes half-closed. He took a deep sniff of Thomas's face, and Thomas hugged him to his own. Whatever was said between the two was obviously private.

MacBride was wearing a puffy red coat, like that of Tony next door, and had a neck warmer and head-cap, too. He was a solid animal, and not so tall as Rob had expected. It could simply be that, like Thomas, MacBride looked shorter because of perfect proportion. His legs, too, were covered by red wrappings. He looked like a Christmas gift, delivered late. "I'd like to take him into the covered arena," called Thomas, and led the horse forward. It stepped carefully. Rob wondered whether a horse's legs could fall asleep on such a trip, as his own legs did.

"And get him a bran mash."

"He's had a number of those already," the driver called out, and looking at the horse's wrapped tail (red, of course), Rob saw the mess down the hind legs and he began to believe that horse deliveries might have more in common with human ones than he had thought.

"I've got one on the stove," called O'Brien. "If you'll just see to the horse."

The driver came up to Rob. "Will you sign for him?" she said. "I have two more waiting in the van."

Rob was startled. "I can't. He's not my horse. I don't know what …"

"I'll do it," said O'Brien, running back to the delivery person and leaving an electronic smear on a screen. He turned to Rob. "We're just saying here that we got him. Not that he's in condition or anything." Then he darted off into the dim light and Rob himself entered into the lights of the arena. He ran the door almost shut, so the man coming in with a bucket wouldn't have to fuss with opening it. Shuffled through the chips of the floor toward Thomas and his horse.

Already the neck-wrap had been tossed on the arena floor and Thomas's hands were busy behind the horse's ears and behind the skull. He was mumbling to MacBride, and Rob wasn't certain, but he thought the horse might be mumbling back. He rested his heavy chin on Thomas's shoulder as the strong hands worked back into the huge muscles of that neck.

Why should he be surprised that the massage he was giving MacBride was exactly what he had received from Thomas over the last half year? Why should that recognition bother him? Rob looked at the brown eyes closing over Thomas's broad shoulder and decided he must never feel any resentment of MacBride. The horse looked kind, and he'd come a long way, and he had so much seniority over Rob MacAulay.

Thomas raised his eyes and saw Rob there. "You want to help?"

Thomas pointed at the bag on the ground, trying not to move his shoulder, and the horse chin on it. "Take out the curry. Clean his tail and around the rectum. Down the legs. You do know what a curry is?"

Rob reached down into the rucksack. The oval rubber tool

was at the top. Curry brushes hadn't changed much since his childhood.

Nor had the hind ends of horses. The previous bran mash had dried into something like fish-batter all over MacBride's dock and down both legs. Not too much like fish batter. Rob worked on it. A twitch of the tail in its bag told him he should press harder and not tickle the poor creature.

It was work much like gardening, in its way. Under the dried mess, the horse's winter coat—and it was thick and coarse, nothing like the gleaming photos—came out yellowed. Khaki.

"Should I take off the bag?"

Thomas glanced up. He himself had reached the middle of the horse's long neck. His face was shining with sweat. "Hmm? Oh, yeah. Probably. Can't be comfortable. But then, there will be more bran mash ..."

"But we can wash him? If it's warm enough ..."

"The wash room has heat." Thomas spoke with complete confidence. Rob undid the bag, and a heavy tail, banged at the hocks, fell out. The tail wasn't completely stainless. MacBride groaned comfortably.

The new bran mash came, and O'Brien with it. The Irishman looked uncomfortable, having nothing to do. Thomas raised an eyebrow at him. "Just tell me where you want him stalled. I'm sure you have enough to do, O'Brien."

Rob was used to Thomas's effect on people by now, so he shot the man a reassuring glance as he backed away.

The place was waking up, and horses were whinnying. One, not far away, was kicking at its stall. Someone opened the arena, then apologized and went out again. MacBride ate, and the two men worked on him. The red blanket came off.

MacBride was a furry, heavy-haired horse. Rob curried and Thomas did his bodywork. Nothing was said, except by MacBride. He nudged the rubber bucket over.

"He seems to be waking up. The old guy always could sleep on the road. Wish I could."

━━━

IT WAS ABOUT A HALF-HOUR LATER, and Rob believed the day would be warmer than yesterday. Thomas was in a small outdoor arena, saddled up on MacBride, who, it seemed, really had slept better than Thomas had done. But both horse and man were relaxed and happy. MacBride wore on his head only a weatherworn rope halter, one end of which Thomas held in his left hand. They seemed to be re-adjusting to the feel of one another. The horse and man appeared to do nothing in particular, although MacBride would occasionally offer a side-pass, to remind the man he remembered how, and Thomas would twist his hips and head around, requesting a spin left, or right. Occasionally Thomas's glance flickered to the far fence, where Rob was slouched. Watching.

Rob was still dressed for the night-cold and thought he might fall asleep there, leaning on the fence. He could feel the sun on his head. On the tips of his ears. People, mostly women, were leading horses behind him. Electric carts carried straw and dung, also driven by women. That same, insistent whinny came from back near the house.

O'Brien was beside him, leaning on the fence. He could just get his chin over, comfortably. They both watched Thomas and MacBride.

"You must ride, too, then?"

Rob leaned his head toward the stable-master. "When I was young," he said. "I was always on old Mr. MacInnes's Eriskay pony, Kinsman. But my legs got too long and then I could only drive him with his daily load of fish. And that was no kind of fancy driving. I just stood on a flat wagon and the pony did the work." He looked over and down at the Irishman and wondered. Had O'Brien been a jockey? It was difficult for a man of Rob's height to know exactly how short was short.

"But you'll be riding now?"

Rob nodded, as MacBride did, from the bottom of the neck. "So I reckon. Thomas assumes it, and I have no objection. I'm at home with the creatures."

They watched the white-haired man on the white horse, moving over dirty packed snow and the wood chips. Then O'Brien said, "I like to see it. A man like that, sticking with one horse."

A man like what? Rob looked over again, curiously, asking for explanation.

"Well, you know. They always seem to be trading up, as though a better horse, like a better car ..."

"Oh, that is so *not* Thomas!" Rob spoke in simple wonderment.

O'Brien looked straight up at the taller man, and seemed to understand he'd made a gaffe. "Oh! I didn't mean to say ..."

Then there came a shout, and a thud, and a sound of skidding, and the drumming of hooves. That insistent whinny repeated much louder. Both men stared. "Shite," said O'Brien, almost without expression, and he stood up. "He can't do it. He'll break his fookin' legs!"

There came a streak of black, down the main aisle, past the enclosed arena, and over a fence. Smooth as a swallow it came, and across that wide arena, around piles of brightly-colored jumps and cavaletti. Over another fence it came, its legs tucked in like the legs of any bird. Into this arena.

It was a tall horse, and a long one, and it was coming for them. Not for Thomas and MacBride, who were stopped still at the other end of the arena, both staring, but for the pair of them at the rail.

In Rob's eyes it was purely lovely. Was it O'Brien's own

horse? It was slowing, skidding over the snow, moving now cautiously, towards …

Toward him. To Rob. He locked eyes with the animal and it nodded, sweeping a fine-haired long mane up and down in the air.

"That was four fences! And over the top of the stall door. Jesus in Heaven."

Rob scrambled up the fence. One fence was the least he could climb to meet this fellow.

The black nose approached Rob's face, and he turned his head to the side, not knowing why he made that particular gesture. It pressed its soft nose against the side of his face and kept it there for a good while. It nickered to Rob. And he remembered out of nowhere doing something much the same, once, to Thomas.

"Fuck again! I thought the horse might bite you, man. He's a stallion! And he's a bad actor, not like that MacBride!"

Rob rubbed his face up and down against the horse's nose. The stallion backed away and blew breath into Rob's.

O'Brien cleared his throat. "His name—his official name …"

"His name is Kinsman," stated Rob.

Rob began as he had seen Thomas do to MacBride, and to himself, behind the ears. He let the horse tell him how deep he wanted the contact. Soon the tall head lowered, and Rob started down the muscles at the top of the neck. He was not aware of O'Brien staring, nor Thomas slowly approaching, from the side, toward them. MacBride was still in the middle of the arena. He'd decided he'd rather stay where he was.

Thomas swung wide, so as not to approach the horse directly. Not to seem aggressive. O'Brien met him at the fence. "Who's is he?" asked Thomas, quietly.

The stable-master didn't meet Thomas's eyes. Not quite. "Well, there's a story."

"Love to hear it."

"Man who owned him disappeared more than a year ago. Stopped paying the board, and when I looked him up he was gone. I did search, you know. A bit. But it came time I should have done something about him."

Thomas didn't look straight at O'Brien, either. "And that would have put you in a difficult position."

"And ... I'd say it has, Mr. Heddiman."

"Thomas. And I don't know why you'd think that. He's a gorgeous creature."

"But not mine."

They watched the mutual seduction of man and horse before them. "Maybe someone wants him."

"I don't want to see your man there get his neck broken."

"Me neither." They watched some more. "Have you ever seen the like of this?" asked Thomas, bemused.

"Not exactly. I mean MacAulay's work on him, of course, I've seen. He's good, obviously. But that stallion ... He's difficult." The Irishman cleared his throat.

"Back home I'd be asking you if Rob there is a Traveler. A horse whisperer. But that's so much superstition."

"He's from the Hebrides. I think they go in for boats there, not so much horses. But he told me that he knew them."

"Ah, he did? And why didn't you believe him?"

Thomas shrugged. "In his own mind I'm sure he was telling the truth. It's just that I never saw any sign of it."

Rob had reached Kinsman's croup. He was shaking out his fingers as though losing feeling in them.

"Maybe he knows more than you think?" O'Brien asked this, hopefully.

"I'd be the last to contradict you on that."

Rob then surprised them all, or at least all the humans, by boosting himself onto the horse's bare back and continuing the massage, leaning out over the long neck. Thomas meandered closer and spoke quietly into Rob's ear. "What are you planning to do with him now, Rob?"

"For now? Make him happy. I don't think he has been happy." Rob sat up, stripped off his navy coat, and handed it to Thomas, who took it and stepped back. Kinsman seemed to take this as a signal to move forward.

This is where he slides off, said Thomas to himself, hoping Rob would not be stepped on. But Rob sat up and put his arms out to his sides, in his familiar gesture of balance. They walked off across the arena, at the horse's will. Rob gave no signals, nor did he clutch with his legs. When Kinsman began to trot, Rob looked concerned for a moment, until he had adjusted his privates and slid back off the knife-like withers. Then he grinned.

Thomas called "Put your arms down, Rob. You look like you're about to take off!"

So Rob did. He put his hands on the black withers before him, folded. The two of them went at a long, easy trot around the arena, avoiding MacBride, who looked warily interested, ears pointed, following the progress. Then Kinsman moved into a canter.

"He's much better trained than he told you," said O'Brien. "I mean, the man. The horse, I knew about."

"Sure." After a few minutes Thomas called out. "When you want him to stop, lean backwards."

Rob looked disappointed, but he did stop the horse. Without giving any perceptible signal at all. They stopped so suddenly Rob did have to lean back. He still slid forward onto the withers, and grimaced. He took hold of the mane and used it to slide down. He almost fell when his legs touched ground. He stepped forward, using the fine black hair to hold him up, and what he said to the horse the humans could not hear. Then he staggered back to Thomas, with the tall stallion's nose fixed between his shoulder blades, following him like a puppy. "I think I'm going to be sore," said Rob. He held out his hands. Lifted his legs, one at a time. Kinsman nudged him from behind.

"To whom does he belong, Thomas? Do you know? I'd like to ask if I could borrow him sometimes."

"'He followed me home? I don't think he feels well?'" quoted Thomas. Rob turned red.

O'Brien spoke. "He belongs to your man, here. To Heddiman. Like everything else, except the boarded horses."

Rob looked entirely confused.

"Did you not know he owns the stables?"

Rob mouthed the words, *Owns them?* "All this place?"

"Not that he's been making any money," added O'Brien, with guilt in his voice.

"One doesn't," said Thomas, shortly. "Aunt Grace didn't. I didn't expect to. Just not to lose too much. And you've done just fine, Colm. If I forgot to say that, I'm sorry."

As the two looked at each other, Rob asked Thomas again. "Can we keep him?"

"He's already yours. That's what marriage means."

"I'll have to tell him so," said Rob. He walked the black horse back to the stallion stable, with only a hand on his back to lead him. He gave him his breakfast and left the blue coat behind in the stall, as a parting reminder. Thomas took MacBride to the stall that had been prepared for him. The fact that they were both stallions didn't seem to be an issue between them at the moment.

Then the two men went along the path towards home, Rob walking stiffly.

"That's one reason we use a saddle," Thomas said.

"He has a pointy back," answered Rob.

As he used the old key to re-fasten the steel gate into their garden, Thomas was using the sun on his head to quiet his mind. Watching his breath helped, also. He was trying not to dig too analytically into the matter of this man beside him. Peculiar, incredibly intelligent, incredibly simple. He wanted to understand Rob MacAulay as he understood other things, and knew that was both impossible and unkind.

Besides, he already had him. As much as a person has another person. As much as a person has a horse. Best friend and lover. Is that what marriage was? Was supposed to be? He turned and met Rob's eyes, intending to say, *So you talk to the animals, too? Like Dr. Doolittle?*

But what came out was instead, "I'm going to change my name to Sullivan. Today. She said I could whenever I wanted to, and now I will."

Both Rob's high eyebrows shot up higher. "Why now?"

"People change their names when they marry. It's an old, established custom."

"To—to Sullivan?"

Thomas found he was laughing. Loudly. His—what was the word Rob liked to use? His "binary," binary star—was undoubtedly finding him as hard to figure out as Thomas was to figure out Rob.

Rob followed him. He himself was not trying to analyze anything. "We could bring the horses through the gate," he suggested. "Let them wander about the grounds. They'd like that."

"We don't even know if they're going to get along with one another."

Rob really *was* sore. Saddles were undoubtedly a good idea. He wondered if Kinsman's back was sore also. He imagined carrying a weight such as his own on his back. If his back were a suspension bridge, the weight would be better carried forward, near the primary struts, rather than at the center, where there was no support, or the rear, where propulsion came from.

He brought his wandering thoughts to heel and answered Thomas's question. "Oh, they'll get on with one another."

Thomas looked over his shoulder at Rob. He was being amused at him, again. Rob didn't mind.

"Did the horse tell you that?"

"Not in so many words."

Thomas slung his bison-skin coat over one shoulder. "They'll wreck the landscaping."

"Only—adjust it?" He caught up with Thomas. Looked around at the winter garden.

"Remember," said Thomas, as they approached the back porch, where the mudroom was. "You still have to meet Sensei."

5

Kyan Sensei

T he light was fading as Thomas drove along State 93
toward the edges of Boston.

"Do I need to remind you that I can drive in this
country? You don't seem so certain of me."

Thomas glanced over, remembering seeing the tall man in
the other half of another car. Reversed. But Thomas had
been driving then as well. "I just remember that I had a
terrible time as a young guy around London. And Boston, in
my opinion, is worse. Worse than anywhere. That's why there
are so few cars used in auto-drive here. Their decisions are too
logical, and Boston. Is. Not. Logical."

Rob leaned toward Thomas. "And I am? I'm not a
machine, Thomas. I'm a lefty. We are all, more than you,
ambidextrous. And I am so more than most lefties. To reset
my mind for right-side driving is the work of a moment. Even
for your dreaded Boston."

Thomas sighed and adjusted the windscreen against the
glare off the cars ahead. "I believe you. And, of course, we do
have to get you your own car."

Rob rustled in his seat. He was anxious regarding the

coming presentation of himself to Thomas's old teacher. "You know, Thomas, when you say that, you sound much like my own father when he would say *we* were going to have to do something about something. It always meant *he* would be doing it. For me."

"And we're crabby tonight," said Thomas, lightly. "Is it the money thing again?"

It wasn't the money thing. It was calling Kyan "master," after Thomas's reaction to being called the same thing, but money was easier to talk of. "It does take some getting used to."

"Even though when you married me you hadn't a penny. You didn't care then."

"And I still don't. Not in that sense. But a man ought to be bringing something to balance the equation."

"I'm sure you will." Thomas was not at all nervous about the coming meeting. He'd talked it all out with Kyan Sensei the night before. And he wondered if a day would ever pass when Rob did not speak Physics to him. And if such a day came, would Thomas be deeply pleased or deeply disappointed?

"And you're chipper tonight, for a man who just got his horse back and had two hours of sleep."

"I am, because tonight I'll sleep like a log. Master class."

Rob wondered what those words meant.

A parking garage stood next to the school, which looked quite prosperous, from the little Rob knew about martial arts schools. "Do you own this, too?" he asked Thomas, as they approached.

"What!" Thomas's anger startled Rob. He looked, not cold, like the Thomas Heddiman he had seen so often, but actually red.

"I only meant …"

"I own *nothing* here!"

Rob stepped back twice, and not out of politeness.

Thomas took a deep breath and let it out slowly. It whistled. "I didn't know that was still in me," he murmured, maybe to himself, and then looked back at Rob. "Sorry. You couldn't know."

Which was part of why Rob looked so white and stricken when he went to meet the teacher.

He knew to take off his shoes, but took them off too early and had to tiptoe over a messy lobby, then rub his socks clean against his trouser legs before entering the dojo. A class was in progress and the smell of fresh sweat hung in the air. Thomas took him by the wrist and led him along the back of the room to a hallway. It had paintings of fishing boats on it. Rob had to stop to look. They weren't his sort of fishing boats, but they were boats.

At the end of the hall was a room with kanji writing, and below it, the words TEACHER'S OFFICE. Thomas patted the door with his flat palm. A thin voice said, "Come in."

Thomas led Rob through the door, still held by his wrist. An old man sat on a simple sofa with a low table in front of him. To Rob's surprise, the sensei was rounded and had a pleasant face. The old man didn't seem dangerous at all. He looked at both of them and said quite clearly, "Thomas, go do something else for a while."

Thomas simply disappeared. The door latched closed. "Now, Dr. MacAulay. What are you afraid of? Thomas said you were not afraid of anything, but here you are, afraid. Can you be afraid of me?"

"No sir," said Rob. "At least not much. But I just now said something stupid, and I haven't had time to make it right."

"Ah. Please sit down and tell me what you said. I hear some stupid things." He smiled, showing many, many wrinkles in that round face.

Rob sat, and he did tell the sensei what he had said. He thought he might have to explain further, but Kyan Sensei immediately burst out laughing. He slapped his knee.

Rob thought, *Thomas is all the time slapping his knee.*

"Thomas goes through life hand in hand with anger. But, of course, I am not saying you have a responsibility to change this."

"Nor is it in my power," said Rob. He found he was holding a cup of green tea. He held it in both hands, as though they were cold. They *were* cold. "And I don't want to change the man overmuch."

"Overmuch," repeated the old man, carefully, looking into his own tea. "Overmuch. New word. Huh!"

Kyan Sensei looked up again, brightly. "He talked about you for more than an hour yesterday! I have never heard him talk so fast. How he could breathe, I don't know."

Rob knew he was staring. Like an idiot. "Thomas did? Of me?"

"Yes!" *Slap, slap,* on the knees. "He thinks you are magic!"

Rob stopped breathing, but the smell of the tea was still going up his nose. "Magic?"

"Oh, my English! No, he knows you are real, but the things he said. On and on."

Rob wondered what color his face was. He could see how red his hands were getting, around the cup. What could the old man think of him?

"It was so good to hear. I have known Thomas a long time. From when he was little Tommy."

"I know," said Rob, and for the first time since leaving home that afternoon, he smiled.

"Has he talked about me, too?" the old man asked.

Rob finally drank some of the tea. "Of course. But I don't want to—gossip—about Thomas."

Kyan Sensei put his cup down. "Someone must gossip about Thomas, sometime!" he said forcefully.

Rob sat upright again, looking down at the man.

"Okay. Not now. We can talk about you. He says you are a teacher. You are a schoolteacher."

Rob nodded.

"Then——" Kyan leaned forward, bright and merry. "Why aren't you teaching school?"

"It's a long story...."

"I heard the long story. I even got pictures of you from a magazine. I heard a song, even."

"Oh no!" Rob hid his head in his hands.

"It was a good song. Delightful!" Rob heard Kyan clap his hands and he put his own cup down and looked at him.

"Are you afraid of teaching, man who is not afraid of anything?"

"Yes."

"No matter. Teach!"

No one had to tell Rob the meeting was over. He rose to leave and Kyan Sensei called to him, "Please tell Thomas to come in." His voice was gentle.

Rob found Thomas in one of the side rooms off the hall. He was doing a kata. He stopped frozen, looking closely at Rob. "You've finished dokusan?"

He had no idea what Thomas's word meant. Rob just said "He wants you now." Rob also did not understand the slight ritual bow Thomas gave him as he slipped by.

Rob sat in the empty room and waited.

———

"–AND the stallion did everything but bow to him! Jumped out of his stall and over four fences and came to a stop as though Rob were royalty. And Rob hopped over the fence and began to do bodywork over him until the enormous shining black creature lay his head down drooled into the flooring! And Rob vaulted up and sat on him to work on his neck and the horse began to walk. He put out his arms to the side like a bird and they went over that arena as if they were born to each other!"

"What color did you say, Thomas? Black?" Sensei was listening as if to a fairytale.

"Black, without a white hair on him, and … Oh damn. You think I'm driveling. Talking like a little boy!"

"No, Thomas, but talking like a little boy is no bad thing. I met your Rob, and you were right. He is a magic person. And if he jumps from place to place, I believe that too. But those things are not so important. For him.

"You remember the story of the man in the old Japanese story who was followed by clouds of butterflies and birds, and he met a wise man who touched him and all that went away, because it was getting in his way?"

"Of course." Thomas went from passionate boy to slightly mulish. "He says they're unimportant, too. Like wiggling his ears. They should go away?"

Kyan Sensei smiled wistfully. "I never liked that end to the story. Poo! The magic goes away. But it is true that it is simply not as important as the thing he is afraid of. Teaching. And that is what is getting in his way, you see?"

"What did you tell him?" The teacher shook his head even as Thomas realized the impropriety of the question. "Your friend refused to talk to me about you, and so, I think, I must give him the same respect. I won't tell you. He can, of course."

"And he will be your student?"

Sensei threw his head back and laughed. "Student, as what? Do you think he needs to learn what it is to hit another being? To know how that blow stays with him for all his life?"

Thomas looked at the cold, half-full teacup. Rob's. There had been no tea necessary for Thomas's conversation. "But if you could have seen him as he was when he came to me, Kyan. There was so little left.…"

"Oh. I didn't say he couldn't learn here. Already you have taught him rolling, you say, and flying over objects. And given him difficult exercises. I just don't believe he needs to learn to hit people."

"Not even in self-defense?"

Kyan shrugged. "There are other ways. But bring him. For my sake, if not for his. I like him.

"And now, Thomas, you will teach the master class along with my latest second teacher. It is Katie, now. I am sure you still remember her? And that you are not going to want to be second teacher?

"Ha! Of course, Thomas. I know you have other work. Always. But it will be good for them all to meet you again. MacAulay can watch. He knows that you, too, are a teacher?"

Thomas nodded. His interview, too, was over.

RIDING in a car at night in a strange city is a chaos of sudden lights and sudden turns. Riding with a sleepy driver is yet more chaotic. Rob tried to keep Thomas talking. He trusted him entirely, but still tried to keep him talking.

"Watching you teach was so instructive," he began.

"I've been teaching you these same things for months," said Thomas.

"But the watching part. It adds another dimension."

Thomas glanced over, blinked, and kept driving.

"And I'm going to resume teaching, also. I don't yet know ..."

Thomas was entirely awake. "You're what?"

Rob hadn't actually meant to say that. Not so suddenly. Not before he had looked at the problem for a bit longer. But he had said it. "I'm going to seek some sort of work. Teaching."

"Teaching ... your stuff?"

Rob was no longer worried Thomas would fall asleep

before engaging automatic. He was worried he might drive them off the road.

"Aye."

"Was that the dokusan?"

"Please look at the road, Thomas."

"I *am*. Is that what Sensei told you to do?"

Rob thought he had left embarrassment behind in that small room with the teacups. But now he folded his hands in his lap and looked straight out at lights that meant nothing to him. "He did—suggest it."

"I've been doing more than that every day for months!"

Rob didn't answer. He was grateful for the dim light, because he was fairly certain Thomas's cone cells were not operating at full efficiency and he couldn't follow the colors on Rob's face.

Then Thomas began to laugh. Uproariously.

"Now you're just laughing at me," said Rob.

"I am. Oh! I am!" Thomas pounded one fist on the steering wheel and laughed some more. "The old man got you. He did!"

"At least I've made someone happy tonight."

The laughter exhausted itself. "Oh Rob. Welcome to my world," he said.

WHEN THEY REACHED HOME, it was Rob who was asleep with his head against the car door, snoring slightly.

6

Neighborly

N ext morning, when Thomas woke, Rob was already up. He found him in the big front room, with a tablet scrolling text in front of him, mismatched sheets of scrap paper in neat piles, and two old pens in his hands. Making severely lined rows of notes across the coffee table.

"Are you actually using both pens?" asked Thomas, rubbing sleep from his eyes.

"For two different things." Rob's voice rang through the room. Echoed down the hallways. He did not look up. "A saddle. One that will fit Kinsman. Do you think O'Brien can provide such a thing?"

"If he can't, I can. That's no problem. Why the rush? You just got the horse."

Rob MacAulay did look up, and a light glowed in his eyes. "I have a responsibility to him. I assured him of it. And I am going to be busy, so I must figure when I can fit it in."

"Busy doing what?" Looking at the books amid the papers, Thomas was fairly sure what the busy-ness was to be, but he wanted it said.

"Finding work. Teaching, of course. I have made a list...."

Actually, he had made several lists. Of Massachusetts local schools, Adult Education. Summer seminars.

Thomas sat himself on the couch, on the far end from where Rob was sprawled. Yes, he was writing with both hands. The penmanship was different, but both legible. Both in block print.

Be careful what you pray for, was the old saying. And in his own way, Thomas had been praying for this.

"Rob. This is Thomas speaking. Thomas Sullivan. Remember me?"

Rob's dark eyes flashed to him, then away, and then back again, more slowly. His hair was bouncing over his high forehead. "You did it, then? Changed your name? So quickly?"

"Took about a half hour, when all the forms were done. Legal name changes are easy. Changing the stationery is the bummer."

Rob put down one pen. Then the other. He scooted over the upholstery and took Thomas's hand in both of his and shook it. As that gesture proved inadequate, he leaned over and embraced the man completely. "I am so glad for you, Thomas," he said, and sounded more like himself—as Thomas knew him—again. "And I'm sorry I didn't even think to ask."

Thomas pulled out of the clutch. "S'okay. Don't matter. But I have to ask you two questions now." He put one hand at the base of Rob's neck, where the muscles were hot and pumped and his pulse beat hard. "First is: how long do you think you can keep this up? This level of concentration?"

"As long as necessary. You, of all men, should understand that."

Thomas grunted. He also knew what it cost. "And the second is, why doesn't your pile of possibilities include the obvious one? You know—Harvard."

"I have no connections at Harvard. My tenure at Edinburgh was revoked. You know that. No University would ..."

"Then get it unrevoked. Or ignore it. Rob, can you still think you are governed by such things as academic rules? Especially that one?"

Rob looked down at the piles. He lined up both pens in the middle of the coffee table. "I will begin with the saddle," he said.

THE DAY OPENED with a thaw and a great sloppiness. For the first time since the travelling pair had landed at the Sullivan house, the area looked mutable. Fragile. Even a bit smelly.

The people who dwelt in the gated community off State Route 93 had attempted, just two years before, to complain about the presence of the horses around them, and been defeated by the long planning of Thomas Heddiman. Much to the satisfaction of the newborn Thomas Sullivan, behind his brick wall. The arguments had been predictable, even ritual, and the defense equally so. The developers had moved into what was grandly described as "equestrian property," and it was so zoned. If the people who bought the houses hadn't been aware of the connection between "equestrian" and the odor of horse manure, that was not relevant. So had the law firms of Thos. Heddiman arranged things. Thomas Heddiman himself, although never actually present, had also arranged that the sanitation of his aunt's old stables be impeccable. It had been expensive, for a man who was working in other places of the world, and in worlds of his mind, but it was his private heritage, and he had maintained it. To Thomas it had been a shrine. And he had pulled in Colm O'Brien, an immigrant from Ireland out of Boston, whose attitude toward the training and maintenance of horses seemed to reflect his own, without ever meeting him.

Heddiman had done so. Now Sullivan was living with it. For once, the laws of cause and effect that were best described as karma hadn't hit him in the face. Thomas could only be grateful.

I did it, he thought. He almost spoke those words aloud as he moved in his wellies over the sodden snow toward the gate. The dripping gate. He wasn't sure he meant he had done the job of protecting the stables, of getting his horse home, or of lighting the spark which had woken up a fire in Rob MacAulay. He might have simply meant that he had remembered to bring the key to the padlock.

It didn't matter what he'd meant, talking to himself in the morning. He went in to talk to O'Brien about a saddle for the stallion.

IN THE GATED COMMUNITY, Tony's family was having breakfast together. Daddy looked out the window and wondered if the roads would be bad. Mommy averred that they were always bad between here and Harvard campus, and he'd better be starting.

"I mean, 'Thena, do you think there's ice under that slush?"

"Do you think you'll be going fast enough to slide on it, sweetheart?" his wife replied. She was toasting waffles for Tony, who was hoping to be allowed maple syrup. Sometimes Mommy said it made her excitable and that excitement would let her down just after first period in school. Sometimes she forgot about all that and Tony got her syrup.

"I think maybe someone a mile ahead of me might be going fast enough, and then we'll all sit there forever."

"Not forever, Daddy. You mean until you're late for your first class."

"Which is why your father leaves at such an ungodly hour. Commute!" Mommy and Daddy both said the word "commute" like other people said dirty words. Daddy got up from the table, closing down his tablet. Only Daddy was allowed to read at the table, because he had to learn about the condition of the roads.

"You're going to invite those people for dinner, aren't you, 'Thena?"

Mrs. Kaye rubbed the backs of her fingers over her eyes—she had not yet put on eye make-up, so she could do this safely. "I will, if you want, but I think it should be you, dear. You're the Professor. You should be talking to the Scotsman. The one who … you know."

"I'll do it," said Tony. "I'm the one who knows them."

Daddy just tousled her head and left the kitchen. Mommy said, "How would *you* do that, sugar? You have got to be in school. And you're not to go trespassing into their property again, you hear?"

"I promised I wouldn't!" said Breton. "But I could write a letter. And leave it on the wall. In a plastic bag."

Mrs. Kaye put the few dishes into the dishwasher. "Oh, they'll take that really seriously, child."

"They *will*! I know them!" Tony hopped from foot to foot, holding a syrup-dipped waffle in her sticky hand.

━━━

THOMAS WAS JUST WALKING BACK from the small boarding-stallion house, where he had attempted to find O'Brien, when he saw the flash of red on top of the wall.

She looked up in alarm as he came crunching up through the snow. "Oh! I'm not trespassing again, Mr.—Thomas. I was going to pin a letter but there was nothing to pin it to so I got a rock."

With her wild black hair flying out over the dangling padded hood, Tony looked less like a transformed cardinal and more like a little girl. How old was she? Ten? Thomas was not good at the ages of children. Especially padded children. "I see. Is it a letter for Rob?"

"For both of you. It's from my parents. But I wrote it." She gave him the envelope: recyclable plastic bag and all. It had a butterfly stamp on the front of it.

He was about to take it, when he looked at her again. "Don't sit up there. You'll get your bottom—your pants— wet." He picked her up as Rob had done just the day before and put her on her feet inside the wall.

"I think you can say 'bottom.' It's not a bad word," said Tony.

Younger than ten, surely.

"May I read it here?"

Tony shrugged, and the whole red ensemble went up and down with her shoulders. "It's yours."

It was an ordinary envelope and at least it was not in crayon. In fact, it was quite readable. "Let's go in and ask Rob. If he's interruptible."

"He's working?" She followed him through the melting snow.

"With both hands."

They did not go to the French doors, which were the only place of access Tony had known. They walked around the corner to a generous porch with vines heavy as a tree growing at the brick wall. "What are those?" she asked him, pointing.

"Wisteria. A cold-tolerant variety. It flowers in the spring." This was uninteresting to Tony, but still impressive.

Thomas paused in the doorway. "Is it all right for you to come in here? Your parents said?"

"Sure," she said, adding. "This house is really old, isn't it? Like a museum."

"No. Not really." Thomas led her into the mudroom and they both took off muddy boots. She followed him through four different rooms before they got to the one with the huge empty fireplace and the couch in front of it. There sat her tall friend Rob. He was writing with a pen in his left hand, tapping with a pen in his right and staring at a screen between them.

"He *is* busy," she whispered to Thomas.

Rob startled, dropped both pens, and turned his head around. "Tony!" He sang out, with a change in demeanor and a display of teeth.

"We've been invited to dinner," said Thomas.

And so it was done.

They led her back to the wall, each holding one of the child's hands. She swung and skipped between them. Mrs. Kaye was standing at the ragged Cyprus tree, and had evidently been there for some time. She looked distraught.

All three stopped in consternation. Thomas spoke first. "We're so sorry, ma'am. We didn't know anyone was waiting for her."

Mrs. Kaye looked at Thomas's silver head. The quality of his casual clothes. The dignity of his being Thomas. "It's not your fault, Mr. Heddiman. I'm sure she didn't tell you she was going to be late for school."

Tony pulled back, held in place by both sides. "Oops."

"You shouldn't have done that, lass," whispered Rob to her, bending.

"I can drive her," said Thomas, quickly. "I brought her over the wall. I didn't think to ask, and I'm the adult, here. Or should have been."

"Oops."

Mrs. Kaye looked at the two men and gathered her

Georgia manners. "No need, Mr. Heddiman. I'll drive Breton myself."

Rob put her over the wall. She clung, a bit like a baby monkey, but he put her in her mother's arms. Her mother dropped her quickly to her feet. "She meant no harm, Mrs. Kaye. She was trying to be neighborly."

Athena Kaye stopped a moment, caught by Rob's singing intonation. "That was our intention also, Professor. To be neighborly."

"Please call me Rob."

"Thomas."

"'Thena. Short for Athena."

And that was also done. The formal meeting. "And y'all will come?"

"At your convenience," said Thomas. He gave her a card— an old-fashioned visiting card, with just his name, and address. He'd written both his cell phone and old landline at the bottom. Rob stared at this. He hadn't known Thomas owned such things.

"And I'm going to have some men come out to put a gate in here. To save the tree, of course," he added, smiling.

Mrs. Kaye looked startled. "Just because of a little girl?"

"And because there are people out there. When I was last here, there were not."

"Which name did you have on the card?" Rob asked Thomas as they stamped their feet on the porch.

"As I said, the stationery comes last."

———

THAT DAY they rode on the trails of Middlesex Fells Park. It was not Thomas's idea of a new rider's first experience on a stallion, but Rob was certain that excursion was what Kinsman wanted. Rob was reluctant to wear a helmet, but Thomas did not bend on that, and Rob forced his head into a battered, borrowed thing. Nor did he see why Kinsman ought to wear a bit in his mouth, when MacBride hadn't to suffer such an indignity, but rode the trail in a rope halter. To Thomas's explanation, that MacBride was an old friend, and that a snaffle bit was not something that controlled a horse by pain to the mouth, but a means of sending signals, Rob replied, "As I don't know those signals, it seems wasted."

"Please? For me? Once?"

The stable-master moved back into the shadows, shielding the smile on his face with one hand against this small confrontation between the two. At last Rob allowed the bit to be put into Kinsman's mouth.

The saddle fit, of course, because it was the one O'Brien had used on the horse. The bridle was O'Brien's, too. The stable-master tied the reins together at the middle of Kinsman's neck. "So the bit won't jangle against his teeth," he said. "If you are sure you won't use it. And if you need to, you can grab it to ask him to stop, or turn."

The tall black horse didn't seem to mind the apparel at all. O'Brien, at Rob's request, did leave the rope halter in place. It was the same sort Thomas had used on MacBride. O'Brien tied the end of it in a loop at the bottom of the horse's neck. "I had to get new stirrup leathers, Rob," said O'Brien. "As mine aren't half as long as you will need. The new ones will stretch a while."

Thomas was approaching, already dressed and aboard MacBride. The two horses regarded each other, and O'Brien and Thomas tried to act easy about the whole event. The stallions were really easy about it. Kinsman stretched out his long neck and whuffled. MacBride, Rob was certain, raised one white eyebrow. His brown eyes warmed. His own whuffle was understated.

"I thought that your black horse might resent the other. He is a bad …"

"Actor, I know. But how could anyone resent a gentleman

like MacBride?" asked Rob, and before the stable-master could give him instructions on mounting, he vaulted up onto Kinsman's back and settled himself into the flat saddle, adjusting the soft parts of his anatomy.

"So all those push-ups didn't go for nothing," said Thomas, observing this as he rested easily on his horse.

Rob owned nothing remotely like riding boots, but his old wing-tips had heels, and Thomas had lent him a set of gaiters, such as the field workers of Rob's childhood had used. As his feet were narrow and long, they found the stirrups easily and dangled down as though meant from birth to just that purpose.

"So we go," said Thomas, and let his white glimmer of a horse walk out of the stable.

"The black might object to going behind," O'Brien called out, but as Kinsman didn't seem to be objecting to anything, they let his voice die away behind them.

Outside the imposing gates was a battered road. It had a button to make a light blink, but as there were no cars in evidence, Thomas merely let MacBride walk over it. Kinsman followed, sharp-eared and high-headed. On the other side was the official beginning of Middlesex Fells State Park: a green wall only slightly broken by a hoof-stamped trail into a wood of maple, pine, and birch. The white horse set a long-strided walk, which was a middle-strided walk to the horse behind, but Kinsman did not forge against MacBride's tail end. Rob heard him snuffle, turning his head right, then left, then up to the sky.

"He's happy," he sang out to Thomas, ahead of him. Rob's hands were still on his lap.

Thomas had a little mirror clipped on to the side of his helmet. He didn't look back. "He told you so?"

"Oh yes. In many ways."

Rob was happy also. The park spread around them, deep but sun-broken. He followed the white tail, the white helmet with white head under it, as though it were a talisman. "I feel I'm in a bloody fairyland!"

Thomas did turn his head, slightly. "You came out of South Uist to Massachusetts to find fairyland?"

"So it seems."

The trail met another, larger one and they rode side by side. Neither horse jostled to be first. Thomas simply blessed his luck in this. He let MacBride shift into a trot, looking at Rob next to him. The man seemed to have no problems with the trot. He didn't attempt to post. Possibly he didn't know what posting was, but his long back moved back and forth, flexible as a snake. He was looking all around at the forest, the half-frozen streams, the mud below. So was his horse. They were moving their heads together. Damn it all.

They came to a hiker, and Thomas raised one hand. MacBride moved to the edge of the path and Kinsman fell behind him. The young man, with a daypack and a utility belt suitable for Batman, looked nervously at them. Thomas smiled politely down, and Rob grinned at the fellow with simple delight.

"People on foot tend to feel threatened by riders," Thomas observed, but Rob didn't reply.

MacBride was warmed by now, and the ground was rising. Thomas opened to a canter. Kinsman was following, at what must have been a difficult, compressed canter. Another blessing, that the long horse was willing to bend to MacBride.

Now Thomas himself was happy. He forgot the situation, the rider behind him, the worry of having a new rider on a stallion on a strange trail. He was with his horse again and they moved together.

At the top of a ridge the forest opened up into sunlight and he sat back to let MacBride take his air. Rob pulled up beside him. His cheekbones were cherry-red with the wind and the effort, and he was still grinning. Squinting in the light and grinning. Around his waist was tied the entire carefully-adjusted snaffle bridle. Rob held one end of the rope bridle in his left hand, as did Thomas. It was limp.

Rob followed Thomas's eyes. "Oh. I don't think he liked it. I didn't like it. The metal."

The metal. Why hadn't Thomas thought of that? He glanced down at Rob's neck, but the winter clothing covered what scarring remained. Rob leaned forward and began to work on Kinsman's long black neck, slick now with sweat. "He wanted to get out. Oh, but he wanted to get out. Not go in circles in a bloody ring!"

Which was the "he?" Thomas decided it didn't matter. Because the horses were sweaty and the wind was getting stronger, he turned toward home.

Cantering downhill was more difficult for a man and more dangerous for a horse. But both the horses were in good shape for it. Thomas had ridden all his life, and Rob?

Well, that horse was taking wonderful care of him. He still had that silly limp rope in his left hand, while his right sat easily on the front of the flat saddle. Long-backed horses were a marvel to ride.

MacBride, still leading, grunted as they came around a tight corner. And at the middle of the path, hidden from sight, was a tangle of orange on its side. A bike. A boy, his face scuffed and staring up in horror. The old grey pulled in his hindquarters for an off-angle jump. Thomas ducked to his horse's neck and grabbed mane as his horse went up, legs tight, veering to the right and over the kid and his bike.

MacBride kept cantering downhill.

Oh. Fuck. Thomas looked over his shoulder at the impending disaster, to see Kinsman also towering up, up, and over the obstacle, ears pricked and legs tucked so perfectly. Rob was also bent forward, holding on to nothing but the little worn bit of rope, peering down at the boy's face. His head, and his horse's head, almost scraped a heavy maple bough that hung over the bend of the trail.

Kinsman lit down like a dancer and Thomas waited for the crash from the horse's back. It didn't come. They were both slowing down, the grey and the black. MacBride became aware how close the larger horse was to his quarters and scooted forward faster. Thomas glanced forward again to check on the road ahead.

The way was fine. Flat, empty. Fine. He leaned MacBride farther to the right, where the hill rose beside the path, and tall Kinsman and tall Rob came up beside them. They broke down to trot, as though they were one horse, one man.

Rob hadn't lost a stirrup. At least, not the stirrup Thomas could see. He was staring at Thomas, wide-eyed. "Was that lad—was he supposed to be doing that? Was it we who were going too fast, or ...?"

Thomas let out an explosive breath, as did Kinsman. "No, Rob. He was not supposed to be there at all. This is not a bike trail. There are lots of bicycle trails in the Fells. This isn't one of them. And we weren't going too fast.

"Are you okay?" It seemed such a tiny question to cover the whole experience. Thomas could feel the beat of MacBride's heart between his legs. His own heart must be much like it. Rob answered.

"We both are. Or if he isn't, he has concealed it from me, and I don't know why he'd do that!" Rob stroked the slick black neck with both hands, letting the rope lie over Kinsman's withers. "He's such a good, kind fellow, and quick on his feet. He could have killed the lad!" Rob spoke nonsense—or it could have been Gaelic—into the horse's ear.

"Of course, so is your MacBride. He saw the accident coming first. We might have gone all pear-shaped but for your example!" Rob showed all his horsey teeth and nodded at Thomas. From the base of the neck, like a horse. Under the helmet he looked entirely gooney.

"I give thanks to all the Buddhas and bodhisattvas in the nine worlds," said Thomas. He let his own head and spine stretch out in relief. He grinned his own sort of grin. MacBride shook his head and snorted, as though at the idiocy of humans.

"I'll just try 'Jesus, Mary, and Joseph,'" replied Rob. "Or just bless a horse who can jump like a good sine wave."

The path narrowed again and Thomas pulled ahead. "Should we call someone about the lad who had the accident?" Rob sang forward.

Thomas pulled out his mobile phone and dialed. "I hate to phone while driving," he said. Rob knew it for a joke.

Thomas did make the call and seemed happy enough with the results. Rob couldn't help but be concerned about the lad, although he hadn't seemed injured, or no more than a fall from a short bike onto soft ground would account for.

Back at the stallion house, they both dried and groomed their horses. Thomas considered the idea of clipping MacBride's coat, but as it was only mid-January he wasn't certain the idea was practical.

"I can't find any scratches, nor heat in his legs," said Rob, huddled under Kinsman's belly.

MacBride was unscratched as well. The two horses were side by side, contently. "Mind if I check him, too?"

"Appreciate it. It's been years since I had the care of a pony."

Thomas snickered. "Are you calling your masterpiece a pony?"

"There's nothing wrong with a pony," murmured Rob, lifting one hind foot. "Until your legs get too long. And that's not the pony's fault, is it?"

The stable-master came through the door. "I heard there was an accident," he said, looking from one horse to another.

"Not ours," answered Thomas. "A kid on a mountain bike slipped out at a turn. Didn't even have the sense to get that thing out of the way. Didn't seem to be hurt ... We went over him and had to go on down."

"Thomas called it in," said Rob, head upside down as he was cleaning the last hoof. "I do hope the police will let us know how the lad is doing. It must have been a fright."

O'Brien gave a tight grin. "I believe the fright will be more once the park rangers find him there."

Thomas brushed out his horse's heavy, stained tail. "Tell me, O'Brien. Who else lives in here: in the main stallion house?"

"No one, since October. That was one reason I was able to leave the black here."

"Can you think of a reason we can't move MacBride in with him? Out of his private building? In adjoining stalls, maybe?"

Colm O'Brien looked at the two horses snatching bites from the same mesh bag of alfalfa treat. "Why not? It was just that your—that Kinsman didn't like his last companion much."

"Why not?" Rob MacAulay asked the question as though he expected a reasonable answer. O'Brien considered. "Can't say. He was a Quarter Horse. Sired a lot of good cutting horses."

"Well, that would do it," answered Thomas, again as though that made obvious sense.

As they walked back home, Thomas asked casually, "So what are you going to teach, Rob? Math? Physics? Flying over invisible or unexpected dangers?"

"I could teach double-handed weeding, I suppose," answered Rob, equally lightly, and then turned to his binary. "Maths and Physics together, to any place that will have me now."

They passed through the steel gate, which moved easier now after a few days' use. "Not afraid of the consequences of it anymore?"

"Of course I am. But the equations will come out anyway.

And besides. As your man said …" The gate slammed behind them. "No Matter."

WHEN A MAN HAS EXPERIENCE, connections, and money, things happen quickly. It was only the next morning when a backhoe was led over the soggy, almost snow-free ground, and the wall came down.

It was only a small part of the old brick wall, of course. Suitable for a human-sized gate. Rob and Thomas had looked online at the immediate options only the day before, but they had not been too picky.

Wrought iron, like the substantial gate that announced the old stable to the world, but so much smaller. Arched up in the middle, with twisted uprights that ended in lance-points, more ornamental than threatening. Maple leaves seemed to be falling down the uprights. They had been chemically treated to show green or orange, or just rust.

"I wonder why the people who ordered it refused it in the end?" asked Rob, sitting side by side on the chintz sofa and looking at the image in the tablet.

"Who knows? Too big, too small, too many maple leaves? It is large for our uses, but I think Grace would have liked it."

Rob liked it. In the middle of the thing was a green box, not wrought iron at all. "That's a combination lock," said Thomas, pointing. "Tony can punch in her code and come in when she wants."

Rob looked slyly at the new Thomas Sullivan. "You're trusting the wee lass a great deal."

"Hardly. I can always change the code. Besides, the kids were climbing the wall already. And this will make her feel good."

They watched the wall come down. The job was so carefully done. Each deep red oblong was punched free from its old mortar, one after the other, down to the ground. Then the backhoe came forward and took the short section of freed wall and wiggled it back and forth, like a tooth in its socket. It gave, almost tilting the backhoe as it turned the piece to a flatbed lorry that had followed it into the Sullivan place. Last came the concrete base, like the root of a tooth. It was wiggled, broken, and came straight up. Trailing dirt. Leaving a long, deep hole.

"I could fill that with topsoil myself," suggested Rob, who longed to be somehow a part of this project.

"Let the locals do it. They appreciate the work. They'll respect you more for it."

Rob looked at Thomas, trying to absorb a point of view he'd never encountered before.

They were at a first floor—no. Now here it was second floor window, where the curtains were linen lace, and they were watching the process with warm tea in their hands. The gate itself went up with remarkable speed. And it fit perfectly. Rob heard Thomas sigh with satisfaction. They were opened to a new world—new possibilities. Literally, into a turn-around in a small gated community with outsized houses and small gardens.

Their own garden was a churned mess. Rob wondered if he ought to turn his hand to the repair, or whether it would offend the locals.

"Have you sent out your feelers?" Thomas asked the question so lightly as he turned away from the window.

"I have. And before you ask, I took your advice and let the K through 12 schools be. Until I'm rejected by the others."

Thomas led him out of the room with the view, which had once been a guest room and then had become one of the bedrooms for people doing those odd things called "corporate retreats." It still had old furniture. An old bed and dresser, all mahogany.

"You would have been rejected by the primary schools,

Rob. You don't have the qualifications. And they would be embarrassed. As though an elephant were asking for work on a pony-ride."

Rob didn't argue the point. He only wondered if Thomas would ever run out of animal analogies for him.

THE DINNER WAS SCHEDULED to be early, because of the presence of nine-year-old Tony. It was the first time the new gate was really used, and the girl punched in the gate-code herself, reaching up and scowling intently. She stepped back as though it was about to fling itself open against her, but it was not so magical, nor so high-tech a gate as that. She had to return and pull one of the tall iron posts backwards. Four adults clapped.

Rob and Thomas stepped out of the Sullivan garden into the Kaye's world. At the end of the short turnaround was a rounded street with sidewalks and pocket front gardens and house-fronts that looked each different, and each a variation on a theme.

"It's just a little walk," said Dr. Kaye, who was wearing a tan woolen belted coat. He was a slim man, shorter than Thomas, with black hair and gold-rimmed glasses. No trace of a French accent, which Rob had half-expected. Tony's mother was taller than her husband by a few centimeters, and her figure was generous. Like her daughter, she wore red. They all touched hands, trying not to seem formal, and Thomas was toting two bottles of wine.

Tony broke free from her mother's hand as they went down the street and took Rob in a hug, which he wore somewhere around his waist. "I'm so glad you're all here," she said. "And made this wonderful gate with leaves on it!"

"Well, lass, we didn't really make it ourselves, or it wouldn't look so wonderful, I think," he replied.

Thomas got a hug, too, which seemed to surprise him utterly.

Athena took from her purse the card she had gotten from Thomas three days before. It was now smudged. "Someone scratched over the name Heddiman and wrote Sullivan. What does that mean, Thomas?"

"I haven't had new cards made," he answered, glancing from one of the Kayes to the other. "I've changed my name."

"Why's that? If it's any of my business, of course."

Thomas gave an easy smile and ran his hand through his hair, and made the joke. "A lot of people change their names when they get married."

Tony's father adjusted his glasses and looked at Thomas. "To ... Sullivan?"

Thomas said nothing. Just grinned. Rob had heard the joke before. If there had been any ice, it was now broken.

"You've done a lot with the place," said Thomas, looking at their entrance, where the carpeted rooms and rounded staircase were all built into the structure in order to give the effect of open spacing, without the disadvantages of loss of privacy.

"You mean the architects did," said Alan Kaye, taking off his glasses and drying the lenses on a tissue from his vest pocket. He looked at the layout of the ground floor with the eyes of a man who thought of his heating bills. "It's 'green,' I'll give you that. Insulation, triple-paned glass, solar panels, and solar paneling on the roof. They all have that, here."

"I think Thomas was talking about the colouring. The rugs on the walls: the paintings," added Rob. Thomas, who had been talking at random, let the comment stand.

"The paintings are Mommy's," said Tony, proudly.

"Are they?" Rob wandered over to the nearest acrylic portrait, which was of Tony herself, some years ago, hanging from a tire-swing, and half-obscured by leaves. He'd kicked off his boots in the tiled foyer and left them there. Thomas had shoved them more discretely against one wall as he entered, and had taken his own boots off more neatly.

"My ma used to paint," said Rob, standing the proper distance from the long painting to appreciate it. It was an appealing painting, both as portraiture and as a work of colour and movement. "She had the luck to have tourists all summer, both for her watercolors and her pottery. Helped the family finance quite a bit. But that was not why she started, of course. Are the weavings yours too, 'Thena?"

"Wish I could say so. I have a friend outside Concord. We barter some."

"Mommy has a gallery!" stated Tony.

"Hush, child. I don't *have* a gallery. Sometimes I display in one. Along with my friend in textiles."

Alan stepped closer. Having taken off his overcoat, he was dressed much like Rob, minus the heavy wear on the sport jacket. "If you want the nickel tour?" Thomas stepped behind him, pulling Rob away from the long painting by one elbow.

"We can't have a dog," said Tony, as though describing a great deficiency in their living style, like lack of indoor plumbing.

"Not now, Breton," said her father.

"Not even a cat," the girl added, and receiving glares from both parents, shut up.

"Every room can be sealed off from each another," Alan announced. That seemed important to him. Thomas looked at the girl skipping and babbling behind them and thought he understood the man.

The back garden was small and high-walled. Few of the trees were more than a century old, but the entire effect was bright.

They ended their tour of the downstairs in a more cluttered back-parlour with audio, telly, and various tablets. This room seemed much more used than the front room. One table was scattered with supplies familiar to Rob. "This is where you do your homework, Tony!" He seated himself at the low table without invitation. His knees rose up remarkably and he took one school ruler into his hand. "Your maths homework!" He looked delighted.

"I *hate* arithmetic," said young Tony with remarkable passion.

"Tony!" cried Athena.

"Breton!" called Alan, at the same moment. "Not that. Not now."

"Well, I do. You can make me do it, but you can't make me like it!"

"Oh, you poor creature!" sang Rob, holding the ruler like an awkward and useless scepter in his left hand. His large eyes were tragic as he looked across at the young girl.

"Can I help in the kitchen?" Thomas broke in, nudging the grown-ups out of the room with his eyes and face. As they left he was murmuring, "Better just leave them alone now."

Tony refused to sit with him. Her hands were clenched militarily at her sides. "I just hate numbers. I always have!"

He shrugged. It was a gesture that bounced his tweed jacket, clinking whatever was in his pockets. "Then you should do it without numbers."

"Arithmetic without numbers?"

"Of course. Numbers are only the final part of things. The way to prove to others you've gotten things right. Right now I'll need something long and round: a cylinder." He glanced all around the room.

"Like a candle?"

"Not a taper."

"A what?"

"Have you got an inexpensive candle? Something for when the power goes out?"

Tony, interested against her own will, sorted around in a drawer beneath the television screen where lurked a jumble of sticks of incense and a few grimy old remotes. She found a cheap white paraffin candle. "This?"

"Exactly. So now," and he placed it on its side beneath the ruler.

"If we get wax on the table, the 'rents will be mad," she warned him.

"No fire. I'm just making a lever."

"What's a leever? Like a teeter-totter?"

He nodded. "And now, two riders for the teeter-totter." He took out two pebbles from his left pocket. "These are the same weight."

"How do you know?" Now she consented to sit down next to him on the sofa.

"Because they're the same weight as the bigger one in my right pocket," Rob replied.

"Why?"

"For balance." She asked no more. "So we have balance on the lever. No numbers, but it is an equation, because the left side and the right make a balance. That's an equation. No numbers at all, but it is balance. And it satisfies."

"Satisfies who?"

"Me. Now let's take the two on the left side inward a bit and see what will happen."

"It'll go flop!"

"See, Tony. You're a natural mathematician already."

"You're trying to fool me, Rob," Tony said in tones of deep cynicism.

"I wouldn't." Rob moved the two left stones inward and the ruler did go *flop*. Then he moved the candle so the balance point was off-center and they had balance again.

IN THE KITCHEN the oven was already heated and various cardboard containers from the local organic shop were being heated. Neither Athena nor Alan were kitchen-proud, which was just as well. They put Thomas to make-work, setting the table and opening the wine.

"He won't get her to like math," said Alan. "We've tried everything."

"Then he'll feel sorry for her. He enjoys it so much."

"Really enjoys it?"

"Oh, 'Thena!" chided Alan.

"Well, I know he's good at it an' all but …"

"It makes him deliriously happy to make equations balance," said Thomas, finding the appropriate wine glasses in the cupboard. Three of them. He spoke about his mate with the sort of amused tolerance that hid his secret pride. "And so he wants people to be happy like he is."

"Good luck to him. Tony is a stubborn little girl." Athena spoke about Tony in the same manner. "And if I know her, she'll try to bribe him."

The first thing Tony said when she led Rob into the kitchen was "If I do my math homework for a week I get a ride on his horse."

"See?" said Athena complacently.

"*His* horse?" Thomas spoke less confidently. "I have a beautiful white horse, Tony. He can do all kinds of tricks.…"

"Rob has The Black Stallion," said Tony.

"Stallion?" Both parents looked alarmed. So did Thomas.

"I said we'd *ask* Kinsman," said Rob, from the doorway. "I didn't say it was a settled thing."

"I won't let her get hurt," Thomas assured them. "Not for a moment."

"Nor would I," said Rob, and added, "You should see Tony's intuitive grasp of topology!"

"And manipulation," said her father.

Two of them drank a fine pinot with their Mediterranean hot casserole and two kinds of salad. Athena had a German White. Rob and Tony had water. Alan had a sausage, which

Thomas declined. It was all good. The conversation soon separated into a monologue about the increasing differences of income between a minority of US wealthy people and the vast rest. This was led by Alan. 'Thena, sensing the presence of Wealth at the table, tried to steer it otherwise, but there was no hope of that. Nor did Thomas object. And Rob, being the foreigner, simply absorbed it all. He did mention his spouse's frequent involvement with the Southern Poverty Law Center. That caused Alan to stare at Thomas for all of five seconds, re-evaluating, and then he picked up where he'd left off.

'Thena listened to her husband's voice rising and felt, as a hostess, a bit unsettled, especially with the repeated phrase "more and more of the country's wealth in fewer hands." He was talking to Rob who was nodding with rapt attention, as one would expect of a man who knew nothing about the affairs of a strange country. Thomas, however, had broken off a friendly interchange about the Hudson River School of Painting to listen.

She put her hand on Thomas's arm, in its grey cable-knit sweater. "You have to understand. My Alan's a sort of an old Leftist. His father was. It's not like he's a radical, or anything."

Thomas crinkled his eyes at her. He put down his fork and laced his hands behind his neck. "Oh, don't sell him short, 'Thena. That was a great comment about the Hoover Dam and how the Desert of the Dead became called the Imperial Valley. I haven't heard such talk since I was a kid on the sloop Clearwater. And it's all true."

Tony realized they were talking politics again. She hated it when her parents talked politics. "Are you going to talk about China, again? Or will it be Russia?

"If we do, I ask to be excused." She sounded formal, for a nine-year-old.

All four adults stared at her, and the conversation died.

"No, honey," said her mother. "We're trying to talk about

things we can do something about. Maybe. We won't do that scare talk in front of you."

"Everyone else does!" Breton Kaye looked at her plate. "At school. In the news. I hate it."

"Me, too," said Thomas, so quietly.

And so they started over again. As they had run through the Hudson River School of painting, Rob started in with tide-pools. He knew a lot about tide-pools.

But with Alan and Thomas there, and with the wine, things returned to inequalities and immigrants.

Rob thought it an opportunity to say something about Italians in the Highlands of Scotland, but Alan's talk about Americans born of Syrian ancestry ran impassioned over him. Thomas laughed and looked straight into the deep brown eyes of his hostess. "You don't have any idea of who we are, do you, ma'am? I mean, you may have read some scandalous story about Rob's escape from slavery in Britain, but you don't know that he was a manual worker for a few years himself. Or that I have spent much of my life doing software for the Southern Poverty Law Center. Would knowing that have changed your inviting us to dinner?"

'Thena sat back in her second best company dress and stared at him. "My sweet Jesus! It would have. I would have kissed you both and dragged you over that damned wall. I thought you were rich and famous in your big house and condescending to visit little old us."

"I don't know what anybody is *talking* about!" Tony had been bored about the Hudson River School and tired of the farm workers again, but at least the grown-ups were laughing now.

"Neither do we, child," said her mother, pouring herself another glass of wine and giving one to her guest. "We haven't an idea what we're talking about."

"I inherited the property from my aunt, Grace Sullivan, and she didn't want it broken up. Since she and I despised the rest of the family—except for my little sister—I've been leasing it out until I felt ready to settle. And to adopt her name.—But that's another story, for another day. Now we're here, and the question is—how to find a place where Rob can tell his incomprehensible story called the Theory of United Fields?"

"A story?" asked Tony.

"Yeah, but I don't think it's written in English," said Thomas, shrugging, drinking red wine.

Their excitement had broken through Alan's monologue. Both he and Rob were now staring at them. "What are you talking about?" Alan asked his wife.

"About some story," said Tony. "But not in English. I don't get it."

"About Rob getting a job," announced Thomas, his face flushed with laughter and good wine.

"Oh, not in front of everybody," cried Rob, his own face flushed for his own reasons.

Alan peered at him. "I assumed you were starting at Harvard," he said.

"You will understand, at least," said Rob to Alan, in the front parlour, while the rest of the adults were in the back, talking music. "I had my tenure revoked, at Edinburgh University. That is a serious mark and carries through."

Alan reared back. "Through changes of policy? Through vindication by the Government?"

"I was not, as you say, vindicated. I was pardoned."

Alan Kaye clapped his hands together on his lap, as though keeping time to a music he did not like hearing. "Pardoned for a crime it is known you did not do!"

"Nonetheless, it was a pardon, and I have worse than no references. And am not a citizen of this country. That is why I did not apply to Harvard. For any position. And, Alan, I am not certain what position I am qualified for."

Alan Kaye had a high rounded forehead and he wore his

hair straight back. He held his head in both hands. "I believe they will make a position to suit you. Whatever you want."

Rob twitched at the thought. "Am I such a celebrity-freak as that?"

"No, you are such a physicist as that. I will make inquiries."

"Please don't."

"Then, will you at least speak to someone in the department? Regarding a seminar, or something to introduce your ideas to the faculty? I believe you represent the Quantum Field Theory people."

Rob smiled faintly. "I was once one of them. I represented no one but myself. Edinburgh was never fond of my ideas. Not enough cosmology. Black holes and such."

"I am a geologist, Rob. The planet that is my specialty is constructed of matter. Is it all not just a matter of fields?"

Rob smiled wider.

"And, I remind you, I am not just a petroleum geologist." Alan said that with rolling sarcasm.

Tony had somehow reconstructed their dinner conversation as an unbreakable promise of a horse ride. She was sent to bed as Rob and Thomas went home. Went home through the pretty gate.

"I do feel for the lass, Thomas," said Rob, closing it behind them. "With her fear of the major nations. I remember when I was a child, on a small island...."

"I do what I can," answered Thomas, shortly. Bitterly. "Just what I can."

Rob followed him into the house, thinking on it.

⬛

THE NEXT DAY Rob did send out a CV to Harvard University. One on paper and one via the real mails. It left him feeling uneasy—exposed. Later that day they went to a shop in Lexington where he was fitted for riding boots, as the gaiters had had a tendency to come loose on his long thin legs. At another shop they bought the light body protection used by riders over fences and a helmet that fit well. Without telling Rob, Thomas also purchased a rubber-coated simple bit—also without telling the clerk it was to be used on a stallion, and not a three-year-old new to bits. Then they returned to the stables and Kinsman showed Rob the beginnings of how one goes over fences.

All this required great persuasion on Thomas's part, as Rob could not see the sense of teaching a horse to go over the fences that were there to keep him in. And especially as Kinsman could already do it so well. Thomas used the explanation that Kinsman, like Rob, enjoyed the experience of flying and wasn't permitted to do it without a human on his back. So it was a matter of obligation.

And with great pride Thomas Sullivan watched his binary go over the short fences of a training arena on his huge horse. Kinsman insisted on over-jumping the three-foot fences by eight inches, but that seemed to be more a statement of opinion on the horse's part, rather than flawed estimation. Thomas didn't bother teaching Rob the beginner's trick of fixing the reins against the horse's neck for balance. Rob hadn't begun jumping that way during the accident on the trail, so why bother now?

Rob kept a careful, slight tension against the horse's mouth with his long arms and the short reins, pulling in and letting go, using the opposite hand to slip in the excess so that any slack might not bang against Kinsman's teeth. His ambidexterity was a great help, and he was careful, imagining what might be painful to the horse. Especially when it was an instrument with metal in it.

Where Rob's face turned, the horse's followed. Or so it seemed, though that might have been looking at the thing backwards. Once they got they got the order of fences wrong, and Kinsman shook his head and roared an equine curse at himself, went back and did it right. Rob seemed unaware of the entire problem.

A tall blond woman wearing tall blond breeches walked up beside him. She watched a while. "Where does he usually ride?" she asked Thomas.

"Here," said Thomas, shortly.

"Huh! He must have been away. I've been here six months and haven't seen him."

"Very far away." Thomas didn't look from the horse and rider as they repeated the jumps.

"He's over-jumping by a lot," she continued, turning her smooth head left and right, evaluating.

Thomas grunted. "I think Kinsman is offended at the three-foot fences."

"Why doesn't the man correct him?"

Now Thomas did look at her. Neutrally. So neutrally. "You'll have to ask him. I wouldn't dare, myself."

The young woman's blue eyes widened. Soon she walked away.

When Rob led Kinsman to the rail, they were both warm and slick with sweat, despite the temperature. "You're right, Thomas," said Rob. "He does enjoy it. I shall have to do it more often with him."

Thomas nodded, making no comment about Rob's proficiency. None seemed to be asked for. "You did notice he was going about twenty centimeters over the top of each fence?" Thomas reached in to scratch the black horse behind the ears, at a spot under the bridle. Kinsman leaned to him.

"I did. Isn't that a good thing?"

"Usually humans want it more exact."

Rob cracked his neck left and right, thinking. Kinsman shifted from left to right in time. "Then why didn't we set the jumps higher?"

A shrug. "We didn't know."

"Next time, then," said Rob, and began to walk his horse forward, cooling him down.

Rob next watched Thomas and MacBride do the same series, only with fences four and a half feet high. He found the horse and rider entirely enthralling. It was so understated. And MacBride seemed to be half-asleep through the whole thing. His hooves, so neatly close they seemed almost tied together as he went over, barely showed air between the tops of the fences and the bottom of the shoe. He began to see the beauty in such exactitude. He felt he had been making all sorts of unnecessary motions, and wondered whether Kinsman was embarrassed to be ridden by him.

He promised his horse he would do better by him.

There were showers at the stable, but it was easier for the two to walk home. Rob, at least, was unaware of the glances of envy the other riders shot at them as they went through their private gate.

"I like riding. I really do," stated Rob, as Thomas fiddled with the old key in sweaty fingers.

"Why? The flight? The perfect communication with the horse?"

"All that, of course. But for them, it's the only way they're allowed out, isn't it? I mean, we're not allowed to give them a road-pass and let them travel the streets and parks? We're sort of like nannies for much more active animals than ourselves. An excuse for them to get out into the world they belong in. It's otherwise such a sad life for a horse."

"Well said." Thomas led the way home.

7

Learning and Teaching

The previous night Rob had had a dream. It had been a bit like the usual sort of dream: one in which he was placed before a room of people to give a speech and found he could not make a sound. Or worse, that his teeth had all fallen out and he never *would* make a sound again. In this dream, he was in his usual dream-lecture room, which was his father's small classroom, and was determined not to give a speech at all. Yet all sorts of dangerous, mean, and insulting things were coming out of his mouth, in a clear, reasonable voice, and he could not stop them.

He had no illusions concerning the mystic meaning of this dream. He was afraid of saying what he had to say. They were the only things he *did* have in him to say. He'd woken up in a heart-pounding sweat, wondering for a moment if the entire last few years had been only a dream themselves—a dream of running, hiding, being chased, ostracized, and almost killed— because that dream was preferable to the speech he had to give.

But here, in this foreign place, had come a change. With two words from a man he had never before met, he had given up his life of passivity and taken up the job of teaching again. Dream or no dream, it was done. And he would enjoy every moment he could.

Late that afternoon he had the second visit with Kyan Sensei. By now he had the basic clothes for workout: an undyed cotton set much like loose pajamas, tied closed with a belt of white batting. The jacket was always folded over his middle with the left side out. That was important, although Thomas could not tell him why. It was tied with a simple square knot, so that the ends both came out high and fell over like fountains. That was important, also. Rob found it simpler than tying one's shoes, although Thomas, who supervised his first dressing, said many people had trouble. Maybe it was something about being left-handed. Or growing up on boats.

He presented himself, barefoot, to Kyan Sensei, and was taught how to bow. Then he was asked to do something he had not heard of by name, but turned out to be the first dance on the mat Thomas had taught him. He looked over at Thomas, but Sensei said he was to do it alone. He did.

He received no correction during the entire thing, which made him nervous, and then was asked, "Do you always go so low? With your knees?"

Thomas wasn't looking at him. At all. He said "Sensei, I just do what I saw Thomas—I mean, Mr. Sullivan—doing."

He was then asked if he knew another dance. He did the second one he had done with Thomas, though he was not so certain of it. Still no analysis, nor correction. Finally, the old teacher said to him. "I think you should work on evasion, Dr. MacAulay. Do you know what that is?"

"Getting out of the way?"

A great smile from the old, crinkled face. "Yes. I will punch at you and you will turn your head right or left so you will not be there when the fist comes. Oh, don't look so worried. I will punch slowly."

Rob looked relieved.

"At first."

They stood beside each other, and after a moment, Sensei asked Thomas to bring a set of risers. Thomas did. It took many risers before Sensei and Rob were more or less face-to-face. Then he pushed his fist toward Rob's face, in dream-like slowness. Rob bent right. Another came, using the opposite small fist, and Rob went right again. That repeated. For many times it repeated, and after a while it was more of a job to evade the little strikes. Then it was a hard job. Left, right, right, left, left again.

Then two lefts came together and Rob was going right and he was hit just under the cheekbone. "I never said I was going to keep going at the same speed forever," Kyan Sensei said placidly. "You had stopped watching."

Rob blinked. That small nothing of a punch was still stinging. The sensei began again. Left, right, left, right. And then a second right. They went on for what seemed an eternity, and Rob was definitely watching. Evading.

Faster and faster. No time for thought. Not even the thought of *When will this stop?*

And the small fist came and he had judged wrong and there was no time except to be hit, but Rob wasn't hit. The sensei threw that last punch into the air where Rob wasn't and then stopped quite suddenly and bowed to Rob, who had barely the mind to bow in return, and who stumbled back from his position.

Kyan Sensei stepped down from his tier of risers, saying, "That is evasion. There are many kinds of evasion. Moving the whole head, as we did today. Turning the face just enough is another. Bobbing. Weaving. And later, evasions of the body. Each is a lifetime's study.

"This you will not practice with Mr. Sullivan. With Thomas. This you will practice only with me. Here. And it need not be daily. You will find you will be sore later, though it will not seem so now."

At the moment Rob's face was acceptably sore, where it had been hit. He was certain the teacher's words would be accurate tomorrow. He bowed again, and finding he was much sweatier than he had expected to be, passed out of the room toward the men's shower.

Thomas had been waiting silently by the wall. As Kyan Sensei passed him, the teacher said, "Yes, I saw."

Thomas only nodded to him.

"Do you think he himself is aware of it?"

"I am not sure. I know he does not *want* to be aware of it."

The old man shook his head and tilted it toward his student. "Better that than if he had wanted it. Men can be proud about unusual skills."

Thomas thought of all sorts of answers, but said none of them. He was simply glad his teacher had seen Rob "flinch." That it was a real thing, and not a phenomenon inside Thomas's own head.

"I will teach him to be aware, in time," said Sensei. "And if I myself am skilled enough, I will teach him control. That will be a new sort of teaching, for me." He bowed quite deeply to Thomas. "Thank you for bringing this to me," he said, then added, "Now get ready for Master Class."

Thomas hurried to do so.

———

IT WAS A WARM WINTER. At least Thomas said so. He said all winters were all warm, compared to his childhood, and that the melting poles were too far gone to be halted. To Rob it was always cold, and most especially so when the snow revealed the deadened earth. But it was not as dark as the winters back home.

And he was kept busy, what with his stringent physical—as opposed to physics—labors. The daily work with Kinsman was, to Rob, important. He found his time with the horse was much like a class schedule: not to be interrupted by small things. And it took place in the huge State Park, with or without Thomas.

There were days when Thomas was unable to show, being locked into the machine from the time he woke until the time he collapsed (with the unmistakable suddenness of a field collapse). A day such as this usually meant that some South-East Asian shrimp fishermen or a shipload of Western Asians had to be delivered from the smugglers of humanity. That was Thomas being Thomas, and Rob let it be.

But on such days he gave Rob permission to hold MacBride's halter in his hand, so Thomas's horse could share the outing, even though the man could not. When MacBride slipped his halter the first time it was half by accident, but as the wise horse did not lose himself or get them in trouble, Rob did not mention the event to Thomas. Subsequent times, MacBride's halter was not even in Rob's hand, and he did not mention those events to Thomas either. He had conversed extensively with MacBride upon the seriousness of this situation, being as it was a matter of trust, and had then reproached himself for speaking. He didn't really believe MacBride understood English, but the horse understood something.

Rob MacAulay found his mind expanding in a strange way. He felt more like the child he had been in the tide pools than in all his years since, and he found it good.

Physicists and mathematicians grew more rigid with age; it was an accepted fact. Rob wondered now whether some of that was not intrinsic to age, but simply that they all rejected this sort of body-learning more and more as they grew in academic learning. Gained "tenure." Well, Rob had lost tenure, and it seems that wasn't as bad an experience as expected.

All this thinking happened in the wide area around the red brick Sullivan house while Rob was waiting for a

Harvard guest lecture to be scheduled. He found he was in no hurry for the lecture. He wasn't sure what he was going to say.

He also kept up with the news of the United States, a place that had been described to him by Thomas as fifty ornery small countries with a government that no one ever liked. The more Rob travelled in the news-streams, city to city, the more he found this to be a good description of things as they were. But as a man born in a small country among many other small countries, he was not surprised.

But the news always infuriated Thomas. After a half-hour of streaming, he could go into full Don Quixote mode, and Rob heard him daily apologizing to him for the absurdities of some ignorant elected official in one far state or another. It did no good for Rob to remind him that he was now the foreigner and did not feel hurt by or connected to one piece of this hurtful nonsense or another, so apologies were not necessary. Thomas was just being Thomas.

And one particular morning, when Thomas sat down at the kitchen table, amid toast and marmalade, and said he was going to be leaving to put out some fire—this one in Nebraska —and that he did not know when it would be put out, Rob was not surprised at all, but rather relieved.

Thomas was returning to his own balance. Rob nodded and wished him well.

"That's all you have to say? You'll be alone here, for I can't say how long. I thought you might be ... I don't know. Upset?"

Rob smiled. "I've been alone before. Far more alone than having you fly away in an airplane. Besides, now that I've bought 'Thena's friend's old car, I can drive at will. Wherever I wish to go."

What he saw in Thomas's eyes was not reassuring.

"You have seen me drive, Thomas. Have I ever veered off into the wrong side of the road?"

Thomas could only shake his head. But Thomas was right handed. Such people could not understand.

The next day, Thomas packed two bags of clothing and one small hard case containing everything that connected him to this presence in the cloud (which was, so disappointingly, made of heavy machinery built firmly on the earth), and he left. He would not even permit Rob to drive him to the airport. Thomas was, for the first time since last summer, gone from Rob.

8

The Big Jump

Rob MacAulay walked the circuit of the Sullivan wall and felt with his right hand the thin band around his left third finger. It was almost unnoticeable on his pale skin. Platinum. Elemental. Round. Orbital. He thought of his binary, orbiting at a new distance to him.

It was all in one's frame of reference.

He opened the gate to Tony's world and picked her up for her mathematics lesson. This time he broached the idea of numbers, promising they would only be as many as the fingers on her hands. He then surprised her by counting, not from one to ten, but from zero to nine. So began a rhapsody on the meaning of zero. And Tony managed to accept that. She even seemed to like zero, and Rob thought that a wonderful bit of progress, so he was glad to give her a reward, which was the walk through the property and out the second gate into the stables.

For her first ride, Athena had accompanied her. O'Brien had seen them admiring Kinsman and offered the girl a ride on his own using-horse, who was Kinsman's son by a

Connemara mare. He was an excellent lesson horse and much more appropriately sized. She had ridden with an adult on either side, ridden proudly, wearing her own new red helmet and bright red rubber riding boots.

From then on, she had been allowed to come with Rob alone. On this ride, Rob rode Kinsman and she rode the smaller version, all around the indoor ring. O'Brien glanced in once or twice, but the animals and humans were behaving impeccably.

Later that same day Rob returned and gave Kinsman a wild ride up and down a sloppy mountain as his own reward.

Two more days passed. No call from Thomas.

On Wednesday, which was his usually scheduled time, Rob drove down to the dojo, where he warmed up with katas in the small room and then engaged in Kyan Sensei's routine of evasion—right, left, right, left—increasing speed leading to the trick. This time he said to the old man, "Sensei, I believe I know what you are doing with me, here."

"Do you?" His eyes crinkled up, but warily.

"You are trying to make me flinch. Only, on command."

"Ha! Good. Then do it."

And he did. It was not such a shock to the mind as he had feared, nor did the teacher praise him for "wiggling his ears" well. Flinch left, right. Sideways.

He simply hated to talk about it. Kyan Sensei seemed to agree it should not be talked about, so that worked well between them.

Thomas had been right about one thing. Letting the car drive him automatically around Boston was ridiculous.

━━

ELEVEN DAYS HAD PASSED since Thomas had gone off. Rob noted the days, not because he was needy in any sense.

Thomas had gone to do what Thomas did, and had he not been the way he was, Rob would likely not be standing on the earth now. No, he noted the days because he was exact in things. That was all. Certainly that was all.

And he still did feel the presence of his binary, orbiting in ways for which he had no words. No equations, either. Not yet. He was not aware he was spinning the little grey orbit on his left hand.

He decided to go for a ride in the hills. Yesterday he had done the dojo and taken Kinsman around the jumps. Today they simply must fly.

It was drizzling. End of January and no snow on the ground at all, and it was drizzling, but that meant the ground was not frozen. He knew Kinsman would not mind the drizzle. After a moment, he was certain that MacBride wouldn't, either. He put on his long black riding coat, which was waterproof and yet called, for some reason, a duster. It was wool-lined. He wore his riding wellies simply because it was raining.

The stable-gate was now soundless with oil and use. O'Brien's stables were well occupied, despite the rain. Horses whinnied as Rob strode by. Sometimes he sang back.

Both the black horse and the white were excited to see him.

By now it was second nature for Rob to halter and saddle up his tall horse, and when he opened MacBride's stall door, the white horse put his own head into his flimsy rope thing. He almost forgot his helmet, but he had promised Thomas he wouldn't scramble his brains while he was away. This was a significant sacrifice, because Rob hated hats of any kind. Likely that had all started because his ears stuck out so.

The three were out of the stallion barn, moving smartly, through the big gate and over the road.

He tied the end of MacBride's halter around the horse's neck so it wouldn't dangle, and let Kinsman set the pace. Rain pattered on the black cotton and off the brim of his black helmet and steam began to rise from his horse's back. He could hear MacBride snorting along behind him.

It was a grand ride, and Rob had nothing to do with the decisions made as they went. It was sloppy, very sloppy, but nowhere near as dark as a Highlands winter day would be. And no bicycles flung across the path.

MacBride let out a grunt, and Kinsman slowed his pace. They were approaching the crest where the trees thinned out and they had seen no one.

But Rob felt as though Thomas was riding there with them. That was good. Proper.

Maybe. Something about the moment didn't feel proper at all.

As he had no work for his hands, he was spinning the small grey orbit that went around his finger and he was *suddenly* aware of Thomas. And it was not good. At all.

It was just a ring. Frame of reference. Binary.

"Wait!" he cried to the horses, knowing all the while they did not speak English.

And Rob fell from Kinsman's back. He fell not sideways but straight down, landing on hands and feet.

But he landed over Thomas.

And Thomas lay on his stomach on a sidewalk. In the snow.

Rob caught his balance in confusion and stood again, his arms out at his sides for balance. His duster's shoulder-coat spread out to each side as he raised his arms.

There were men in front of him, in this sudden, bright daylight. Staring at him as he stared at them. He heard himself cry out, wordlessly. Then the men were running away. He swiveled to look around, and men were running away behind him, too.

Thomas groaned and without a thought Rob bent down and picked him up. Thomas was unexpectedly heavy.

There was no confusion in his mind, as the possible clashed with the impossible. There was only need, and Rob answered it simply.

"Kinsman!" Rob screamed, and though the horse did not speak English, he did know his name.

There was no sense of time or of passage. Only the weight in his arms and Rob's confidence in the horse.

But they were back in the drizzle and the slop, and he was sliding down the side of the horse he thought he had already fallen from. Rob sat on the trail, with his arse in the wet, holding Thomas. In Massachusetts.

Two noses came nuzzling close, one white, one black. Rob looked helplessly at them.

Thomas tried to lift his head. Rob assisted. "Thomas? Thomas? Are you conscious, man?"

Brown eyes opened and then closed against the rain. Thomas's face was bloody. "Rob? Are you ..."

Thomas looked around him, at the horses' heads, legs, the muddy trail. At Rob. "How'd I get—?"

Rob tried to think as Thomas would think. Practical. Practical. "Thomas, we left a number of people in—wherever. Nebraska, was it? Do you need a phone? I left everyone but you behind, if that matters."

Thomas stared unfocused for only a moment, and then he did take his mobile out from his trouser pocket. He made connection and left a short text. Rob had no idea how a man so hurt could accomplish this.

Then Rob helped him onto MacBride's back, told the horse quite severely he must not drop Thomas, tied the end of MacBride's rope halter around both of Thomas's wrists, to attach him to the neck of the horse, vaulted onto Kinsman's back, and carefully walked them all down the sloppy trail to the stable.

O'Brien asked no questions. He called the ambulance.

ROB SAT beside Thomas at hospital (*the* hospital, they said here), still with his black duster lying on the floor. His binary went from semiconscious to completely unconscious as he entered medical care, which seemed only practical to Rob. Thomas *would* wait for help to arrive before giving in.

It had been hours: tents filled with doctors, gurneys leading to X-ray, even an MRI. Rob had waited in lobbies, holding the useless duster and then napping under it. Now he sat by the hospital bed, waiting.

He found the entire experience difficult to believe. Not so much the shift to Nebraska, pulled by Thomas, and the shift back, anchored by the horses. Not that. That was the part of Rob's peculiarities that he himself tried not to think about.

What he could not believe was that men had brought Thomas down on some street. His Thomas. He was slowly, oddly, getting angry about that. That such a thing could happen.

The light was getting dimmer when a doctor came in and told him that Thomas had suffered a concussion and a hair-line fracture of the skull as well as what he called a "green-stick" break to his left clavicle. He had been battered in other areas of the body.

"It must have been a terrible accident on that hilly trail," she concluded. "Rolling him over and over."

"It was not the horses' fault!" Rob sang out sharply, surprising her. She was of Asian descent—he knew no more about her, except that by her gestures, she was attempting to placate him. Rob allowed himself to be placated. He was showing his anger to exactly the wrong person. "But Thomas is not conscious. He was for a few minutes. Now he is not. Is it what they call a coma? I am ignorant of these matters."

The doctor, who was very small, dragged a plastic chair

next to his and looked up at him. She touched his hand lightly, three times. The hand with the platinum band. "No, no, Dr. MacAulay. We don't call this a coma. There is no damage to the brain we can see. When a man is hurt like this, his brain hits against the insides of the bone. Back and forth. That always causes swelling, and the body's reaction is to sleep. We are working to reduce the swelling."

Rob took her hand in his. It was also small. "Thank you, Doctor." He looked for the nametag, by habit. "Doctor Nguian. Thank you for that."

The doctor seemed overwhelmed by the sincerity of his response. She smiled up at the tall man, but she edged the chair back a few inches. "We have also stabilized the clavicle, which is the bone in the front of the shoulder. And given medication to reduce the bruising from where he hit the trees."

"Hit the trees," he repeated after her, slowly, his eyes shifting. "When do you think he will wake up?"

"Probably not today. But I think he is safe. You can go home."

"I'll just stay here," Rob said softly, and he gave her a wide, gentle smile. With big teeth.

⊏⊐

FIRST, Rob called Kyan Sensei to leave a message that Thomas was in hospital. He could think of no one else to tell. The hospital staff served him dinner as though he were a patient. He couldn't eat it. Asked the nurse if he could have another glass of water.

No one who depended on him was at the Sullivan Place. O'Brien took care of the horses and Rob repeated and repeated to them in his mind that things were well. That they had done brilliantly. He was so proud of them. He found he was saying these things on his rosary, which had happened to be in his trouser pocket.

If they came to cast him out, he could slide under the bed. He wouldn't make any bother, and surely the hospital had more urgent business than to bring men up to force him out with brooms. He would be no bother.

As he was thinking these things, there came another visitor. It was Kyan Sensei, accompanied by a young person Rob did not recognize. He entered the room and looked at them. Rob found the chair the doctor had left and brought it over for the old man to sit in while Sensei looked at Thomas.

"What happen to him?"

Rob answered the question first by saying he was assured Thomas would be all right. Awake soon. Then he made certain that Sensei had known of Thomas's trip to Nebraska, so that he would not be spilling any of Thomas's complex secrets. Once this was established, Rob told him, in the only language he had for it, what had happened. Including the participation of the horses and the fact that the people here thought it a riding accident.

Kyan Sensei looked at Rob for a while, and then down at Thomas for a longer while. At last he said "I have known him since he was a little boy. I thank you for his life. And I thank the horses, too, though I don't know them."

Rob looked across the unconscious body at the only other man who really knew about Rob's ability to flinch. And he didn't talk about that at all.

"I'm just so happy he's back. With us. And will be better." Rob found he was stammering and began again. "And I believe I must thank you also. For Thomas. For him being Thomas."

Kyan leaned forward and stroked the battered face. "He was such a hurt little boy. And it did not get easier for him."

"Tell me, Sensei." Rob was feeling the anger grow again,

though he was bone weary. "How could those men bring him down? How could *anyone* bring *him* down?"

The old man smiled and clapped his hands together. "Oh, Dr. Mac—Rob! Everyone loses fights. We lose fights all the time! That doesn't mean he's brought down. Not at all."

Then he got up and his diffident attendant took him away.

No one made Rob hide under the bed that night.

9

Jan

The sun was up, but Rob was asleep in the plastic chair. Thomas was also asleep, in his own fashion, and his face sadly discolored. The people who came in and out to change the bags on the IV post or empty the catheter could not wake either of them. Someone had pulled a hospital blanket over Rob, and put a small pillow under the place where his head touched the wall.

Into the room came a woman: brown-haired, green-eyed. She was neither tall nor short, and seemed to be in her mid-thirties. She stared at the man in the bed for a long while. She touched him, but did not shake him. She walked around the bed and stood in front of Rob. Him, she touched on the shoulder.

He opened his eyes. Remembered things, slowly. Looked up at the woman in front of him, who was wearing a parka, blue jeans, and trainers. She was standing with her legs slightly bent, in good readiness. He focused on her face.

As she was saying, "Rob? Rob MacAulay?"

He was saying, "Jan. The sister."

"Got it in one." The smile was so familiar.

Rob began to stand, and the blanket and pillow fell to the floor. She shook her head, which had loosely curled hair. Much like Thomas's hair, but longer and not grey. She moved the chair—the one that had been Kyan Sensei's—forward, and she sat. She whispered, "I've wanted to meet you for so, so long. But I told Tommy not to be a bridge between us, because I wanted to meet you myself."

Another mystery. Another secret. And this secret seemed so friendly and innocent. After a few seconds, he had to smile at her. "They did tell you he is going to be well, despite all this?"

Jan nodded. "Or I'd have made a more emotional entrance, believe me, Rob. I'm allowed to call you Rob?"

"Oh, Jan. Janet. You are allowed to call me anything you please. I, too, have waited to meet you. But now ..."

"Yes?" She leaned closer and looked entirely intent. Very still. Like Thomas.

"Now I must beg leave. To use the facilities." He pointed behind him, at the bathroom door.

Janet Paddiachi put one hand over her mouth to stifle her laughter, and let him unfold to his true height and squeeze through, by habit ducking his head, to go under the lintel, closing the door quietly.

She looked at her brother's battered face. At the narrow hospital bathroom door. She sat down again, opening her parka against the heat, and resting her legs on the other chair.

Rob came out to encounter, once more, the unknown. The unknown dropped her legs again to allow him to sit down in the chair facing her, and he realized how close to knowable she was. It was amazing.

"You're grinning at me," she observed. "Has he been talking about me so much?"

"Not so much," he whispered back. "Frequently, but with

a wish, I think, not to invade your privacy. It is your face and body that are talking to me. I see so much of Thomas in you. He calls you both 'The Rogue Heddimans.'"

"Although neither of us are Heddimans at all. He's a Sullivan, now, or so he's told me, and I've been a Paddiachi for years. And you're still grinning."

Rob shrugged. "I have such large teeth, that I think they make the expression more obvious. Still, I am pleased to have made the introduction, although I hadn't expected it to be in such a situation."

"So you *do* talk that way!" Now she was grinning, too.

"What manner—what way?"

"Very formally, as we Yanks would call it. And like you're always singing. I heard you in the videos, but I thought maybe you turned it on and off."

At that moment Rob closed his mouth and stopped smiling. Perhaps he would never speak, or "sing," again.

"And you're blushing. That's true too!"

In a very small voice he said, "In another moment I will escape back into the toilet and refuse to be seen or heard again."

"Oh, damn, Rob! Here I've pushed so hard, when I wanted to be just like family. We *are* family … But that's just me." She pushed her chair back from him, as he himself did for people. This small woman pushed herself, and pushed her great confidence, like Thomas's great confidence, away from him.

He was grinning again, regardless. "You are quite welcoming, Janet. Jan. It's just that I'm still not used to being described by people, as a public—thing—yet. Please put up with me."

And as she pushed forward again he noticed what he should have noticed from the beginning, but for the parka. "Ach—Ah! You're going to have a baby! I thought that was part of a dream, or a code of some sort, from the first day I spent with your brother." He remembered snatches of conversation. In an airplane. A Boinger.

"We are! But that's one of the things I didn't want to talk about until I met you."

Rob stared unabashedly at the prominent round bump in her trim body. Grinned like a village idiot. This was the closest thing to a baby Thomas would have, barring high-tech tinkering. And it was no part of him, but still he felt he might jump up and down from sheer happiness. "I will be an uncle! Of a sort. I mean, if the idea doesn't—offend you. Or your husband."

"Paddy would love it! *I* would love it!" Looking back at Thomas's unconscious figure, with all the machines attached, she lowered her voice again. "It's a boy. Gods willing, we're going to name him Thomas."

"How splendid! How lovely!" Rob put out both hands, splayed wide, and made circles with them, trying not to hit anything.

She sat back. Complacent, her own small hands over the bump. "And now, Rob, can you tell me, exactly, what happened to Tommy? I'm sorry: to Thomas?"

Rob's hands froze in motion, collapsed into smaller things, and settled themselves into his own bony lap. He looked at Thomas, at Jan, into himself, for some sort of guidance. Found none.

"I think," he said slowly, "it would be best if we left that to Thomas, himself. When he wakes up."

Jan Paddiachi stared for a moment and then let out a burst of laugher she did not even try to smother. "Oh, he's trained you already!" she said. Then her brain caught up with her mouth and her eyes widened. "Gods! I'm sorry. I didn't mean it the way it sounded. I clean forgot!"

He waved away the apology. "I know exactly what you mean. He has a habit of secrecy."

"We both do," she said, with a new tone of bitterness. Like

Thomas, once again. And at that moment, Jan, who was facing in the proper direction, noticed her brother's eyes were open.

Thomas looked about the bright hospital room, and at the improbable faces of Rob and of his sister. He briefly considered the possibility that he was dead, or near death, and then a blast of pain caused him to reject so spiritual a solution.

"Oh, Jeez!" he shouted. Or it ought to have been a shout. He wasn't certain it had even come out as words.

Rob's finger was already on the nurse-call button. He pressed it repeatedly, and in pattern, as though it were Morse code.

Both visitors were standing together when the man bustled in, and looked down at the patient lying there, with tears leaking over his discolored face.

"Do something!" shouted Rob, and it was a true, full-lunged shout.

"I will. I will. It's just that we don't go around giving pain control to an unconscious person. You can see the problem in that, right?" The nurse was tall, African-American, and he shoved both Jan and Rob aside to get to the IV post. In his hand he held a syringe. "By rights, I should wait for the doctor," he mused, holding the insertion point in one hand and the needle in the other.

"If you do, man, I will bloody throttle you!"

The nurse looked at Rob MacAulay with calm amusement. He was already depressing the plunger. "And if you think I'm doing this under threat, Dr. MacAulay, you might ask yourself why I came prepared with this thing already."

Rob defused immediately. He backed away from the nurse, with garbled apologies.

Still calm, still amused, the nurse extracted the needle. "No problem, man. I get it. S'matter'a'fact, I get it all the time around here. Be too bad if no one cared about the patient. And that does happen, and then I have to care all by myself."

Jan spoke up. "How long before he feels anything from this?"

"Not so long," he said. "Differs. And it won't make it all go away, you know. We can't exactly erase pain here."

"I know," she said. "Thomas knows too." The nurse disappeared.

She held on to the bed rail. Rob held on to the bed rail. They were like two different-sized birds perched over Thomas's leaking face. He was looking at them. Finally, although he was still leaking, he began to smile.

"What the hell, what the hell," he said weakly. "So. You've met?"

"Just now," said Jan. "And you'll be glad to know he spilled no State Secrets."

His eyes shifted to Rob, then closed. For a minute, both thought he had gone to sleep again.

"There. I'm feeling it a bit," he said. "What'd they give me?"

"I've no idea," said Rob.

"None in hell," said Jan.

Rob noted that even their curse-words were much alike.

"How's the pain?" Jan asked her brother. It had the feeling of a familiar question.

"Unbearable," he answered. "But I'm lying here about three inches to one side of it."

A pause, and Jan rocked back and forth a bit, hands on the bed rail. "Now?"

"Uh. Four. Maybe five—six. Talk soon."

Rob turned to her, and was aware that some sort of point-position in this room had been taken away from him. He was grateful for that. In the light from the single hospital window he looked from her face, which was backlit, her hair a glowing drift of brown, to Thomas, so white now against the white sheets. Except for the bruising.

R.A. MACAVOY & NANCY L. PALMER

"You seem to have been in this situation before, with your brother."

Her expression was both fierce and exhalant. "Oh yeah. And not always with him the one hurt."

She turned her body to Rob. "My older brother is the closest thing to a father I ever had, and that's—well, that's odd."

"I thought only nine years older."

"It was enough. It had to be."

"Talk now," said Thomas, and both shifted back to the man in the bed.

"A good twelve inches away, and I bet I've got a few minutes before I'm going to nod off again, so. Progress report."

"Give, or take?" said Jan.

"What?" said Rob.

"Rob. Listen to me. I remember you there, where you weren't. I mean, couldn't be. And then I remember the horses. I made a call, didn't I?"

Glad to be of some use in the conversation, Rob said that he had. "I don't know to whom," he added.

"He says, 'To whom?'" Jan broke in, delightedly. "He really does!" And then she answered. "You did make the call. To Kathleen Maloney Applebee. It got bounced to me and I found it when I got off the plane. I was in the air coming here when—whatever—happened."

"And the people I went to Omaha for?"

That was the question Rob had wanted to ask for almost twenty-four hours. He never thought it would be this stranger to answer it. "She says they're okay. For now. Something really scared the Nativists. She doesn't know what."

Rob had been trying to follow this strangely elliptical interchange. It was as new to him as his journey of the previous day. "Nativists? You were attacked by Native Americans?"

"Two feet," answered Thomas, from the pillow,

announcing the position of the pain in relation to himself.
"Wow. That's better."

"Rob. You tell Jan everything you know. Things I don't
know. She already knows about flinching."

"She—she does?" Rob's voice broke.

And then the doctor came in.

A LONG CONVERSATION followed in the hospital cafeteria,
while they ate food Rob did not remember ordering. It was
disjointed, much like the conversation in the room above,
when Thomas had woken up. It was, however, much longer.

"So, then. Your brother has told you about my occasional,
eccentric 'flinch?'"

"Oh yes. Must be a month ago he started mentioning it."

Rob looked down at his plate. There was food there. "And
you didn't simply think your brother crazy?"

Jan Paddiachi put down her flatware with a rattle. She
snickered and used her napkin. "Tommy is crazy all right.
As Don Quixote was crazy. But his enemies have never
turned out to be windmills. No, it's not the sort of thing he
would make up because he's had his head rattled too
many times."

He didn't know where to begin, but as she seemed to know
so much—more than Rob did—of the history, he began with
his ride on the hills, with the two horses. And he told her
everything he remembered, including the snow on the ground
in whatever place he had found himself, and his surprise at
Thomas's weight, and Thomas's use of the mobile phone, and
his being tied by the halter-end around the neck of MacBride.
He spoke his piece without looking at her, feeling only,
because of the heat in his ears, that he must be colouring
wildly. When he did look up Jan was regarding him with
unusual composure. Like Thomas's own.

"Well, well. You really are the Magic Man he talked about."

He looked down again. "It's *not* magic." He heard himself sounding stubborn.

"Physics, then. Can you explain it in the physics language? I wouldn't understand it, but …"

"No, Jan. No. I can't. I can't at all. It is embarrassing!"

"Dragging toilet paper down the hall on your shoe is embarrassing. This, on the other hand, could be useful."

In a small voice he answered. "That is what I fear."

"Yeah. Me too."

Rob looked up at her, and her face—that strange variation of Thomas's face—was straight and serious. "But it's there. Already there. So …" She contemplated something that might have been tuna casserole. "You did it with Thomas. Which means he did it too. Can it be taught?"

Rob only shrugged.

In his turn he asked about the American Indians who had attacked Thomas in Omaha, only to discover Nativists weren't that sort of person at all, and that the imperiled people in this particular effort had been immigrants from the hungers in Western China a few years previous, and the matter behind it had been, as usual, ignorance, competition for too few jobs, and decreasing natural resources. It was all so familiar to Rob.

"I was simply astonished to see any number of men could hurt him in—in battle. My expectations were unrealistic, I suppose."

Jan grinned. She smiled so much more frequently than Thomas, but it was so much the same smile. "Then you and he are a perfect match," she said.

They left the cafeteria. He discovered he had eaten all his food, and still didn't know what it had been.

Walking toward the elevator, he found himself asking Jan if she were interested in Quantum Field Theory.

"Never before," she replied.

"It's never too late," he said, hopefully.

"Never is."

In the hospital room the doctor was long gone, but so was Thomas's brief foray into wakefulness. He was snoring, softly.

They went to what Jan described as "Old Aunt Grace's place" in their separate cars, with Rob leading the way. Together they found fresh sheets in the linen closet and put them on one of the many unoccupied bedrooms. Each showered away their mileage and then slept. Jan, too, could be heard softly snoring.

When he woke up, she was already wandering through the rooms. "So you two live here now. Wow."

"Is that of special significance? I admit I have never lived in such dignity, before, with the huge gardens, and all, and Thomas spoke of Aunt Grace Sullivan so often...."

"Well, of course he would," Jan said, fingering the ornate mantelpiece in the room where the incongruous table with screen and piles of paper sat so close to it. "She was the only sexually—well—less-acceptable person he knew as a child. Made all the difference in the world to him."

Worlds he had not known existed were opening to Rob. "Oh. That he didn't speak of so much. Just something about Maria."

Jan sat down in the couch, her arms folded crossed over her chest. Staring at the blank screen. "Together for so many years, here, after her husband—the Heddiman—died.

"That's why she left Thomas this place and her legacy. Small, by our families' standards, but enough to get him a start. And she told him he should live here after she was gone, because he loved it so much. The stables, the quiet. Everything. When he was ready."

"Ready?"

"Yes. Seems it took him a long time to be ready. A long time to become Sullivan."

He had nothing to say to this.

After a sigh and a pull up on her bump, Jan went on. "In the beginning, I was jealous. He had a way out, I thought, and I didn't."

"Oh, I am sorry." He sat down beside her.

But as she turned to him her face was bright. "Don't be. I was only six when she died, and Thomas split the legacy straight halves with me. I didn't love the house as he did, and I wasn't gay, either. Hardly knew Aunt Grace. And instead of her, I had my brother. Don't be sorry at all!"

Before he could respond she continued, "I know that you, Rob are not to be 'classified.' Sexually or otherwise. I've been told so by Tommy many times, but I didn't have to be told. People are simply people. Or they aren't."

Rob wasn't sure what she meant by that, but appreciated not being classified, and was fairly certain she had included him amongst the word "people."

She stood up from the sofa, holding the bump up with one hand. "Pregnant women, now, can't escape being classified. By every stranger. They come up and ask to touch my belly."

Soon they returned to the hospital to see Thomas.

He was awake: both feeling better and looking worse. The discolouration of his face and exposed arms was a sunset of blues and reds, which Rob knew would soon begin to alter to the family of greens and yellows. For a moment he had to wonder what his own very pale skin had painted, after the incident in The Meadows Walk, in Edinburgh.

He looked at them both with the calm warmth and acceptance only found in a person of high spiritual development. Or a good deal of morphine.

Before he could speak, Jan began, "My Knight of the Woeful Countenance! Once again! And where's the pain today?"

"Somewhere near Ashtabula, Ohio, I believe," he answered her, his voice buzzing slightly with the effect of the oxygen tubes inserted into each nostril. "I wish it would stay there, but … unlikely."

His brown eyes flashed with yellow as he focused from his sister to Rob. Rob reached forward, made shy by the presence of the sister, and put his fingers on Thomas's right hand. Even it was discoloured. Rob's touch was tentative, but Thomas snatched those fingers with a grip surprisingly firm, for a man so badly hurt. One who was also as diffident as Rob.

"So both of you know more than I do about the incident. That should worry me, I guess."

"Don't worry about Omaha, Tommy. Thomas. Kathleen has it in hand."

Thomas closed his eyes. Even the eyelids were swollen. "I said *should* worry me. But not yet."

Jan spoke up again. "Since you've done it, Thomas. Flinched, or whatever, all the way from Nebraska to here, I don't see why you can't learn to do it yourself."

Thomas seemed completely surprised by the idea, and shifted his gaze to Rob, who added, "She may be right, Thomas. I, too, have been thinking. Your idea of body-learning, which is so different from what I knew as learning, and yet did work, seems to indicate that possibility."

"But you still can't control it."

Rob found he was smiling. He hadn't expected to smile at Thomas this morning. They were still clasping hands, too. "Not yet. But Kyan Sensei has hopes, I believe."

"Oh. Well. If he thinks so, then it's all settled," said Thomas. Possibly he was joking.

He paused for a full minute, either out of weakness or deeply thinking. Then he told Rob he would be going home in a few days, and would be bringing with him a personal nurse, to oversee his recovery.

Rob's automatic offers to be that nurse were cut off sharply. Fairly sharply. "I want someone trained for the task.

Not your well-meant efforts, Rob. Besides, insurance will cover it. And more importantly, you have other things on your plate. Harvard, for one. Kyan Sensei. And making it all up to the horses. Gratitude of that depth is an important thing."

"They are important in another manner, Thomas. They were the anchors that allowed me to come home with you. They seem to be—I don't know—naturals at this."

Jan leaned against the rail. "I'm sorry I had to leave Sonny Boy behind."

"Don't be," said her brother. "Your horse is now O'Brian's work horse, and he's doing important work, and he knows it. These people—uh, creatures—aren't made to be pets. And he's not called Sonny Boy anymore. O'Brien calls him something else."

"What?" Jan asked the question of Rob, who was embarrassed to admit he didn't know. Had not asked O'Brien, nor the small horse O'Brien rode.

There wasn't much more to be said. Thomas didn't seem eager for them to extend their looming presence, and Jan had to make things ready for Paddy's arrival. She said she planned to stay only a day or so at Aunt Grace's with her husband, and they would spend the rest of their visit in the privacy of their own quarters.

Rob did as he was told. He returned home to find a brand new housekeeper already cleaning up the rooms, and a landscaper assessing the winter's damage to the gardens. Rob hadn't been aware of the existence of either individual. He wanted to chat with the landscaper, and to tell him the place would be intruded upon by a pair of large animals frequently, but his immediate goal was to go through the gate and express the requisite gratitude to the black and the white anchors of their lives.

THOMAS SULLIVAN, who would always be Tommy to his sister, stared at the bright ceiling of the hospital room and wondered what part of the feeling of great satisfaction that he felt belonged to the morphine and what part would be left to him when the drug wore off.

His memory was so clear and beautiful—except for the part where he was beaten to death.

There had been the thought, so clearly remembered and accepted, that he would never see Rob again. That it was possible that Rob would never discover how he had died. The last thought of that lifetime was that at least he had met Rob MacAulay and he had finally become Sullivan.

Then there was the image above him of the spreading black figure, all black. Like Yama, God of Death, only wearing Rob's face. And it had picked him up. Great last scene before the lights went out.

And they had gone out: all the lights, and next he was on the back of a horse, white and shining. The imagery was also perfect for death. If he had to design his own death, he couldn't have chosen better. But the voice—Rob's unique, singing voice—interrupted it, telling him to send a message on his mobile. That had required choice and the effort to move. And led to pain. Not a good death-scene at all. Luckily, the message required was pre-coded and accomplished by reflex. Evidently he *had* sent it, for Jan had used Kathleen Maloney's name.

So as a death-scene, it was pretty much a washout. As a near-death experience, it made sense, but how much stranger it was in its reality. It had been a touch of death, most certainly, but it was really an omen of a future life. Thomas Sullivan tried to laugh and decided it was better not to do that.

He had been so uncomfortable with the way in which his connection with Rob had begun—with a long, and strange effort to save the man's life. He was now comfortable with the manner in which Rob had saved his. Rob's role as savior was strange, but not so long lasting as to be awkward.

And as someone had said to him once, after the first exchange of lives, there is no more counting.

Thinking only of future healing and not about the approaching painful part of it, nor even the perils of the world, Thomas allowed sleep to take him.

AS FAR AS anyone in Massachusetts knew, except Rob, Jan, and Colm O'Brien, Thomas had come off a horse. And though the stable manager was not kept abreast of the daily activities of the people at the Sullivan Place, he did know that Thomas Sullivan's helmet was still hanging on the hook by MacBride's stall, slightly dusty. That made a complete hash of the accident story.

He sidled up to Rob as Rob was crooning to his horse. "Now, Rob, it is none of my business, strictly speaking. And being from Mayo, I am comfortable with conspiracies. So I know to my bones that Mr. Thomas Sullivan did not go riding up that hill in the rain without saddle nor helmet. You can tell me what happened or not, as you will. But it will be easier for me to keep the story straight if I know it."

Rob and Kinsman looked down at the short man. Kinsman flattened his ears for a moment. Rob put an arm around the horse's neck and comforted him. "I'll tell you, Colm. I mean, I trust you entirely to tell you. But it will leave you feeling I've told you a lie. Or that I'm a lunatic."

O'Brien's blue eyes brightened. "Now after saying *that*, you have to tell me."

Rob thought of the long story, the story involving physics, and a short summary. He weighed each in his mind and said at last, "On the hill, I felt he was in trouble. So did the horses. All three of us. I—I flew to the place where he was. It was in Omaha, I've since learned. There were a large number of men beating on him. He was down. I picked him up and they scattered. I saw what I had done and was frightened and called Kinsman. The horses pulled me—pulled us both—back. I tied him to his own horse and we came down. You know the rest."

A long silence held, as O'Brien looked from Rob to Kinsman, then over his shoulder to white MacBride, who glimmered in the dim light of his own stall, and finally to the dusty helmet.

"So are you going to call the nice men with the butterfly nets?" asked Rob.

O'Brien pulled the left side of his mouth into a smile. He didn't look directly at Rob, but in that single expression Rob felt he understood what the man had meant about being a conspirator. Colm O'Brien put out his hands. In the dim light of the winter day in the stable Rob couldn't exactly read his expression. "Now why would I do such a thing? Even if I thought you were as mad as my Grandda, what would I gain by it? When you could so easily in turn say I'd made up the story? And you the one with money?

"But I don't think you're mad. From the day I first knew you, I knew that you, Rob MacAulay, were not an ordinary man—but mad? Hardly. And I have the evidence to back your story."

"You do?"

"Thomas Hed—Sullivan, never, ever rides without a helmet. That's enough for me."

"It is?" Rob felt foolish, with his two word questions.

"Combined with Kinsman's behavior to you, and the way you ride together, heads moving as though there were one mind between you, I do credit it."

"I must admit that mind is not mine," said Rob. "I doubt I could do anything with the horse he hasn't done before." At that moment, the stallion was rubbing his chin back and forth over the top of Rob's hair. It was not an elegant picture.

"But you can," said Colm O'Brien. "You can get the old fellow to behave like a lamb. But leaving the matter of horses aside, there is the matter of your disappearing and appearing as you said. May I ask, is it a thing you do often?" He spoke so casually, one would think O'Brien discussed teleportation on a regular basis.

"No," admitted Rob, sighing. "Not so much. Not so far. Before now I've just sometimes been a bit flinchy. And never at my own volition. This was new."

O'Brien dared a hand on Kinsman's withers, which the horse allowed. "Do you think the difference was the horses? There is a power in horses. I know it."

A whinny came from the other stall, and O'Brien went to answer it. MacBride was less perilous to stroke, anyway.

Rob called after him, "I don't know what to think. I certainly did call out Kinsman's name, and after that we flew from that snowy street like … the channel being turned from one telly station to another. And in the new channel both Thomas and I were sitting on my horse's back. Except we slipped right off into the mud.

"Before that time, Colm, I simply thought of it as a form of field theory, in practice. I hope it still is, for the sake of my own brain!"

Again the Irishman turned his light eyes on him. "Well, then. I'm all for field theories, myself. Rotate the turnouts regularly. And with the grand new manure digester your man bought for the place, even the flies are no problem. No more complaints from the rich neighbors."

Rob felt comfortable with O'Brien, but still considered mentioning the importance of secrecy in the matter. Colm O'Brien forestalled this by adding, "And if I wanted to tell my mates over a pint some evening, just who do you think would wind up in the mental home? You or me?

"And certain, it's more the craic to me just knowing about it."

———

JANET PADDIACHI DID her own circuit of the enormous garden she still thought of as Aunt Grace's place. That a new wrought-iron gate stood at one spot did not disturb her memories, because she hadn't been here more than a few times since childhood. The fact that there was a small, bi-racial girl opening it was a slight surprise. That the child turned to her and glared, however, was a larger one.

"Who are you and should you be here? This is some peoples' home now, you know!"

She looked almost fierce, standing there in the dead grass. Fierce and cute. And sure of herself. Then the child put both hands to her face and exclaimed, "Oh! You are going to have a baby!"

"Quick to spot that," said Jan, perfectly calmly. Speaking easily. Perfectly Thomas's sister.

"My name is Jan Paddiachi. I'm Tomas Heddi—Sullivan's sister."

The child pointed at her, broke into a great smile, and jumped up once. "I do that too! Forget he changed his name."

"Well, it's been so recent," said Jan, returning the smile. "And who are you, I mean, besides a friend of the family? What's your name?"

The girl, who was wearing a red jacket, took Jan's hand without asking. "I'm Tony, and I come here for arithmetic. And horses."

Their joined hands began to swing back and forth. They continued walking. The weather was fine for a day in

February. The gardeners were working on the other end of the property.

"And because you are Thomas's sister, I can let you know a secret," giggled Tony. "My daddy says that Harvard wants to offer not just a lecture, but a faculty place to Rob, so he can teach somebody besides me. I don't like that so much, but Daddy thinks Rob will."

Jan looked down at her, her composure coming more difficult. "Then I will tell you a secret in return, Tony. My brother is hurt and is in the hospital now."

The small face, so fierce, then friendly, became horrified. Quickly Jan tried to adjust the expression. "He'll be okay, don't worry. I didn't mean to scare you. It's just that if you were expecting a lesson today, it will probably have to wait a bit."

Tony gave Jan a powerful hug, just at the part of her body now widest. "I'm so sorry," she mumbled into Jan's coat.

"It'll be okay, Tony. Really. He'll be home in a few days, with a nurse. Just a few bones broken."

"We'll be ready," said the girl and began to run back towards the gate. Then she turned on her heel. "He had a car accident?"

Jan was good at deflections of this sort. "Not a car. Ah— Oh, he'll tell you." And she watched the child fade into a spot of bright red against the dark red wall.

Janet Paddiachi smiled again, staring at her own protruding belly. Then she said, "Oh, Tommy. You've certainly widened your circle of friends."

⊏⊐

THOMAS SULLIVAN LAY in a hospital bed thinking nothing.

Jan, his sister, thought about the child she had just met, and about the approaching arrival of her husband. She held her uncomfortable belly (which had a name) close to her and thought about all the varieties of trust. And about reality. She didn't herself cling to any particular reality. She'd encountered so many.

In Nebraska, a woman named Kathleen Maloney Applebee petted her deaf Sheltie and told him not to nip, even knowing he couldn't hear her. She waited for the last of her high school students of Chinese descent to call in safe. She was more certain the student was safe than she was that the dog would not nip again, but it was good to be certain. She wondered how urban legends got started in immigrant communities, but was grateful this last school story sounded so positive, and that the community was out of immediate danger from the Nativists. (Native of what, she'd like to know!) Also wondered how Heddiman—no, he was Sullivan, now, had gotten home. But he was rich. Thank God he was rich, amid all this nastiness. So often rich people didn't care and—ouch! The dog had nipped her again. But not badly.

⊏▭⊐

IN BRITAIN, there came a Vote of No Confidence.

And on the same day, the weather in Massachusetts changed, and it snowed again.

The Uses of Clouds of Birds and Butterflies

Jan hadn't gone to visit her old teacher, Kyan Sensei, since returning to the states, and asked if she might come along the next time Rob had his personal lesson.

Rob knew she had a double motivation in asking this, and he was wary, but the teacher agreed; he had known Jan since she was a toddler. She was also unusually informal with him. It could have been simply because she'd started out as a toddler. Very unlike the behavior of Thomas or Rob. Kyan Sensei didn't seem to care either way.

After warm greetings and reminiscence, she followed them both into the small back room where Rob spent his time avoiding being hit. It was his first lesson since the incident on the hillside, and he wondered if he was now expected to be able to pop about the room at will. Instead, the teacher set him on his bare feet on the mat, had a student assemble the tower of risers, and began the drill as before—except with the woman watching.

Rob knew what would happen. He would be distracted. He was already distracted by her, and he'd wind up with a bloody lip. Or swollen eye. Kyan Sensei seemed unaffected by Jan's presence and went about his drill—his drill with surprises —as he had before.

Rob was glancing at her, though he shouldn't, and was grateful that at least this room hadn't a mirror on the wall to make focus harder, when she spoke right up and asked Kyan Sensei if she might be allowed to punch Rob.

"He won't think I'll hit him, Sensei, so when I do the surprise might be more ..."

Rob was glancing at her when the blow came, directed somewhere below his face. He couldn't tell, because at that moment he was leaning against the wall next to Janet Paddiachi and he had one hand locked into the hair of her brown-gold head. "I am finding you simply ... irritating, Janet!" He said, before he could put a lock on his mouth.

Her mouth dropped open. He released her hair and stepped back. Jan stepped forward. "You—you could have hit me. Hurt me. Hurt the baby!"

Rob slapped the already smudged white wall with one open palm, cursing silently.

Kyan Sensei jumped off the risers and walked calmly the distance necessary to reach the pair of them. "Yes, Mrs. Paddiachi. He might have. So I wonder why you were so insistent to be here. Did you not believe the stories? Did you not believe at all? With three people you know saying a thing was happening, why did you stand here?"

She shouted "Why the hell did you *let* …?" and she shut up suddenly. Her hazel eyes were wide and fixed. She took a deep breath and encompassed her belly. "Oh, Jan," she mumbled. "You're the idiot again!"

"Is the baby distressed?" asked the old man. He did not try to touch her.

She shook her head and looked around. "No. No. Just Rob is distressed, I think."

Kyan shrugged, in western fashion. "I think it's something he will have to live with." He turned his eyes to Rob's.

Who was upset, and leaning against the wall for support.

"Good control," said the teacher to him. "In two ways, I think. Good control." He smiled broadly and bowed to Rob MacAulay. "No need for kata here tonight. You have done enough."

They drove home with Jan attempting in different ways to explain or apologize. Rob couldn't think of a thing to say.

TRIGGER'S PUB & Eatery was located where the last milk-wagon horse of Edinburgh had been housed. When she looked at the place, Yownie MacManus was never certain the place really had been a stable until 1990, or that the eponymous milk horse had been born on the day Roy Roger's Trigger walked down Grove Street. Yet photo posters of both animals decorated the walls as one walked in. And it was her local public house.

Tonight a table of her confreres was already sitting in discussion. It was well-lubricated discussion and moved quickly, although at times the lubrication tended to slosh out onto the table when people leaned inward or pounded on the tabletop.

She looked from the tabletop to her sketchpad. Decided it was not worth the risk and stuffed the pad in her bag as she pulled a chair over and sat.

"Duffy, aren't you worried about your tablet there, in the wet?"

Her editor turned to her and acknowledged her arrival. "It's waterproof."

"Alcohol-proof, too? Those wee yellow spots on it aren't …"

Across the table sat Fran, another Splint writer. "It's Yownie! Up MacManus!" Francine was fairly high up herself, and the glass she raised did not have beer in it. "Yownie, the question of the night is how quickly we're going to get the re-seating of the Scottish Parliament, now the Splinter is no more."

Another man whose name Yownie couldn't recall voiced in, "It will all depend on the Welsh. Whether they stand with us. And to be frank, have they ever?"

"Ah, but you're not Frank," Duffy shouted out sideways. "You're Jimmy, and you don't have the slightest idea about the Welsh. Any Welsh."

Yownie settled herself and lifted one hand to snatch the attention of a waitperson. "It's too bad Geoffrey is visiting in South Africa with Nelson, then," she said to the table at large. "He'd be the one to set everyone straight about the state of affairs. I'm just hoping to understand a glass of something."

Fran was still looking at her with a sort of bright intensity. Or possibly the brilliance was something reflected in the small amber glass in her hand. "You do hear from MacAulay these days, don't you, Yownie? Or at least Heddiman?"

Something in Iona MacManus went suddenly protective. "Sullivan, you mean. He's now Sullivan. And of course I chat with them. Both. They are my friends."

"Important friends, at the moment."

Yownie pulled her sketchpad from her bag. She had an

irresistible impulse to draw Francine as a ferret. "Important at every moment. That's the thing about friends. What is it you think Splint wants out of them?"

"Dr. Rob MacAulay is extremely important to us all now." Duffy grunted in agreement at this, and Jimmy, the man who was not Frank, nodded also.

"We think he should come home," said Fran in a tone of perfect, whiskey-buzzed authority. Around the table rose a general murmur of approbation.

Yownie chatted with Rob about once a week; Thomas maybe twice that often. They spoke about the cold of Massachusetts. About teaching one interesting small girl mathematics whilst avoiding numbers. About riding his horse in the hills. About the patterns in which snow could fall, according to temperature: a subject that evolved, with Rob, into too much maths for Yownie to follow. About learning in a manner involving the body without use of the forebrain—a subject about which Rob seemed child-like in his enthusiasm. She always initiated such emails and they never involved politics, either the British or the American variety.

"I will not aid you in turning the man into a figurehead again."

Duffy snorted. "You gave him away to Rolling Stone easily enough."

"I was trying to save his life!"

"And you did," said Duffy. "I would think he owes you for that."

Yownie couldn't speak a coherent word. She couldn't even curse. The waitress was at her side, and she managed to apologize to the woman for disturbing her on such a busy night when she had decided not to stay. She was up and out, her chair blocking the aisle behind her.

The table of journalists merely watched her go. After about twenty seconds Jimmy said, "I think the problem there was she was too sober. She should have caught up with us before talking."

No one else mentioned Yownie's departure, although Duffy did think to wipe the surface of his tablet dry with a cocktail napkin.

⌗

THOMAS WAS DRIVEN home in a private medical van. The driver, because by Massachusetts law the vehicle had to have a human redundant driver when carrying a passenger, was in the front compartment. Rob sat next to Thomas's cot as they went blindly from road to road, looking out the rear windows of the vehicle. It was sleeting. Soon it would turn to snow.

"This must be what it's like for a dog in a crate," said Thomas, peering down his nose. "In the back of a car, I mean."

Rob looked out the speckled length of glass, where only receding pavement could be seen. "If I were lying there like you, I'd be feeling nauseated right now. Ah! Probably I shouldn't have brought up the idea."

Thomas grinned and asked for an extra pillow. He couldn't move his arm to get it himself, because of the collarbone restraint. Rob unsnapped a cupboard and pulled one out and then paused, with it hanging in his hand. "What about the skull fracture? I'm thinking about keeping the spine straight and all those things we're taught …"

"Hairline fracture. Gimme the pillow." Rob helped him lift his head and pushed the pillow under it so that he could look out the window. At not much.

"Janet told me about the jump in the back room with Sensei."

Thomas saw Rob tense and look up for a moment, so that his green (at the moment) eyes caught the grey light coming in the window, and by the shimmering of the eyes' movement he could tell Rob was thinking, or remembering something. "You mean when I might have blown up Janet, the baby, and who knows *what* else?"

He had expected this reaction from Rob. "Actually, she describes it more as her asinine stubbornness to be somewhere she didn't belong, or to prove something, and that Sensei let her fall into her own trap. He does that sometimes. But I wasn't there, and to me that part of it is not at all important. Really."

The changes in the colors of Rob's face really were the semaphore Thomas had first imagined them, so long ago. Early autumn. A past life. "Not important? But I might have ..."

"You didn't hurt anyone." Thomas cleared his throat. "Let me start again, Rob. From my frame of reference. When I died in Omaha."

Thomas saw Rob's eyes go black with shock at what he had said. He took a breath and tried again. The sound of sleet had stopped pattering, as it turned to snow. "Sorry. I'll rephrase that. I know that in my own frame of reference, I died on the street there. I remember it—the grief, the letting go of it all, and the dark figure picking me up as though I were weightless. And I remember what came afterwards, though I don't have words to describe it.

"And I remember being on the hillside, after. With the horses all around me. And you. The rain. That was a return. From something."

Thomas closed his eyes and the movement of the van pushed him left and right against his odd seatbelt built for horizontal people. "The thing is," he said. "Besides all the— the satisfaction of that satori ..."

"The what?"

"Doesn't matter. Jargon word. Like your Physics babble that I have to go look up later—what I mean is, I think I can do it too."

And Thomas's battered face went soft with wonder. And with speculation.

———

ROB WAS HAVING difficulty in the swaying van. He was glad that Thomas was happy, despite his injuries. In fact, his Thomas was radiating contentment from every pore. But he wondered exactly what narcotics they had him on. He remembered his own experience with narcotics and tried to think how best to speak to the man. To make sense, without hurting Thomas's feelings.

"Oh, I see you looking down at me," said Thomas. "So worried." He laughed quietly into the echoing van. "Don't be worried about me, Rob. I'm not in a drug haze, nor have I gone soft in the head. I'm saying I know now that I—that this new me—am able to do it."

"Do what, Thomas?"

"Wiggle my ears. Flinch. Whatever ..." He drifted into silence, into stillness. Rob leaned closer, peering into his face.

"Hah!" Thomas blinked, staring into the falling snow and receding past out the rear windows. "We're going to need a new word for this."

———

WHEN THEY GOT home and installed Thomas in a recliner in the room with the grand fireplace, Rob allowed him and his home-care nurse to become acquainted while he had a look at Thomas's allotted medications. It was actually short, compared to what he had received simply for a pair of abraded hands late last summer. Nothing in it to explain strong mood changes.

He didn't minimize the effect of the scientifically inexplicable travel from Omaha, Nebraska to his Massachusetts home. Rob had had all his life to think about his random "flinches." Or rather, to become accustomed to *not* thinking about them. He wasn't proud of his habit of turning away from the subject, especially since it had become impossible to deny. But what was a scientist to do with a thing that could not be disproved by science? Especially a quantum field physicist. They were a minority in physics and were always being accused of allowing intuition to outpace evidence. He'd had to be so careful to maintain any credibility.

Now here was his own binary, Thomas, who had the habit of diving into studies where there were no boards, no panels, nor journals to flay him raw for an error. He envied Thomas for this freedom, and he had had enormous success with it in his own different line of work.

But it made Rob profoundly uncomfortable. More uncomfortable because the matter at hand was evidential. It had happened, and Rob had supplied the evidence.

He did not know how long he had been standing by the sofa, folding and refolding the medication guidelines, when Thomas called him over. The nurse was gone.

"Cheer up, Rob," he said.

Thomas was covered in a soft woolen blanket, from which only his head and hands could be seen. "I said I felt I had died, you know. Not that I *was* dead. And I know what's got you worried."

And how could he know that, when Rob himself wasn't certain? Rob gave an attempt at a comforting smile. He looked for a place in the form under the blanket that might not mind being touched, and settled for one hand on the uninjured shoulder.

"I do. You're thinking about the possibility of jumping from one place into another already occupied by quanta of the baryon or lepton fields. In other words, of superimposing matter and going 'boom.' Or of simply getting lost."

Rob hadn't exactly been thinking of such things, but they would do as objects to worry about, so he just shrugged.

"See. I've picked up a bit of the language," began Thomas, with a deep breath, placing his right hand over the one in the sling. "And I've had time to think about it. If it were going to happen, I think you'd have done it by now. Every small flinch has that possibility, and you haven't become part of a wall or floorboard yet. Or dissolved into the waters of the tidal zone of South Uist, when a child.

"And it makes sense. I don't have the equations you feel necessary, but I do know that matter fields don't superimpose. Just as a person doesn't bump into a table and become the table, you didn't jump into Jan and become Jan, a few days ago. The air around you, I don't know. Do you hear a *whump*? Feel a displacement?"

Rob sat himself down on the arm of the sofa and wrung his hands together. "Thomas—you're going from one sweeping statement to another, and ..."

"And you're going nowhere at all with this. And have been doing it for years."

He didn't care for the light of enthusiasm in Thomas' eyes. "Would you rather I donned a spandex outfit like a comic-book hero and went popping around, grabbing people out of danger? Super-Physicist? It is such a limited sort of power."

"Better than Ant-Man," answered Thomas, jovially. "And actually, I wasn't thinking of you at all. You already have enough on your plate."

"You are thinking of you?" Rob looked at the battered figure in front of him. He hoped he did not sound scornful.

"Maybe me. You've got your kind of training. Your private obsessions, as you call them. I have thirty-three years of practice in meditations. Concentrations. They have their own discipline."

Rob leaned forward. "I don't want you to be disappointed, if your grand ideas don't work."

Thomas smiled with the confidence of a young boy. "Oh, don't worry about me, Rob MacAulay. But there is one way in which you could help."

"If I can, Thomas."

"I think you can. Help me up. I want to take a shower."

LATER THAT DAY, Rob received a call from a woman named Francine who said she represented Splint magazine. It seemed odd to him that it was this stranger and not Yownie coming to him with so many unpleasant ideas.

He said he was too busy at the moment to come to Scotland. Or even to talk.

And he was busy. The next day he was due for a meeting with certain of the Physics faculty of Harvard University. Rob was too concerned about the new, peaceful Thomas Sullivan to worry about the old, tenure-revoked Professor Robert MacAulay, and so all his hopes to conceal his collapse equations simply seemed less important. He allowed the little Volvo to self-drive halfway to Cambridge, but with the snow falling it seemed to be so conservative in its decisions he cancelled it so he wouldn't miss the meeting. And luckily, the woman who had given him directions had been clear. Had reserved him a parking spot, actually. Almost like a handicapped spot.

It seemed interesting to Rob that the older buildings on the Harvard Campus were the same shade of red brick as was their own house. Was it the colour of the local clay? Red like the autumn maples of the area?

The faculty assembly, however, was in a modern glass and concrete structure. People liked to see physics and astronomy as contemporary. As though the nature of reality was a faddish thing.

Certainly mankind's understanding of it was all of that. And here he came, bringing what he hoped was a new fad with him.

He was led to a round, blond-wood table, and there were a dozen chairs placed around. As he was nothing like King Arthur, he could only expect to find himself in the Siege Perilous.

Seven people were already seated. To his surprise he knew four of them personally, though he had to go through every trick in his mind to get their names right. For the most part he had previously mostly Skyped them.

This was going to be tricky, and Rob knew too well that he was not good with tricks. But his confidence was in his equations. He had bet his career on them, and though his career had less meaning to him now, the equations were still the center of everything.

"Hello, Brian," he said to Professor Scherinhoff. He was finding himself delighted to see the man. It had been four years. Another life. "And Professor Babisha. So good! I believe I last saw you in Jakarta!"

Shira Babisha smiled at him widely. "And I am so glad to see you, Rob MacAulay. Glad you are alive, in fact. I have prayed for your safety."

The rest of the table shifted and squirmed at that statement. Rob supposed one wasn't supposed to talk about prayers when engaged in faculty meetings.

But a man he did not recognize chimed it with "Yes! Let's hear it for sanity winning out. Survival of the Physicist!" There was actual applause.

It took Rob a moment to catch the pun, because he was distracted by the fact that the man spoke in pure Oxbridge. He must have been staring, because the man continued, "Come on, man. You can't believe any of our tribe believed the things they were saying about you."

Rob supposed "our tribe" were physicists. Or mathematicians. Or simply sane Britons. But he was caught by the use of the phrase "saying about you." As though Rob had simply been the victim of a rumor campaign. This would once have been depressing, but after the past six months, it felt minor.

He shook his head. People were still drifting in, taking chairs. "Well, Shira, your prayers seemed to have had power, and I am grateful. Extremely grateful. But I didn't come here to talk about such things. I hope never to talk of them again, to be truthful.

"I did come here with some equations to share with you. I think they're interesting. Now I haven't had access to the block-frame machines to proof these. These are all old-fashioned and so I'm hoping someone can help me proof them, for better or worse …"

And without further conversation, he opened his briefcase and handed out wee-drives. Each of the people at the round table took out a book, tablet, or in one case, a wrist-phone, and plugged in. Rob had brought a couple of paper prints, in case they were necessary, but no one needed one. Nor did anyone use intelligent glasses, which he thought interesting. He himself had just gotten used to them. But that was Thomas's influence.

It was a quiet meeting for some minutes.

<hr>

THOMAS SAT ALONE in the empty room, a blanket wrapped around his shoulders, the recliner as upright as possible, and tried to feel his spine leading up to his head. He had not had to meditate off-kilter for some years, but this was not the first time he'd been beat-up and had to make do.

He ran through the simple steps of Dogen for Zen sitting. It was surprising how much he had lost in a few months by the autumn's distractions. His mind kept slipping to Rob and his trip to Harvard. He watched it nibbling at his worries until the idea of watching that was simply too boring and his thoughts wandered back home again.

Here. Now. Breathe. After fifteen minutes or so, the bell chimed and he slipped from open sitting to concentration, and the moment of his concentration was the moment of his letting go on the pavement of Omaha. He did nothing with the moment, though it called to his memories, his emotions. As the blackness took him in, in Omaha. One moment.

It hurt like hell when he fell onto the sidewalk. It was freezing. His head …

He cried for MacBride, as Rob had called for Kinsman. And it was not pavement at all, but the rubber matting of the stallion hall, and his horse—both horses—were screaming high in their noses. MacBride was clambering his hooves over the open stall top. Kinsman's box was locked closed. He was kicking the wall, hard. A tall blond woman came running in from outside and saw him lying there, in a wet blanket, stocking-footed, and she shouted something he couldn't understand, because at the same moment his phone was ringing. It was Rob's signal.

⎯⎯

THE PEOPLE at the table were distracted from their perusal of the document by Professor Rob MacAulay springing back from the table so fast as to send the chair skittering. He was pulling the mobile phone from his pocket and turning away from them by the time anyone focused on his tall, lean frame.

More than one of the Harvard faculty wondered whether the traumatic events of the last few years had caused the man to become unreliable. Certainly that was forgivable. To be expected. Such a man must be sympathized with. Supported. But he had not come to them with a story, but with equations. And here, sympathy could not matter. Then Professor Babisha murmured, "His new husband is in the hospital, I heard. Accident. He must have gotten a call."

The people seated around her accepted that excuse. Although it was remembered that Professor Babisha had already used the word "prayer" at a faculty meeting, so, tentatively.

The table returned to its equations. A few hands were tapping in notes. Two men were talking, quietly.

Rob withdrew to a corner and waited for Thomas to answer. He whispered "What is it? I felt—something—and then it was gone. Tell me you're all right."

"I'm all right," came Thomas's voice. The connection was not good, but Thomas could be heard. And another voice behind his. "Tell you later. Sorry I disturbed you at your meeting."

"And that's all? You'll tell me later?"

Thomas was laughing. Rob thought he was laughing. "Yeah. Really. All is well, here." And Thomas was talking to someone at the other end. Casually. He rang off, leaving Rob with the phone in his hand.

He slipped it back into his pocket. Shrugged an apology to the table in general. Pulled his chair in again.

By now Professor Hsien, who had been in Singapore, the last Rob had known of him, was ready to respond. "Mac-Aulay, these are indeed interesting equations, about the baryon-field collapse, as you call it. But I have to say this is not the first time I've heard them. Are you sure they are yours?"

Rob swept his memory for his last sentence. "I am, certainly. But you yourself might remember them—some of them—as having been first seen in a text from a graduate student named Chandalati. About two years ago. When she was asking whether you had thought about those after your publication in the East Asian Journal on what you were describing as the Higgs boson interference pattern."

"Yes, I remember that, although I have never met the

woman since." Professor Hsien was old and set in his ways, but he did still think, and that was why Rob had touched him with that one idea, soon after things had gone to hell in Edinburgh.

"Well, Professor Hsien, you aren't likely to hear from her again. Please consider I was not in a position to chat with you under my own name a few years ago."

Hsien regarded him long and calmly. A few others at the table did the same. "That is a good argument, MacAulay, but certainly you see how I can imagine that you use it to claim someone else's posting as your own."

"Ah, I do see how you might. But it doesn't matter."

"Doesn't matter?"

"Not at all." Feeling much more confident now, Rob stretched his long arms onto the surface of the table. "Because I don't care whether you believe the equations are mine. Only that you look into them."

Another voice chimed in. "That's a bit too innocent for acceptance, Professor MacAulay. There is no man born who doesn't care if he gets the credit for new work."

It wasn't a matter Rob wanted to argue. He turned back to Hsien. "Then, if it matters to you who sent you the packet, I can simply tell you what the cover letter said. How I described seeing you at a seminar in the early summer of '38. How I was sitting at the back of the hall, but was impressed by what you said about the interference patterns the day before. Although, of course, I wasn't sitting at the back of the hall, but on the platform to the far left of you."

Hsien gave a tight smile and steepled his fingers. "I do remember that. And I never felt it worth spreading about … But it would be so much simpler if you simply explained how you got the posting sent from India instead of Britain."

"But that's one thing I can't do, Professor Hsien. Because although the British government has pardoned me for things I never did, still I haven't heard of them, with their vastly strange law about the guilt of people who had contact with me over those years, pardoning those individuals. And I can't simply give out the identity of anyone who took the risk of helping me bounce my posting.

"That's why I'd rather accept your belief that the work isn't mine. As long as you accept the figures. And that's why I needed you all."

He looked from one set of eyes to another. From the Iranian woman to the two Americans he had texted in the last few years. "I haven't had access to any good computational equipment at all. It has been simply unbearable! You can imagine, I'm sure. If my equations are wrong, I'd like to know that. If right, we'll all have a lot of fun with them. Won't we?"

"Oh, I'll have fun either way," said the man who had spoken about caring for credit. Rob finally remembered him, if only by that tone of voice. His name was Alexander Poddley, and he had been a teaching assistant at Inverness for one term at the same time Rob had finished his undergraduate work. "It's been a long time since I've had a Quantum Field Theorist to tear apart."

Rob found he was laughing. Heartily laughing. He had used to be so afraid of confrontation with people like this one. Now it seemed such an attitude was like a child being afraid of the doctor's needles. "Oh, Poddley, tear away! I am simply so happy to be doing physics again! I haven't had access to the fast-frames in so long, and having no university life at all. Neither the good nor the bad."

Things at the meeting grew far looser and more convivial after that. Only four at the table seemed pleased by his offerings, but that didn't matter, for mathematics was not affected by approval or disdain. If the equation was in balance, all was well.

Rob got a few invitations to go out for lunch in Cambridge, which he had to put off because of what he said were family difficulties. But everyone left with his mail address and mobile. He counted the meeting a success.

Rob left the meeting and headed back north pleased with the idea of having his new findings "torn down" by Poddley. By anyone. He was sure of them. As certain as that he could wiggle his ears.

He let the Volvo drive him home through the increasing snow, and sat passively. As long as Thomas was safe, there was no hurry.

⸻

"YOU DID WHAT?" he was shouting at Thomas, who was lying flat out on the bed now, having been brought home in a three-wheeler by O'Brien. "Where?" Rob heard his voice rise until it cracked.

Thomas's wet clothes lay in a heap at the side of the bed, where they'd been left. Evidently it was the stable-manager and not the nurse who got him the pill bottle and the glass beside it. Rob was still not certain what the professional's hours were. But it seemed Thomas had waited to be alone to try this—this stunt.

"Do you ever really look at your face when you're in a mood like this, Rob?" Thomas asked. "The colors …"

"I don't know that I've ever *been* in a mood like this before," Rob answered. He stalked twice across the width of the bedroom and then sank onto the foot of the bed. "You're sure it was Omaha? Not just the stables?"

Thomas was smiling like a happy, white-headed boy. "Smell the wet trousers, Rob. That's not urine, horse or human. Yes, I'm sure I went to the place where they knocked me down. I was concentrating on that moment and I remember the sidewalk. The alley. And I did what you had done. I called a horse. My horse, but I'm not sure you can separate them.

"It's just a good thing I didn't wind up back on the hill-trail, all alone. Of course, I could still have used my phone to reach O'Brien. I wasn't unconscious or anything."

Rob just stared at him. His long fingers were laced together on his lap. "The horses. Exactly what function do the horses serve in all this? Anchors?" He shook his head and let out a huge breath.

"I guess. Maybe people could be anchors, too. But humans don't always know who and where they are, ya know? Horses always do. I don't think I'm making much sense right now, Rob. But. You have to give me credit; as a first attempt at flinching I did pretty good."

It was difficult to remain angry at Thomas, lying there in the enormous bed, but Rob was succeeding. If he had not been so damaged, Rob would have been tempted to simply shake him.

"Well then, Thomas. I pronounce you the official ear-wiggler. Flincher. Odder-bird of the pair of us. Are you happy now?"

Thoughtfully Thomas answered, "I think I am. We'll have to consider this some more. Implications. Worldwide implications and all. But I think I am." Then he focused again on Rob, sitting at the foot of the bed.

"Oh! I forgot to ask you. How did your meeting go?"

"My meeting? You're asking how my day went?" After a few moments the both of them were making sounds approaching laughter. Or hysteria. Thomas winced, stopped, and lay quiet first.

His meeting? Oh, Rob thought it had gone better than expected. Considering he had laid all his cards—equations—on the big round table. Those equations could speak for him better than he could do in simple English. Before his peers. Or people who had been his peers a few years ago. Now he was less than a tenured Professor.

And more. And for once, he wasn't afraid of the sniping,

the ambitions. How could he be? What exactly could a man who had come through what he had been through be afraid of now?

Well, there were men like Colonel Landry, for one. It was easy to repress thoughts of his first "welcome" to the states, and the calls, but it was impossible to forget them. (Scotland. US. Frying pan to fire, as Thomas had warned him.)

Actually, there was a whole new basket of dreads to carry now. And if he had help in hefting the basket, that same help was creating new worries. Thomas, the superhero, for one.

The time was past for Rob MacAulay to float along, letting others make decisions for him. To coddle him, protect his shining "mind" from the big perilous world.

This jumping. It was a piece of the big perilous world, and he himself had created it. Or if someone else had done so before him, they hadn't published. "Published!" He was thinking in Academic again.

Did the phenomenon somehow validate his collapse equations? Or was it an independent oddity, with no correlation to Field Theory? That seemed unlikely, but in the end, Rob had no goddamned idea what was going on with this special displacement. Had spent years trying *not* to know what was going on, because it hadn't suited his idea of science.

Which made his behavior, ironically, bad science in itself.

Now he had Thomas, lying damaged and discoloured in bed, and seemingly better at being an odd-bird than Rob had ever been. First attempt, and he'd flown the continent.

They ought to make a bloody odd-bird nest. The two of them.

Feelings of protectiveness began to grow in Rob MacAulay again. Once again, he was putting others in danger, simply by existing. But this time, passivity was no solution. Nor simple self-sacrifice. Both were cowardly, when seen from a distance.

Look at Thomas. He was not going to consider simply ceasing to exist, one way or another, because he might be a danger. He was going to fight. It was his nature. It was why Rob was still alive. Being Thomas, he was bound to follow his path, wherever it led.

He must call Kyan Sensei. If Thomas hadn't already. And Jan would be returning with her husband Paddy. Rob hadn't Wikied Paddy at all. That had been rude. A new, contemporary variety of rude.

Things were moving so fast now. When exactly did winter break, in snowy Massachusetts?

10

Paddy

efore Rob could research Shiva Paddiachi, he was there at the door, with Jan proudly at his side.

It had often seemed to Rob that there were more students in his classrooms from the Indian subcontinent than any other single place on earth. He was familiar with both the appearance of the people of India and their manner of speaking, which to him was pleasant, as they seemed to sing their English pronunciation. It was a different style of song than his own, but still, it felt familiar.

Paddy sang in a style of his own. He also looked a bit different from the students Rob was used to: leaner faced, hawk-nosed, taller. He reached his hand forward and grasped Rob's. Paddy's grip was unexpectedly strong, and his hand, calloused. Together they sang to each other the words, "So glad to meet you." The harmony of the two voices was as unexpected as the strength of Paddy's grip.

Jan, standing to the left of him in the doorway, announced, "Paddy's an explorer."

"Botanist," he stated, his dark eyes flashing sideways at her. It seemed this was an old joke between them.

"Tour guide." Thomas's voice came from behind them, as he moved slowly into the front parlour. Another old joke, it seemed.

When so much private language was being thrown around, Rob had always found it better to remain quiet until he could form context.

And it seemed there was a great deal of context among these three people. Rob watched Jan's young husband exploring—and that was the perfect word for his movement—the rooms and halls of the Sullivan place, using hand-touch and foot placement as quickly and carefully as rock-climbers that he had seen on educational telly. He talked as he maneuvered. Squatting without effort to chatter with a recliner-tucked Thomas. Rob had never seen anything like the way the man moved.

Jan was at his side, as though called by all these thoughts. "Paddy designs habitats. They're amazing." Her green eyes narrowed as she heard his suppressed laugh. "Not habitat-towns for rodents. Not that. Real habitats.

"His habitats are based on ultralight aircraft design, combined with greenhouse tradition and solar power. They started out as a way to preserve endangered orchid species. But now they're being used for humans in inhospitable climates."

Rob was trying to hear her while watching Paddy talk, which he accomplished by much use of his hands waving around the still form of Thomas, who listened intently to the man. Rob was willing to bet Thomas was also aware of Jan's conversation with him. Thomas could multi-task.

"Too much information at once?" said Jan, grinning up at Rob and holding her increasingly stretched-out belly with both hands. She was no longer standing quite straight. The room seemed unbearably busy.

"It will take me some time to catch on, Jan," he said as

mildly as he could. "You have all known each other much longer than I have."

"Oh, poor Rob!" She took his forearm in one of her hands. "We are a sort of shock-wave, all together." He thought for a moment she was going to lead him to a comfy chair.

"Ah, I didn't mean it was unpleasant. Your husband is a delightful man."

"Oh good." She released him and began to walk awkwardly toward the other pair. Over her shoulder she called "You know, Rob, when you first came to the States I was going to give you a puppy. You had been so alone. Paddy convinced me it wasn't a good idea."

Thinking of his present involvements, Rob was grateful to Shiva Paddiachi.

The evening arrived, and it was centered around a dinner for the five of them. Rob had invited both the nurse and the housekeeper, as he had never had employees other than teaching assistants, and he wasn't certain what the protocol was for such people. They both declined. The kitchen work fell to Paddy and himself, as the siblings were both disabled in their respective ways. It was all interesting.

Paddy fell into the role of chef, and he did it with great enthusiasm. He had been hoping to get Thomas's new husband alone—although he had learned quickly that the pair did not use that word to describe their marriage bond. Paddy found that idiosyncrasy interesting, as he found almost every-thing in life interesting. He darted busily around the roomy kitchen, though he did not know where anything was kept. And he talked to the very tall, very pale man who found him the proper pots and introduced him to the pantry.

He talked and he talked.

"So, what are we to one another, Rob? I mean officially. Is there a word for our relationship, or are we just in the old British sense *connections*?"

Rob MacAulay was thinking about this. By his lowered

brows and by the changing patterns of red and white on his face—Paddy had been warned about this aspect of Rob—it seemed he was thinking deeply. But Paddy was inclined to suppose the man thought deeply about most things. At last he replied, "I have no idea, Paddy. Does it matter?"

Paddy leaped forward and embraced his new connection in a spontaneous hug, which took Rob somewhere in the middle of the rib cage. Then he sprang back again and said "Of course it does not! Such terms are meaningless. Though, having touched you, my mother would insist I wash my hands and face, or even my entire body, before continuing to cook."

"Because of—of caste issues?"

"No, no, no! Because the one who cooks a meal must be absolutely clean. He or she washes completely before entering the kitchen and does not leave before finishing."

"And you follow this custom, Paddy?"

"No. Rarely. It is a story of my mother's. Even she does not anymore—not with hot water and soap available. And antibiotics." He flashed a smile at Rob. "Don't forget I have a doctorate in the life-sciences."

Rob MacAulay's face went through all colors of confusion. In his hand was a pan in which he was about to rub some garlic. He waved it around, meaninglessly. Paddy went on.

"Isn't it ironic that the two of us are vegetarians and we are about to cook for two flesh-eaters? Sometime we must discuss why you are vegetarian. For me it is more expected."

Rob opened his mouth, but shut it again as Paddy continued, "But that is for later. Now I wish to speak of the Heddiman world of secrets. I notice you are already contaminated by these secrets. When I first met Thomas, and then Jan, I was quite mystified by why it would be necessary to keep so many secrets."

Paddy was chopping vegetables with great accuracy and speed as he spoke. He spoke also with accuracy and speed. "They have reasons, of course. In the great attempt to save you from the temporary insanity of Parliament, I know my friend Thomas had many reasons to keep quiet. Did it bother you?"

Permitted an answer, Rob hurried out with, "Sometimes it did. I didn't understand his project at all. But it worked, so I can't resent it."

"Oh! But the secrets began long before that. From childhood. I think the two of them grew up trying to survive a tyrannical government." He swept carrots into a bowl and began on onions.

"Government?"

"The government of the Heddiman family. They might as well have been august Brahmin children of old India. Their lives were decided for them when they were infants. Had not Tommy—Thomas—been such a free spirit, they might have become simple wraiths. Money wraiths. Floundering in politics …"

Rob simply interrupted Paddy. "And are you an august Brahmin, Paddy, that you know such things?"

"I"—and he put one hand out over his heart, not touching himself—"do not believe in such nonsense as caste. Of any sort! I am fierce in that.

"And that is how I first met Thomas. In the mountains of Nepal. I was engaged to show him and a following of young unfortunates a way out of India to new lives. He had thought to pay me for that. To pay me!" His voice swelled with outrage. Thomas, who could hear from the next room, gave an apologetic smile and pretended to hide his face behind his hands. Another bit of history between them.

"It sounds like quite a story," said Rob, grinning in spite of himself, rubbing the garlic on the pan.

"Yes, it is, my dear Rob. Involving rappelling, translation, and the abandonment of some rare specimens of epiphytes. But it is not for now. More important, now, is to know how you saved Thomas in Omaha, Nebraska." He fixed Rob with dark intensity.

"Ah, dear," said Rob, his heart sinking. "There are reasons for some secrets, you know, Paddy. Some really are dangerous. And they aren't Heddiman secrets. They are mine."

"So tell me yours." Seeing that Rob stood tall and motionless, his eyes darting from one side to another, Paddy added, "Just because I don't approve of secrecy doesn't mean I can't keep a secret. I already know much of it."

It was dark outside, but the kitchen was bright with overhead lighting. Rob had the now familiar feeling that the ground was sliding out from under him. "Do you, then, know that Thomas himself flew—or jumped—back to the place where he had been hurt and came back again? Without me at all. Just MacBride for an anchor."

"Who is—never mind who is MacBride. That is new and different. How does he say that he …?"

"He says he used meditation. As I don't meditate, I have no idea what—"

Shiva Paddiachi raised both hands toward heaven. Seeing the chopping knife in his right hand, he lay it down on the table and repeated the gesture. "Then there is hope for all of us."

"Hope?" Rob sighed and leaned against the butcher block. "That's the optimistic view."

Paddy shrugged. "I am an optimist."

Rob's phone rang. He hadn't bothered with creating identifying signals for various callers. He rarely got phone calls. He answered it.

Paddy watched the tall man hold the phone in one hand while dangling the fry pan in his other. He reached in and took the pan from Rob's hands, fearing he would drop it. Perhaps drop it on his own foot. Rob seemed intent on his call.

Paddy's curiosity, never entirely asleep, woke up smartly. He stepped back, but not so far back that he could not hear

Rob's side of the conversation. He was speaking to someone he called Professor Babisha.

"He said he had found simple errors in my maths? Already?"

That sounded dire to Paddy, as he was aware of Rob MacAulay's position in the world of physics. Aware of the bloody infighting of scientists in general. But Rob did not seem angry, or even defensive. He had merely leaned his hip against the butcher block and listened with great intensity.

"And you? Ah, then. Well, I don't know, do I? I said I had had no access to the big machines. That's why I gave out the equations. And I don't agree that it was foolish. The maths will stand or fall. It doesn't matter how I feel."

There was silence. Silence was just as well, as far as Paddy was concerned, as he doubted he would understand Professor Babisha's end of the conversation. "You don't? Your results back my own? I'm not sure you ought to have told him so. Not so baldly.

"Why? Because you are still in the University system, and spite can do you damage. Especially—forgive me for speaking —as you are a woman in the sciences. As I was a poor fellow-ship student, I understand these things. Don't charge in being a ..."

Paddy could almost hear the woman's response. She was speaking loudly. Rob's voice remained low. "Indeed. The mathematics will stand or fall. As I said. You are right. And I think you are unusually brave."

And Rob then smiled. Paddy thought he had a lovely soft smile. Men in the west did not usually dare to smile so openly. "I'm not brave at all. I am simply beyond caring. Thank you so much."

He slipped the phone back in his pocket, beneath his kitchen apron. His large eyes were vague and not looking at anything in the kitchen. Not looking at Paddy until he spoke up.

"Departmental squabbles?" he ventured.

Rob visibly reset his mind. "Ah! But not my department. I don't have a department. Or a University. I merely shared some equations explaining field collapse to some Harvard faculty. The woman was getting back to me."

Paddy leaned close. "So you are not affiliated with any University at the moment. That is to be expected, after all you have been through. But why do you act like a ghost who cannot care any more about things?"

Rob MacAulay gave the smallest of sighs. He washed his hands in the sink and went to find his fry pan again. "Because I am a ghost, I suppose. I am more than unaffiliated. I had my tenure revoked. Revoked."

In that moment Shiva Paddiachi—Dr. Paddiachi, among people who cared about such things—understood what that word had meant to Professor Rob MacAulay.

DINNER WAS FESTIVE, and the four partook of it in the dining room, which Thomas and Rob had not yet used. It had modest chandeliers and an old mahogany table that tonight sported a damask cloth. This last was Paddy's idea. The paneling and wallpaper were understated and warm in color. More importantly, the room tonight was filled with human light and warmth.

Rob declared sincerely that the entire menu was Paddy's. It was not actually necessary for him to say this, as neither Thomas nor Jan believed Rob had the skill to produce food both so colorful and so stringently healthful. The four of them sat in one corner of the long table, giving an unbalanced look to the assemblage. Not even Rob minded this particular lack of balance.

They served no wine, and each of them had a different reason for avoiding the stuff, but there might as well have been wine to smooth the evening, as they chattered on about nothing and everything: about everything except impossible skills that resembled teleportation. Rob assumed such conversation would come later.

During the dinner came the occasional interruptions from Rob's mobile. Thomas knew how unlike Rob it was to keep the phone on during dinner. To keep the phone on at all. Thomas listened—without looking—to each short half-conversation. They all involved the equations and the calls were not from one person, as was obvious from the differences in Rob's manner as he spoke. Thomas's curiosity was such that he was tempted to do something technically rude, to allow him to eavesdrop. He refrained. From the glances of his brother-in-law at each call, and the slight breaks in the flow of Paddy's conversation, he knew Paddy knew more than he did of the situation. That was slightly irritating to Thomas. If he could get one of them alone, either Paddy or Rob …

Thomas realized he was falling into old habits. Bad ones. Instead of continuing being devious, he simply asked Rob who was calling and why. He spoke as the non-fish course was being taken away, carefully, as the china was Grace Sullivan's original tableware.

Rob looked down at Thomas as he was picking up Thomas's plate and the three-tined fork. Rob was removing from the wrong side, as table service went, but no one had corrected him. No one at this table would. "It's people from Harvard. They're getting the results from the fast machines. On my equations."

"And?" Thomas was leaning back into the armchair at the head of the table. He was not placed there as head of the household, but because it could be stuffed with pillows so that he might sit up for so long.

Rob fitted the silverware from the plate he held into the sprawl of his hand. He was not certain how to translate the conversation from the academic bits that came from the phone to the deeply personal that bounced around the table. It made him sound awkward. More awkward than usual.

"Some are happy. Some are not. That isn't really important. I mean—what the Harvard people feel about it. That's not important. What is important is that I finally got someone to look at them."

"Brave of you," said Thomas.

Rob shrugged.

Jan could not believe that Rob was worried about his reputation, so the comment puzzled her. "Why brave?" she asked the room at large. She had already eaten more than she usually ate at dinner, but was eager for the next course. Pregnant and eager.

"Because of what use they might be put to. For years I didn't share them. Only recently have I had the—the faith in the future to dare. Although I'm not certain that faith really is the right word."

She smiled slyly at her brother's colorful damaged face. "Maybe you had some persuasion," she ventured.

"He did not." Thomas's words came out sharply, and invited no banter at all.

Rob disappeared into the kitchen, and they heard his mobile phone singing out again. Paddy followed him, carrying his plates with greater dexterity. Sister and brother locked eyes in the room, alone.

"His usual explanation for his reluctance is Einstein and the bomb," Thomas said to Jan. She leaned back against the pillow stuffed into her own chair. Laced her fingers over the baby.

"Ooohh! Nothing is ever simple, is it, Tommy? No simple fun?"

Thomas tried to shrug and thought better of it. He smiled slightly, and that, too, had an odd appearance with the chandelier light and his swollen features. "There is always fun.

We've had fun in the wildest times and places. When you were a kid and I was—whatever."

"And now I'm on the edge of Mommy-dom. You know, Tommy, the baby's a boy."

"Were you hoping for a girl? Our family runs so much to boys."

JAN GRINNED BROADLY. This was a moment she had been waiting for: to tell her brother that he was going to have a namesake. It was a shame it had to happen while Thomas was so injured. But looking at her older brother sitting there, propped by pillows, Jan decided it wasn't a shame at all.

THOMAS WAS ALSO LOOKING at the color of a face—Jan's face—and he thought it was true after all that pregnancy brought out a bloom in a woman. "We were hoping for a healthy baby. So far, so good, too. And we have a name picked out."

Thomas raised his eyebrows and waited.

"He's Thomas. We both chose Thomas. Put our choices on little papers and folded them and traded. He's Thomas."

She added "You look like you've just been hit on the head. Again."

THOMAS DID FEEL he'd been hit on the head again. But this time, it didn't hurt. The idea of a baby being named after him rendered him speechless. He wondered if he were flushing semaphores. Like Rob.

IN THE KITCHEN they could hear the phone's little signal.

This call was not like the others. Rob was not surprised that he did not recognize the voice, as he did not know most of the people who had been at the meeting, and the callbacks were often from affiliated mathematicians. In two sentences he was aware it was some sort of University official speaking to him.

And the caller was speaking as though his connection to Harvard University was a done deal, and it was only a matter of scheduling specifics to be worked out. And apologizing for calling during the evening.

"Doctor … Wembly? Do I have your name correct? Thank you, I can be forgetful in such matters. But there is, I think, a misunderstanding here." The phone was slipping in his hand. He used his other hand to steady it. "I'm not employed by your University. I have not even made an application to it."

Genteel laughter came from the other end.

PADDY STARED AT HIM CLOSELY. He had raised one hand to Rob's shoulder. He heard the words "Not at all. I am merely saying I did not think it possible and so did not—did not consider employment at Harvard."

Poor Rob was actually sweating, and not from heat in the kitchen. Paddy pulled a paper towel free and dried his forehead, and his hands, one by one, steadying the mobile phone, while Rob continued the conversation. "You do know about Edinburgh, Dr. Wembly. Don't you? I had my tenure revoked. I am not at all sure your university would …"

Shiva Paddiachi wanted to give his "connection" a hug. To pat him on the back. In India, he would have done so, regardless of culinary cleanliness. But people such as Rob MacAulay were as skittish as wild cattle. He just listened and watched.

And prepared the next course. He did not expect there would be much help in the serving.

━━━

PADDY EXPLAINED to the siblings as much as he understood of Rob's call from the bigwig at Harvard, and his sad—to Paddy's mind—confession of his lack of tenure. To Paddiachi it had seemed an almost comical situation, but as an ex-academic himself, worthy of sympathy.

Thomas Sullivan attempted to raise both hands behind his neck, to support his head. He wound up with one hand behind his neck and the other resting on his lap. He made a sound much like the growl of a dog. "That man in the kitchen," he began, and then he cleared his throat. And cleared his mind. "That man in the kitchen, there, last week broke all the rules of human possibility. He brought me from death back to life. He is changing the world!"

Thomas expelled air from his nostrils forcefully. "He *has* already changed the world, almost as a side-effect to his thinking about a problem in physics. And he's just begun."

His sister leaned across and put her hand over the passive one on Thomas's lap. He shared a wry, sympathetic glance with her and continued. "If that man, there, has a problem with the university-shaped world, he's allowed to. I will see he's allowed all the little quirks—or quarks—that come with the package. I am not going to permit anyone to stand in his way. Or bother him."

Jan squeezed her brother's hand. "Tommy, I don't think you're going to need such ferocity."

Thomas looked from one to another in surprise, discovering he was indeed going in the direction of ferocity. Past simple irritation. Past anger. He took a deep breath, or at least as deep as his bandaging would allow, and composed himself. "You're right, Jan. After all, why else did I go to Britain? Scotland. Whatever."

"I don't know," said Paddy. Both looked at him and he rolled his dark eyes. "No one ever tells me anything."

Jan snickered and cut her cheese mattar into smaller pieces. "Of course not, Paddy. We keep you entirely in the dark."

"To control my anger," said Thomas. "That's why I went. And you can see how easily that lesson went down. Unlike your cooking, which slides down so well I am going to gain two kilos by morning."

In a complete non-sequitur, Paddy replied, "So who shall go next?"

"Hmph?"

"Who is going to break the laws of physics and travel at the speed of light so dramatically? Shall it be your sister, or my poor, inadequate botanical self?"

Thomas looked from one to another. "That is the question, isn't it? I don't think it's a matter of inborn talent. Rob and I have no genetic connection. I believe that the big problem is going to be control. Rob has the skill naturally. I learned—if it was learning—by following him. Literally following him. But I know that it worries him. That ability to 'flinch,' as he called it, or to jump, or fly, will be discovered by a person without moral control, and then all hell will break loose. He has a right to be worried. Think of it."

"I have thought about it. Lots," said Jan, again stroking her belly absent-mindedly.

Paddy was no slouch at thinking. "You both accept the word 'control,'" he said, waving his fork around, "But what you mean is simply purity of heart. We must pray that no one without simple purity of heart discovers this."

Thomas reared back, or reared as much as his condition allowed. "Well that would have let me out from the beginning, my dear brother. I'm as impure a fellow as you could dredge up, but I flew."

"Don't demean yourself again, Tommy. How many times have I told you?" Janet Paddiachi glared at Thomas with a severity only half in jest. "I'm not at all pure. Or in control. But that's not why I resist the idea of being the next one to jump off the cliff. I fear for young Tommy here." She patted her belly. And belched. "Sorry."

It seemed that Paddy was going to speak, but before he could open his mouth, the door to the kitchen swung open and Rob came through, ducking unnecessarily under the lintel and slipping the phone into his jacket pocket. He had forgotten to take off his cooking apron.

"Forgive me for disappearing like that," he said. His voice moved erratically from note to note—from key to key, almost, from his suppressed excitement. "It was Harvard. They want me."

"It's what you want that matters," said Thomas, in a subdued growl. Rob, having not been part of the dining-room discussion, stared at him blankly, wondering why he was angry.

He also stared at the food on the table, as though he had forgotten what it was and why it was there. He sat down at an angle beside Jan, placed so his left-handed eating would not interfere with her own.

Thomas had to remind him, as the meal continued, that he was supposed to be eating.

11

The Government Man

T he next morning Rob opened the north door, where the wisteria grew over the brick porch uprights, to find a world dusted with new snow. Two individuals stood there, waiting for him. In front was the small stripe of red that was Tony Kaye. Behind her, like an oversized, flat white backdrop, stood MacBride. Both had their breaths steaming into the light. MacBride's breath was so significant a cloud that the open space of the garden beyond the porch was obscured.

Rob glanced from the horse to the girl and back again, squinting against so much white. He began his goofy grin and could not suppress it. The child didn't seem to notice.

"Oh, we aren't together," said Tony, as though that short sentence would explain all. "He was here before me. And I am so happy you let the horses play in the yard, as though they were children. Human children. It must be so much more fun than being locked in a box."

By stepping out onto the heavy porch floorboards—just enough snow had blown in to *crunch* under his foot—Rob could look sideways to the rim of red wall that enclosed the

Sullivan garden. Being far-sighted, he could make out the wide steel gate that led to the stables. It was closed and locked, as it had been when the sun set last night. There were MacBride's perfect round hoof-prints coming up the stairs, trampled over by the longer, messier prints of Tony's sheep-skin boots. There were prints at the foot of the porch. The hoof-prints ended about ten meters out. Simply ended.

Rob had good vision. Very good powers of observation. The implications of this simple picture were enormous. He dared not show what he felt in front of the child.

He said, "I should call Thomas. Thomas is MacBride's. I mean, MacBride is …"

"I know what you mean," giggled the girl. "I think you said it right, though. And I don't want to get MacBride in trouble. If he's not allowed on the furniture. On the porch. You know."

Rob pulled Tony into the house along with himself. He almost asked MacBride to wait, but realized the idiocy of that in time. "MacBride is not in trouble, lass. The porch floor-boards may be. I don't know."

They found Thomas just as the day-nurse was done with him. He was ruddy and clean and dressed in robe and slippers. He greeted Tony with a smile and then noted, by the girl's expression, that she had not seen his face and arms in full color since the "accident." He began to explain that the green and purple were just bruising, and nothing to frighten her, but she broke in.

"I just feel sorry for you, Thomas. So sorry. And MacBride is on the porch." She looked up at Rob, uncertainly. "Maybe I shouldn't have told him?"

"No, Tony. He ought to know." He echoed the child. "MacBride is on the porch."

Morning light—almost a glare of snow light—made the tiny motions of Thomas's eyes into a sparkle as he thought.

Thought quickly. "Well, he hasn't done that before. I'd better see what he has to say. Right, Rob?"

Rob nodded forcefully. "And do look at the snow whilst you are in the doorway. It's so pretty this morning."

Thomas had a cane to support his good hand and keep him from falling on the old oak floors. He was supposed to ask for help when walking, but as he was Thomas, Rob hadn't even begun to argue that point. As he went—step, step, thump, step, step, thump—slowly north, toward the wisteria porch, they could hear him saying, "Oh, I always like to look at the snow. To look at anything interesting, really."

Tony squeezed Rob's hand. "Is he going to be upset at MacBride? Tell me the truth."

He remembered what it was like as a child, when one feared that the parents were going to be "upset."

"He will not, Tony. For one thing, no one has ever told MacBride it is dangerous for him to come up on the porch. Never thought of it. But he is curious. Thomas is. And MacBride is curious, too, it seems."

"Maybe he'll come in the house, next," she said, grinning. To Breton Kaye, nothing could be more entertaining than the sight of a big white horse walking through the house. "Maybe he will," said Rob, forcedly neutral.

They went into the south parlour, which had been cleared of ordinary furniture and made into an impromptu school-room. They worked on geometry. Tony had found herself, against her will, liking geometry. She was losing her battle against mathematics.

"We call it 'plane Geometry,' not because there is also a sort of fancy Geometry, Tony. But because everything we do here is done on a flat surface. Two dimensions."

"Mama has a plane to make things flat, too. She said the kitchen table was hopeless and she got out a thing she called a plane and it made big curly things of wood. Flat surface. Of course, she did a lot after that, with sanding and a finisher to make it pretty."

"So your mother is a wood-worker?" asked Rob. He wasn't surprised at all. Mrs. Kaye did many things. Although Mr. Kaye had the degree in geology, it was his wife who had set the patio stones. Rob and Thomas had admired the patio stones a few weeks ago. When the winter broke, it was promised that they could have a barbeque out there.

"Oh!" Tony put one finger up in the air, in a gesture Rob had seen in her father, when making a point. She was holding her kiddie calculator, which looked like a magic wand, in pink and purple, in that same hand. "I forgot. I was going to tell you about the government man who came to our house about you. But then there was MacBride on the porch and I forgot."

Rob was digesting this information when she asked, "Are you really a refugee, Rob? Like he said?"

Rob's mood dropped like a stone. He tried to control his expression and hoped the nine-year-old couldn't yet read his facial colours. "No, Tony. I'm not a refugee. Not at all. The government man must have been mistaken."

Tony was looking at him closely, her round eyes seeming so large. Likely she could read his colours, or at least notice them. "He was a nice man. Or Mama said he *seemed* to be a nice man. That may be different. I don't know." Rob shook his head, indicating he couldn't know either. "He said the United States, which is *us*, ought to be good to you because you had some hard times. Which was, I guess, why he thinks you're a refugee."

"Tony—a refugee is a person who comes to a foreign country to escape another country. I am not a refugee in any sense. I was born on an island off the coast of Scotland and I came to the United States to live with Thomas. I had been in trouble in Britain, but that was over when I came. I arrived legally married to a United States citizen. I came to see his country. To live in it. I don't know for how long.

Wherever we live, we will live there together. It is that simple."

Tony nodded as he spoke. She put down her calculator. "And he said maybe you got married so's you could leave England. Scotland. Britain. Whatever!" She shook her braids in irritation over the complexity of politics.

Rob MacAulay knew his face was going liver-red. He restrained himself from making fists of his hands, because he was now a teacher in the presence of a student. "Tony. You have seen Thomas and me together at least twice a week now. Do you think—can you think—that I'm with him merely to be protected from something?"

Tony grinned at him, and it was so like her mother, Athena's, grin, that all Rob's anger melted away. "No way in —in the bad place—do I believe that! Nor does Mama. She said so. And when the man wanted to talk to me alone—"

"He wanted *what?*"

She laughed. "You look just like Mama did when he asked."

"And your da—your daddy?" Rob felt he was breaking some sort of rule in asking the child about her parents, but he wanted badly to know where he stood.

"Daddy just looked at him. Said hardly a word. He's good at that, not saying anything. But meaning something. I don't know how to explain it." She laughed again and gave Rob a sly look. "But that man left faster than he came in. That's how Mama said it."

There was a presence behind them. Tony saw Thomas enter first, leaning on the wall, rather than using his cane. Rob turned and saw that Thomas had something to say to him.

Rob spoke for Tony and himself. "We also have something to say to you, Thomas." He rose and gave Thomas his chair. Pressed him into it. "Tell him, Tony."

"It's about the government man," she said, evidently pleased to have her audience expanded.

She repeated her story, almost word for word. Well done, for a nine-year-old. Thomas listened as Rob stood behind him.

When she was done, she pointed at Thomas and looked at Rob. "That's what I meant. About Daddy. Not saying a word but meaning it. You know?"

"I do know," said Rob, with his hand on Thomas's one undamaged shoulder. Unfortunately, it was over-time for him to be leaving. For Harvard.

THOMAS SULLIVAN HAD his own need for achieving balance. It was different from Rob's quirks, certainly, but it was also useful at times. If he could not explain the phenomenon of field collapse, and did not have the mind-set to operate in the weird world of physics, he had a skill at keeping the man who did understand such things alive and functioning in the world of humanity. Which had to be at least as weird as any other science.

He made a battle-plan in his mind, much like the tabletop displays he had grown up with, describing famous and complicated conflicts. Gettysburg. Stalingrad. But instead of artificial dirt with roads and tiny toy people, his was a clear table of ideas, expressed in people and possibilities.

There were the Forces of Academia, where Rob was general. Rob was a powerful general. Once he had been indecisive, and who could blame him for that? But no more. Not after he had put his equations on the table at Harvard, thrown down like so many playing cards. Tarot cards was a better analogy. Thomas wished he'd been there, to see the man do it. To be a fly on that wall. Rob was surrounded by enemies whose weapons were pride, greed, and ignorance. Enemies only an academic like Rob could believe had the power to do him damage. But then, belief was what it was all about.

And there seemed to be some allies at that table, too. Mustn't forget that.

And in another corner of the game table was Magic, whether one called it flinching, jumping, teleportation … Rob would simply explode if he called it magic, but Thomas felt he had gone from life into death and back again and no longer cared what people thought of his use of words. It was magic, and he had experienced it. He had even done it. Hell, his horse had just done it.

Which of these was most important? The scientific theory, or the magic? At this point in the game, Thomas was not sure it mattered. And he suspected they would discover the two oddities were the same at base. Occam's razor, sharp and glittering, pointed that way. Two huge thought-shifts, happening at the same time—and coming out of one single man—was ridiculous. They were one.

Proving that was Rob's concern. Thomas was a pragmatist.

And now, as expected, from the edge of the table came his oldest game enemy. The one little Tony was now calling "The Government Man." Always, when the game was in full progress, there came the Government Man.

This was Thomas's constant opponent. In Scotland, in Thailand … sometimes you could call them Government Men. Sometimes simply criminals. In the end, there was no difference. In Thomas's mind, he could represent them both with the same game-icons.

The goal of the game? Had to be a goal, as it was a game. As always, for Thomas, the goal was freedom.

Leaning on his cane and leaning on the wall of the Sullivan house, Thomas felt himself not crippled, but empowered. He was not angry any more, despite the intrusion of the NSA and its attempt to re-construct the language of his life with Rob: to reach its clumsy hand into the small and perfect happiness they were building in his aunt's old house.

Without any machines at all Thomas stood alone, leaning against old wallpaper, feeling the game-board build itself within his head. He was smiling. He could be useful.

He would have liked to go to Tony Kaye's house. That would be only polite. But with the state of his bruises and the freezing ground, he was forced to call and ask that the Kayes come to him. As it happened, only Athena Kaye was home. Dr. Kaye was in Baltimore for a conference. That suited Thomas, as she was the one he imagined would open up to him most easily.

He waited for just a few minutes.

Out of a window he could see her punching in the combination to their gate. The woman punched with authority. He met her at the wisteria porch, which by now had its peculiar hoof-prints overlaid by human. The sight of his multi-colored face, arm sling, and cane obviously opened up her every protective instinct, and Thomas guessed she had many of these. He welcomed her, offered her tea or coffee, and did his best not to totter his way through the house while she talked about the visit from the government man.

What a solid new connection was 'Thena Kaye. Throughout his working life, Thomas had made such connections: people he could trust instinctively. People with skills. Her in-built distrust of the police and government had likely grown out of her history in black America. Brave, protective, and solid. Quick as a whip was a bonus, of course. As she repeated to him her daughter's story, only with an educated, adult viewpoint, it was obvious what was happening, with the nudge, nudge, nudging of the NSA to turn Rob MacAulay into something they could make use of. Something to have in their pockets politically. Even though Britain and the US were now supposedly the best of allies, Russia and China between them could turn the best of allies into something different on the board.

He told her, over coffee and biscuits, that no, Rob had not

entered the country as a refugee. He had come with no idea of claiming refugee status. Thomas offered to show her good copies—for the originals were in deep storage—of the papers that had freed Rob from His Majesty's legal system. Marriage license. Passport. She had waved all that away.

Athena had the card the man who had visited left. She'd kept it in her wallet. It was a nothing sort of card, with the florid NSA logo covering most of the front, and the Refugee Assistance attachment icon filling the rest. At the bottom, the name of the local Boston representative.

Not the name of the "government man" himself. That she had written down, having asked the spelling to his face. He was Al Hinkley. Spelled that way. Of course, a black man, she said. They *would* use a black man. And she had asked the man why he didn't have his own cards. Some bullshit about not being important enough to have his own cards. When she had been a young social worker in Atlanta, Athena Washington had had her own cards, with a chip in each one. And as she knew well at the time, she'd not been important at all.

Oh, Thomas thought, she was a marvelous addition to the web of protection he had built for himself over the years. She could be as useful as Paul Corey, given the right circumstances.

And that was the problem.

He leaned back in his chair in the kitchen nook, using his cane as prop. Athena Kaye was protective, reliable.

And a neighbor. And most of all—a mother. Tony's mother.

Slowly and carefully Thomas spoke to her, looking her in the eye. "I am sorry you became involved in this nonsense, 'Thena. I can't say how sorry. Because you live here. And because of your family.

"Rob and I—well, we have lived for a while on the sharp edge of things."

She told Thomas quite sharply that if he mistook her for

some reality-show addicted housewife he was mistaken. She had her elbows on the little table and her head resting in her hands. Her face was dark, warm, and alert. Like her daughter, she was a creature dressed in shades of red.

"Not for a moment did I believe that," he answered. "Never. But you have a family. Roots here."

"And you don't?" she replied.

Thomas sighed. He found himself attempting to run a hand through his hair, but he didn't have a free hand. "My family is small and—uhm—easily transplanted. Rob has always worried a great deal about having the misfortune to be dragging trouble behind him. Being the cause of danger to those who have befriended him. I used to laugh at this aspect of him, but …"

'Thena pattered her fingernails over the wooden tabletop. Four-four time, he noted. She stated, "I'm not going to allow anyone to drag my girl—or my husband—into more trouble than I can help. No, Thomas Sullivan. If I ever was such a fool a few years of social work burned that out of me.

"But I know that neither you nor that lovely child of a man you are married to brought this trouble into our lives. Tony and I were born into it."

"We'll be taking care of ourselves. And you—I know you're really good at that, too." She finished the last of her coffee and put the cup down. "I just want to keep the channels clear. You take a photo of this card, now. And of the name I wrote. They could be useful."

Thomas did as he was told. Then she added, "And you tell Rob that he's done us a tremendous favor, and that we appreciate it."

For a moment Thomas could not sort out which favor she could mean.

"The math. Or maths, as Breton's begun to call it. She's actually shot forward like a rocket. Not so much that she learned, because that girl could learn anything, but because she likes it now. And since she's as stubborn as I am, I didn't think anyone could change her mind on that."

Thomas found he was smiling broadly. It hurt, but he still smiled. "Rob is a born teacher. I think that is more important to him than the field theory stuff."

"Should be! Teachers and librarians. If we survive at all, it will be because of those."

She stood up, and gave Thomas a hand to do likewise. He took it.

"And the horses were a part of it, too. But that was no surprise. Every little girl loves horses."

Thomas stood braced before her. "And a lot of little boys, too. If they can stand being made fun of."

'Thena shook her shining, braided head. "I can still remember when cowboys were big stuff to the boys. Now it's just the cowboy's guns."

Thomas followed her to the doorway. Told her to be careful of the porch stairs. There was still ice under there.

Mrs. Kaye promised she would be careful. Very, very careful.

WHILE THIS WAS GOING on up north in the refuge that was the Sullivan place, Rob was driving to his long-awaited interview with the dean of—what was it? Scheduling? No, it must be a more important title than that—about his original idea of teaching one simple class at Harvard.

Here he stood in the old red-brick quads of the University, where the tall, leafless trees and the rows of evergreens made their patterns over the dead grass and reminded him so much of University as he was used to it. Only not with this dark a brick. But the waiting for the dean was the same. It served to show the academic his place in the world.

He smiled to himself. The waiting didn't bother him

anymore, for he had no place in this world, nor wanted any. But to teach? That was a different thing entirely.

This dean's name was Lorenby. She greeted him in an office where the machines arcing around her desk should have been decorated with old-fashioned book-bindings, to make the picture more fitting. The walls of the room were lined with books behind glass casings. Old books, with leather coverings all much the same. He spared a moment as he approached, using his far vision to sweep over the binding to see what was so important as to cover the walls. It turned out they were yearly school records. How dull.

He noticed the three chairs in front of the desk. Obviously he was intended to choose one. Instead, Rob MacAulay chose to stand behind the middle chair, using his height to gaze down at Dr. Lorenby, who hadn't risen to greet him.

He could play this game. All his life, it seemed, he had played it.

Dr. Lorenby was a woman of European descent. Greying hair, worn short. No glasses, but with the window behind, he could not tell whether she had the glassy surface of contact lenses in her eyes. Rob himself was wearing glasses—his new glasses, to which Thomas had trained him, which were almost rimless and had at the left corner a connection to the wee-drives that powered him with telephone, GPS, and so much more. When his eyes focused closely, they became real glasses, with lenses designed merely for vision.

He had come so far, technologically, in the months since he'd looked scornfully at the glasses in the shelf of Morrie's shop in Inverness.

He smiled at Dr. Lorenby, and put his hands onto the back of the chair before him. He said he was glad she could find the time to speak with him. He was as warmly courteous as he knew how to be.

In return she surprised him. She surprised him greatly.

"Dr. MacAulay. I'm glad to see you at last. And sorry you had to wait."

Oh certainly. Rob didn't believe her words for a moment.

"But first I wish to discuss with you a visit I had yesterday from a man at the NSA, concerning your refugee status."

Rob held a bit more tightly to the chair-back. He had not expected this. He hoped his face did not show the level of his irritation, and was aware that the light was shining through the tall windows of the office directly upon him. "Dean Lorenby, I have no refugee status. I don't know who came to see you, but there was an error somewhere in the American— I mean the US—bureaucracy. I entered the country freely because of the man I married. I am fleeing nothing and need no help. Nor will I encounter any hindrance, or I so hope."

Dean Lorenby scratched under one ear and looked up at him. On impulse he moved around the chair and sat in it, attempting to remove any appearance that he, too, was gaming her. "When I arrived at Kennedy Airport, a man tried to convince me to sign some sort of document requesting refugee status. I refused. I still do not know why he wanted that of me. I'm not in any difficulties with the British Government...."

"Not anymore," she broke in, with more humanity in her voice. Yes, she was wearing contact lenses. This much closer to the woman, he could see them. Could see her. "Like the entire world, Dr. MacAulay, I've been aware of your strange and actually tragic last few years."

Rob tried to brush aside his last few years with a sweep of his hand. "Please, Dr. Lorenby. That is over. So much over. This tale of 'refugee status' makes no sense and is like a can tied to a dog's tail. I don't understand it and would like for it to be gone."

"So you have encountered it before?"

"Two or three times since I landed here. It makes no sense at all. I want nothing from the US Government, except to be left alone. As the spouse"—and here he paused a moment, because he hated the word "spouse." It sounded like what happened to a garden hose when left under water-pressure after a hard freeze. "As the spouse of a US citizen, I am legally dwelling in the country. If a university feels I have something to offer, I can be granted permission to work."

He thought to add that he was not even looking for reimbursement for teaching a class at the University, but that seemed off-issue at the moment. He simply closed his mouth and waited for Dean Lorenby to speak.

Lorenby's eyebrows rose. She had dark hair pulled back and a square face. As she was backlit, he could not tell the colour of her eyes.

"Frankly, Dr. MacAulay, I think you are being unusually restrained about this. If I were in your shoes, I would be furious at the entire United States."

The statement left Rob without words for a moment. He had expected anything except simple humanity. In return he offered, "But I do understand there is fear here. In fact, a little girl I have been tutoring is fearful of the world situation right now. So I can't go into some state of outrage …"

The dean leaned forward in her chair. She rested her head on one hand. "I have children, too, Dr. MacAulay. I sympathize." She raised her head again. "But still, we at Harvard want as little involvement with the government as possible. And we do want you. Your participation, I mean. After your recent past, the last thing I imagine you want is for Harvard University to sound—grabby—to you.

"I know little about physics. That may be an advantage to you, right now. But I've heard you come bearing gifts. In the form of a new analysis of Quantum Field Theory. The subject of field collapse, to be exact."

Dr. Lorenby pronounced all these words carefully. It was clear she knew little about physics. And it was an advantage to Rob, as she had said. So he immediately proceeded to tell her that he wanted to teach a class. A rather unorthodox class. And he described it to the woman, leaning in close over her desk, leaning between the machines.

"A class without credits? Graduate level? A sort of a seminar, then?"

"You can call it what you will, but a seminar is generally a more closed thing. I would like the situation I used to have at Edinburgh, when I had tenure there...."

"Oh—you still do, Dr. MacAulay. The revocation of your tenure was an obvious mistake and the whole thing was erased. Are you saying you don't know that?"

Rob looked down at his own hands. For some seconds. "No one has said a word of this to me," he said at last. "Are you certain, Dr. Lorenby?"

"I am. And no one told you? That is unforgiveable. The whole thing is unforgiveable!" The woman's voice was shaking. He raised his gaze to hers and the two professors, from different countries and of different backgrounds, shared a similar emotion.

"Dr. MacAulay. Rob, if I may. And I'm Catherine. We will see if we can arrange a class for you, to your specifications. I don't think it will be difficult."

Shortly after that, Rob's interview at Harvard was over. He let the old Volvo drive him home. He hugged the memory of Dean Lorenby to himself and grinned until his face hurt.

⸻

HE DID NOT GO IMMEDIATELY into the house, because he had been free to think during the entire trip north from Cambridge. The time he had spent on the run, which had begun to recede in his mind, filled by finer things, by close ties and hope, started to bleed back into his consciousness. Rob was determined there would be no repeat of that period.

So he did not require that the car take him home. He had

the car take him through the main gates of the stable and park itself close to the little stallion barn, which now had three residents. Only two of them were stallions. He sat on the black flooring of the central aisle as Kinsman and MacBride clattered in from their substantial paddocks. He was glad O'Brien had decided to let the horses in and out of their paddocks at will—and with their warm breath clouding his glasses, he began to use the glasses for one of their many purposes.

A simple rightwards flicker of focus brought up the phone menu. The left earpiece divided into two, one of which could be pressed downward to serve as a mouthpiece. He could use the eye-phone without the mouthpiece, but then he had to sort of bellow, so he preferred the extra work.

He called Yvonne of Rolling Stone.

Rob expected he'd be leaving a message, but he got her immediately. Perhaps she was wearing eye-phones also.

After exchanging greetings, which grew into conversation warmer and more personal than he'd expected, Rob found he was smiling to himself once more, and he was holding his knees in his hands as he asked her his favor.

Her response was worried. "Yes, Rob. Rolling Stone has served that purpose for Thomas Hed—Sullivan many times. And last year, you were put in the 'pouch,' as it were, with him. He has also used the Washington Post, in this country, and other agencies I don't know about. But may I ask why you are asking this yourself, instead of going through his …"

"I'm not trying to hide anything from Thomas, Yvonne. Not at all. It is simply that this peculiarity with your NSA— I'm sorry, I know it isn't yours in any sense. But in this I feel I ought to … what is that expression? Take point. For once in my life. Thomas can't be my eternal guardian. It becomes, well, embarrassing. And it isn't his job."

There was hardly any silence, but he could hear the three horses breathing, almost in concert. As though they were following the conversation. "I understand. And you think this mistake about your immigration status is more than some glitch?"

"I know it," he said. "I don't know what on earth they could want of me, as all I have of value is my collapse equations, and I gave them away purposely. They're already in machines all over the world. And this started long before I spread them out. Like seed, actually, if you recall the Bible story."

Yvonne's laughter created static on the line. "I'll have to look into that. Rolling Stone has never been heavy on the Bible, but as to your value to the government, I can speak. These people spread out a broad net. Don't underestimate your value. It exists simply because you were in the news. Or because you are a person. It could be no more than that.

"But, my dear Rob, we are ready here. Send away."

From his wallet—a thin flap of an old-fashioned wallet in his trouser pocket—he pulled his passport card, and attached to the back of it, a wee-drive containing all his immigration information, a copy of the passport itself, and the recording, which he hoped the officials never knew about, of his first interview with Wembly when he was pulled out of the line at entry into the country. The recording machine was one of Thomas's tiny prizes, which had been embedded into Rob's shirt collar. The wee-drive was now inserted into the left hinge of Rob's glasses and the information went, at electronic speed, to Yvonne Perrin, and thence wherever she wanted to send it. There was nothing in it Rob MacAulay felt ought to be kept secret at all.

It was an old saw that the correction never catches up to the error. He hoped that saw was broken.

When he was done, Rob rose from the rubber floor without using his hands. He remembered how Thomas's ability to do so had first impressed him. But it seemed even a scarecrow could gain coordination, when made to work at it. He strolled over to the stalls and spent some time with the horses. Kinsman told him, in a number of ways, that spring was coming. Spring was an energetic feeling of movement. And of mares.

That was something else for Rob to think about. But not now.

⊏———⊐

THOMAS WAS in one of his long sitting rooms, looking out at the bare trees and the edge of the wall. Sunlight had melted the morning's frost, but exposed faint rings on a folding table in here. There had been tea. And coffee. An overstuffed armchair was still placed in front of the sofa that sat opposite the row of lacey windows. Rob observed all this.

Rob held his news to allow Thomas to reveal his own. And so he learned about 'Thena and her own view of the "government man." As Thomas spoke of the woman's value to them, Rob saw beneath the calculating front that had been Thomas Heddiman, that this man felt a real warmth toward her. An appreciation of Athena Kaye in herself.

"Value" was such a flexible term. Rob sat next to Thomas and put his arm carefully over the back of the small chintz sofa, so as not to touch the damaged shoulder. "You sound better, Thomas," he said.

"I am better. Every day."

"I mean, you sound—I don't know—younger. I'm glad you like 'Thena."

"I like the entire family," Thomas responded. He settled back against Rob's arm. "I didn't expect them."

Rob thought back to the cardinal bird in the snow that had turned into a little girl. "Who could?"

If Rob MacAulay could, in any sense, teleport, he could not telepath at all. Out of the corner of his eye he observed Thomas and was almost gleeful to think he had been a part of opening up this lonely, too self-sufficient man to sudden strangers. He would have enjoyed sitting there and just thinking about that, but he had his own news.

He told Thomas his own day's story, from his meeting with Dr. Lorenby to his conversation with Yvonne Perrin in the stable. And about his using the eye-phone, in all its complexity, really for the first time.

He expected from Thomas some reaction to this—to his taking measures for himself. Possibly a negative reaction, for Rob had not yet touched the world of politics on his own. "I didn't mean it to be a secret, Thomas," he said, looking into the brown eyes gone amber by afternoon sun. "I just wanted to do it and have it done."

What was Thomas seeing in Rob's own eyes at that moment? Thomas would always be difficult to read. But then he grinned: a lopsided grin because of the swelling, but an honest grin nonetheless. "You sneaky bastard," he said, and he leaned his head back against Rob's long arm. "You're becoming so much like me."

"I hope so," said Rob. "I need to catch up on sneaky-bastard-ness, I think."

He felt Thomas's snort shake the small sofa. "Not too sneaky, please. Two in one household would be too many." Thomas closed his eyes as he said, "And are you now getting paranoid about it? About the NSA? The government men?"

"I'm not," Rob said. He stretched out his legs, pulling off his shoes—each heel with the opposite toe—and settled his legs up on the armchair across the aisle. "I'm remembering International Geoffrey.

"And I'm thinking," he added. "That I'd like to visit Scotland now. It's time. And I'll be teaching a course, soon, so I ought to go now."

"Alone? I mean you'll be travelling alone, not teaching." Thomas's one eyebrow was up, but he didn't seem bothered by the idea.

"Alone. If you don't mind." As Rob spoke these words, he found himself in an inner grimace. Asking permission again.

Thomas sighed and shook his head, reading Rob's face more easily than a book. He put one of his own legs on the seat of the same armchair. It barely reached. "Don't talk as if I have some sort of say in the matter. That's sort of insulting to me, Rob. After last year.

"But I think it would be a good idea, myself. As what you did with your data was a good idea. You should visit Edinburgh again. Give my best to the MacManus clan. Sometimes I miss them. The old man, especially.

"But first," Thomas whispered dramatically into Rob's ear, "I have a trick to show you."

Rob gazed at the man with his swollen face, his arm in a sling and the cane leaning by his side, and said, "I hope it's a sort of mental trick. I know you're Superman and all, but even Superman—"

"Just watch," said Thomas, and his face had the expression of a twelve-year-old boy. A proudly naughty twelve-year-old. He raised his right arm, with a wrist-phone on its flexible metal band. "I started with my clothes, first, but—"

"You're learning to dress yourself?" asked Rob dryly.

Thomas merely waved him off the sofa and heaved his weight forward, scooting along the upholstery to one armrest, which he leaned against.

"At no time do my fingers leave my hands," he began, and Rob stood, amused, waiting for the trick.

It was a simple and un-dramatic trick. The wrist-phone fell from Thomas's raised arm to the cushion of the sofa. Rob was about to enquire what the trick was, when he noticed that the sofa cushion was also rising a few inches to Thomas's left, and Thomas himself was sinking into the sofa as though he had just now sat down.

It took a moment for the meaning of these small things to sink in.

"You—you moved. Didn't you? You jumped and left the watch behind!"

Thomas looked modest. Falsely modest. "I've been working on control. I didn't want to worry you, but control is what we've been missing in all this."

"And that's what you meant by starting with your clothes?" Rob's heart was pounding so that he could hear it in his own ears. "Oh, you are still the sneaky bastard, you—you—"

"Sneaky bastard," Thomas finished for him. The modesty was gone. If he had had the strength to crow, Thomas would have done so. "And you know what the wrist-phone symbolizes?"

It took Rob only a moment. "Restraints?"

"Handcuffs, to be exact."

Rob sat back down, facing Thomas. "You are so quick at this—this oddity. It's marvelous."

Thomas's expression sobered and he reached his good hand over to take Rob by the arm. "No, Rob. You have been slow...."

"Now stop tightening up those shoulders! I don't mean through any lack of ability. You invented this whole thing. I mean, as far as we know. In our circle, you were first. But you have lived in such a stubborn denial for so long...."

Rob shook his head in stubborn denial, or maybe merely in confusion. "How could you be sure you wouldn't wind up with the strap halfway through your arm, Thomas?"

Thomas had the answer to this ready. Long-ready. "Because you didn't wind up with a bullet in your body before I met you. In the wharfs at Inverness. I saw the videos. It was either that I was to assume you could move around something quickly, or that you had pre-cognition as well as all the rest of this mish-mash. Occam's razor led me to believe you can't see the future."

"I'm so glad I can't," replied Rob. He closed his eyes and

wound his fingers together in his lap. "That isn't a gift I want. No one would."

"No, Rob. No one would. But now you must be willing to learn. From me, as there is no one else I know of."

"I will," Rob whispered, and he leaned his face against Thomas's in his peculiar, equine manner, and rubbed up and down. "I am always learning from you."

They fell asleep that way, together on the sofa, in the last afternoon sun. Jan came in and found them like that. She maneuvered a tartan throw over them and quietly took away the folding table, which bumped lightly against her belly.

12

A Father's Lecture to His Son

That evening, after dark, after a great deal of maneuvering of schedules and airlines, Rob felt he ought to spend some time with Kinsman, as he would be leaving him alone for the first time. And because spring was coming, and his horse was a stallion, there were bound to be issues.

March had come in like a lazy lion. The ground was sodden again, but the steel of the gate in the wall was still cold to his hands.

The considerable enclosed arena was lit, and many of the outdoor arenas and round-pens were also in use. The winter had meant little to these horse-people. He could hear hooves coming down with a heavy, wet thump as horses still went over fences and were encouraged through the patterns of whatever discipline the riders had chosen. He made squishing noises with his wellies as he dangled his brand new riding boots in his hand.

He didn't encounter O'Brien, but went into the stallion stable, where three horses were ready to greet him: MacBride, Kinsman, and Kinsman's small son, who had once been Jan's and was now O'Brien's. They were always well informed of his arrival.

Kinsman was a shine of eyes and nostrils in the dim light. He spoke to the horse in English. Why not in English, Rob considered. Probably the animal would understand Scots Gaelic as well, or as little, but Kinsman had grown up hearing English.

"O'Brien and yourself shall have to be preparing for the mares. I'm told there are quite a few scheduled this year, and I'm sure you know what that means more than I do." Rob was sitting on a chair and changing into his gear. The three horses rumbled in reply to his natter.

He opened the stall gate, allowing Kinsman onto the rubber-floored aisle, and held his rubber curry in his hand. He didn't bother with a halter yet. The horse knew where to stand, and always enjoyed the prep work. Who wouldn't enjoy being pampered by a smaller being? By a friend?

"A father of horses—ach, a father in general—has to be a responsible person. Don't you agree?" He worked energetically at the glossy back and Kinsman lipped Rob's cowlick. MacBride made a more opinionated remark, leaning his neck against the bottom half of his stall-door. Sunny, being both younger and gelded, just pricked his ears attentively.

"So the fact that you can get yourself to a willing mare does not necessarily mean that you ought to do so. There are consequences."

What a strange version of the "father's lecture to his son" this was. Rob had never yet seen Kinsman display any prowess in the transfer of himself to other places as MacBride had done in the garden, but Rob assumed the horse could do it. Assumed that the horse would be impelled to do it when the first pheromones hit. Hell, they must already be floating about O'Brien's establishment. It was a good thing O'Brien didn't go in for artificial early mare stimulation, such as was still done with flat-track racehorse mares.

Rob's lecture was done, and he felt himself a fool for having given it. And the brushing was done and the hooves checked. The saddle pad went on and then a minimal saddle —the one with poleys, which was the new saddle Rob used when they were going out without a particular plan or discipline in mind. Only then did Rob offer the colourful rope halter to Kinsman. He waited for the horse to put his head into it. Rob couldn't bear tying Kinsman up, as though he were some sort of—

Slave.

Kinsman stuck his head forcefully into the halter, as if to say *get it over with*. Rob tied it behind the horse's ears and tied the end of it in a loop at the base of Kinsman's neck. Then he hopped up into the saddle. It was easy to do now, because of Rob's height, and the intense workouts he had begun less than a year ago. Easy as a monkey onto a goat, he thought.

And there he was, in the middle of the closed-up stable, sitting on his horse. He breathed mindfully, as Thomas had taught him. He tried to feel himself becoming one creature with the horse, as Kinsman himself had taught him. And he pictured the bare dead grass in front of the wisteria porch, where MacBride's footprints had sat in the snow so recently.

Aloud he said, "Good then, Kinsman." He settled them both deeper into the image. "Let's go." He squeezed his legs just a bit.

There came a shifting of weight as the horse's hooves found uneven ground beneath them. The sudden wet cold and night breeze. Kinsman started, filled his lungs, and went stiff as wood. Rob was ready for that and leaned forward, pushing his fingers deeply into the taut muscles behind Kinsman's ears. He sang out through his nose in a lullaby he remembered from early childhood. "It was good, Kinsman. You and me together. Good, wasn't it?"

After a while the horse's head lowered. He agreed it was good. Kinsman looked over his shoulder back at the stable, where the steel gate was closed as Rob had left it, and around at the Sullivan garden. Kinsman always liked being in the garden.

Rob breathed mindfully for the both of them and did not restrict the horse as they moved over the grass and under the trees. Somewhere in the new housing development a small dog was barking.

"You and me. Together. That's how we do it," he repeated, and his hand massaged the long neck until it lowered further. And Kinsman's legs, which had been high stepping from insecurity, went back to their long, smooth walk.

Rob did enjoy burying his identity into Kinsman's. As though the four legs were his, and the warmth and horse-strength were a part of him. They moved north into the more heavily treed section of the garden.

He remembered how he had rambled on the pony of old Mr. MacInnes of Eriskay, who had been a fisherman, when Rob was a small child, in some lazy afternoons. The pony was left free to stravage the shore for dulse and whatever other seaweed was pleasing to a pony in Eriskay. Little Rob used to sit on the pony's back just like this and lean forward. It was a good memory. Clear.

Suddenly there was another shift of the land under Kinsman's hooves, and this one was stranger. He seemed to be sliding in sand.

And it was early morning and the air was sharp with salt and it was warmer. Rob heard the sea in his ears.

In the next moment, Kinsman was bucking and leaping like a rodeo pro, and, had Rob not grabbed mane before thinking, he would have hit the sand and stones of the beach.

Of Eriskay.

Rob descended into deeper and deeper breathing, meditation and an attempt to connect with the frantic animal. It was good the horse was frantic, so that Rob did not have to be. "You and me together, Kinsman," he said again. And again.

The horse was slick with sweat. Pastern deep in water, they were facing back to a shoreline Rob remembered somewhat. He didn't have time to think what had changed in the landscape of his memory and what had not. He felt understanding of the event seep into him and he allowed it to seep into the horse beneath him.

"Good, Kinsman. Oh you did well. Now let's go home. Home.

"To MacBride," he said firmly, and he thought of the calm white horse and how the winter coat of the animal was beginning to drop, so that white like snow was left wherever MacBride leaned or scratched himself. The image of MacBride changed in his mind into something a bit different, with more smell to it and width of back. A physical MacBride, and welcome and waiting and …

They were back. Not in the garden, but in the aisle of the stable from which they had originally started, so recently.

So long ago.

Kinsman was chuffing like a locomotive. MacBride had his neck out the stall top, lipping at them. Rob put his right hand out and touched the white nose. Rubbed it. His hand came away dusted with white hair.

He slipped to the flooring, and his knees almost gave way under him. He released the girth and let the saddle and pad simply flop to the rubber matting. He found the neat supply of towels and began to dry his horse, rubbing hard, crooning to him. When he got to the head he wrapped it in a clean towel and rubbed it dry.

Rob held Kinsman's head in an embrace so motherly and affectionate he would have felt awkward showing such a display to Thomas. Kinsman didn't mind a bit.

The water on the horse's legs was definitely salty. Not that Rob needed proof of what had happened. He walked the horse back and forth along the short aisle, holding to a bit of mane, singing an old lullaby to him, until Kinsman was calm.

He didn't apologize to the horse. What had happened had been accidental, but who could call it a mistake? No harm, no foul. He just repeated "You and me, Kinsman. You and me." Then he led Kinsman back into his own stall and went to the hot-water tap and made all three of the horses a small bran mash. With just a bit of brown sugar. Sonny seemed puzzled but eager for the snack.

Somehow Rob didn't think Kinsman was going to be jumping through the—the whatever—by himself to get to mares. Not any time soon. He smiled to himself.

Smiled wider as he recalled, though all the frantic leaping about in the dawn light, that he remembered seeing a man coming out of a shed that he remembered as once having been used to store fishing tackle. Just for a moment.

Did that man have a story to tell, or had he just wiped his eyes and went about his business? It was early morning, after all, in Eriskay.

<hr />

"YOU DID it just to show me up!" Thomas had fallen asleep in his recliner, and his tablet fallen to the floor-rug.

Rob swung a light armchair over beside him and sat down. He was breathing hard, now that he didn't have to be responsible for the horse. "Like each oddity I've accomplished, love, it was involuntary and not exactly with the control you're searching for."

"What *were* you trying to do?"

This was embarrassing to admit, as Rob knew less about stallion keeping than Thomas, let alone O'Brien. "I was trying simply to convince him not to teleport after the nearest welcoming mare—

"For that would be more than inconvenient. It would land us all in a world of trouble."

Thomas stared at him, absorbing all this. At last he settled back in the chair. "Well, you could simply have him gelded."

After twenty seconds had passed, Thomas added, "It was a joke, Rob. God! I don't think I've ever seen your face go through such a range of colors!"

Again Rob tried to reply and nothing of sense came out.

"It was a bad joke, Rob. I'm sorry," said Thomas.

⸺

LATER THAT NIGHT, having gotten Thomas into his side of the bed—and it was getting easier every day—Rob said, "I'm worried."

"As you always are."

"I'm worried at how easily this thing can spread. First me, then you, then both horses. What happens if such a trick can be spread throughout humanity? That is a worse concept than anything achievable by unifying—"

"It isn't that easy," Thomas announced firmly, turning on a reading light. "Paddy's been trying for days. And he's quite the yogi. Been meditating all his life. No luck at all.

"No, Rob, I think it involves some connection with you. You took me. The horses anchored us both. And by the way, you don't seem anywhere near as exhausted as you said you were after your Omaha trip. Getting practice?"

Rob thought about it. He wasn't particularly weary. Emotionally exhausted, but that was all. He changed into his flannels, because the bedroom was always chilly. "Actually, it's Kinsman who was asleep on his feet when I left, as though he'd run a race."

"Damn long one." Thomas was smiling. Rob could see his teeth shine in the light. "But to get back to you being the center of teleportation ..."

"I do hate that word," Rob grumbled. "And about Paddy. Did you attempt to take him with you? On a short hop somewhere? And what does Jan think about her husband attempting this?"

Thomas found his book. He was brushing up on physics while resting. "Jan thinks it's a great idea. Jan's my sister, remember? And did I try to take Paddy with me, along the couch?

"To tell the truth, I never thought of it."

———

ROB DID STOP PADDY, as he rappelled himself down the front staircase of the Sullivan house. (It was, of course, not rappelling Paddy was doing, but such images always occurred to Rob at the sight of Shiva Paddiachi in motion.) He described the conversation he had with Thomas the night before, concerning Paddy's unsuccessful attempts to—flinch? Fly? Teleport? There was no word that satisfied Rob—and he asked Paddy whether he had considered using Thomas as co-pilot in the endeavor.

Paddy's bright eyes widened. "Oh, my dear brother-in-law. Or brother-in-spirit, which is so much more perfectly said; I did not wish to broaden the parameters of my small experiment. It is not as if we are under a deadline in this. It is merely one of my yogic meditations."

Jan came down the stairs behind him, holding on to the handrail, moving with great concentration. Every time Rob saw her, now, the lump which bore the name of "Thomas" seemed to be more prominent. Rob had the strong sense that there were now four people involved in this interchange on a staircase. He had to remind himself of the words of the conversation as Paddy continued, "Besides, we are on holiday here, in the romantic forests of Massachusetts. I must keep a light heart, to make my sweetheart's temporary but delightful increase of mass bearable!"

Paddy kissed her, and Jan's face went pink to red.

She was much like her brother, and yet not. And Paddy was just a bit like Rob. They had both survived academia, at any rate. Rob felt comfortable calling the pair of them a binary. Obviously, no two stellar objects were identical and so no resulting orbits could be the same. The binary—no, it was a trinary—went on down toward the beveled glass of the front door.

Although the exchange of information regarding jumping had been minimal, Rob was left with a strong feeling of satisfaction.

Brother-in-spirit.

Term of little meaning, really. But Rob did not bother to delve into his sensations regarding this new title, or those regarding the bump named Thomas. Jan's bump felt in Rob's mind much like the warm back named Kinsman, somehow. Even the trained mathematician and physicist named Rob MacAulay refused to analyze some things.

13

Returning to the Auld Sod

H e had never thought that his approach towards a seat on a flight to Edinburgh would be easy, and it had not been. Delays, luggage, proper placement of the proper passport page onto the reader, anxiety of waiting for the sky to fall before the unit lit up with the simple word "AUTHORIZED."

Rob was authorized. To travel. Over an ocean. Alone. With his tumultuous and confusing personal history is seemed absurd for the little flat screen to declare him authorized.

But he did not argue with the screen. He went to his airplane.

He had also not expected that his physical presence in the airplane would be easy. In this matter, he was somewhat mistaken. All his life, except for the time he had fled Britain with Thomas, he had sat in coach. He was often told the experience was miserable for everyone, but for a man of Rob's elongation, coach had been more of a package than passenger service. Never had he had the luxury of a tray-table lowered over his knees. Always he had bent down his head for hours in the position of a man in penitent prayer. Universities did not pay for their instructors to travel in splendor.

This seat, in whatever they called this class, actually was not so bad. With a small foam pillow, it was almost like sitting in someone's cramped and noisy house. His seat neighbor was inoffensive. And Rob had an aisle seat, so the ceiling was higher. Still, as the window shutter had not been lowered, he could see out.

So much sky. Black and filled with stars. No moon.

This was not the sensation of flight that he loved—not this rumbling high over the earth. That was more closely found in the mat room, where he had progressed in his practices to ten imaginary men to soar over, coming down on one hand and a roll to his feet again. So lucky to have a ballroom to be converted into practice space in the Sullivan house.

So lucky to have Thomas Sullivan.

Rob saw himself smiling in the reflection of the window glass. He knew he was, in most senses, a "kept man," ridiculous as it sounded, given his age and appearance. Thomas had all the money. Even his suit, new and perfectly tailored for him as his old one never had been, was a careful gift from Thomas.

But, in retrospect, Rob knew he had always been a kept man. For seventeen years, Janet had formed and managed him, and for a few more it seemed to him that most of Scotland had been keeping him.

Despite his contentedly solitary habits, Rob felt he had spent his life supported by countless hands.

He felt a bit sleepy. Dozed. When he woke up the sky was lighter and he could see clouds, but below them was ocean, so far down. Shining like metal, it was so even. And in the distance—land.

Someone on the speakers was announcing something; Rob wasn't listening. He recognized the curve of that land. No clouds in that direction. He had leaned absurdly far over and had both his hands on the window plastic and was making some sound.

His seat neighbor spoke. He was actually arching over her legs. But she didn't seem bothered by it. By her voice, she might have been Glaswegian. "Ach! Do I hear an islander coming home?"

"Passing over home, certainly," he replied and looked at her brightly.

Her comfortable, middle-aged face warmed to him and then sharpened.

"Dear Lord!" she whispered. "You're—"

"Yes I am. And coming home, for a while."

HE HADN'T TOLD anyone he was coming. No one except Father Tonio Scala, of course, who would tell Mary Banks and a few of the Italians he had worked with last year, while hiding at the golf course. It would be a simple, discreet, in-and-out visit, done more for the sake of proving that he could still do something by himself. All the winter he had not felt what he might have called homesickness for Scotland. He had had so much to see, and to learn.

So Rob had no idea where that bit of drama had come from, when he had been surprised by the arc of the Outer Hebrides appearing in the little plastic window. By character, he was not a dramatic man.

And at the other end of the flight, during the process of British acceptance of his passport, Rob wondered if the tension of that moment—when his passport card was inserted into the machine and might not come out—might end in a catastrophic cry of "Kinsman!" and great, unexplainable confusion ... But no. He would not panic. He had become stronger than the flinch that had used him and saved him last year. If the machine kept his pass-card, he would look irritated like any other righteous traveler. Any free traveler. And he would sort it out.

As it happened, the machine spat out his passport card as neatly as a different sort of card is used buying cabbage at a grocery.

He hadn't brought much luggage. He wouldn't stay long, and if they'd lost it he'd just go dirty.

Rob had his feet on Scottish soil. Scottish concrete, vinyl, and whatever, actually. With dancing lights and arrows on the floor and walls of international rune symbols that would be equally appropriate in Bangkok. But he was sufficiently confident it was Scottish.

He found his way to his bag, and it was not shredded, and if it had been ransacked by any evildoers he did not much care, as there was nothing in it he would much miss. He wheeled it out smoothly like a dog walking at a reluctant heel.

And he passed through a set of doors to a hall that was filled with milling people. People with flashing signs and glowing signs and speaking signs and old-fashioned crayoned signs who were awaiting arrivals. This was the last airport barrier one had to break through to get to the shuttles, of course. He wondered if he had made the mistake of landing at the same time as some important person. That would certainly slow things down.

But one of the glowing signs caught his eye. And another. And many more. They were of all sorts, from the flashers to the cardboard ones to simply people jumping up and down in place. And they all said some version of "MacAulay" and voices were even shouting "Rob! Rob! Rob!" as though his name was a sort of football cheer.

Rob MacAulay was the important person?

"Jesus, Mary, and Joseph," he murmured. There was a moment he almost called for Kinsman.

THOMAS SULLIVAN WAS PERFORMING a rickety kata—off-balanced by his useless left arm. But to him it was a statement of intent. He was doing better, no longer needed the visiting nurse, and could more or less make it through the day alone.

How much his situation reflected that of Rob's—minus the air-travel and plus a fractured clavicle. They were moving in parallel. To independence. To Thomas's mind, they both needed a dose of that.

He knew he must be missing Rob's presence more than Rob was missing his. Rob's day had been filled with structure, movement, border-crossings …

A flake of alarm moved down his mind, thinking of Rob, the passport, and the political border. He watched that flake move through his awareness as he moved his left leg, shifted, and breathed. Breathed.

Rob would be okay. Jeez, if any man had the resources to deal with a government snafu now, that man was Rob MacAulay. Thomas shifted his weight and moved his right arm in a circular motion. And breathed.

If idiocy piled on idiocy and he was trapped at customs, in some encore of last year, he had the ability to dismiss the entire problem by disappearing. *Poof*, like in some film. It would destroy the attempt at normality that Rob was so intent of preserving, but it would not destroy Rob.

No. It would be just one more call from O'Brien, maybe. Or even the man ass-flat on the living room floor.

Breathe.

Thomas Sullivan found he was smiling at the thought of Rob's burning so many bridges because of a government snafu. It was a naughty smile. He simply was not as decorous and personally careful as his binary. He had enjoyed burning a few bridges in his time. The smile did not leave his face sore at all, he noted. And the tooth that had wobbled a bit no longer did. So far, so good. Thomas disliked being limited.

Breathe.

And when he was done with the kata (he should *not* be doing so much thinking, dammit) he would shower and then, maybe, sit down with the tablet and follow what was happening in Scotland. What was the time there, exactly?

Oh, damned silly man to be fussbudgeting. Rob had been gone for about a day. Grow up, Thomas.

No. Don't grow up.

Breathe.

<hr>

IN HIS MOMENT of panic at this wall of inexplicable people, Rob found his foot was moving forward, almost by itself. The habits of a teacher took over from the instincts of the shy man he was. And at the same moment, his eyes, looking far as always, saw the figure of Tonio Scala, dressed in black trousers and puffy blue coat, squirming through the mass and toward him. He slid between two enthusiastic bouncers by darting under their arms, as Rob never could have done. Rob remembered something spoken by his friend the priest in a different time, about the virtues of being "a middling man."

He sprang up to Rob and reached both hands up onto Rob's shoulders, as though to stop a horse from bolting. But Rob had not been bolting; he had been stepping forward.

But then, how could he know what his own stupid telegraphic face was doing, even as he was moving forward? Rob breathed as Thomas had taught him and put on as much of a public persona as he knew how to wear.

Tonio was already talking into his ear, bouncing up and down to do so. "I am so glad to see you, Rob, and I had no part in this!"

Rob reached his free hand down onto Tonio's shoulder and answered, "And I'm so glad to see you, Tonio. So glad. What is this thing you had no part in?"

"This—this exhibition. I know how you feel about such displays."

Rob looked over his friend's head at the wall of people. Most were young. All were smiling. None were rushing at him. "I think it depends a good deal on what they're displaying."

He felt his grin broaden. It seemed to encompass his face, exposing every big, boxy tooth in his mouth. He hugged Tonio to him one-handedly with a grip so strong the priest lost his breath for a moment. Then Rob stepped forward more confidently. He tried to meet every eye, as though they were students and this was first day of class. He raised his head and filled his lungs.

"Hello," he said. He heard his voice ring though the impossibly huge airport outer chamber. He had not known he could be so loud.

And they cheered.

As he strode forward, with his wheelie-bag behind him and Tonio heeling more closely at his side, the wall of bodies and faces broke, but not so much like that of an attacking army as a crowd of friendly dogs. Each face could be made out from the mass, and although he could not immediately recognize anyone he knew, they looked like people he might be about to begin knowing.

It was much like a first day of class.

Most of the people who looked up at him—and it was a fact of life that people did look up at Rob MacAulay—were young. Adults, most of them, but few of them as old as his own age. And they were not as international a lot as his usual classes. By and large they looked like the range of human being one was likely to see in Edinburgh. In Scotland.

The flashing, the glowing, and the simple signs were disappearing down into the crowd of bodies. And they were waiting for something from him. The pull of their waiting was strong and warm and not to be denied. To have denied this group whatever it wanted would have been cruel. Cruel as to a child, or a puppy. In fact, he could imagine this vast gathering of strangers as one puppy sitting before him, wagging its tail.

Rob gazed about again. He was thinking fast. Organizing. Deciding what he could make of this assemblage. He tried to gather all the eyes into his, and with his hand on Tonio's shoulder, he called out, "Is there anyone here who wants to tell me what it is you want from me? At this moment I have no idea."

He tried not to make his question in any way formidable, but welcoming. And hoped that he would not be answered by an inchoate roar of voices. Instead of that, a young woman pressed herself out of the crowd like a pip coming out of an apple, and she was apple-cheeked and smiling.

"Dr. MacAulay? We've come here to welcome you home."

Rob looked full at her. She was a brown-haired person of average size and she had clever eyes and a not-so-confident smile. His own smile met hers and the meeting of eyes grew and bloomed into something larger.

The past three years whirled around his head and all the world whirled beyond it. He put all that time aside and put on again the mantle of teaching. He filled his lungs and spoke to the assembly. "In this world of so much pain and disappointment, that so many people should come and welcome a stranger home is a thing to be treasured. It's certainly something I myself will not forget.

"Thank you."

And the huge puppy made of people leaped and jumped around Rob MacAulay, as he wheeled his bag and walked with Tonio Scala out of the airport and into early morning Edinburgh.

"What am I to do with them all?" Rob whispered to his friend as the March wind whipped through his hair.

Tonio's own hair, slightly thinning, blew in circles as he leaned upward to whisper back. "You mean, where are you to find the loaves and fishes? No, I'm not being sarcastic, Rob. I'm muddled about it myself."

Rob had intended to wheelie toward a shuttle stop, but stopped on the concrete. He was still grinning, not even aware that he was, and there were so many human bodies surrounding them that they broke the wind a bit. He didn't feel a bit of the cold or the wind, though his overcoat was unbuttoned and snapped at his calves and ankles. "I know. I'll begin by sorting them into categories."

Tonio mouthed the word "categories," but it was lost in the wind.

Rob sang up at full voice against the wind. "Who here has come to discuss my field collapse equations?"

That will bring out a few of them, he thought to himself, but instead many hands went up, as though they were still in early school, and even one sign went up—a cardboard thing containing the words "FIELDS OF," but that sign spun off half-read down the lane of shuttles and taxis and was lost to sight.

That display of interest in his dearest subject warmed him more than the first welcome, if that were possible. "I will be so happy to do that. But possibly not at the taxi stand?"

Laughter bubbled then, but through it an older man pushed his way, ruddy, grey-coated, and with seamed eyes behind glasses. He, too, was smiling, but more formally, and he pressed into Rob's hand a card. His words were lost in the wind and laughter.

Rob read it. "You represent the University, then?" Rob shouted down at him. He nodded.

Memories rose up like a wall inside Rob's head. He found he was saying, "And do you also represent all these young people here? Did they arrive with you?"

The man shrugged noncommittally. Was he saying that he could not know whether he stood for those friendly faces, or was he intimating that it didn't matter whether he did or did not? The difference between those two meanings was, for Rob, profound.

He put the card into his overcoat pocket and said, "I shall definitely call you soon. Quite soon." His smile, too, had become more formal.

Then he raised his eyes to the assemblage and said "The rest of you lot? What can I do to make you happy?"

Things went nicely from there.

———

ROB ENGAGED in three different talks with people as the morning passed into afternoon. Going to the first, on a public bus, he spoke a hurried bit with Tonio, who had his own day to live and hadn't expected to be the sidekick of a man leading small hordes. Tonio left him with a scribbled sheet of paper as to where to expect to find him. Rob hadn't time to enter it all into his mobile, so he put the paper in his pocket, where it rubbed against the formal card of the man from the University of Edinburgh.

It was in a bustling chips shop that he remembered from past years where he addressed the first of his questioning groups. It was, entirely by chance, that these were the ones who had questions about politics. He had expected such questions, as he remembered well his role as a figurehead for one thing or another. He hadn't been expecting to like it, as he hadn't liked any of his former figurehead position, but he would run from it no more.

A well-groomed woman tried to turn it into an interview, right there and then, invoking the people's right to know. As he was surrounded by at least eighteen people at the moment —and God assist the owners and operators of the chips shop in seating and feeding them all—he swept one hand around and invoked the people seated around him. He gave her no priority. He did offer her some of his chips, however, which was more than a token gift, for he had been already hungry upon landing.

How did he feel about coming home? Happy, of course. Was he frightened to be back in the place where he had been hunted, shot at (so that was known), and enslaved?

No, he was not frightened at all, for he had a passport and a pardon, and as far as he knew, not an enemy in the world.

Rob knew that all those phones were not out because people were calling friends, but were photographing and or recording him. By now he was inured to being recorded. He was entirely back in the mind-frame of teacher, where such things were to be expected. He waited for the next question and hoped it would not be too terribly intrusive.

It was, "How do you feel about the position of Scotland as part of Britain, today, then?"

It was from a young man with ginger hair. He did not announce himself to be a journalist. It didn't matter to Rob if he were. His answer was simple. "I'm glad certain changes in the law have been overturned. I am sorry one of the five of us who wore collars is dead and glad that all the others have been struck off. Sorry one man is back in the dock for another crime, but I know nothing about that."

And he didn't. It might be that the fellow had really been a bad hat, but he remembered Geoff Mfume's dismissal of the idea of black hats and white hats. So all he said was, "As for the new negotiations between our re-instated Parliament and that in Westminster, I can't know any more than anyone here. And politics are not my talent. They never were. Anyone here could speak as much about it as I could."

So they did speak. He listened to many ideas, some of which involved separatism, but most of them more close to the ground. Homelessness. The Russian problem. The reconstruction of the burnt Middle East. Rob finished his chips, snagged some from neighboring plates, and learned much. Had Thomas been there, he could have added a lot to the discussion, but Thomas was in Massachusetts, so Rob sat and listened.

His glasses sparkled over his left eye and told him it was time for the next meeting. A madness of separate checks flurried and then he was up and off.

This time he folded into a taxi and headed for the University, to an open spot where young folk were assembled to talk about his equations and their implication for Quantum Field Theory. He took his wheelie bag from the taxi boot and he still had no idea where he was to lay his head, but he was a happy man.

There was no one officially representing the University in the ring of benches in one of the grass quad where Rob met the young folk who wanted to talk physics. Nor were they all of one level of expertise. That, in itself, made him feel comfortable. He always had liked mixed classes.

He had learned—or relearned—a few things while teaching young Breton in Massachusetts. He began by calling out, "I'd like the women to sit closest to me." They rebelled some at this, and most of the rebellion was from the young women, who claimed they didn't need special treatment. That they were as good as any other student in the sciences.

"I know you are. I know it well," he called back, against the wind. "And I also know that the lads will outshout you and pretend they haven't heard you talking. And that gets wearisome. For me as well as everyone else. So as you're not paying for this little talk, I suggest you do it my way. It won't hurt a bit."

The people—he could not call them students, or at least not *his* students—shuffled. The girls and young women seemed more reluctant to slide forward than the males did to slide back. It was purely symbolic, as there were a dozen bodies there at most, but as they moved, he told them about young Tony in Massachusetts, and about how he had been learning how much a person's attitude can affect their learning. That he hoped these advanced lovers of the sciences here on the windy quad could be the beginning of a new movement to encourage others who might be left behind. By their own examples, they could encourage them.

With his hands in his pockets, Rob swayed back and forth in the air and became enthusiastic. Finally, one young woman sitting close to him called out, "But about the collapse equations! Your Theory of Balance?"

Rob came to himself with a blink and a start. "Of course! You didn't come all this way in the weather to hear me talk about early students, did you? Well, is there anyone here who hasn't obtained a copy of the information I left at Harvard?"

One and all, they shook their heads. They had the equations.

"And are you satisfied that they are all integral, and there is no error in the computations? That is not like that man in Russia—Bielovsky—said?"

One and all they nodded. Forcefully. "That's why I bussed down from Inverness to be here," called a young man in the back.

"Then are you waiting for me to give out some wee thought-picture that will make it all plain to the public and raise the media to an uproar? To change the way that people see the nature of reality? To alter the paradigm, the phrase one hears every day now, even in the movies? For this moment to be like a movie?"

Silence fell. Rob sat down, as to be closer to them. Less confidently, the first young woman ventured, "And that bit you're saving for the University itself? Sure they deserve a good hit from you Professor, after the cowardly way they threw you off, but …"

"That," he said, and he thumped both his chilled hands on his long thighs in a gesture he'd picked up somehow from Thomas, "is not something I'm saving for the University. It's something I'm saving to be accomplished by you. And that is because people like you are the representatives of all the young physicists coming along. The equations, and the need for them, came to me as I was walking the roads of the Highlands for two years. Like those songs a fellow can't get out of his head. And I didn't even want to be the person who distributed them. I kept sending hints under different made-up names to old colleagues, hoping to spark them into publishing the whole lot themselves.

"Once I was safe and had a home, I lost patience with that and simply gave out wee-drives instead of addressing a faculty meeting, as I was expected to. Which is a large step further than I ever wanted to go. Listen to me, my true colleagues. I wanted these findings, unless someone with more computing power or a better mind than I have could negate them, to come from elsewhere. To come from everywhere, I'd hoped. So that no university, or worse, government, could claim them.

"It's one small mental hop from the equations to a model for unity. It is. I hope it is your hop."

"Are you saying that you yourself have not made that hop?" asked a new voice, that of a young lad, whose voice cracked. The question was so appropriate, and so unexpected, that Rob knew he was looking to them all as a man caught out in something. His face was hot. God only know what colours it was. He heard a titter of laughter. Rob was so used to that. But it did not seem cruel laughter. He didn't have time to answer. Or to refuse to answer.

The dark young woman, sitting closest, said, "They're talking about the Nobel Prize for you. You know that, didn't you? Don't you want it—some vindication—after all this?"

Again he stood. He whipped his head, neck, and upper body back and forth. "I do not want it! What I want is to be let be!" Rob realized he was exhibiting too much feeling here. No one was likely to understand how much he did not want the Nobel, nor why. He wasn't sure himself. He tried to deflect the question without any outright lie.

"Physics is a young person's game. It's your game. My own mind is now, well, elsewhere. I'm hoping I can hit to you this particular ball and you can pass it along. To one another." He hoped the sports analogy was not too forced. Sports metaphors did not come easily to him.

"Have I asked too much of you?" He watched each chapped face closely. A few looked rueful. A few smirked. "I didn't mean for this to be some sort of test. A game, aye. But not so as there might be losers."

Rob glanced from face to face. An even dozen faces. And he himself wasn't sure of what he was asking of them, so he tried to seem respectful.

In the driving wind, and with only certain of the trees budding, interest was the perfect response. And he saw it in their eyes. Or he thought he saw it. He grinned until one chapped lip split and he tasted a bit of blood. That tiny sting and taste was the perfect offering to the future. Give and get.

Then he heard the *teedle* of his mobile sounding over his left ear. "And I have to go, now," he concluded. "Another meeting I scheduled. I didn't know, you see. Whether anyone would be interested.

"But I'll leave you all with an address where you can reach me. If—nay, when—you have something to say."

"Us? All of us, just sitting in the quad, here? You're giving us your email?"

Rob thought of Thomas's careful arranging of Rob's mail-structure. He did not need to tell these youngsters how carefully his own privacy was being protected. And Rob himself found that sort of talk depressing.

"Why not you? And why not here? I have more than one email address, now. I've become just a little bit canny over the last few years. And it's for my sake, too, that I give it.

"I'd like to know if some young prodigy changes the world

around my ears. Before I read it in Rolling Stone." Rob linked his email address to "open" and they all clicked it into their various machines.

Then, still trailing his wheelie bag, he headed for St. Francis of Assisi rectory.

———

IT WAS ALL SO different and new, taking the train in full view of others and getting off at the nearest stop, which was just north of The Black Isle. It was not so many kilometers from there to the church, and once he would have walked it without thought, trailing his wheelie-bag over gravel roadways. But he was running late; he'd scheduled things too tightly.

He called Tonio to tell him he'd be waiting for a cab for a while, only to hear that fraction of an Italian's forgiveness which could be translated over a simple phone. He was informed that it would waste far more time to involve a cab, and that he ought to have simply called from the University. He was commanded to wait where he stood, and that someone would use the GPS to find the wandering sheep and bring him home.

Rob had to wonder what sort of sheep he would make. Perhaps a mountain goat, as he had read somewhere they were narrow in the chest and long-legged. But he didn't feel too secure imagining himself that sort of animal. Not so close to the North Sea. To Dornoch, and the fall over the edge. Remembering Jacomo, the confusion, the fear. A mountain goat likely had little of that sort of fear.

He was still thinking of the goat idea, with the wind playing a tattoo between his long legs and his fine blue over-coat, when a quiet car drove up from behind him.

The driver, in bright silk headscarf and bright, colourful smile, was Sophia Benneli.

He turned, as much as he could in the harness of the car,

and stared at her face as though he were a child seeing St. Nicholas and knowing him to be real. "Sophy! You are Sophy —my team leader. I haven't made a silly mistake because I wanted to see you so badly, have I?"

She looked at him in wonderment. As the car was driving itself, this was quite safe. Her lovely oval face closed its eyes and she reached out to touch his arm. "Oh, my sweet Francis, why would you be wanting to see me so badly, when it is you who have saved my own son from death? I asked—I begged— to be the one to drive you back to the church where you received your name."

There was too much in this one statement for Rob to find sense. "Your own son? Sophy, are you telling me that Jacomo at the golf course was your boy?"

"I am. By all the saints I am, Francis—or Professor Rob— and had there been more time you would have known it. But you were standing there and bleeding and crying out for whoever had pulled you up with my Jackie and we had no time to be anything but practical."

This beautiful woman, all black hair and features like some Renaissance Madonna, was weeping as she looked at him. They were the sort of tears that come out of the face like a small spring out of the rocks, disturbing nothing. "So I drew out the emergency syringe and knocked you cold, hoping that Antonio could put it all right. And he did."

Rob wrapped his hands over each other and pulled himself into the smallest package he could in the little car, because he feared his emotions might drive them entirely off the road. "Oh, he did, Sophy. For me he did. He spent an exorbitant amount of money to re-surface my hands and to rebuild me in other ways, but always I was thinking—what about the rest of you? What about Jacomo, especially?

"I had an odd, strange time after that, but it seemed most of the world was paying attention to everything I did. Every day. But all the rest of us—of you—I've been so worried, and so afraid to say anything in public that might call attention to you, up here in the Highlands of Scotland, when I know ..."

Sophia rolled her large dark eyes at him. "You are worried about us? About my son and I?"

"About everyone there at the Royal Dornoch. And all the people I worked with through Tonio. Homeless people. People with nowhere to go. When the passports collapsed, perfectly blameless people had no recourse.

"I myself," and Rob stopped to think of a short way to describe his monumental good fortune at having discovered— been discovered by—Thomas. He could not think of any way, short or long, so he simply shrugged and said, "I received the mercy of God. But I didn't forget you."

Sophia sighed and smiled and shook her head. "Antonio knows that. The money has come every week."

Money? Rob blinked twice and remembered the involvement of Thomas.

"And the British idea to kick every child raised in Britain out of his own country simply because he went to a hospital in Italy to be born—well no one is making that an issue. Not since the National Elections. So there are fewer EU citizens homeless in Britain than last autumn. Other groups of people, of course, Francis. It will always be that way, somewhere in the world."

"I hope not," said Rob to Sophy, with unexpected forceful-ness. Then he added, "I've wondered, Sophy. What is it you do for a living, when not running and hiding?"

Sofia smiled widely. "If anyone deserves an answer to that question, it is you, Professor. I was training to be a medical doctor. But I dropped it to come to Scotland. I made that choice myself. It was nothing Britain did to me."

"I thought you were something like a doctor. More formally schooled than the average gardener, anyway."

Her dark glance swept by him again. "And may I ask you, Francis—do you still flinch up off ropes and ladders?"

Somehow he felt easy in answering her, "Now, more, I go from city to city. Or across oceans. Sometimes on horseback." The look in Sophia's eyes was so wary he had to add, "I haven't hurt anyone, Sophy. Not a soul."

He gave her a grin, with almost half of his teeth. Now one more person knew. Knew for certain. Unexpectedly, Rob found this to be a comfort.

14

Things Go Wrong

The little rectory, no more than a hundred years old, was bright and filled with warmth and food smells. Gathered in it were the people who had been creating the warmth and food. Rob had never known it so crowded. It was as though no one in it were hiding at all. Not from the law or from anything. It was glorious.

"Bless you, Rob," called a voice he didn't quite recognize.

"Bless everyone here. In fact, bless everyone in the world," he cried out in reply, and immediately fell silent, for he had never before felt himself to be a character out of Charles Dickens.

He knew all these people. Or thought he did. Somehow he expected it to be Christmas, instead of the early days of March. His eyes were swimming. He opened his overcoat and dropped his wheelie-bag, regardless of its harness, and regardless of the floor.

The church in front was not an old building either, dating back only a little older than the rectory. But it was of brick and was solid, and even the length of the rectory's kitchen was considerable. But fifteen people did manage to fill it, when it was their intent to expand and fill.

Besides the priest himself, there was Rob's old silent driver, still seeming as rigid as a soldier on parade. This time Rob dared ask him his name. It was Sinclair. Art Sinclair. He was, when not engaged in subterfuge, a postman. And he could and did speak. He was rigid, in fact, because he had four of his vertebrae fused surgically some years before. It was no more than that.

Smiles were traded and hands pumped. There stood the leader of the men's team back at Dornoch. He was another Antonio. And Jacomo, of course, who was wide-eyed and not at all now surly. One season can do much for a young fellow. Clear up his skin, for example. And a blonde woman in a simple dress the colour of the local brickwork, who was introduced to him as a real Franciscan—unlike Tonio, who was secular clergy officiating at a church named for the saint. Her name was Clara. That made three of them in the parlour attached to the name Francis, one way, or another.

"And what of Mary Banks?" asked Rob of Tonio. "I'd hoped to see her here. I have written to her in the past few months, but—but what, Tonio? You're looking everywhere but at me."

Tonio shook his head sharply. "Nae, Rob. Mary just couldn't make it here tonight. That's all."

Rob took a deep breath and let it out. "Good. For a moment you had me worried. I'll just look her up afterwards. Unless she's moved after all this time. I have a true debt of gratitude to the woman. All the care she gave me, the risk she took just to share shelter and sustenance with a fugitive man."

The priest still evaded his eyes. "I think it's better you don't, Rob. Not just yet. Mary has her own issues."

Rob blinked twice. The nun wandered discreetly away. "Have I offended her in some way? If I have, it was by accident and I—"

"Not you, exactly, Rob." A young child bounced into Tonio's side and was deflected back into the room of people like a pinball. "It's more ... Thomas."

"Thomas? I don't think she's ever met Thomas or spoken to him. In fact, I ..."

"Oh." Now it was Rob who dropped his glance from Tonio's. "Oh, I can be such a simpleton! And I'm just not used to thinking people might have an attitude about the two of us! And if it comes down to that, Tonio, it's you who are a priest of the Franciscan Catholic Church, and though I'm not abreast of the dogma these days, I would imagine it would be you who—"

"*Don't* you go imagining such ideas of hate and putting them on me, Rob MacAulay. My best of friends. It isn't fair!" Tonio was flushed and sweaty. His eyes sparkled.

"You're right, Tonio. I'm sorry I spoke. I'm still not used to the whole thing. Of all the things people have hated me for, these past few years, that's one I haven't had to think on."

"And you should not have to! Oh, Rob, I'm so bloody sick of people's hate. And of dogma." Tonio flung himself into a wooden kitchen chair, which squeaked in protest over the wooden floor. "Enough of Mary Banks."

THOMAS SULLIVAN ANSWERED THE PHONE, seeing that it was Paddy. That name on the phone-sheet made him nervous. His sister and her husband had come and gone so frequently in their stay that they did not usually bother to check in. Last he heard they were visiting the site of the battle of Lexington and Concord. He had not understood why Paddy would want to see that bit of overdone historica, but then, Paddy's curiosity was boundless. Thomas answered the phone and then listened hard. Paddy was attempting to explain where he was at the moment. He wasn't doing too well, and Thomas had never heard him incoherent before.

He asked Paddy why he wasn't at the battle-scene, and listened for a little while, inscribing addresses and phone numbers in the computer that Thomas's mind became when he was under stress.

At last he told his brother-in-law he was on his way to him.

THOMAS HUNG UP. He had a desire to kick Paddy. No. Really. To kick his sister. But he couldn't do that, could he? Not her. Not now. But kick someone. He found he was squeezing the phone until it was flashing random lights at him. He whipped together the clothing and keypad he'd need for driving and was out the door. He heard MacBride whinnying in the distance and paid him no mind. He drove.

ROB LOOKED AROUND THE ROOM, where conversation had faded, and faces were staring at the both of them. "I have come with another topic for discussion."

"Which is?"

"Which is my—my flinching. I guess you could say I've come to entertain the party. Or to make a great fool of myself, which might be entertaining in itself." This part of his speech, although rehearsed in his mind, seemed awkward to himself. He knew he was shifting from foot to foot.

"Oh yes," called Tonio. "I've been waiting to hear about that. You have half my secret congregation here thinking you can perform miracles."

Rob stepped back into the kitchen doorway. The dining table had been moved to one wall. "Tricks, rather. Or one kind of trick. Now," he said, a bit too loudly, "If everyone is willing to hug to the walls, we may all see this trick. Or we may see me banging my head against the floorboards.

"I must first explain. Thomas has been trying to teach me a sort of acrobatics. And I've been working, myself, on a different sort." He stripped off his jacket. His vest was not so tight. He cracked his back left and right.

"Rob, don't go hurting yourself for a party trick," whispered Tonio. "You're not a teenager anymore."

"No. I don't think I'm even that mature. I'm just an overgrown lad and always will be. But Thomas has been trying to teach me how to take a fall without hurting myself. And it has come in handy. But I've added some of my own trick to it. Watch!"

He looked around at the room, in which were gathered people he'd had reason to trust before. To trust with his life. He imagined eleven different men in white practice uniform, gathered in a line. Then he added five more. More than he could ever leap. He stepped back a few strides for momentum, caught Jacomo's eyes intently, and then leaped further than his own legs could take him.

And jumped.

He ended his roll at Jacomo's feet and slammed into the lad forcefully, but not hard enough to knock them both down. He looked at him and nodded. Jacomo nodded back, his dark Italian eyes perfectly round. From the assemblage came a shuffle, a murmur and then excited chatter, some in English.

"Could everyone see what I did?" Rob called to the room in general.

Sophia answered. "I saw you disappear in the air and appear again beside my Jackie. Is that what you meant me to see?"

"*Is* that what you meant us all to see?" asked Tonio.

"It's what I'd hoped," answered Rob, feeling both relieved to have the secret revealed before so many and terribly embarrassed.

"And is it a trick?"

Rob nodded. "I'm sure it is. But of what sort I have no idea. Let me try one simpler." He turned back to the priest, mumbled to himself and said. "Please stand there and don't move. Thomas is better at control than I am."

"Thomas can do this thing too?" As Tonio was speaking, Rob appeared at his side, without sound or light or anything except—appearing.

Rob swayed a bit, but didn't need to catch on to Tonio. He said, "What did you say about Thomas? I only heard half."

Tonio did grab on to Rob. "How do you do that, Rob? It is physics?"

Rob chuckled. Guffawed. He took back from the priest his jacket and shrugged into it. "Everything has to do with physics, Tonio. And I don't know what it is I'm doing. I think I started when I was just a lad, but Thomas says I've been in denial about it. Because it's so much not science, you know."

"But you saved my life! Do you want to deny that?" Jacomo's—Jackie's—voice broke as he spoke.

"No, lad. Never think so. I'm just uncomfortable with things I don't understand."

Arthur Sinclair said, "But you said anyone can learn it?"

"I said Thomas can do it. And his horse, MacBride."

"Horse?"

"We're just beginning to study it, you see."

Jacomo blurted, "And you trust us all with this?"

More calmly the priest added "Why not? Who would believe us here, with such a story?"

"But I do trust you." Rob looked ruefully at Tonio. "Who could I trust more? But I didn't want you to think I could work miracles!"

Father Tonio Scala began to snicker, then laugh aloud. Then all the room was laughing except for Rob.

"Oh, no. It's never a miracle. Not our Rob!"

"Our Francis," added Sophia.

As they laughed at him, or with him, Rob's face went from looking irritated to improbably cold and distant. The party mood was gone. He was pale, and was spinning the thin ring of platinum on his left hand. He began to shake his head, asking for silence. He had just begun to quiet the racket when his mobile rang, in his glasses.

"Aren't you going to get that?" asked Sophia.

Rob continued to shake his head, and then he shouted, full voiced, "Kinsman!"

And Rob MacAulay winked out—disappeared—leaving his overcoat and wheelie-bag on the floor of the rectory. Young Jacomo cried to Sophia, "And what does that mean— that word, 'Kinsman?' Is it physics? Sacred? Magic? What?"

———

THERE WAS THE PULL, the jump, and then it shifted. This time, the—whatever it was—was not instantaneous. Was not the speed of causality. Causation. But instead it went a wee bit off-kilter, and this time there was an unmanifest *something*. Had Rob had enough time, there would have been confusion. Fear.

But there had not been that much time. Just a knowledge to be filed away for later. If a later came.

And there came the shift again, and he was skidding over floor tiles and into a set of legs. Familiar legs. Rob grabbed the familiar and let the knowledge and the almost-fear go, to be sorted out later. He was flat out on an institutional floor, with an institutional sofa and the legs were not the sofa's but—

"Thomas?"

The legs rose. Retreated, rather. A face came down. "Rob! Whatthefuck? I mean how did you get here? Why?"

"You called me, I thought." Rob tried to climb off the floor and found he was tired to the bone and shaking. Thomas pulled him up by one arm instead, and he was sitting on the stiff sofa beside him.

"I did call. Just now. But you weren't answering," Thomas replied, staring at him wide eyed, but watchful. Rob glanced around them. Many similar sofas, some chairs. A distant desk. Doors, a television without sound on.

Hospital waiting room.

"I am answering," he whispered. It seemed no one in the sizeable room noticed the man being picked up from the floor. "I came a long way to answer. I thought you were *calling*, you see."

Thomas still had only one arm to use, but that hand gripped his own arm firmly, squeezing twice. "Yes. You're right. I'm scared, and when I can't do anything about it I react. Most people don't even notice that about me. I'm sorry."

"But what happened?"

"Jan went into labor. In the middle of the fucking Battle of Lexington-Concord tour. But didn't you get the message already?"

"It's probably beeping in my glasses," said Rob, as though that made perfect sense. "I came just as the things were sounding. Because I thought you needed me."

"And who saw?" It was the old Thomas speaking, completely tamped down and in control. Even panting and limp as he was, Rob was having none of that today.

"It doesn't matter who saw. Tell me about your sister! Where is Paddy?"

Thomas took a deep breath. Then another. "He's in the room with her. And there are things we didn't know. That I didn't know. Jan is A positive. Paddy's O negative. A few years ago, they had a stillbirth. That baby, and this one: both A negative. Do you know ..."

"Yes I do. There is a danger, once the mother's blood stream recognizes the baby's. But there were shots she could take. I know that much."

"Well, that time they were too confident. That's Jan. This

time they've done everything right. But she wasn't supposed to have the baby in a battlefield, ya know? Even a battlefield that old. And I'm not allowed in there. We have to wait until they tell us. Tell us something."

Thomas watched Rob stand up. He realized once more how tall a man Rob was, especially when slightly swaying. "I have to place a call," he whispered down at Thomas. "It's legal to do it out here, isn't it?"

"Oh yeah. I did. Just look around you. Everyone's on their phones."

Rob tapped his left lens. Looked hazily forward, found a number, and tapped again. He stepped away, lowering his mouthpiece.

<hr/>

TONIO WAS STILL TRYING to control everyone—to make sense of what they had seen—when he received the call. He almost cancelled the ring before noticing who was calling and from where.

Rob's voice, somewhat static-ridden, said, "Tonio. Forgive me. Forgive all that. The odd business. I'm home. In Massachusetts, I mean. I need you lot there to do something for me, if you will."

"Rob! We were so worried. You just—"

"I know. Believe me. I know. But I need you to pray for a baby. Will you do that?"

"A baby?"

"He's having trouble being born. That's why I was called. Please?"

"With whole heart!" said Father Antonio Scala, and he closed and called his small flock together for instructions.

15

Deliveries

Many floors upstairs, where visitors were limited to the necessary, Jan Paddiachi was coming back to full consciousness, with the warm touch of Paddy's hand encompassing hers. She sent her eyes on a reconnaissance of the room, and followed that exploration with one regarding her feelings and memories. The second trip into the outside world was more frightening.

"Baby?" she asked him. She had intended her words to be clearer and more adult. She was surprised at the paucity of her voice. "How's the baby?"

"He is doing well. Our young Thomas is doing well. Although it's only two minutes since I could not have told you that. But the shot caught up well and your own Rh positive blood had not had much chance to attack the child."

Her eyes caught his and sought out any possibility he was trying to protect her: to save her for bad news in the future. But she found none, and, anyway, such falsehood was not in Shiva Paddiachi's makeup. She relaxed back into the bedclothes with an outtake of breath much like that of a fireplace bellows.

"Of course, no one knows that good news yet but you and me. And the medical staff. But that's enough. Though I did call your brother when we were deposited here. I felt he deserved so much from me."

Jan winced. "Ouch, yes. Thomas. The elder Thomas. I should have told him. Warned him about the entire history. He knew nothing."

Paddy remembered well his brief phone call to Thomas Sullivan, and the man's huge reactions. "That may be true, oh sweet goddess of my days. But remember also how much he has kept from you, over the years. There was some justice there, I think."

"We wanted to be better than that. You said so, Paddy."

He squeaked his chair forward and petted Jan's arm. He rose and kissed her lips. They tasted a bit like chemicals. And like pain. "I'm sorry it was not the earthy memory of childbirth that seems to be the fashion, these days."

"I'm not sorry." She gave a different sigh. One of relief.

Paddy added "In the interest of full disclosure and transparency, my love, I must say that I did a great deal of praying for you and the baby in the past few hours."

Jan grinned at him. Weakly. It was an old subject to them. "Praying to whom, may I ask?" Paddy was, by upbringing, a polytheist. It fitted him about as well as did double-breasted suits: useful in certain circumstances, but not many.

"Oh, to whomever might be listening. I really wasn't signing a formal address. And intent is a powerful thing. I know Thomas says that. He who will now be 'Thomas the Elder.'"

"I wonder how he'll take to that?" Jan grinned naughtily. "And how soon will we be allowed to—?"

She heard a scrape and a disturbance in the foot of the room, and something—someone—hit the metal foot of the bed. Jan could not see who or what, but Paddy could, and she watched his eyes.

Paddy expected to see Thomas, evading the security of the hospital. Or even, somehow, Rob. Dr. Paddiachi had become broad-minded about such happenings. He did not expect a rumpled boy of fifteen years, clothed in a rugby shirt and khaki trousers, with tousled dark hair, holding something like a mala clutched in one hand and staring wildly around him. He locked eyes with Paddy and said, in a broad and somehow lilting Scots, "I've come to pray for the baby."

"Well, young sir, your voice is more than welcome," announced Paddy. Jan tried to raise herself, but failed. Jacomo crawled up the bottom of the mattress until he could see her. "You must be the mother, then?"

"I must be." She grinned at them both. "And your prayers are obviously powerful, because we've just been told young Thomas is well, despite his unexpected arrival."

Paddy almost whispered to Jan something about now not being a time to be sarcastic, as sarcasm was one of her small failings. But he didn't think that this time she was being sarcastic. Instead, he took matters in hand.

"So, young man. By your accent you've come a long way—"

"From the rectory of St. Francis, north of Inverness. Where we were asked by Rob to pray. For the safety of a baby. This was by mobile phone, just after he went pop and disappeared from amongst us."

"Did he?" asked Jan.

"Did you?" asked Paddy.

She added, "That certainly sounds like Rob."

"Is this your first flight?" asked Paddy. The lad nodded forcefully, causing his hair to flop. "I didn't even intend to—to move. Just to concentrate in prayer. Although I did jump with Rob once before—"

"You're the boy at the golf course," said Jan in sudden understanding. "Jacomo! I'm sorry. I didn't mean to call you 'boy,' when you're obviously a grown man." Jan wasn't sure what she was trying to say, and her head was spinning. "I didn't have a clear idea who you were, but we'd heard the story."

Jacomo was entirely standing now, although wobbly. He stared at the hospital room, at Jan. At Paddy. The beads looped in his right hand were now clearly a rosary. His face, too lean to be cherubic, showed pride. "I'm here. All the way!" Then the bubble of accomplishment collapsed.

"My Ma will murder me for this."

━━

AS HE WALKED into the waiting room a short while later, the effervescent personality of Paddy displayed itself again. He inserted himself between Thomas and Rob, pushing them both sideways on the hard sofa. He was cheerful, which was the best of news to Thomas, but he also did not seem surprised to see Rob there.

"All is well, my dear family! Little Thomas is born, injected with the magic drug and is even now nursing from his mother. They have these hormones, you see, that can quickly cause a late-term pregnant woman to begin secreting milk, and—

"Oh, Rob, I forget myself! I am glad to see you here. Jacomo was wondering where you had gone, and I knew it must have been to Thomas or to the horse."

"Jacomo?" asked Rob, who was weary and feeling how he'd been pressed sideways against the hard armrest.

"Jan is okay?" asked Thomas. "And the baby, too? Oh, shit, Paddy, I've been so—Jacomo who?" It took a long time for Thomas to call from his memory stores the story and the name of the boy Rob had pulled up from the North Sea. Paddy intervened.

"He's the boy upstairs, hiding in the bathroom, because Jan is supposed to be alone to bond with little Tommy. But I saw him and he is so beautiful!"

Thomas almost asked him if he meant Jacomo or the baby was so beautiful, but sanity reasserted itself somehow.

"If they discover him, the boy is to say he is my half-brother and no one had stopped him at the door. It will be simple."

Rob was beginning to catch up. "Are you saying that Jacomo followed me here from Scotland, Paddy?"

"Yes. No. Really he was following the baby you asked him to pray for. And he must have prayed hard. Intent is a powerful force, I agree, Thomas. He says you had the entire rectory of St. Francis, there, praying for our baby."

"Yes, I did," said Rob, in a small voice for a man his size. Paddy rose and embraced him so strongly he sat him straight up again. "Thank you so much. Thank all of them. Our child is well. Janet is doing remarkably well. All is well!"

"But what are we going to do about this Jacomo?" asked Thomas, always the pragmatist. "Or about you being here, Rob? Sans passport? Sans plane?"

Paddy waved it all away. "These are small things, surely? Compared to our fears an hour ago? But I must tell you both that the Scottish boy wants to be called Jack, although his mother calls him Jackie. And he has wanted to talk with you for months, Rob."

"Because he's been 'flinching'? 'Jumping'? Since last summer when I pulled him over the edge?"

"No. Or maybe that. He didn't say. He does need advice though. Because he is fairly certain he is gay."

Rob stared from Paddy to Thomas and he opened his mouth to speak, but nothing at all came out.

"IT WAS SUCH AN ACT OF HOPE," whispered Paddy to Jan, over their son's tiny head.

"Isn't any baby?" she replied. She counted again the five,

perfect pink-brown fingers balanced over only one of hers. The other ones were inserted, like pretty hydrae, around the aureole of her breast. Ten fingers. Ten toes. Two incomprehensible eyes: the lot, as expected.

Tommy.

"No, Jan," Paddy was saying. "I think most babies are acts of ignorance and energy, with—one does hope—some love over all to seal the package. It is the rare mother who knows beforehand what she is doing and does it anyway."

She took her other hand and put it on her husband's: also a perfect hand and attached to a face she found perfect as well. "Why do you speak only of mothers? Paddy, you are the most involved father I've ever known."

He placed a reverent kiss upon her forehead. "But you have known so few fathers, Janet."

Before she could reply, he continued, "I speak of mothers because you have carried him under your heart for so long in a manner I can only appreciate from a distance. A close distance, but still …"

Jan laughed softly. It was surprising how easy it was to do everything softly with young Tommy around. "Still, we had better not let him know how we had wanted a girl."

Shiva Paddiachi's own laugh was utterly silent. "Why not, when so many young daughters all over the world are quite baldly told they are a disappointment to their parents because they are girls? But we shall wait, I hope, until our son is old enough to appreciate the humor of it."

"The humor of it! Yes, I think there was more than the usual amount of comedy involved in the birth of Thomas Paddiachi. What with strangers bouncing in from nowhere like that."

"We must admit there was only one stranger, and he came from a church's rectory in Scotland. It was only *through* nowhere that he came. And like a wise man from your western bible, he came bearing gifts! The perfect gifts, better than gold, let alone the various aromatic saps from trees."

Janet shifted in bed and chuckled. "His good intentions?"

"Prayers, he called them. And not only his own. Those of a distant congregation. They had seen a star, I think."

"Heard a beeping phone," said Jan, but she spoke to complete Paddy's metaphor, not to diminish it.

It was strange to Jan how Paddy's expansive public persona shrank and softened when they were together alone. But she had long come to understand that the brilliant man she'd married was by nature an entertainer as well as inventor. Explorer. Whatever else. She ran her hand through his shiny black hair and placed his head on the bed next to the warm, drowsing figure of her son.

Her two men. Somehow, by chance, fate, or perfect luck, she had them.

———

ROB RODE down the lift with Jaco—with Jack. His hand lay on the lad's shoulder, for the lad was vibrating like the skin of a horse and he needed to reassure Jack. There was too much unpredictable power there, and Jack needed—deserved—acknowledgement. Even praise, if that wouldn't make the situation even more dramatic.

There he was, visible in the random mirrors of the hospital lift. A gangling lad in his mid-teens, dressed in a hand-knit jumper over a rugby shirt. Jeans. Perfect international teenage footwear. Looking down directly, Rob could see the enthusiastic black hair, standing all-ways. So much like his own. The top of a less-aggressive nose, much like his mother, Sophia's. Seeing him from the top and from a mirror Rob could get a more direct view of the lad's face. Again, it was like that of his beautiful mother, but it would be stronger.

But looking in the mirror gave Jack the option of looking back at Rob, and the glittering excitement and adoration in those eyes made Rob wish to be anywhere but in a lift alone with him. With doors closed.

Despite the impossibility of the boy's arrival, Rob was in a more familiar awkward position again. He was a teacher alone in a closed lift with a lad who had an obvious crush on him. Who wanted to talk about being gay.

Rob attempted to say all appropriate things at once, both to please the lad and keep them both out of error. What he came up with was to take his hand off that shoulder, take a step away, and look down at him. In his deepest tones he said, "You have done well, young Skywalker."

And Jack crowed. He laughed. Exuberant. Only half in fun. For he had done well—if not shooting through the crack in the Death Star by intuition alone, it had been something as inexplicable and pure-hearted and fine. And as dangerous.

Rob's glasses signaled him and he saw the address. He winced and hoped the expression was hidden from his companion by his left hand raised to the hinge and so covering a part of his face.

He said, "First we must call your mother and hope she is still at the rectory."

Jack's glowing face fell a bit at that. "I was hoping, since I was here, to have a chance to see Boston. I have never been here before."

"That you can do at any time, Jack. Using the usual methods. I would certainly not close the world to you, now that you have so competently flung yourself into it. But certain things ..." and now he was going to give the whole "power and responsibility" message to the lad, completing another trope of fantasy. It felt so false, and was still so true. He settled for saying, "First things first," as the door to the hospital hall, lobby floor, opened.

Rob had not felt so glad of a door opening since the door

to the London official building had opened and he had walked out with a fragment of a slave collar in his old jacket pocket. As though Rob's own sexuality had ever gelled into anything describable. He still kept the printing of Yownie's sketch of himself as a gaseous mass of everything in the solar system. Plus a few atomic symbols. Minus a bird. But Rob's gravitational field was locked around a revolving body called Thomas Sullivan, and Rob was not ready to address one more three-body problem.

He pulled them both into an alcove containing a water-dispenser and something in pottery he assumed was a work of art. He pulled down the mouthpiece of the glasses and tapped the appropriate symbol for Tonio's rectory, hoping that Sophia would still be there. Not much time had passed: had it? Time expanded and contracted greatly, and not only because of the effects of different relative speeds.

For instance, it felt an eternity since he himself had arrived back in Massachusetts. (Allowing for a momentary, yet cataclysmic bounce in direction.) And news of Jack's arrival seemed to be something from a conversation one paragraph removed from the present. Yet here and now a phone was ringing.

Tonio answered. "Rob? Thomas just called."

Of course. For once Rob was happy for his plans to be scouted out by Thomas's quicker wit. "Then you know young Jack is safe here."

"We do, and we are grateful. His mother would like to speak with him."

"Sophy is still there?"

Rob could not see, but could feel the lad's eyes rolling at the mention of his mother. Such a reaction was as predictable as any in good, solid physics. "Is anyone else still left there after my rather childish and dramatic departure?"

Father Antonio Scala huffed. The rest of the Italian response was lost to the poor information transfer of the mobile telephone. He could imagine it, however. Then the priest added, "Everyone is still here. Can you think for a moment someone would claim a previous engagement and motor off now?"

"Good, Tonio. Because I'm going to have to ask you for another favor, of the same sort."

"To pray for you? I am told the baby is safe. So blessedly safe."

"Ah!" said Rob strongly, speaking on the intake of breath. "And his parents would agree with you. And are most properly grateful. But this time I need you to pray us home again. Quite frankly, our sources here are weary. My soul-friend Paddy calls it prayer and also 'the force of intent,' interchangeably, I think, but I believe the two of you would get on grand."

At this point there came a sound of scraping, as the phone was grabbed out of Tonio's hand. Sophia Benneli took over the conversation. "Why cannot the two of you come home in the usual way, Rob MacAulay? On an airplane. There has been exploration—tricks—enough today, and my Jackie is gone. He is gone. I am a mother!"

Rob thought that as a parent of either sex she had been unusually tolerant with all the shenanigans of the day. He said so, but added, "I'm thinking on the problems of Jack being here without a passport. Or even identification or overcoat, as it seems. It's a difficulty that is always in my mind, and I don't believe I am over-suspicious in thinking of what will happen to a lad as honest and sensitive as he is when confronted with government of one sort or another. We've had a long history of suspicion, haven't we? And the trouble that his unusual gift—a surprise even to me—might wind up with your not seeing him for a good while. Do you understand?"

There was silence. Had he just now broken whatever faith the woman retained in his words? Then she replied, "If I ever do see him again at all. I'm neither slow nor gullible, Rob. I understand."

"And I've never lost a passenger yet." That sounded so false in his own ears, but it was all he had to offer.

"When are we to pray?"

"Just now. In a few wee seconds. Like Tonio said, do it 'with whole heart.'"

Rob turned to Jack, who had been listening warily. "Now Jack ..."

"Take us home!"

"There is no trying. Just doing or not doing," whispered the lad, and Rob hugged him tight. That bit of Star Wars memorabilia was as good as an Ave Maria, to Rob's mind, and he remembered where they had come from and together, they jumped.

Coming down together half on floorboards and half on a throw rug. Once he'd looked around him and placed himself, Rob pushed Jack Benneli away from him as though he was too hot to hold. He looked around for the face of Sophia. "Take him," he panted. "Please take him back."

Then Rob really was too tired to stand up again.

16

Kinsman

Thomas Sullivan, who felt something odd had just occurred, amid all the other odd things of the day, was pausing in mid-sentence with Paddy in the waiting room, when his phone signaled him. It was the four tones that indicated O'Brien was calling. This was completely off subject and not part of the major issues around him. Thomas's hand wanted to shut it off.

But his mind did not, for somehow it was not off subject at all, and it was with a sudden chill that he turned away from the new father and he answered the call.

O'Brien's message was like the end of well-written mystery novel; it seemed unexpected and yet inevitable. He listened to the words that Rob, just minutes before and five thousand miles away now, had decided not to hear.

Holding the arm of the exuberant Paddy in one hand and with the wrist-phone to his mouth, he made arrangements to leave for home.

He knew that Rob was gone. He knew young Jack had gone with him. He needed no one to tell him those things. He smiled at Paddy as sincerely as he could, and said he would be back as soon as possible.

━━━

ROB WAS BEING HELPED off the floor by many hands. Why was he was always at his weakest in the presence of Tonio and all Rob's other Italian friends? He couldn't catch his breath. He felt he had run, or even flown, all the distance from Massachusetts to St. Francis parish with Jack on his back. In a way, after all, he had done just that.

And he now understood more than he had ever wanted to know. To know about the nature of this business called flinching, or jumping, or simply wiggling his ears.

Sophy and Jack were talking to each other in Italian, and talking much too fast for Rob's brain to catch. But she was so worried about her son, and so proud of him, and so glad he was back, that she threatened to crack the lad upside the head to express her feelings. Rob didn't need to understand the words to get all that. And Jack was also visibly excited, and a bit full of himself, which was only to be expected. And a bit seasick.

It seemed to be the middle of the night. One dip into the mathematics of his mind assured him it would have to be that time, in Scotland. Still, there remained in the room a good half-dozen of the people from the original welcoming party. Perhaps they were friends or relations of the Bennelis. Rob had done more than entertain these people. He had worried them terribly.

Again.

Tonio was telling him he should eat, and he knew he should. He wasn't certain he could eat, but somehow cheese and biscuits were in his mouth and went down easily. And other finger-food, somewhat old but all of it tasty.

His hands were still unusually cold, and he could hear

himself apologizing to people. Not for pulling Jacky away through time and space, because he really hadn't done that, but for his setting up the scene which had somehow made such a mad and passionate act possible.

When someone—not Sophy, and certainly not Father Antonio Scala—used the word miracle again, Rob's hands began to shake and he found he was getting angry. He did not know at whom.

But he did know. He was angry at Rob MacAulay, for being an idiot, an ass, an irresponsible child who had wanted not only to explain his oddities to these special people, but to show-off.

He met eyes with Tonio, and the priest was alarmed to find his friend wearing his natural war paint over his cheek-bones and between his eyes. The eyes, themselves, huge, sparking between green and violet. This, more than the habit of popping in and out of rooms, reminded Tonio of Rob's essential other-worldliness.

There was a reason for that war paint, and those eyes. Rob had somehow received another message, and not through his glasses. He felt himself receding from the people around him. He felt himself begin to shiver.

"I'm sorry, Father," he said. "But I'm going to have to go back. As soon as I can."

Looking at the changeling sitting beside him, with his long legs propped up on another chair and an afghan over them, his face under the war paint more fine-cut than ever and the hands with the shreds of biscuit in them, still trembling slightly, Tonio said, "Rob, are you sure that is safe? Safe at all?"

Rob's eyes narrowed in puzzlement and the war paint faded. "As safe as any—ah! You thought I meant more of—this. Nah. No more of this, believe me. I must be on the first plane home."

Tonio settled. Somewhat. "So something is wrong? With Thomas?"

Rob wiped his hands on a paper towel. Dropped his feet to the floor. "Not with Thomas. But wrong, and it's my fault. Believe me, I must go home. I shall have to make my apologies to the MacManus people. I did want to see them. And to the University, although that's not such a great matter. But I must go home."

Jack was beside them, his young body just beginning to feel the result of immense exertions it had not done before. But that was youth. Lovely thing, youth.

"Did I do something wrong?" the lad asked. "In coming to you? Did I mess things up somehow?"

Rob looked at the boy with cold honesty, and Jacomo Benneli knew he was going to be told the truth.

"I don't think it had anything to do with you, Jackie. I did it all by myself. But you are going to be sore for a while. In the body, sore. Shaky in the mind. If you're anything like myself, you will be. Let your mother take care of you and be glad you have her right now."

The young fellow who had prayed his way to Boston stood and clenched his hands at his sides. "I don't need my mother to—"

"Yes you do. Pay attention to the man. Pay attention to someone, for once!" said Sophia Benneli.

"I'm not denying you did a remarkable thing, Jack. Perfect and heroic. You did. You came to save a baby and the baby was saved. I don't know the intermediate steps. The methodology. But that is my lacking. You did what I asked and far more." Rob looked from the lad to his mother. "And you, Sophia. I am sorry I caused you such worry. Don't make that hushing noise at me. I caused you great anxiety, all because I didn't understand.

"I didn't understand the simplest thing involved in any sort of work, which is that for every action there is a reaction. Or to say it more plainly, everything, even a thing that seems like magic, will have to be paid for.

"And that is why I'm taking an airplane home. Like any other traveler. And paying for the ticket."

All three gathered around Rob nodded at his words, for they had understood him perfectly. Understood him on an emotional level, although they had had no idea what he'd been talking about. It was something with which Rob MacAulay, as a quantum field physicist, was quite familiar. Then he sat down again and began to fiddle with his magic glasses, until they could buy him a ticket home.

He called Thomas for the first time since his return to Scotland, but he received only the answer-bot.

▭

THE FLIGHT BACK, Rob could never remember. All the explanations, the apologies to Clan MacManus, to the University of Edinburgh, were left to Tonio. Or were not done. He was alone with a shapeless memory that it was all expensive, and that he didn't care. Some pen-pushing labor was done, and he did not care about that, either. He was driven to an airplane, and whether or not the flight was comfy or horrid he did not remember. His passport and his pass-card were injected into the machinery of the process and worked as expected. He cared enough about that part of it so that he was particular to have both small symbols of identity back on his person before he left the ground. He cared that much.

He emerged from the airplane in Boston and went through the passport ritual once more without unusual irritation. At the other end of that he found Thomas waiting, and he opened his mouth to speak to him, but couldn't think of any appropriate word. Because Thomas was Thomas, he did remember the existence of the wheelie-bag and led Rob to the place where it would be spat out. It seemed meaningless activity to Rob, but he went along with the process because he deeply needed some organization in his mind at that moment.

As they trundled it along, toward whatever goal Thomas had in mind, Thomas announced, "He's not dead, Rob. Whatever—message—you felt, Kinsman isn't dead."

Rob skidded to a stop. "That's not. I mean, I know already …"

Thomas looked warily at Rob's face, from an angle. "I can't know whatever it is you know, or how, but I left him in the vet's surgery not many hours ago and he was breathing. Unconscious, of course, after that much intestine ripped out and re-attached. It was a close thing and a few years ago they couldn't have pulled it off, but—"

"Explain it all!" Rob's voice was angry and rude. They stood there together on the airport walkway.

Thomas Sullivan reacted with a powerful mildness. His eyes shone amber in the grey March light. "Kinsman was found shaking with colic and sent immediately to East Mass. Large Animal Veterinary Hospital. About four feet of his gut had swollen and rotated and sealed itself off. That part died quickly, and even a few years ago there would have been no hope for a horse like that."

What Thomas didn't have to add was that even today without a significant amount of money and the owner's will to use it, survival still would not have been possible.

"He's been hanging in half-suspension in a surgical stall for recovery. Heavily sedated. If you've had some feeling he was dead, that could explain it. I can't say."

Rob looked at Thomas for the first time, really, and saw a man bone-weary and shaken. His left arm was not in a sling any more. Rob's sense of remorse spread outward. "I'm sorry you were left with this whole thing, Thomas. So sorry. Especially now, with the baby and all."

Thomas shook his head: a simple gesture that said nothing

and everything. "Let's go to him," he said aloud. "To Kinsman. Little Tommy is doing well enough."

———

AS THE CAR drove them north, even Thomas—vigilant Thomas—was fading toward sleep. Rob looked at him.

Thomas's careful mind was relaxed and Rob had the experience of looking at the man he had married. This time he did it with almost a stranger's eyes.

Rob's mother had first told him about physical beauty, as humans generally accepted it. She was the painter, after all, and though he had followed more in his father's footsteps, Rob hadn't forgotten what she had said. Beauty of face and beauty of body are a matter of symmetry and proportion. Of geometry, really. Flesh overlies bone and puts the shape to it, and although wear and misuse can conceal it, the symmetry and proportion are there.

Thomas must have been afflicted with an extreme case of beauty since birth, and neither his way of life nor any accident had interfered with that. In middle age he was awesomely beautiful, and with a sudden shock, Rob wondered how much suffering this had caused the man. This man born to money and therefore in the public eye since birth. Nowhere to hide that face, except under a mask of business and bluntness. It explained so much about Thomas, all in a moment.

How strange it was that a mind like Thomas's, fierce and challenging, should be packaged so. What cost had he paid for it in youth? Rob remembered that Jan had hinted at the difficulties of Thomas's youth, but in certain ways Rob was a blockhead when it came to hints like that. To gossip. To the entire language of human beauty and how one was supposed to respond to it. And here was Thomas, beautiful, angry, and gay. That now meant something new to Rob.

Perhaps it was because he had not understood before now

why they had gotten on so well together. It had never occurred to Rob to dig at the wounds that must have been caused in Thomas by this condition. In fact, Rob didn't remember he had ever mentioned the fact of Thomas's extreme beauty aloud. Good thing.

Being unusual in any sense was always so painful for a child. And Thomas had been unusual in so many ways.

WHEN THE CAR drove them into the surgery lot, Thomas was asleep and Rob had no idea where he was. It seemed to be more a medical center than a veterinarian's, except for the proportions of the building. Rob unfolded from the car and Thomas woke up with a start and a grab for the steering wheel.

"The GPS worked right for once," he mumbled to himself as he got out also, and then he led Rob along a sidewalk lined with early spring plantings toward an expensive and confident-seeming doorway. They may as well have been visiting an orthopedic surgeon or an oncologist, except that the murals in the hall walkways were not of humans but of horses.

And it was bigger. The reassuring impression of a human medical facility became blockier and more barn-like as they walked into the building. The people walking to and fro along the halls looked less like medical technicians and more like Mr. O'Brien as they went on. Thomas led Rob through an outsized glass doorway into one more hospital waiting room and suddenly Rob could smell horse.

A woman sat at a long desk. She was competent, young-seeming, and strong. Thomas said to her, "Rob MacAulay, concerning the horse Kinsman. The one with the re-sectioned bowel."

As Thomas spoke, Rob heard uncertainty for the first

time. Possibly Thomas was not as sure of the horse's condition as he had pretended to be.

The medical receptionist—taller and more athletic-seeming than the ones Rob was used to finding behind such a slick desk—looked from one of them to the other and her face brightened. That one expression meant a world to Rob. "Oh, good. Dr. Kessinger has just come in about a half hour ago." She looked up at Rob and measured him.

"You're the man who flew in from Scotland when you found out."

Rob just nodded.

"*Very* good. It will just be a few minutes before he can speak to you." She looked into his face with approval. Approval for what, he could not know. For flying across the ocean because his horse was ill? Thomas led him back to the row of chairs. He pulled down on Rob's sleeve until he sat in one.

"I still don't feel him," said Rob, as though that sentence made sense.

"And would you expect to?" Thomas responded. "I mean to say, do you always feel you are in some sort of … contact with Kinsman?"

That question sounded like something from a child's story. "No. Of course not. But now. Just now. After using him as I did.…"

Thomas glanced left and right. Everywhere but at Rob. "You take a lot on yourself, you know. First everything is science to you, and now you sound like it's a world of magic. Wizardry. Kinsman's been through heavy surgery. Unconscious. Had you any sort of feeling from me, when I was unconscious?"

Rob knit his hands together between his knees. He sat stiff and alone. "I know. I'm ridiculous," he stated. Thomas did not try to touch him.

Dr. Kessinger came walking down the hall, wearing the

usual white lab coat. He was a compact, bony, dark man, not much taller than O'Brien. He shook hands with Rob, and his eyes, too, measured him in some way. He spoke straight and to the point.

"It was good you came so quickly, Dr. MacAulay. But as it turned out, the hurry wasn't necessary. Your horse has pulled through surprisingly well. We took out a meter of intestine that had twisted around itself, like a length of sausage casing. Ugly analogy, but accurate. Because of the situation, we were able to almost eliminate spillage of waste matter into the abdominal cavity."

Rob opened his mouth to speak, but the vet went on. "Still the shock of the thing was enormous to him. I wasn't at all sure he would pull out of it."

"But he did?"

Kessinger's taut face softened almost into a smile. "His eyes are open and he's trying to find his feet. That's a good sign, as long as he doesn't panic. I'm told he's high strung...."

"I am told so, too."

The vet tried to make sense of that response and gave up. He continued, "And that's good in a horse in many ways, but not always in recovery. So we're keeping him sedated. Doped up. Until he adjusts to his new circumstance."

"He's had a great deal to adjust to," said Rob, knowing the vet could have no idea what he was talking about. "May I see him now?"

Dr. Kessinger looked Rob up and down again. Rob wondered if the vet was seeing another high-strung creature that might become a problem. "I won't upset him, doctor. I won't raise my voice. Or try to touch."

"You won't be able to get close enough to be able to touch, as it is," said Kessinger. "But certainly you can see him. He's your horse."

"Who belongs to whom?" Rob mumbled, but carefully, so that the vet couldn't hear him. It would sound too sentimental and absurd. Rob, with Thomas behind him, followed Kessinger from one hall to another, to a juncture of buildings, where the floors became suddenly not at all like those of a medical complex, for they were dusted with shavings and the walls lacked murals or decoration.

They passed through a set of automatic doors and then the smell was all animals and antiseptics. The side doors were now huge. They passed into one and were in a room that was half stall and half ICU. Lights were blinking on panels of machinery and there were IV tubes and a heavy sling-affair and in it was the long, ungainly body of Kinsman, shaved to the skin over his entire abdomen and cut and sewn like a product of taxidermy. His eyes were slightly open and his ears flopped down to the sides. His head hung as low as his knees and his feet barely touched the floor. A string of drool dangled down to touch the shavings.

Rob stepped as close as the tape-woven barrier allowed and looked at the horse, who did not look back. He said nothing, either to the horse or to the doctor. He just stared. At last he made a noise deep in his throat and bobbed his head up and down from the base of his neck. He pressed forward against the barrier. He nickered again.

Kinsman just drooled.

"You can't expect much," said the vet, as though the horse had been somehow criticized. Behind his few words was the message that it wasn't all about Rob MacAulay at the moment. That it was about this horse, who had been through as extensive a surgery as horses ever received, and had lived.

"I know," whispered Rob, and was surprised to find his voice softening as he spoke. Without knowing it, he had begun to weep. "I know." He turned to Thomas, who hadn't spoken all this time. "Is there somewhere around here I can bunk, do you know? For a day or so? To be on hand, if—"

"There is," said Thomas and the vet together. Dr. Kessinger continued, "We have a cubby, just like in a human hospital, where a human can stay while his horse is in recovery. A lot of people want such a thing. It's not sophisticated—"

"I'm grateful," said Rob, and he looked at Dr. Kessinger. "Grateful for everything." He hoped the vet could not tell he was crying. How much a fool he must seem. Kessinger slid his eyes away from Rob's face. "I'm glad we were in time," was all he said.

———

THE TWO MEN sat next to one another on the cot in the little room. Rob's wheelie-bag had been brought in.

"He doesn't know me," stated Rob.

"And you thought he would? With all the drugs and shock and—"

"He doesn't *know* me. It has nothing to do with the drugs. The shock—oh yes, I suppose. But he has always known me. More than I've known him."

"And you think that won't change? Or at least, that you can't, maybe, begin again, Kinsman and you?"

Rob shrugged. Or shivered. "I think you believe I'm feeling sorry for myself, Thomas. That my horse is rejecting me. That I'm selfish enough to …"

"No I don't! Give me that much credit, Rob."

Thomas didn't try to touch Rob.

After a minute Rob added, inconsequentially, "They cut him."

"I noticed. I imagine they thought they had to, what with his quick-trigger and the problems of recovery. Plus the probability …"

"I'm not objecting. Just noting."

Diffidently, Thomas asked, "Should I stay with you?"

"No," said Rob, and then more forcefully. "No, Thomas. Go back home. To your people. I ought to be alone anyway. I have to think." He looked at Thomas.

"I've learned some things. I have to sort out how I can talk about them."

"What kind of things?" asked Thomas, and Rob could feel Thomas's tension as he spoke. Rob tried to smile. It didn't work.

"Not about that scary thing people call 'us.' Much simpler. I need to think about Newton's first law. Or about karma. Cause and effect. I'll explain when I have the words in line."

Thomas stood up and he did touch Rob then. He rubbed his hand into Rob's mop of hair, forward and back. "Whenever," he said. He turned toward the door.

"And, Thomas?" Rob added. "Thank you. I forgot to say that. Thank you for all you've been doing here, all by yourself."

"Thank me? Oh God! Don't bother!" Thomas waved all matters of gratitude away. He kissed Rob on the top of his head and went out the door, leaving Rob staring at the wheelie-bag on the floor, thinking it had never even been unpacked since he left Boston.

———

THOMAS DID LEAVE THE ROOM, but his footsteps faded to a stop on the industrial flooring along the outside hall. Something in him didn't want to go any further from Rob, so he found he was not moving at all. He was standing in place and breathing and not thinking, when he heard Rob's voice.

He was being called back. No. He wasn't. Rob was talking to himself. More like singing to himself. But in no words Thomas recognized as words at all. And the barest excuse for a melody. But out of his memory Thomas pulled a name for the thing Rob was doing. He'd heard that it was called keening. Rob was softly keening. And Thomas could not move away from it, nor for the life of him could he have gone back to the source of the sound. He stood in the veterinary hallway and listened to Rob MacAulay keen for the death of something or other, and he wondered what this music was, and what this person was, whom he loved and had married. After a few minutes the keening stopped and Thomas found in himself the ability to walk on.

SOMETIME LATER A MEMORY came up into Rob MacAulay's mind. It was the fragile, unbreakable, soap-bubble sort of memory that can't be argued away nor explained. Rob remembered a moment, somewhere between a rectory outside Inverness and a stable outside Boston. Somewhere that was nowhere at all. It had been a change—a kick sideways—a re-direction. Had it not been for this instant of change, there would now be no memory of that moment at all.

No memory and no more understanding than there had been all the other times when Rob MacAulay had slipped sideways from one place to another. But now there was the soap-bubble memory and the sick misfortune and only a wee bit of understanding.

He sat there holding this bit of understanding balanced on the tip of his mind, while the black horse swayed in his suspension harness, groaning occasionally.

HE WAS STILL THERE when the attendant came in to monitor the tubes and clean the horse a few hours later. It had been quiet in that cubby in the corner of the recovery stall for so long that no one had any idea that the horse's owner was still present. A camera was mounted on the ceiling, but it was pointed at the horse. When the attendant spoke, the man didn't immediately respond. He was sitting on a hay-bale and when she touched his skin, it was chilled.

Before this healthy, young, compassionate woman could become alarmed, Rob focused his eyes on her and apologized. He cleared his throat and apologized again. Then he stood with some difficulty, looked at her again, and left the room. He didn't look at the horse at all.

17

The Government Men Return

I t would have been unkind, and maybe even impossible,
for Thomas to try to talk to Jan about the things he had
in his head right now. Yet Thomas Sullivan had a strong
need, for once, to talk to someone. It was something he'd
picked up from Rob MacAulay, and as Rob was the issue at
hand, he sought out the nearest person who might listen. That
was Paddy, who was upstairs in the Sullivan house, shining-
faced and dashing about.

Thomas grabbed him by the hand. This was such an
unusual action by Thomas that Paddy stopped dead and
looked at him with his dark, startled eyes.

"Will you listen to me for a moment, Paddy?"

"Of course. By all means. Why wouldn't I?"

Thomas, gathering his long habits of organization,
attempted to describe all that had happened, and was
happening at the moment to Rob. It involved emotional
descriptions, and Thomas wasn't good at those. And the organization of his narrative seemed utterly false to him, as inside
himself Thomas was not organized, but a bucket of
confusion.

Horse, emergency flight, the damned Scottish-Italian boy, and Rob at the center of it all. The vet's.

Both men had settled themselves into whatever chairs were available in an ornate, long-unused room in the old house. They could hear Jan cooing to young Tommy somewhere.

"So. Thomas. You are saying to me that your Rob came flying because he thought you were in trouble, as you were in Omaha? And that all the rest happened as a result of that?"

Thomas had hoped for a different reaction. Some sort of empathy, or sympathy. Not this process of having his own words summarized and explained back to him. As though he was not able to do as much himself.

Thomas was only vaguely aware of their surroundings. He hadn't bothered to re-do this level of the house. It was much as it had been for the corporate renters. Cold. Formal. He felt this conversation would go the same way. He had a strong feeling he had made a mistake.

"And are you saying that in some way, Jan and I and the baby are responsible for his present sorrow?" Paddy's quick, bright manner of inquisition hit Thomas on the raw.

"Of course not. I just need someone to talk to."

"Oh! So then." Paddy was obviously surprised to hear that Thomas could need a thing like that, and was re-adjusting his mind around the idea. "So, do I understand that the difficulty is that a dear horse has been injured?"

Thomas had hoped for so much better. To whom else but Paddy could he approach the topic of "jumping?" Teleportation. Metaphysics?

In short, the topic of Rob.

Paddy was answering him. Thomas tried to follow what he was saying. It was so simple, really. It was about how the horse might be important, but the baby was … was the baby.

"I understand," said Thomas. He did understand. He was bitterly disappointed in Paddy, or in himself for expecting more, but he did understand. As Paddy bounced back to Jan, he sat in the ridiculously small Queen Anne chair and felt tears leaking out of the corners of his tilted eyes. A year ago he would have been able to say he didn't remember the last time he had cried. Now he was only glad no one saw him doing it.

Thomas Sullivan felt small and young and helpless. For that reason, he thought of Master Kyan. He thought he might go to him.

———

OUTSIDE THE GATE to the main entrance he found a car parked sideways, blocking him. And he found a member of his private security team leaning into the window of that car and talking with the female driver. Thomas Sullivan's home security team was an understated thing. They wore no uniforms but had intense education in being civil and in keeping the peace. In his own mind, they were just like the best sort of bar bouncer: non-irritating and able to minimize the importance of anything that required their presence. Trained for less civil interchange too. They were the best.

The young man in the light jacket saw Thomas's car approaching and began to back away from whatever conversation he'd been having with the woman in the exit-blocking car. It was not in his job description to stand in between trouble and the boss, once the boss was present.

With a press of a button on his dashboard, Thomas caused the long iron gate to recede into the wall that could conceal it. He got out and stepped forward through the open gate. He pressed another button—this one in his pocket—and the gate closed behind him. He took the same position as his security man had taken, leaning forward, and looking down at the driver of the other car. He caught her looking at the gate closing: her face showing contempt at his daring to close the place again. He added that look to what he had already learned though his glimpse of the massive, dark blue car, and the language of its license plate.

"Ma'am?" He spoke with extreme sweetness and extreme care. What should he call her: Officer, Government Official, Illegal Blocker of a Private Drive? Bully? No—Ma'am was the better word to begin with.

She met his eyes with a look that wasn't exactly measuring, because by that woman Thomas had already been measured, catalogued, and found wanting. Thomas wasn't yet certain if the woman's entire body language was meant to draw him out in anger, or whether she simply came stamped with it. If this was her usual approach, then she was merely stupid. Stupid, in this instance, would be a good thing, as Thomas was the opposite of stupid and would have an advantage.

"You are Thomas Heddiman, who have now taken to calling yourself Sullivan," she informed him.

"I've taken to it so well that it is now my legal name," he informed her right back. Casually.

"You're not the one we've come to talk to. It's Rob MacAulay."

For the first time Thomas was actually offended by this pretentious little woman. Professor MacAulay was the way people referred to Rob, unless he told them not to. He always told them to call him Rob once he had met them. Few did, however, as he was now the Magic Man of Physics, and Thomas was damned certain Rob had never encountered this creature before.

Because he was offended he spoke even more mildly. "Doctor MacAulay isn't in," he said. "Ma'am."

Her dark eyes flashed and one side of her mouth showed teeth. "We know that isn't so, Mr. ... Sullivan."

So. Stupid. Outrageous and stupid. Thomas felt a certain relief. He let his eyes move slowly along the empty seats of the big blue car. "Two things, Ma'am. First. I must repeat, he is not home. And second—well, who exactly is this 'we' you speak of? All I see is a woman in a car. By herself. I find it confusing."

Now she showed all her front and side teeth, in delight at having confused him. Surprisingly stupid.

"I'm not alone. We are guarding every entrance to your walled property and we haven't seen him leave all day and last night."

Every entrance? Who were the "they" who were still not identified, and were they also guarding all the ways in and out of the small village where Tony and her parents lived? That would make everyone there irate. Angry at the bullies, or angry at Thomas and Rob. The two of them had tried to be neighborly, and Rob could make friends, it seemed, simply by looking at people. Not to mention that having a man who seemed to be a shoo-in for the Nobel Prize as a neighbor didn't hurt with them. But still, Thomas had found you couldn't be sure of people in a group. He did not want any excuse for resentment between them and the Kayes' neighbors.

And for a moment Thomas almost forgot O'Brien's stable. Were they also attempting to bully the riders? Thomas knew it was almost impossible to bully a competent horse rider.

"He's been away for longer than that," said Thomas, dropping the ma'am, as she seemed to be taking the title as a form of submission.

"Then we will search."

"Our premises? You have a warrant, then, whoever you are?"

"We are the Federal Government. And we can get a warrant."

We are the Federal Government? For a moment Thomas wished he had that idiot statement on video. Then he remembered that he did have it; he had had video installed in the maple trees on either side of the main gate. The expensive kind with audio.

Speaking louder, but not contentiously, he said, "Lady, you must be off your meds." Shaking his head slowly, sadly, he began walking down the street, crossing the road to be among the houses that lined the road on the other side of the Sullivan's brick wall. His legs ate up ground without him having to break into a run. And as he expected, she started her car and followed him.

She leaned out her window, from the other side of the street and said, "The man has a debt to us!"

He almost broke his pace, trying to imagine what she could mean. He settled on looking directly at her: looking at the small, pinched-faced woman wearing some sort of dark blue suit. Not quite a "Men in Black" suit, but it tried to give the same impression. Her overwrought face, however, negated the power of that icon. Thomas wondered what on earth was happening.

"Rob owes who what?" And he thought. *The man owes many kind, nameless people everything. I can't imagine he owes this woman anything.* "What debt?" he said, still walking, and noting the street he was passing on. It had been lined with spacious and elegant houses when his Aunt Grace was alive and he was a small boy. Now it was still lined with houses. Different houses.

"He was granted asylum by the United States!"

This piece of nonsense, rather than angering him, settled him further. Any branch of the government must be fully aware that their new prize physicist came in as the spouse of a US citizen. This insanity must be small in scale and not the government incursion he had feared. For a moment he had a perfect image of what he wanted to do: he could bounce into the back seat of the woman's car, pull her jacket up and over her eyes, and then bounce them to the entrance lot in the Fells Park, where there stood a baroque fountain, complete with spitting dolphins, and leave her in the blowing water, shrieking indignities. It was close enough for a jump, and he knew the way from childhood. *Pop pop pop* and even by cameras he would never be seen. Never suspected. And he would break no oath, because he was not even angry any more.

And then the woman shouted out, "We need him! We need him!" This was another thing Thomas didn't want to hear again. Not now.

It would be heard again, echoing in his mind, later.

Because of the pathos of the last words, Thomas did something far less like the games-player Thomas Heddiman. He didn't respond to the woman in the car at all. Instead, he raised his phone and called the police. Out of some strange impulse, and maybe because he was still thinking about horses, he called a number that was still on his address list from years ago.

Amazing luck was with him, for in a few minutes of walking down that street, pursued by the woman in the car, rescue came galloping to him. Well, it came trotting. A man in his huge list of acquaintance, who was on the local mounted force, came up on a bay Quarter Horse and asked, "Is there a problem here?"

It wasn't, "What's all this, then?" but it was the closest American equivalent. The woman threw her car into park with a deadly, thwarted expression, and Thomas raised his hands to this friend with a bewildered Whiskey-Tango-Foxtrot equivalent.

The man on horseback was Reginald Foster, one of the few local mounted policemen in the area. He was also the only one who did not privately refer to himself as a "pony soldier." He was, instead, a "buffalo soldier," being the only black mounted policeman north of Boston. They had met through their interest in horses, and that was now perfect luck. For Reggie had just come off duty doing public relations at a local primary school. The Quarter Horse he rode was named Cochise. Thomas remembered that, as he remembered the man. In the three years since Thomas had last ridden with Reggie, Cochise had not aged visibly. Nor had Reggie. If

Reggie had gone gray, or even begun to lose his hair, it was invisible under his riding helmet. The full-face visor was up.

The peculiar, wasp-like woman behind the wheel of the blue car looked flummoxed, as well she might, her own car being blocked by the solid mass of the bay horse. She honked, and that was a bad idea. Police horses are not spooked by honking cars. Mounted officers, however, are infuriated by them.

Thomas did not wait to see what happened next. He knew his riding buddy would let him know the results. Sometime. And the guard would see that Jan, Paddy, and young Thomas were protected. That left them doubly buffered.

Thomas ambled back to get his car and drove on toward Boston. This entire oddity was wrapped up in a bow and sent to the back of his mind.

18

Revelations

Kyan Sensei listened to Thomas's story during the time he would usually be eating his midday meal. The plates of rice, vegetables, and the ever-present seafood sat in front of him, and he held his chopsticks in his hands, but all grew cold as Thomas spoke. Outside Kyan's small personal room echoed the sounds of people in workout and the thump of old punched bags, and the smell of fresh human sweat intruded and mixed with the smell of fresh fish. It was a comfortable place for the man who had once been Tommy.

He knew to talk to Sensei slowly, because the old man got lost in rat-a-tat English. The entire narrative, containing Jan's baby and a boy from Scotland, both of which were peripheral to the heart of the story, took over an hour to relate. The overly-organized Thomas realized he had been reduced to babbling, while Sensei's lunch grew cold. He also realized he was sniffling in front of his sensei again.

During the entire story, his teacher made no response other than the occasional soft grunt, and a waving of the sticks in the air in a circular pattern, as though to wind up Thomas when he was running out of power.

In the end, he was facing Kyan and a table-full of cold food, and he heard the tap on the door that meant someone was expecting the old man to supervise a class. Thomas felt both dull and wrung dry.

Kyan raised his voice to call out to the person on the other side of the wood to go on without him. Then he put down his chopsticks, cleared his throat, and began to speak to Tommy —to Thomas Sullivan—softly.

"When a person like this Rob—our Rob—encounters people like us, I expect there to be a few mistakes."

Thomas could make no sense of this, but then Sensei had never been fluent in idiomatic English, and he knew how to wait for him.

"Most, because Rob is so young, he can't know. Like any child, he cannot always know what will happen. He must learn."

"Rob may be young in spirit, teacher, but he's almost forty years old."

Kyan waved his small hands in the air dismissively. "Yah! I don't mean age like that. You know. You look in his eyes every day. You *live* with him. No one else does. He is a different sort of person."

Thomas shifted in his chair. "Of course he is. In many ways. He has solved what they've called the Unity Theory. The theory of Everything." He didn't want to be bragging about his binary. His man. Not in front of Sensei.

But Kyan shook his head. "He doesn't know *everything*. Or he wouldn't be in grief now. Grief I know, too. I have lost people. But you are maybe too close to see too much about your Rob.

"Your sister, Jan. She was angry that someone was more important to you than her. I saw that. That is why I let her be silly with Rob."

"Jan has Paddy. I didn't have anyone. Sensei, what you're saying …"

"Makes sense. You were going to say it doesn't make sense, but you are wrong. I'm almost eighty years old and people are people. They are often silly. But now Jan has a baby. She won't be silly like that again. Or not silly in the same way." The sensei's smile was rueful.

"And I know, too, that Rob would not hurt her, no matter. He has good heart. That is most important."

Thomas felt the conversation was getting out of hand. But often his conversations with Kyan Sensei had taken days or weeks to percolate through his brain, so he simply let him continue. He listened to the sounds in the room, put his hands in his lap, one over the other, and breathed.

"The horse named Kins Man I never met. Horses are too big for me and I like boats. But the horse had a part in his own getting hurt, too. May be his heart was good but his thinking was not careful. Many of my students begin like that and I must teach them better."

Thomas thought of the nature of that tight-wired half-thoroughbred. He could think of no response to his teacher except to say, "He was Rob's first horse. They were so beautiful together. Everyone said so. They moved like one animal. One mind."

Kyan looked at Thomas intently for a long time. He sat back in his chair. Slowly he began to smile. "And you have never been able to see yourself with Rob. How could you? I can say the same about you. It is beautiful, too." Then the old man giggled. "He even has a long neck and big teeth! Like a horse. But I am sure he won't hurt you like he did Kins Man, because you have common sense. More than your Rob, you have common sense. I am proud of you, but sometimes I wish you had less common sense and more fun."

This was not a new topic between them. Thomas drooped his head and said, "I'm trying."

"I know. And about the worrying that this flying through nowhere may become a danger by spreading like the flu—it is not true."

Thomas looked up, all alert again. "How do you know, Sensei?"

"Because I have tried it. If you accept I am good at such things, you may believe I have tried it, with every sort of mind in my head, and I can't do it."

"Paddy can't, either," Thomas murmured, too low for his teacher to hear.

"It belongs to Rob. I think he touched you deep in your heart and you can fly, too. And that boy over the ocean you talked about so well ... There must have been deep feeling for Rob to touch him so. To leap off a cliff for a person means some kind of love, I think. I hope the boy, too, has sense and doesn't make trouble."

Kyan Sensei rose, with a popping of his old knees, and he threw the cardboard containers of his uneaten lunch into a can next to the chair. Feeling his long interview was over, Thomas hurried to say, "But you will talk to Rob. Won't you? To give him comfort, at least?"

Kyan cracked his neck in the same rolling motion Thomas used so often. "He doesn't need comfort, Tommy. He needs grief. I give him soft words and the sadness will come back later. But I *would* like to talk to him about what he saw when he was Nowhere."

And the interview was over. Thomas walked slowly out to his car, his hair blowing in the spring wind. Like all his talks with his teacher, this one would take time to figure out. But he did feel better—unwound. It was only halfway home he remembered he hadn't mentioned MacBride showing up on the porch. But then he remembered Kyan Sensei's words about too much common sense, and stopped worrying about MacBride.

He arrived back at his gate and only then did he

remember the government idiot. (There seemed to be so many idiots to be taken into account that it cluttered his thoughts.) Standing at the gate was his efficient security man, trying to be taken as a casual pedestrian. This time he greeted Thomas with a hand-scrawled letter, folded and without an envelope. Thomas rolled down the window and took it.

"I didn't read it, of course, Mr. Sullivan. It was left by a policeman on a horse." The man seemed to find this fact more remarkable than the letter itself. Thomas, sitting before the gate, replied, "Call me Thomas, please," and added, "Thanks for handling the thing today." Then he opened the gate and drove in.

He put the car into self-drive and read as he approached the garage. The message was simple:

Car's plates Fed. Gov't, but I don't know more than that, yet. Driver resisted arrest. Don't know more than that, either. Cochise didn't like her and I didn't either. Tell you more if they tell me more.

Happy Trails,

Reggie

Thomas sat in the garage, the door closing behind him and the light dimming, and he imagined exactly how the woman had resisted arrest. Did she wind up thrown over the croup of Cochise, the easy-going, broad Quarter Horse? Pleasant to think of, but unlikely. Probably he simply kept her there, haranguing him while backup arrived. Motorized backup. Again he had to consider what was happening to Breton and her parents' gated village. And O'Brien's stable. He got out of the car and went into the house, listening for sounds of Jan, Paddy, or young Tommy.

Damn! A young Tommy existed, right in his house. He cheered up as he climbed the stairs.

To Thomas's surprise, he heard instead the bright chatter of machine keyboards in the east parlor. He strode through the rooms, forgetting he had ever suffered an injury at all, and found Rob, his tragic, keening binary and heart-mate, sitting by the coffee table and typing with one hand and writing with another.

Thomas approached him slowly, fearing that the man's grief had turned into some sort of psychotic break. "Rob?" he asked, casually.

Rob lifted his head and his uncontrollable dark hair went every which way. "Thomas!" he sang, in the key of A. "I am so glad to see you. I wasn't certain where you had gone. Jan and Paddy are upstairs with the bairn, but they didn't know where you were either!"

"I was visiting my teacher." Thomas didn't look directly at Rob as he spoke. "When I last saw you, you were ..."

Rob swiveled around on the sofa to meet Thomas's eyes. "I was grieving. I still am. I'm not ashamed of it. But I'm now doing something else also. I'm working out a model of my experience in going sideways between the rectory in Scotland and the hospital lobby in Massachusetts. Because, as I tried to say so badly before, I was aware in it!"

"More equations?" Thomas was also aware. Aware that his voice was coming out slightly bitter.

Evidently Rob didn't notice. His eyes, fixed on Thomas's own, were blazing in colors: green, purple, and more, too quickly for Thomas to see rightly. "*Not* equations. Modeling. Making theory, which is different. Which is backwards, for me."

"But not for Einstein," said Thomas. He had no idea what Rob was talking about, but he had that bit of information in his head from reading a biography. "For him the idea came before the math." He sat down on the couch at the other end from Rob, out of the way of those impossible long, waving arms.

"Ah! But he was previous to Quantum Physics, Thomas, and so I am different from Einstein."

Sure you are. Not going bald. Taller, too. Thomas put one hand over the other in his lap and hoped Rob would begin to make sense.

And Rob did, in his own way. "I'm writing down what I said before I had any continuity in my thoughts. About the nature of that thing we were calling Travelling, but is as much contraction as travel. Which is why it can propagate so rapidly. And the transformation of energy inherent in it, which we may as well call karma."

"This isn't physics, then?"

Rob stopped waving. He was taken aback at Thomas's words. "My love, everything is physics. Your fingers on the grand piano next room over. The mind telling them how to work. The crying of the baby upstairs, and by the way I must certainly keep my voice down now. But everything is physics.

"I just don't know what sort. Yet."

Thomas and Rob reached out their hands then, and touched.

And Thomas's phone vibrated.

Rob leaned back again, watching as Thomas shot his cuff back to look at the screen. He pressed once, and held the thing up to his face.

A movement flickered outside the French windows, where the Japanese maple was exhibiting its red glory. The motion caught Rob's eye as Thomas began to speak into the phone, a half-dialogue that made no sense. What Rob saw did make sense to him, however. He looked at Thomas, who was looking back at him startle-eyed, and then they spoke in perfect unison.

"We've got a visitor."

Rob rose and approached the French doors. Two things occurred to him as he saw Athena Kaye coming past the maple tree. The first was simply that, unlike the tree and unlike her previous appearances in their lives, she was not wearing red. In fact, she seemed to have a caftan and bathrobe over her feminine body. The second was that she was also wearing a thunderous brow.

He pressed the palm-print security latch that disabled their house system and cracked open the door. The sound from without was full of the singing and twittering of birds. Their friend, however, didn't match the bucolic scene. The woman was bloody furious. Rob left Thomas's phone problem behind him.

"'Thena!"

Tony's mother stepped over the doorway and kicked off her dusty clogs, where they rolled over the rug and clattered to a stop on the bare wood floor. Rob reached one hand out and down to touch her shoulder. Athena Kaye was as tense as though she were made of wood herself. "What in God's name is wrong? Is it Tony?"

She shook her head and made a fist, which she brought down forcefully—and noiselessly—on the back of the over-stuffed sofa. "It's those goddam government men! Again!"

Thomas, who had been using his right hand to cradle his phone-wearing wrist to get some privacy, lifted his eyes to hers for a moment. He realized that his first conversation to his binary had missed some important bits.

Rob saw their eyes meet and realized the same thing, in a floundering fashion. "What men? What ... government are we ..."

"They are blocking the gate! The whole damned community gate! And flashing some sort of nothing badge at my neighbor Stella, who can no more tell a real official or cop from the man in the moon! So, of course, I get called."

"I'm glad you recognized the badge as meaningless," called Thomas, putting his hand over his phone.

"Damn right I did. And damn good thing I did, too!"

Rob had never heard a word of vulgarity coming out of Athena's mouth before. Her face was so flushed it looked like a terracotta statue. He found himself comforted to see that a person of such different complexion from his own could turn red too, while at the same time he asked the obvious question of her. "Was it about me? Have I made more trouble for you?"

She turned her eyes to his and they were swimming. She said, "You, you poor thing, ain't made no trouble ever for anyone and don't you forget it!"

Rob was so astonished by the forcefulness and the bad grammar coming out of his friend that he scarcely heard the fluting whistle that indicated there were other people at the door: not the French doors, nor yet the one down the hall with the porch and wisteria, but the other door, the one that led from the drive to the garage.

And then Thomas raised both arms like an orchestra conductor. His eyes flashed from Athena to Rob and back to the woman again. He called, "Stay here. Please stay," and then he ran, quick as a boy, down the length of Grace Sullivan's old house and he disappeared.

Mrs. Kaye leaned against the back of the sofa and growled, "What's this, now? On his phone? More lying government men?"

Rob had been watching Thomas's face, which had seemed to shine. Rob had educated eyes, when it came to reading Thomas Sullivan. "I doubt it, 'Thena. I don't know who it is, but it could not be someone Thomas doesn't like." He turned to face her and his own eyes were smiling. "Let's just wait a moment and cool down. Shall we?"

He was thinking that the call must be Kyan Sensei. Few things set Thomas bouncing down the hallways like that, and his old teacher was surely one of them. "'Thena, I don't think things are as bad as they seem."

Athena Kaye settled down onto the arm of the old chintz sofa, and her expression adjusted itself, shading from outrage slowly to curiosity. Rob stood where he was, listening.

He heard the sound of the garage door, and of other

doors. Excited talk, both Thomas's and other voices. One of them he remembered well.

Then down the long side passage of the house, passing under framed pictures, some of which were pricey oils and some of which had been taken by a Brownie camera, Thomas returned, shepherding before him Yownie. Rob stepped over the whole sofa in one stride, past the low table and the baby grand piano, and he ran to meet her.

When their meeting came, he was, of course, staring down at the top of her head. He was used to this, and he was delighted to find the top of Yownie's head was completely unchanged by their few months' absence from one another. She wrapped her hands around his midsection and he dropped his over her shoulders, where they landed low on her back. It was a peculiar embrace, but neither minded. They made a few Scottish-sounding cries and then Yownie pulled her face away from his vest and said, "The mountain would not come to Mohammad and so ..."

In reality, she had intended to say those words. She had rehearsed them on the flight over, but when it came time she found herself stuttering, "The mountain. Mountain ..."

In good-natured reply Rob began, "Ah, I am tall, Yownie, but surely not so wide as to be called ..." But then he was staring in blank silence at the man who had walked in behind the others. He was a middling man, no taller than Yownie, black-haired and dressed in jeans and a simple shirt. He was smiling, awkwardly.

Rob stood full upright. "Father! Tonio! Ah, Ah! What a distance you have come. And how happy I am to see you!"

At the other end of the room, Thomas was doing the introductions. "Athena Kaye, may I present, direct from Scotland, Iona MacManus, and Father Antonio Scala. You two, meet our friend and dearest neighbor, Athena Kaye."

As the five people gathered together in the parlor, scattered between Aunt Grace's old baby grand and the coffee table laden with screens, machines, and scattered paper, only Thomas heard Scala's voice murmuring, "And I hope you will be still glad of me an hour from now, my dear Francis." It was so odd a statement from the priest, and there were so many people trying to talk at once, Thomas wasn't certain he had heard the words correctly. But being Thomas, he filed the words away, to be investigated at a more convenient time.

━━

ATHENA KAYE, being a lady from Georgia, felt herself thrust into the position of showing hospitality to these strangers from Scotland. 'Thena did believe the bright young woman was Scottish. She wasn't sure about the accent of the man Rob had called "Father." He certainly didn't look as though he could be gangling Rob's father. He wasn't old enough, nor tall enough to have been the father of Rob MacAulay. So he must be a clergyman. 'Thena didn't know how to place him as a clergyman, let alone as a Scotsman. But he was clearly loved by Rob, and that counted for a great deal in her heart.

She looked at Thomas, and he looked at her. She saw the gleam in that strange, wealthy man's eyes and felt allowed to be hospitable to the visitors. If it wasn't her house, it was certainly her country. Her poor, half-crazy country. She gave a surprising and genuine smile to the woman with the foreign-sounding name, and another to the clergyman behind her.

Yownie shot a dozen quick glances into the room around her. Thomas was uncomfortably aware that some of these would come out, somewhere, in pen-and-ink. He hoped they would not be recognized as his home. He hoped he would not be in them. But then she spoke out, and what she said to the entire room, and so loudly that the strings of the piano echoed her, was, "I have brought him down. Not only his bloody splinter government, but the man himself!"

A moment's respectful silence greeted this, and then Athena Kaye spoke. "The government man? You did?"

Thomas said, out of the corner of his mouth "Wrong government, 'Thena. Wrong man."

Rob swayed back and forth, looking from Yownie to 'Thena and sparing a glance for the priest who hung back in the parlor doorway. "Is it Ferris you're talking about now, Yownie? Andrew Ferris? How can he *be* more brought down? I heard he was in complete disgrace. Of course, I am so far away now...."

She pointed both index fingers into the air. The right one was stained indigo blue. Her black hair shook in the fringe over her blue eyes. "Now he's for the dock!"

"The dock? You mean he's escaping your country?" That was 'Thena, who spoke, and as no one responded, she shut up again.

Thomas ran across the room, found a shabby Queen Anne chair, and tried to insert it under Yownie's knees. She stepped forward, refusing to sit. "Rob, ducky, listen to this. I have tied him to your personal persecution. He is the one who decided there needed to be a symbol of Scottish independence, and that he must so be a terrorist. It was in this manner he gained the votes in Parliament to put his band of hatefuls into power. I can prove it, and I have proven it! Next week it will come out. And I have tied him to Parks, and to some piece of scum in Inverness Police, who was always waiting for a sight of you."

Rob only stared, mouth open. Thomas, who was always quicker in such matters, was standing beside Yownie, holding the oval back of the chair, and he said, "In the Splint, Yownie? You're going to do all this from a comic column in The Splint?"

Her eyes shifted away from Thomas's and spent a moment looking up and to the left. He knew from experience what that meant. The truth was not going to come out. Not completely.

"I wasn't alone, Thomas. No one could do such a research independently.

"I had sources." Now she looked straight ahead. Stubbornly. Every bit her father's daughter. "Every journalist has sources." She seemed to notice the chair for the first time and backed into it. "And, of course, we're not coming out with it in The Splint. It's The Guardian."

"Wow," said Thomas.

"Ach," said Rob.

"I think I want a chair, too," said 'Thena. She planted herself on the stuffed arm of the flowered sofa.

In the moment of silence, all in the room heard a patter of footsteps. It was Shiva Paddiachi, coming down the stair. "I am so sorry, all you delightful people, whom I will shortly know so well, I'm sure. But the baby is having difficulty sleeping with all this loud talk."

For the first time the priest spoke. "That baby," he said with a peculiar reverence.

Paddy bowed. "That baby," he said, with pride.

━━━

IT WAS four minutes and fifty seconds later. Rob knew the time so exactly because he had tapped the left hinge of his glasses and looked up and left twice, thereby causing the time to appear in the top of his visual field. (It looked to others as if he were simply cogitating.) He was sitting with Yownie and Thomas, discussing the impending destruction of the man who had hounded him and, if all this was true, attempted to have him killed.

"I understand," said Thomas, leaning over Rob to Yownie as they sat on the sofa, "why he would have preferred Rob dead than sitting in jail, able to explain himself. Or produce an alibi."

"Probably not. Have been able to produce an alibi, I

mean," murmured Rob. "Can't think how I could have timed anything to be able to produce an alibi." He tried to think of his time on the run in terms of calendar days and failed miserably. No one paid attention to him.

"But have you been able to tie Ferris directly to Parks? He's the only one we can attest to having made a shot."

"Thomas, we've got him within three men, by email and confession. That's closer than Kevin Bacon."

Closer than Kevin Bacon. Rob had been hearing that phrase most of his life, and it occurred to him now he had never known the origin of it, except that a Kevin Bacon was a sort of numeral six.

"And what I need from you, Rob," she continued, prodding him in the kidney with her elbow, is the assurance you will testify against this man."

He looked down at her in surprise. "Testify that someone tried to shoot me in front of the Inverness Library? Of course. Why wouldn't I?"

"I will too!" said Thomas, more forcefully.

Yownie looked closely at Rob. "I had a wee bit of trepidation about it, Rob. Sitting in a British courtroom isn't the most pleasant thing for anyone, and there would be cross-examination."

"I don't care."

"Rob is good speaking to groups," said Thomas, grinning proudly. "And with facts. If he speaks at all, no one can shake him on the facts." He put one hand up to Rob's shoulder and thumped him soundly. Rob swayed into Yownie, who hit the sofa arm with her hand for balance.

Another small conversation eddied in the room, consisting of Father Scala and Paddy. Rob presumed they were talking about the baby. It occurred to Rob that Paddy was making as much noise as anybody. Twice, as he glanced over, Tonio was looking at Rob as he spoke to Paddy.

Athena Kaye moved between one group and the other, her

hands resting on her opposite elbows, clearly fascinated. Whatever frustration she had felt about the blockade of her neighborhood by the government men seemed to have been forgotten.

"And at the same time we're pulling Ferris down, we are working towards a new vote on Scottish independence. It's the perfect time!" Yownie was glowing, and her blue eyes held a martial sparkle.

"But are you sure it is?" Rob spoke quietly, leaning forward close to her. "The perfect time. For independence?"

She met his large, improbable eyes with confusion. "How can *you* ask such a question, Robbie? You? After all they've done to ..."

"Aye. After. That's the important word here. What has happened has happened, and the future is an unopened box. Likely it is appropriate, what with the attitude of Western Europe and all, but are we so sure that England herself isn't feeling things the same, now?"

Yownie didn't speak a word, and Rob heard the slight sound of Thomas chuckling, in his left ear.

But Rob was looking up and over the room to where the priest and Paddy were sitting, on dining-room chairs, right by the passage Tonio had come through. More and more his old friend and protector was staring with intensity in his direction.

Rob rose and excused himself. "You know the mysteries of politics far better than I do, Yownie. It's a failing of mine. But at the moment I realize I haven't even said hello to my other friend."

She looked across the room also. "Ach, Aye. The man attached himself to me. It was a matter of saving money on the airfare, he told me, and also that he had ..." But Rob was not hearing her. He was walking away, stork-stepping over the furniture. "Tonio," he began, holding out his hand to the man. "I am so glad to see you again, and sorry you had to go to such trouble."

Father Scala rose. He didn't take Rob's hand, but embraced him around the entire body, somewhere about the bottom of Rob's ribcage. "I hope you will be," he said, and that statement made no sense at all to Rob. Meanwhile, Shiva Paddiachi was scuttling backwards to allow them privacy.

Rob dropped himself into the vacant wooden chair. "I am now told you came flying here in some haste. I can understand that. I could also understand if you'd wanted to wash your hands of me, after the uproar I must have created in the rectory."

"No, Rob. Never." He took one of Rob's outsized hands into both of his. "It is simply that I have come with news. Information, really."

"About young Jack? His return must have caused—"

"Nae. It's about you, Rob. About you."

Tonio's brown eyes in his oval face were so earnest and serious that Rob had the sensation he was at a physician's office and was about to receive unexpected bad news. Suddenly the conversation around him faded away as he stared at Tonio.

"You'll remember your time at the clinic at the end of the summer last?"

"I couldn't well forget it."

"Well." The priest dropped his head a moment, and Rob saw his friend's dark hair slipping forward. This was too much like the interview with the doctor for Rob's comfort. What news might have been withheld from him all this time?

"Well, I've had the results in my drawer all this time. Hidden, of course. First, because they were dangerous to you and to me also, and later, simply because they were private."

Rob could wait no longer. "Are you going to tell me now that I've got cancer? Like Janet? And you didn't think to say because—oh, I can think of so many reasons why you wouldn't want to say such a thing to a man in my position. But if I have—"

"You don't have cancer!" Tonio overrode Rob's words. A moment's complete silence stilled the busy room, then Tonio waved his hands to all in a placating manner and gave an apologetic smile. People began to talk again.

"Nae, Rob, I'm making a mess of this. I thought I would. It's just that the results of the bloodwork were unusual."

Rob thought of his time in the private clinic, of the heavy medication, the contraptions on his hands, and the silly conversations he had had with the priest during his visits. "The entire procedure was unusual, as I remember it, stuck in some secret room with my hands tied up like that old movie about the man with hands that were gardening shears. I'm not surprised that the paperwork was scrambled at the end of it."

Tonio looked at him again, and the eyes he met were the same huge, impossibly purple-green ones he had seen then. And the spikey dark hair and ears standing out like half-moons to each side. But the boxy teeth were hidden, because for once, Rob MacAulay was not smiling at his friend. Tonio took a breath and continued.

"I did nothing but file away the medical work and ask that the people in the clinic keep it secret as well. Even after you were cleared of all accusations."

"Pardoned, not cleared," Rob inserted in a pointed manner.

"But after your performance at the rectory, my researches upon your past increased."

"Increased? You were already researching me? My past is an open book!"

Tonio straightened in his chair and sighed. "Hardly that, Rob. Hardly that."

One more awkward pause strained the small space between them.

"I looked up the birth records for South Uist in the year you were born, as well as those of Eriskay, and you weren't there."

Rob's mind raced and his head shook, right and left, from the neck up. "No great surprise there. Have you any idea how tiny a place is my island? And when I was born, just twenty years or so from buying its independence from a corporation. And choosing to keep its records in Gaelic? God and Mother Mary, Tonio, you should have simply looked at the baptismal records."

Tonio nodded. "Of course I did. And if I'm not mistaken, your birthday is May first."

"It is."

From the inside pocket of his blue windbreaker Tonio drew a packet of assorted papers. It was a hefty packet. He sorted in it. "Here. A photocopy. In both Scots Gaelic and English. I had someone from the University go over the Gaelic to be sure it matched the English. You were baptized by one Father Douglas MacRonald. Do you remember the man?"

Rob didn't need to think. "Of course I do. He was the only priest we had when I was a lad. And a crotchet of a fellow, too. I remember him as ancient."

Tonio's oval face crinkled in a grin. "That ancient man was not much older than you are now. But that's how a child thinks. But the important thing is the date. Look."

Rob did. He had seen this document before. In fact, he remembered using it to apply for his first passport. But if he had ever paid attention to it, really, he didn't remember. "May 1, 2001. So?"

"You were baptized on the day you were born."

Rob shrugged. "So I was a sickly bairn! You know how important it is for people like my parents to get a child baptized."

Tonio grinned. "Better than you do, Rob. And do you remember being told you were a sickly child?"

Rob shrugged again, returning Tonio's smile, and after a bit the smile went away. "I don't remember anything like that.

That doesn't mean it wasn't true. I have a poor memory of my early years."

Tonio sighed and flicked through the sheaf of papers. "So does the local hospital. According to the clinic on the North Island, you weren't seen by them except for your vaccinations."

Rob heard his chair squeaking over the floor as he pushed himself away from the man he so regarded as a friend. "Tonio, I don't know what has gotten into you, with all this. I'm getting two ideas in my head. One I find loony and the other offensive."

The priest simply raised his eyebrows and waited.

"The offensive idea is that somehow you think I'm illegitimate, and if you think that, you never met my parents and so I suppose I must forgive you for that."

"I don't think that, Rob."

"And the second is that you suppose I'm some sort of space alien. A Martian mathematician, possibly."

Tonio grinned again, but tightly. "I don't think that, either. Before you jump to conclusions, please let me finish."

Oh, finish and be done with this.

Aloud, Rob said nothing.

"I visited South Uist myself and Eriskay, too. For the first time, I must say. And there are still a number of older people who were there when you were baptized. Who must remember you. Oddly enough, they all seemed to forget their English when I tried to speak to them."

Now Rob did grin, showing his front teeth. "As well they might. My people don't like intruders asking questions about one of their own."

"So I went to old MacRonald."

It was Rob's turn to raise his eyebrows. "He's still with us, then?"

"In a retirement home in Inverness. I didn't approach him as a fellow priest, because I didn't know what the old fellow might think of a follower of the 'Argentine.' I just approached him as a friend of yours."

And so I thought you were.

Rob locked his teeth over his tongue and let Tonio go on.

"The old man also lost his English. Although he's spoken little else for twenty years now. So I approached him again. In Latin. And he did admit baptizing you, when confronted with the photocopy. But he claims he can remember nothing else about it.

"No one will tell me anything about your birth and child-hood, Rob. In fact, they seem not to recognize your name, although you were all over the local paper just a year ago. And ten years ago, with the nomination for the Nobel. They seem to have all developed a sudden and particular amnesia."

Rob shifted in his chair and ran both long hands over his head. "They simply didn't like you, Tonio. To them you must have seemed like one more ... what does Athena call them? Government man."

The priest put all the papers back into their hidden pocket. He looked around the room, where other conversations seem to have died down. He lowered his own voice further. "No doubt you're right, Rob. But tell me yourself. What were you told about your home-birth?"

"Actually, I was told what every child is told when young. My ma said they found me under a thorn bush. But you must remember being told such a story yourself."

Thomas was strolling over to Rob, carefully listening as Scala went on. "Actually, I was told I was born in a hospital in Torino. But my parents don't seem to have had the imagina-tion of yours."

Thomas butted in. "I don't remember anyone bothering to spin me tales of any sort. But if they had, it would surely have been of a stork. I can easily imagine another long-legged odd bird bringing Rob to his parents." He looked brightly from one to another, seeking out the reason for the strain that lay so heavily over this conversation. "Why are you two going on about this?"

"The man here obviously thinks I'm some sort of space alien. I can't think of any other reason he'd be here with his mental ideas."

Thomas looked at his binary with great amusement. "I actually can see that, Rob. You'd make a great ET. But taller."

"I never said that!" Tonio hit one fist on the chair arm. He pulled out the papers one more time and searched through until he came to the records from the very private clinic. He held them out uncertainly, but Rob refused to touch them. Thomas grabbed them up.

"What is this—blood work? From last August?" His amber eyes slid along the medical documents like a man reading sheet music. Then the eyes narrowed and stopped. He looked down at Tonio Scala with doubt and challenge. "I can't make any sense of this. Where did the guy mess up?"

Scala spread his hands on his lap. "I don't believe he messed up anything. There was Rob, a week after the procedure, safe and healing. Healing far faster than expected. If the doctor had failed in that procedure ..."

"Rob'd have no hands at all now. I know that much. But you're giving me nonsense. No blood type? Doesn't that just mean O Neg?"

"The doctor couldn't type his blood and simply used the red blood cells and mitochondria he pulled from Rob to feed back into him." Rob cleared his throat, loudly and obviously. "I'm sitting right here, Thomas. Tonio. Don't talk over me this way."

"And the mitochondrial type. That's the issue that caused the doctor to come to me, Rob. The mitochondria didn't fit with the rest at all. They didn't fit with any human mitochondria. I don't know a lot about medicine, and less about genetics, but ..." Tonio was now wringing his hands and blinking at

Rob. "He said they were strangely—strangely assorted. As from many different creatures."

Thomas sank down onto his haunches to be level with Tonio. Rob looked at the tops of both men's heads. "What did the doctor do, then? All I remember is watching the news on the ceiling. Laughing a lot."

"He took the blood out of you, added saline, and fed it back in. With the synthetic pads. No more than that. And in a week you were well, Rob."

Rob stood up, pushing his chair back as he did so. "It was a lot longer than that, and you know it. This is shite about my being well in a week. I spent a month in your cellar, if you remember."

Tonio stood too. "It was expected to be six months, my friend. When you left me that note and disappeared, I feared for you."

Thomas rose lightly as a cloud, and put a hand on each man's shoulder. "So what are you leading to, with all this, Tonio? Rob is as upset as I've ever seen him. Give him the bottom line."

Father Antonio Scala smiled. He actually smiled at Rob and took again one of his large hands in both of his. "My dear friend. My brother. Think of what you can do. Of what you have done. I love you dearly, and I do not believe you are entirely human."

Now Thomas dared intrude. "What's this? What's he implying, Rob?"

With fierce disgust Rob replied, "The man seems to think I'm some sort of fairy! A fairy physicist! Can't say I fancy the idea."

19

Birthday

R ob MacAulay stalked down the porch stairs and
stood under the wisteria. Its purple petals were
raining down all over his head and shoulders, but
he didn't notice. He was wishing with all his heart he could
erase the last minute or so of angry, violent words he had
thrown at the priest in the parlour inside. He hadn't known he
had it in him to be so hate-filled, however insane his old friend
had been behaving. He, himself, had behaved worse. He took
a deep breath of the windy spring air and almost got a purple
petal up his nose. He sneezed. Walked forward into the
garden, away from the busy house.

How they'd all been staring at him. His face was hot. God
knew what colour it was now, but no one was here to see.

Rob walked forward through the thick grass and the smell
of the new growth filled his lungs. He did what Thomas said
so frequently that it had become a joke between them. He
breathed. And he entered the north end of the Sullivan
garden, which was less managed than the rest, and more
closely planted with trees and shrubs. The stable gate passed
behind him and he was alone with his roiling mind.

THOMAS SULLIVAN STOOD in the doorway, unwilling to follow Rob. He watched his friend and lover brush by the bushes, covered in pale purple wisteria petals, like so much confetti. In Thomas's hand was the paper from the Inverness doctor, which he had scrunched up in a ball. He didn't even know he'd been ruining it. Erasing it somehow. As though he could erase the results.

ROB CAME TO A SHORT HAWTHORN, and wondered briefly what had made the old woman plant such a tree in her elegant estate. He put his hand on it and remembered how his mother had cut a blackthorn down and woven the branches carefully into his first cradle. She had cut it down on Beltane, of course. By tradition that was the only day in which a good superstitious Hebridean was allowed to cut down a thorn tree. It was also his birthday.

In fact, today was his birthday. May 1. He had forgotten. When a man turns forty, birthdays don't have the same meaning they did for a child. He wondered, suddenly, if the thorn tree she cut down was the same one under which she claimed to have found him as an infant. But that would have meant she cut down the tree on the same day she bore him, and that made no sense. Rob rubbed his hand up and down the branch of the little hawthorn tree, absently, between one long thorn and the next.

THOMAS, still watching from the doorway, saw his aunt's old hawthorn burst into bloom. Silently, it bloomed. Perfectly, it bloomed as Rob touched it. He saw Rob standing beside the tree, not looking at it at all. He heard the man give a great sigh and droop his head down where he stood. And Thomas blinked and rubbed his eyes, because it seemed that Rob's hand, and even his ears, had begun to glow.

ROB'S MIND was suddenly full of that moment when his flight from Scotland skewed sideways. When he was aware of being somewhere Other. Somewhere Other, but not completely unfamiliar. It was a body memory, like those Thomas had taught him to recognize on the mat. Or on the piano. And Rob gave another great sigh and raised his head up again.

Everything was the same as it had been a moment before. Everything was totally different.

He went back toward the house to apologize to Tonio. He saw Thomas looking out the door at him. He saw Thomas's jaw drop.

Rob laughed.

20

Rob As Himself

D r. Robert MacAulay strode back through the garden much faster than he had come, his arms held only slightly out to each side. It seemed to Thomas Sullivan that the gesture was not so much the one of the gawky and over-tall man he knew, but one of floating, as a wild animal floats over the ground. His face was ruddy and happy and oh-so-young. Thomas knew his eyes were slightly wet, but that couldn't have been the sole reason that every movement of Rob's body trailed a corona of light as the sun in eclipse has a corona. His feet made no noise in the grass, but the sky was filled with the song of birds. In the distance horses whinnied. Nothing made any sense and Thomas sniffled and he laughed with Rob. Like Rob, he was fully happy, but unlike Rob, he had no idea why.

His binary met him on the porch boards and embraced him, whirling him around in the air. And there was no martial arts trickery in that upset. Rob had picked up Thomas as a grown man picks up a child. In his rumpled shirt and linen vest, Rob smelled like the wind. "Thomas—Tommy—I must apologize!"

"To who?" he gasped. "Not to me."

So he was Tommy again. Like his namesake. Like his own childhood. Thomas Sullivan embraced the perfect silliness of it.

"I must apologize to everyone. To the world." Rob ducked his head and entered the house, dragging Thomas in his wake.

The vestibule was crowded with staring people: Yownie, Paddy, Athena Kaye. As Rob entered it was decidedly a brighter place, and he moved along it, embracing one body after another, although he didn't swing anyone else around. What he said to each was incomprehensible. Possibly not in English, although no one asked for explanation. Every eye saw a man glowing, and every eye accepted it.

In the parlour had remained the priest, and with him now was Jan, sitting on the sofa with her infant. She turned her head in time to see her brother-in-law stop walking and kneel before her. "The wee bairn!" he sang out. He put his hands out but did not touch young Thomas, except by a field of gentle light. The baby kicked and bubbled contentedly. Jan, without considering the matter, held him out to Rob, and little Tommy tried to grab one long finger in his hand, staring with blue baby eyes.

In that manner, on his knees and held by the baby by one finger, Rob finally met Father Antonio Scala's eyes. He asked him for forgiveness. He spoke in the perfect Italian of Torino, or so Tonio Scala heard it. Scala locked hands over Rob's free hand, and what he answered he never remembered, except that he ended by exclaiming, "Dear Lord!"

"And Mother Mary, for isn't it her feast day, too?"

Shiva Paddiachi was standing beside his son. With bright interest he asked his wife, "Were we not told that a baby could not smile this early? That it must be gas pains? And yet I do not think …"

Lovingly, Jan whispered, "Shut up, Paddy."

Rob rose, or rather floated, to his feet and looked around

the assembly. "'Thena! You said you were having difficulties at the community gate. Do I remember properly?" He looked for all the world as if he were holding a class of students and taking questions. Except that he was glowing.

She looked confused. "That's why I came here. Yes. Seems a long time ago, but …"

"That ought to be the first item on our agenda, I think." He looked around the Sullivan parlor, seeking dissent. Finding none, he put his hands up, index fingers raised in a professorial manner, and led everyone back toward the north porch.

"Thomas, Yownie—please get your audiovisual equipment ready."

They all walked after him—all except Jan and the baby, who sat back on the sofa and cooed to one another.

It was such a beautiful day and the grass was sweet under their feet. At the intricate ironwork gate to the neighboring community, Rob bent his legs and spread his arms and sailed over it.

"Hope is a thing with feathers," whispered Father Scala to Thomas.

"I think Rob would call it some sort of field," Thomas mumbled in return.

Thomas worked the combination lock to let the rest of the crew pass through more normally. To the priest he said, "Somehow this is reminding me of the story of the man with the golden goose under his arm, who pulls along …"

"Or the pied piper."

Thomas glanced at Tonio. "Well, he's got the pipes for it, anyway."

The coiled streets of the gated community were dotted with people, standing glumly outside their homes.

———

YOWNIE THOUGHT the place looked just a bit like Old

Town Edinburgh. Streets that went nowhere at the slowest possible rate. She wondered at this new American develop-ment. Was it supposed to look medieval? Her only "audiovi-sual equipment" was her mobile phone, but she needed no other. She caught up with Thomas. "What are we about to do here? Is it political in nature?"

He grinned, and she thought him twice as lovely a spec-imen of the human male as the one she had met in the rain in Edinburgh only half a year before. It was the happiness that did it. "If Rob is involved, politics becomes impossible."

She fell back again, fascinated by the repetitive three styles of house surrounding her. Three bland colors, also. In a way, that reminded her of decent council housing. But these houses were far different from those built with public support. The size of them spoke money. Who with money would spend it this way? To look like council housing?

Noise from in front startled her out of her reverie.

There stood the opening to the outside world. It was bordered by something that attempted to resemble a stone wall, though that attempt only went a few meters and was replaced by chain-link. A round, impersonal flower garden sat in the center of the opening and a gatehouse presided. All of this was difficult to see because it was crowded with milling people, and a long sort of town-car was attempting to block the entrance to the community. This car, in turn, was blocked by a policeman on a sturdy bay horse. There was some talking going on that Yownie could not hear. She saw the car edge forward, almost bumping the side of the horse, who put his ears back but did not move. She saw the policeman's hand edge down to his holster.

Then out of the crowd appeared the head of Rob MacAulay, seeming taller than ever in relation to the people around him. And the sun shone down on him. He was moving forward toward the scene: a scene that crackled with tension.

She remembered she was supposed to be a photojournalist and used her phone.

Rob stood beside the long car. One heavy fist knocked on the top of it. A window slid down.

And Rob sang out. He sang so loudly she thought her ears might pop. The horse moved nervously.

"I believe it is to me this piece of theatre has been directed. My name is Rob MacAulay, if you have any doubt in the matter. Speak with me and let these people pass!"

Yownie was so glad she had turned her phone camera to video and mic. It had been a beautiful moment. Not the equivalent of "Let my people go," but it had much the same flavor. And better tuning. A sudden, inconsequential thought came into her head. Through the First World War, it had been considered a benefit that a British officer had a high voice, because his orders could be shouted farther. A bellow was imposing, but didn't carry.

But maybe it was not such an inconsequential thought. The people in the forecourt, or whatever it was called over here, began to raise their own voices in support. She heard the word "commute" and the word "dinner" and the important words "school bus." She hoped her phone picked it all up.

She could not hear what the people in the car said. As the window sank, Rob raised his head a moment and caught the eye of the nervous police horse. He spoke to the animal—or at least, his mouth was moving. From one moment to the next the horse went from a case of the jitters to complete and solid fascination. The animal's head turned to Rob's and his ears were pricked so far forward it seemed they might snap closed against his forehead. The head of the Mountie also swiveled, although with the full-face helmet lowered, she could see nothing but sun-glare and a dark shape beneath.

Rob was listening to the person, a man, in the driver's seat. No, here it was the passenger seat. Rob put both his white hands on the black car's top and lowered his head. "I have heard all that nonsense before, you stupid men, and I tell you that you represent no Government of the United States that I am familiar with, and I highly doubt you will find a branch of said government who will now admit to having backed you in your ridiculous enterprise." He pointed at the mounted man. "Now I show you there a representative of the local government and the local people."

***

IN ALL HIS days being used as a public service, the cop had never received a rousing hand, which he got, not for standing against this illegal imprisonment of a gated community—which deed had been, frankly, scary—but by being pointed at by this friendly giant. He didn't much mind. Applause was applause. The giant's accent was definitely peculiar, and his operatic singing might have seemed absurd if it had not been so obviously impromptu and genuine. It came to him that his was his friend Thomas's new husband. From Scotland.

***

"AND YOUR IDEA of coercion is so lacking in power that it has already failed in this town. I am told there is one of your own ilk in the local lockup at this minute for blocking another, similar gate. If you are not aware of that it is likely that the woman has been denied contact with you this wee while."

Having no idea what Rob was saying, except that the black-car-people were trying this stunt at other gated communities in the area, the people exploded again.

Yownie managed to wiggle up to Thomas. He, she was glad to see, had an honest-to-God camera on his head, focused over one eye. "Have you got this?" she whispered.

"Aye, I have," Thomas sang back. She stared at him, but

he didn't seem to be mocking her. It could be Rob was simply that contagious. Thomas was smiling widely.

"And … and can I have the footage?"

"Ach. Aye." Yownie stared at the transformed Yank again.

Rob had another thing to say. He raised one hand and pointed at the sky above the mounted policeman. "And that, up there? Do you see it? It is a drone. Them I know well. This one is marked by the local police department. So you are being watched, and not only by me and the local policeman here." He looked up a moment and added, "And of course by the local police-horse, too. And there is nothing you can do to erase your faces, nor your license plates, from public record."

"He can't really read the writing on that drone, of course," muttered Yownie to Thomas.

Thomas answered her, smiling even broader. "But he can. He can."

The car backed out, to wild hurrahs. Most of the enclosed community seemed to be out here now, under the sun. Under the eyes of this man who was almost a stranger to them, but now adopted so quickly.

Then, in perfect timing, the school bus pulled up. From out of it piled a dozen children, one of them dressed in red. Breton Kaye trotted up in astonishment to stare at the assembly, and of course, noticed the tall figure of Rob in front of them all.

"Rob?" she asked, staring up. And up.

"Tony!" And he plucked her off the ground and swung her in a great circle, the both of them grinning. Her school bag, on its strap, flew in a wider circle.

And that was the image that made the news that evening. The local news. And then the national.

———

SITTING on the raised border of the round garden, Rob and

Thomas found Father Scala telling his wooden rosary, seeming oblivious to all around him. Rob stepped up but did not interrupt until the priest raised his eyes. "Which mystery are you praying, Father?" asked Rob.

To Thomas the question was meaningless, but Scala answered, "Joyful, of course."

Rob raised his head and his arms and gave one glorious sniff. "Perfect day for that," he said.

Most of the original small procession receded. Athena pulled her child away and home. Father Scala followed, still saying the rosary. Roses were blooming on the brick wall— blooming out of season. The gate sprang open and they walked through.

"I have another errand, yet," said Rob, quietly.

Thomas had removed and folded up his camera. "You're still glowing, you know."

Rob shrugged. "I'll calm down, Tommy. It takes so much to rile me that I suppose it will take time for it to fade."

Neither Yownie nor Scala were certain the two men were talking about the same thing. Neither of them knew, either, how extraordinary it was for anyone to get away with calling Thomas Tommy.

"I must drive back to see Kinsman again."

Thomas looked up at Rob. "I have things here to finish, Rob."

"No matter. I'll be fine on my own."

No matter. How often Rob said that now. Like Kyan Sensei.

"May I come along, Rob?" asked Tonio Scala, feeling some sense of responsibility.

Yownie said nothing, but she got into the car in the back seat.

DIFFIDENTLY, and after looking again at his friend's grand and glorious face, Tonio Scala suggested he allow the car to drive them, or allow himself to drive the car, his excuses being that Rob had been under a great deal of stress that day already, and that he had spent a few years of his priesthood in the States.

Rob turned to him, and in the dim light of the garage his eyes were shining a full, distant sort of heather, speckled with green. "Seems you don't trust my driving, either, Tonio. Thomas has the same quirk, though I have never come close to bending a fender in this thing, automatic or no. But it is not possible you could drive, as the seat has been converted for my ungainly size."

And as they pulled down the drive toward their own private gate in the Sullivan wall, he added, "Besides. I never saw the difficulty in switching right to left, in a car. With the wheel on the other side of the car, all reverses itself in the brain without conscious effort."

The gate slid open, and if there was someone guarding it, that person was not obvious. They started down the lovely wooded road, overhung with maples and birch. Shadows of branches dotted the road before them. The windows darkened subtly at the tops, but not enough to diminish the beauty of the drive.

"And don't you both, Scots as you are, find it odd that this huge country should still be so stuck in its ways that everyone is driving a personal car and public transport seems an idea undiscovered?" Rob murmured complacently as they went.

"I've always thought that to be a simple function of the size of the place, you know?" answered the priest, looking not at the pretty scenery but at Rob himself, placed so far back into the car that he looked like some racing driver, half-flat on his back. Yet his head still touched the padding above. "I imagine any huge, continental country, such as Russia, for example …"

And why are we talking such bullshit. Now? NOW? thought Yownie MacManus, from the rear seat.

After a few minutes Rob must have noticed that his friend was still not looking out the window, but at him, and he programmed and engaged the automatic function of the car and took his hand off the wheel. "There, Tonio. If we are to be smashed, it will be by software malfunction and not my own."

Neither of them had thought to question where it was they were going. The name "Kinsman" was still vague in Yownie's mind. So they looked out at Massachusetts on a May evening, while the car, by programming, evaded all cities that might disrupt traffic or disrupt the mind.

Shadows were growing long when the car approached the hospital. The veterinary hospital. Yownie then recalled all the particulars associated with the name "Kinsman." She had not known that Rob's horse was ill, but then, if the beast were ill, she would expect no less of Rob MacAulay than this visit. "What if the place is closed to visitors, Rob?" she asked. "Did you call to be certain …"

"It will not be," he answered. He parked in the back of the sprawling building, which was less imposing than the front. More stable-like. They got out of the car, Rob walking behind, as he had to unfold himself. In the dimming light, he shone brighter than he had before. And the light was not confined to his person, but trailed out behind his movements, golden.

I am in a fairy tale. Yownie left her photojournalism packed away in her mind.

The rear door, scaled to horse proportions, opened to Rob's hand. They entered a wide passage less brightly lit than what she'd expect in a human hospital, but with her father's lifelong team-driving practice, she knew this sort of place well. Scala and she followed Rob down the rubberized floor, trotting to keep pace with his strides. They turned twice, heard nickers from both sides, but saw no human being.

Rob opened another door, this one with a window at the top. He took a breath and entered a room.

And there was the tall black horse, held up in a sort of sling that tracked along the ceiling. His head was down, almost to the floor, his ears outwards and his mouth hung open, his belly shaved from mid-section to between his hind legs. He was such a pitiful sight she couldn't resist a small sound of sympathy. She heard the priest draw in his breath.

An orange mesh fence was snapped from one side of the room to the other. Rob walked to the near side and unsnapped it. Let it drop.

Yownie knew that fence was there for a reason. She also knew she would no way in hell say anything about that. Rob stepped in over the layer of shavings to the head of the animal and didn't speak. He raised his hands above either side of Kinsman's wilted head.

And the horse did lift that head. Half a meter. Their eyes, the brown and the—whatever color—engaged. The glow of the movement, clear in the dim light of the room, fed itself into that drooling black head, which raised farther. Then Rob MacAulay stepped one step forward and embraced the horse's head in his own arms and put his bright face sideways against the dark one.

They rocked, from side to side, constrained by the sling, and Rob whispered, singing a lullaby to his horse. Yownie first assumed the words were nonsense and then threw out that assumption as so much nonsense itself. Was this what they had always meant by "horse whisperer," that overused and now meaningless term? She saw Tonio Scala step gingerly forward. He dared to put a hand on the animal's withers. For him it was a bit of a reach. Scala grinned like a delighted child and flashed a look at Yownie, who, herself, could not stir from the spot. Kinsman took a great breath, and then another, and each time it seemed to her the beast was inhaling the golden— whatever—that Rob expelled as he breathed.

Horses smile much like humans. And these two had such similar teeth.

"Oh, my heart," said Rob, sincerely. "Oh, heart of my heart!" He sounded like a young man in first love. The horse pawed and tried to put his feet under him. The sling slipped and now hung under his girth. It seemed to have come loose. Kinsman gave out a powerful whinny for an animal in such poor circumstance.

Rob looked directly at Tonio. "God be praised," he said.

"Always," answered Tonio. His voice was choked.

Rob backed away from the horse again. "You need your rest, my friend," he said firmly. "I know you don't think you do, but you can trust me on this." He walked away from the horse, with Tonio following. When they reached the orange mesh, he replaced the fence in its slot. And he took them back toward the door.

There came another whinny as he opened it. He called over his shoulder, "Those parts I can't give back to you," he called, and neither human had any idea what that meant.

Then they were out of the room and kicking their feet against the rubberized flooring, to remove shavings and anything else that might have clung. All the way back to the car they saw no one. It was now dark. Beyond surprise now, Yownie noticed that Rob was no longer glowing. Or not much. Nor did he seem so impossibly tall. But the rest of the change remained. He was not gawky. He seemed the perfect size and shape for himself. As they got back into the car, Tonio Scala suggested she ride shotgun this time. It was only fair.

They rode home to the Sullivan place. They didn't talk much. Yownie was stunned by it all, but not at all unhappy. All in all, it had been a long day.

⊏━⊐

TWO DAYS later the drones were back. It was almost Edinburgh autumn redux. The difference was that the laws of privacy in the Commonwealth of Massachusetts and those of Scotland were different. A property-owner, or renter, had the option of destroying a drone within a certain altitude of their house. In practice this meant little, as a good, high-functioning camera drone had lenses powerful enough to focus from above the designated property line. But enough drone handlers were careless that something could be done, if the dweller did not use a weapon that might endanger anyone but the drone.

Thomas Sullivan was good at this sort of shooting, and amused himself with a system of disruptive power surges that landed all sorts of valuable equipment on the Sullivan acreage. Rather like a man shooting quail.

He had little else to do in the interim, because Rob MacAulay had led in all things regarding himself without bothering with discussion. Having done the same all his life, Thomas could scarcely object to this. Nor did he want to.

Rob allowed Thomas to work out a phone system that allowed certain calls to go through to him and blocked the rest. Rob chose the list himself, and it included many more public media sources than Thomas had expected. More than he had even known Rob was aware of. So Rob chatted calmly with interviewers from major US news sources and also an assortment of peculiar ones. From what Thomas could over-hear, or heard later on the news-streams, it was a simple repetition of what had happened that day in the community gate, in which he patiently—with a teacher's acceptance of repetition—asked the interviewer to refer to the immediate video taken by Thomas, as that could only be more accurate than human memory. He also willingly shared the recording that had been made for him at his entrance into the country, adding no comment to it except the repeated statement that he had come as the spouse of a US citizen and had had then and now no other political motives.

The one question, which might have been a bomb in other

hands, was why he had given his equations to the Russian and to two Chinese, as well as Harvard physicists from other unfriendly nations, at his afternoon session over an oval table. The answer, so obvious to Rob, was that upon giving the data up as public record, it would have been nonsense, and poor nonsense, to make certain of his scientific colleagues go to the extra click and drag to grab it from a secondary source. It was almost impossible to get a soundbite out of Rob MacAulay. The recording from Kennedy Airport customs, however, received wild notoriety. Upon this Rob did refuse to comment, stealing Thomas's line. "I am a foreigner here. It would be better for you to get your data from people more closely informed."

When he chose, Rob could even be a pedant.

Otherwise he went about his business, working out chord inversions on the old piano, which no longer bothered his ears with its equal temperament, and learning from Thomas the secrets of turning the mathematics of music into emotion through inserting minor accompaniment into major keys and the use of suspended fourths. To Rob this seemed like so much magic.

Like so much magic.

Rob MacAulay had ceased trailing streams of glory, after his encounter with Kinsman. And had seemed to shrink back into his usual six-foot-seven height. But there was a definite physical difference in his appearance. It was as though a Great Dane puppy, or a foal, had grown into his adult proportions. Not that he looked older. He looked ageless. And his eyes were now a constant, faded purple, with a green ring and radiating lines around the pupil.

IT MADE perfect sense for Jan and Paddy to take their newborn out of the besieged Sullivan house. Perfect sense, except that the well-behaved infant began to squall immoderately whenever they tried to depart. Young Tommy bathed in the presence of Rob MacAulay, as did MacBride and the recovered Kinsman, both of whom lived most of their days in the garden, adjusting the landscaping to their taste.

Thomas, too, bathed in his binary's presence. He was aware he had taken to following the man around the house, as though he, Thomas, were some sort of younger brother, or disciple. Had Rob behaved in the slightest like a superior, this would have been intolerable to Thomas Sullivan. But Rob did not. He was, in fact, less self-conscious, somewhat cuddly, and more demonstrative than Thomas would have believed one week ago. The most amazing part of the entire transformation was the day Thomas discovered Rob's left pocket bulging in his new suit because his wallet, keys and other trinkets were all in one place. Regardless of balance.

At the end of the two days he cornered Rob as he was about to leave the bedroom in the morning. With forced casualness he asked if Rob were planning to leave.

The man's arched eyebrows went higher. "But you know I must, Thomas!" And Rob saw Thomas Sullivan began to shrink before him. Attempting his mask of stone-face without success.

"I did think so," he said, and began to turn.

Rob took him by his healed upper arm. "But you knew it. I promised Yownie I would go to Scotland. To testify. You will have to go also. You are an eyewitness to a shooting, you remember."

"Yes. Of course. I meant permanently, Rob. To go elsewhere."

In complete alarm Rob's voice sailed up. "Why on earth would I be doing such a thing?"

"Because you are different now. Very different."

Offended, Rob huffed. Chuffed. "Not *that* different!" He took Thomas in a strong embrace. This time there was no whirling of one around the other. It was an orbit that shrank in size until the binary was almost one star. And it did not last for only a moment. Nor an hour.

⬛

IN A FEW WEEKS the drones were gone again, as world news, which by definition is never good, overtook the notoriety of the obscure local scandal of the government men. There were threats from Russia against both sides of the ever-changing Chinese situation. And vice versa. These were things with which even Thomas dared not concern himself.

To escape it, this aspect of the world, the two men and the two horses amused themselves in brilliant weather. As all parties, except Kinsman himself, had decided that the horse had best be kept from strenuous work, they spent hours in an open arena together, engaging in a sort of impromptu dual dressage work, involving much side-pass, close circling on various leads and anything else Thomas remembered that didn't involve airs above the ground.

Rob didn't wear his glasses for riding, so Thomas kept his wrist-phone for possible emergencies.

This dressage was accomplished in the rope halters they had become accustomed to using on the trails. It was a sight to see, and people saw it.

"I feel like Donald O'Connor or Gene Kelley," said Thomas to Rob as the two horses shuffled past each other.

"Don't know the gentlemen," answered Rob on the next close passage.

The white stretched out and the black minced closer to match gaits in a manner most horsemen and horses never perfect. A line of riders, and even horses, watched them over the arena fence. Rob thought this attention much preferable to that of the drones. Not to say there did not come the occasional hovering drone. There is, however, a definite problem with drones over any area of horse-work, as they resemble insects too much for the feelings of the average horse. Because of that, there were safety laws.

"How old is MacBride, again?" asked Rob, as they passed in a reversed figure of eight.

"Twenties. Never knew," answered Thomas, when he could. He heard Rob chuckling at this and began to wonder what the joke was when the wrist-phone vibrated and Thomas called a halt.

"It's for you," he called out. Kinsman spun on his quarters. "Sweden or Scotland?" asked Rob.

"Scotland."

Rob dropped his head a moment. So did his horse. "Then I'll be going," he said.

21

Solitary Confinement

R ob was mildly surprised that he was flying Aer
Lingus, with a brief stopover at Shannon Airport.
He still wasn't used to the intimate connection
between Ireland and Boston that everyone else seemed to take
for granted. He no longer felt guilt flying first class: only relief
that he could almost fit the seat. The stewardess was a woman
from the west coast of Ireland and he listened to her asking
him his drink requirement and found she was answering him
awkwardly, in poor school-girl Irish. He had unknowingly
spoken in Scots Gaelic. He asked, in English, for her forgiveness and for a cup of tea.

It was an awkwardly-timed flight, as he was supposed to
arrive at Heathrow at about six in the morning. But it did not
hurt at all. He looked out the little window and felt he was
flying through the dark beside the ship. And then he slept.

▭

ROB AWOKE ONLY with the bump of landing. He had never
had such a restful flight on an airplane, and the dreams which

remained were all pleasant. He remembered something absurd about sitting in the dark on the wing of the plane with the wind blowing through his hair (Hair? Feathers? Dreams were not analyzable). As he waited for everyone else in his class to get off first, which was his habit, he heard someone discuss an ancient television series where the actor William Shatner had the experience of looking out an airplane window to find some monster sitting on it. It must have been an important piece of old telly he had missed. Two people mentioned it as he sat there.

He had known the testimony he was to give was before a London court, and not one in Scotland, but he had not expected the reception he received upon landing. He might as well have been some sort of foreign dignitary. Nothing like a pardoned criminal at all. But the limousine was every bit as uncomfortable as though it were a paddy-wagon.

All his needs were attended to, and he went through a deal of preparation with the prosecution. How odd, to be a witness. He had hoped for some sight of Yownie, but he was insulated by officials who seemed to be all from south of Hadrian's Wall.

His testimony was everything the prosecution wanted to hear and wanted the jury to hear. What was more, he was unshakeable in his simple statements. He also had the backing of videos and of statements prepared by Thomas and even by MacManus the elder. He was certainly not the central witness to the case against Andrew Ferris et al. He was simply a man who had had a bad, extended experience, and never claimed to know much about the essentials of whatever had happened to England for a short time last summer and autumn. These seemed to include massive corruptions and direct links to murder and attempted murder. His own tribulations not being so bad in comparison.

That did not seem to mean they were the least notorious. But as Rob MacAulay was a new man, perfect and un-

balanced, he did not care about the cameras, the questions, or the snarls of the future. He sat in his hotel room, with a sharply-dressed guard at the door, and he looked out the window at a London West-Side street.

Thomas would be coming to the trial, but they would not be together. Thomas was a US Citizen.

Rob went to bed and dreamed of flying over London.

———

TO BRITAIN this was one of those "trials of the century," which occurred so many times every century. Half a year spent in the United States, and in other places less easy to describe, had put Rob MacAulay out of touch with the importance of such events. He had always known that about himself —that he tended to hear the news-streams in a sort of translation, of language or of time. He sat in the witness box in that same manner, watching a magistrate wearing no horsehair at all on his head, and he wondered more about that change than he did about the court case.

And it was such a huge court chamber around him. Filled with people who cared so much about the outcome of this trial. A man sat in the dock, and from the witness box he could see him and did not recognize him as Ferris, the once Prime Minister of the Splinter group. He didn't recognize him at all. A year ago this might have embarrassed him, for he was always so careful to remember people's names and faces. Now it did not bother him. It wasn't his job to recognize the defendant. He recognized no one in the chamber except one face, and that was of Tonio Scala. Evidently Tonio would not have to testify, and so was not kept away from the proceedings. He was in a balcony.

———

FATHER SCALA RECOGNIZED Rob MacAulay and gave him
the warmest encouraging smiles he could. He had wrangled a
little seat in a balcony corner, but he knew Rob was seeing
him smiling. It was those eyes.

Surely everyone in the courtroom knew about Rob's eyes
by now. Could feel the light of him, the pull toward him. His
own friend Rob was now Pied Piper to a huge British courtroom, and Scala was there simply to see how that would
work out.

It was working out well. The prosecutor asked his questions, about when Rob had felt a need to run and why. And
Rob's answers were child-simple. He had been advised to run
by friends and he had run—or rather walked—out and up
into the Highlands. And had done so for two years.

Having been part of those two years, Tonio hugged
himself, but just a bit. He didn't want to take credit that wasn't
his due. He, too, looked around the London courtroom for
faces he could recognize and didn't see a one. Not even a
parishioner from St. Francis.

Tonio hadn't known Rob had been shot at twice. He'd
only known of the once. It was so like his strange friend not to
have mentioned it. For both shots there was video evidence
shown on the screen above the jury box, although it was
blurry, making it look like Rob had actually been shot, or had
been out of focus. Seeing these, Tonio rocked back and forth
in his seat and hid his grin. Rob looked simply at the images,
showing nothing in his pleasant, placid face.

Yes, that image on the screen was his. No, he had no idea
who had been shooting at him. Yes, he had been frightened.
The story of how he had finally made connection with
Thomas Heddiman, US Citizen, was tight and short. Rob
remembered the strange communication with Thomas word
perfect, as it had been found on the records of the Inverness
Library Computers. With no strong emotion he relayed his
experience as a captive of Thomas Heddiman and then as

chattel. And his narrative skipped over the entirety of the great change that had come about in that relationship, and courteously skipped to the pardon.

Tonio, peering out and down, was now feeling stressed and weary by the whole thing, but Rob, it seemed, might have gone on forever, sitting there, too tall in the wooden box. Giving a seminar. Or defending a dissertation.

The cross-examination of the defense would start the next day. Rob was led away, with only one glance met between them.

———

THAT NIGHT ROB dreamed again of flying over London. When he woke he felt sorry for the place. For the people.

———

IT WAS EXPECTED that the defense would attack him personally in the cross-exam. After all, there was little other use they could make of Dr. Robert MacAulay, with his fame and popular history, but to tear that sympathy down. So his contacts with the prosecution gave him breakfast and conversation with emotional support outsized for what was a professional and legal interaction, and even the snappily-dressed guard at the door suggested he comb his hair once more.

Rob seemed not to recognize the seriousness of the day, but indulged the important men who were trying to help. He even combed his hair for the armed guard, knowing it would make not a bit of difference to the springy covering on his head. He allowed his suit jacket to be adjusted and donned the archaic collar tie, which was somberly striped in academic manner. The tie seemed to him to be as odd an ornament as the horsehair wig that the magistrate had abandoned, but the tie remained even as that headpiece had disappeared.

It was one more collar. He smiled gently at that thought, and the assistant to the prosecutor petted his shoulder, as though she were comforting a large and valued animal. The sharp-featured and sharp-minded woman in her power suit actually crooned to Rob as she led him into the chamber.

Such was his effect on people this day.

The media was prepared for a grueling cross-examination of the former victim and slave. It was certain to be an attention-grabber and the beginning of a jolly series of call-and-response from sides of opinion. Like that of any political conflict. Or sports team.

But it didn't come off. It simply didn't come off as expected, much to the media's mystification.

The defense approached the serene presence in the witness box with subtle conflict in mind and he smiled at her. The woman—and common sense required it be a small woman to assault Rob MacAulay's popularity without coming off the bully—asked of him whether he could be certain that it had been an appropriate action for him to have fled from the first hint that he might be accused of treason. That an intelligent man ought to have stood and confronted the police and explained his innocence.

Rob thought about the question for ten seconds. "Quite likely that would have been more appropriate, Ma'am. But my tenure had been revoked and my wife was dead. I cannot claim I was behaving as an intelligent man at the time."

With that admission, so simply said, he muted her thunder.

The lack of confrontation repeated itself again and again as she approached the weak spots in his two years of fugitive behavior and he admitted each one. Serenely and without much emotion, he admitted himself a fool to have run.

Standing against this, of course, were the videos of the gunfire. She could not attack those as she intended to attack MacAulay. And he sat there for hours under her lash—a whip which was slowly turning limp. A fool who had run and hid and repeatedly been shot at. He offered no explanation for the gunfire and produced no personal theories about the motivations of his assailants. His perch in the witness box was unassailable because he did not defend it. He sat patiently, under the personal gaze of hundreds and the news-stream of countless, and regarded them all with patient, compassionate, purple eyes.

TONIO SCALA, in his high remote chair, wondered why people were not seeing the impossibility of Rob's presence there. The color, the glow, the way all eyes shifted to follow his, as though his old friend was a sort of saint or guru sitting in the box next to the magistrate. His worry of the afternoon before shifted to amazement and then to simple entertainment, watching Rob happen to the court as he had happened to the community by the Sullivan estate in Massachusetts.

But people see what they are prepared to see. It seemed even machines saw what they were prepared to see, or their viewers did. No one rose in the middle of the cross-exam to shout that there was something inexplicable—something magic—sitting there.

And when Rob's cross-exam was over, the defense barrister was sweating and shaking, and Tonio half-expected Rob to ask her if he could help the woman in some manner. That would have been the corker. Tonio even hoped it would happen. But Rob had been prepped by his managers. Prepped by a lifetime in front of a class. He spoke simply, and before the day was done, the long-awaited cross-exam was concluded.

Without theater. Or without theater of any conventional sort. None that could be used for the news-streams.

Tonio stood in place, though the court had not been

recessed. He was so ready to meet Rob again, face to face. But then the defense reserved the right to recall the witness, and he was taken away again. And Father Tonio Scala had a parish to shepherd, many kilometers to the north. As Rob was led away once more, he lifted his face to meet Tonio's eyes. That moment was enough for his two days' investment.

Father Scala travelled home a happy man. He called Sophia Benneli and told her all about it.

———

IONA MACMANUS HAD SPENT FAR LONGER in the hands of the prosecution than had Rob MacAulay. After all, she considered this entire trial something she had started, but her creation was completely out of her control by now. And it wasn't the triumph she had expected.

Yownie had been conflating the trial and Rob in her mind. That made no sense, but she had been hoping to see Rob again, not remembering such an interaction would be impossible.

After her mind-bending time at the Sullivan estate and its peculiar gated community, she was less steady in her thoughts than usual. If she could see Rob again, she might be able to decide if her mind had been playing tricks on her in Massachusetts. Or not.

Glowing? Flying over fences? Impossibly tall? Healing?

And now the legal proceedings were so dreary and prolonged. She was losing interest in punishing Ferris. Losing interest in the politics of Scotland.

But she was maintaining a strong interest in the nature of reality.

How often Rob used that phrase: the nature of reality. And now Yownie looked in her own hotel mirror and wondered what that reality was. She had seen her Dad since coming home, although not Geoff. Could she tell either of them she'd seen something impossible, and would she be believed? Maybe another time she could, because they were special people, but not in the middle of the trial. They would know she'd gone mental.

So Yownie paced her room, drank whisky from the personal fridge, and tried not to think about it at all.

Her own snappily-dressed guard was not friendly.

———

FOR SOME DAYS, Rob had no part in the trial. Neither was he allowed to leave his hotel room and participate in anything else. Nor could he watch the news-streams, lest somehow any further testimony he was required to give might be coloured or warped. The guards did not well understand the difference between political news and that of science, so he looked out the window and once more felt sorry for the people of England going by. Then one of them was carrying a sign, and even before Rob could read it, the man was dragged off and the window obscured.

So Rob entertained himself. Answered certain questions in his mind. And elsewhere. It was working well until the guard came in and seemed to find Rob absent from his hotel room. By chance he appeared from the bathroom and all was well in that quarter. For now.

Rob was not bored any more.

One night he dreamed he was with Thomas, crossing the Atlantic. He was not in a jetliner but in the same Boinger that belonged to Paul Corey. It seemed it was a dream relating to last autumn, and the two were talking about him again. When he woke he didn't remember what they had said exactly—that being the nature of dreams—but it was that old argument about not categorizing Rob MacAulay. But in this dream Thomas turned in his co-pilot's seat and saw Rob behind him. His eyes widened. Paul Corey also turned.

And then he woke up. It was a short dream. But when he woke he knew Thomas was on his way to London.

━━━

THOMAS SULLIVAN DID arrive in London. He went through the same procedure of convincing an assembly of lawyers that he could be trusted on the stand. Prosecution—defense—it had become much the same to Thomas in his many years of involvement with the law over the world. As he went through this almost automatic process he was aware of two things. First, that Rob was a certain direction and distance from him at that moment, and second, that he could no longer put on his accustomed stone-face.

It seemed his stone-face had altered into another thing. He wondered how much of Rob was contagious. He wondered if he himself was glowing.

All of it was distracting.

Breathe.

In his hotel room, with his own snappily-dressed guards, he experimented by closing his eyes and rotating, to see whether Rob's presence remained in the same direction. Was he now a human GPS system? If he was being monitored, did the people monitoring think they had imported someone crazy as an important witness? He decided it didn't matter much. They could not do without him, sane or insane.

He expected his own "cross" to be more brutal than whatever they had given Rob, as he didn't have the public sympathy value. But that didn't matter. He was used to this sort of thing.

Breathe.

22

Visitations

Father Scala had just finished Mass and gone out into the churchyard to feel a sea breeze when Rob appeared beside him. His shock at the apparition died half-formed, because his friend was standing there so utterly normal-looking he might have ambled in from the road. He didn't even seem to glow.

"Father. I hope I didn't scare you," Rob began, and the first thing that struck Tonio Scala was that Rob had gone back to calling him by his religious title.

"Surprised, aye. Last time I saw you, you were being pressed hard in the witness box."

"That's just it. Thomas, Yownie MacManus, and myself are now under lock and key in hotel rooms, going mental with the isolation."

Tonio sat himself down on a convenient tombstone. "But you are all witnesses for the prosecution."

"All the worse. The defense has kept its right to recall any of us, so we're isolated. From the world. And each other."

Tonio looked at Rob standing there in his shirt and blue

jeans, with his hair all over in the wind. "Obviously you're not isolated."

"I've a few moments," Rob said. "I'm supposed to be on the pot, and if their cameras can't find me soon, there may be trouble. So I would like to ask you a favor."

"Ask."

"I'd like you to hear my confession. Wait, now. I'm not trying to use your own faith as a falsity. Not so much as will concern you, I hope. I *will* take an honest confession from you. But I so need someone beside myself and the visiting barristers to talk to. And I think Yownie needs it far worse."

Yownie MacManus? Tonio Scala did not believe the woman had ever been baptized Catholic. But that thought slipped in and out of his head in a moment. "And they'll allow me in?"

The tall figure lifted his head and took in a lungful of the sea breeze. "I can't say. I'm hoping."

And then Rob was gone from the churchyard. There was not even a pop of displaced air.

THOMAS, who was a bit vain about his teleportation control, and confident about his ability to track his own binary star, appeared in Rob's suite soon after Rob got back from the Highlands. Before he could speak, Thomas took him into a loose embrace and led him into the bathroom.

Thomas whispered, "I've been studying things. I don't believe I am bugged. I am a US citizen. It would be too much of a scandal if it got out. And I stated my concerns about my being called to witness overseas a long time before I left.

"And I brought a sweeper. See? It's in my belt buckle. You are likely not bugged simply because you are you. And I've come prepared to sweep your rooms …"

Rob put his hand gently over Thomas's mouth and whispered, "Ah, but my guard at the moment is a man called Colin, who often comes in after a short knock to entertain me with the songs he is writing. Somehow he values my audience. I didn't intend that to happen, but I am, by nature, a teacher, and I listen to people. So, love, I ask you to go back and wait for Tonio."

Thomas listened carefully to Rob, while he remembered the outlines of the hotel bathroom. It had no clear window to the street. It was the same with his own bath. "Tonio?"

Rob's hair had grown out and half covered his eyes. At the moment they were green. "Tonio. And if necessary, can you express an interest in the Franciscan Catholic Faith?"

Thomas nodded, thinking hard, and he touched Rob's face. "Have you seen Yownie? I feel her. It's gotta be sheer murder for her to be so ..."

"I will be seeing her. For a moment. That is more difficult, because this entire trial is her show, you understand?"

"Not yours, Rob?"

"Not even a wee bit. Please go back now."

And Thomas did.

━━━

IT WAS NOT forty-eight hours later that Tonio Scala drove into the Inverness Airport, expecting to find some sort of charter flight waiting to take him to London. What he did not expect was a lanky, balding Australian with an accent so overblown he could scarcely understand the man who was waiting for him by the long-term parking.

"G'Day, G'Day! You must be the fella Tommy said was coming south with me today."

Tonio looked up at the man: pale and ruddy, baby-faced and balding. "Tommy? That would be the baby in Massachusetts?" He felt he was not getting his lines right in some sort of theatrical event. A spy movie, possibly.

"The baby? Naw, that's me old mate himself, the newly begotten Sullivan, Padre." And the tall fellow put his hand between Tonio's shoulder blades and steered him through the disorganized halls of the private plane airport toward what was the most impressive private plane Tonio had ever seen, let alone ridden in. Up the stairs and into something even more impressive. And empty. When Tonio Scala drifted toward the small rows of seating, the man pressed him gently and inescapably toward the cockpit, where he found himself ensconced in the co-pilot's seat.

The complexity of the lights and buttons was daunting. The expanse of window around him, inspiring. Tonio strapped himself in.

"I'm Paul," said his pilot, the jolly, bouncing accent fading to one more realistic in a moment. "I'm going to get you to Heathrow. What you're doing there, I don't need to know."

Tonio turned to Paul, to tell him he wasn't doing anything that required secrecy, but was just going down to hear confession from an old friend. Remembering the nature of the sacrament of confession, however, he held his tongue. And then the engines started.

Paul handed him a pair of noise-cancelling headphones, so the roar of jets turned into something like silence. Soft rain spattered against the plexiglass wall, and soon after lift-off, the rain was gone, leaving no smears on the window. It was like going through a car wash. Tonio was looking down at a layer of shining cloud when the pilot reached over and pressed a button on the headphones. He could hear the man's voice. And, in the background, he could hear ground control.

"How are you doing over there, mate?"

"Ach! Well. Very well. Had a wee scare when we hit the cloud. I've always been in the seats down along the aisle, before, but this is something to remember!"

Paul Corey looked at him. "I thought you'd sound Italian."

Tonio could see the man's mouth move, but that movement didn't seem connected to the sound he heard. "I don't properly know what I am," he said to Paul Corey.

Corey's smile stretched from one earpiece to the other. "Welcome to the club."

The trip was thrilling. And short.

─────

THE CONFESSION, however, was ridiculously long. Rob MacAulay had not been to confession since before the death of his parents, which meant twenty-five years. After half-an-hour sitting across from Rob in chairs over a small table before a window that had been made opaque, and listening to the list of large sins and small misdemeanors Rob had assembled, the priest broke into the monologue.

"We don't do confession in that manner much anymore, Rob. In fact, it's been quite a while since we have done."

Rob MacAulay looked widely at Father Scala. Today, his eyes were mostly green. "What is it that you *do* do, then?" Dr. MacAulay waited for instruction.

And they had a pleasant chat for another half hour, which ended with the both of them fingering absently the fringes at opposite ends of the priest's purple stole. And Tonio let Rob take his hand and send them into the bathroom of Thomas's hotel suite. That mundane jump, for the priest, was both simple and astonishing. His knees gave out.

It was Thomas who grabbed him up when he began to fall forward, as Rob had forgotten that Tonio hadn't flown with him before. And both Rob and Thomas shushed his yelp of laughter as he stared into the small mirror, seeing the three men, with their three different heights, reflected. And then came a three-handed bounce into yet another drearily identical room where Iona MacManus was waiting, as nervous as Tonio had been. Thomas and Tonio remained in that room, while Rob bounced Yownie back to his room for just a moment. She returned with her hand over her mouth, and Tonio thought she was about to be sick.

She was laughing. "Is this a side-effect of your procedure?" Tonio whispered up into his tall friend's ear. "Getting the giggles?"

⊏⊐

"THERE COULD BE WORSE," said Rob. The two men were back where they had started, and alone but for each other. The stole still lay on the table like a limp purple snake.

Tonio looked around him at the blank hotel room. He felt a strong desire to tear the screening off the window. "And what did you need me for, in all this?"

Rob shrunk into himself and the red patterns began in his cheeks once more. "I'm so sorry, Tonio. I needed a pattern. An algorithm. An 'and gate,' perhaps."

"What does that mean?"

"Without you with me I couldn't be sure I wouldn't be interrupted. I had never moved Yownie before. Nor you. Now we all can do it, if we choose, and we are not really prisoners."

Father Antonio Scala wrapped his stole into his small bag. "You're saying I can go popping back and forth now, as you do? As Thomas does?"

The eyes were now purely purple and Rob's face did shine. "If you study at it. If you're open to it. But it was not for the sake of any conspiracy that I asked you here. None other than as an act of kindness. This has been hard on them, and I don't know how long we'll be kept here."

"Harder on them than it was for you to wear the collar?"

Rob smiled broadly. "Ah, so much so. I wasn't alone, then."

⊏⊐

THE TRIAL of Andrew Ferris dragged on, and the prime witnesses were kept isolated. Even when the unending civil disturbances in China grabbed the news-streams again, and when Russia threatened, in Britain the trial remained the daily headline. The prosecution came to visit their encapsulated witnesses more rarely as the summer ripened and began to pass.

Donald MacManus was dropped by the defense, as the public hue and cry about his health overwhelmed his need to be recalled, and what public sympathy the defense had had was stripped from them by this treatment of an aged witness. Still, neither he nor his grandson Geoffrey were allowed private audience with Iona MacManus.

23

Escape

I t was just as well that few visitors came, because the three witnesses were often not in their hotel rooms at all. They were on an island far to the north and west, where the people spoke a different language. Thomas was never certain when they came to the shores of South Uist—or was it Eriskay?—that it was really the island as it existed presently. The sea level seemed not to be as high as he had expected. The people ignored them unless addressed personally, and seemed impossibly unconcerned with the strangers who appeared and played in the tide-pools, and sometimes watched as the long evening light, grey, green, and purple, stretched shadows into the dark hills behind them.

Only two at a time could visit the island, because someone had to be back in London, ready to send a message of alarm in case these idylls were about to be interrupted. And it worked best if that sentry wasn't Rob MacAulay himself. And the Catholic priest Tonio Scala was often there, in that profoundly un-canonical setting. Scala clearly enjoyed his own relief from the stresses of life by his visits to somewhere, some-when in the Hebrides.

Thomas began to think of the place as Tir na n'Og, although the only fairy presence was Rob himself, who was more interested in explaining the Latin names of the various starfish and anemones than he was in uttering mysticisms.

When Yownie was the visitor, she sketched. Thomas could not see her sketching, because he was never there at the same time, but Rob would display choice little bits of paper to Thomas. Papers he kept in his suit jacket. These sketches were not all of landscape, or of invertebrates. Sometimes there were human figures in them, and Thomas never asked Rob, although he did wonder, whether these people were the dead.

24

Yownie in Battle

When the defense released her from possibility of recall and so she was free, Yownie discovered that her father had spent long weeks in hospital, diagnosed with COPD as well as his recurring prostate problems. She was enraged, or at least as enraged as her strange summer had left her with the ability to be. That he was now home and feeling much better only made her own position worse. She had been in fairyland and not been there for him.

Geoffrey had been. The three of them had long chats in his rooms above the rugby field, and Donald MacManus was far more interested in comforting his daughter than in discussing his own health. His continued anxiety, however, was quietly betrayed by his new habit of reflexively checking the fingertip blood oxygen meter every few minutes. The man tried to be discreet about it. Each time he glanced at the flickering red numbers, though, a tiny shard of guilt pierced his daughter. Yownie looked out the window and saw by the pattern of shadows that she had missed the long light entirely, and that it was well on its way to becoming autumn.

She felt a slight resentment toward Rob, who had made

her confinement so different from solitary confinement, and therefore one more thing she couldn't say to her own family. If he didn't know what was happening in the wide world when he took them out into his own slice of another world, then he should have known.

As she thought these things, drinking black tea and staring at the shadows on the ball-field, she realized she was having the resentments people normally felt toward God. And whatever Rob MacAulay was, or had become, he had never shown any sign of thinking himself to be God.

She was ashamed.

She prowled about and looked into the local where the writers of Splint used to congregate. As Splint had no physical address, it was the best way to get back in touch. As she waited there, on a Friday afternoon, she used her machine to catch up on every issue she had missed. The trial was, of course, the running news, and she herself was being treated reverently in her absence. Yownie knew that being treated reverently by her colleagues was one short step from being put on a shelf. She had no intention of letting herself be put on a shelf. She thought she might announce her return with a sketch, showing the witnesses who had been put into isolation as so many chained people, wearing collars like the one Ferris had had put on Rob just about a year ago.

And then she found Fran had already done such a sketch, or had used someone else who could wield a drawing pen do so, while she was locked in the hotel. Francine, the same bitch who had tried to interview Rob under the guise of representing Yownie herself. Becoming angry at Fran was just the right-sized anger in which she could slide herself into her accustomed life. But no one from Splint showed that afternoon, and as she wasn't much of a drinker, she used the time to text Fred, the fellow who now had the rotating job of editor of the 'zine.

It was easy to reach Fred, but not so easy to chat with him, as he said he was busy. When she asked him what business he was busy with, he replied, *hard 2 say. Talk soon.* And he cut her off.

Yownie was steaming. So were the windows of the place, because it was raining outside and the weather was already cooling from summer. She was in a corner by the entrance-way, with no one at the table but her. An ale half-drunk and a few bills under it. She remembered those days when she hadn't known so exactly what the news contained, but had at least felt a part of it, and she wished hard for the fellowship she had known with her two friends on their private island, whilst a third stood guard.

And she found it—not the island—but the fellowship. She discovered that she was sliding off some piece of stuffed furniture and hitting the carpet with her bum in a room she had known, briefly, just one season ago. One hand was clutched tightly around her tablet, as her eyes darted around and found Thomas Sullivan, who was craning his neck to see her over the top of the sofa. "Feeling pissed-off, are we?" he asked.

Yownie was speechless.

"You're not the only one. Rob's been in a foul temper for days. He won the Nobel, you see."

She let her machine fall gently onto the woolen rug. Outside these windows, the weather was clear, but the maples were beginning to think about turning color. She edged away from the seat of the Queen Anne chair, because it was beginning to stick into her upper back. "I know. That happened over a month ago. Everything about the prizes has been skewed since they had the assassinations of the winners and switched the giving of the prizes to summer, leaving the old day as a memorial.

"The acceptance speech was a real zinger too, with the woman from Syria and the little girl. Talking about teaching arithmetic and the equations and human trafficking and the inability of Rob to make it to his own prize."

Thomas got up and walked around the sofa. Sat himself on the rug beside her. "That's just it. Rob had no intention of accepting the Nobel. Never had. But he was completely unaware of the whole thing, and now what can he say, with his little Algebra student and his physics colleague supporting him so passionately? Little Breton with her simple statement that when she met him she could still see the scars from the collar around his neck. I watched it. Brought down the house."

Yownie looked around the pleasant, cluttered room. She thought she might cry and didn't know why. "And where's our personal fairy-man now?"

"I'm here," said Rob, who sat with them, making a triangle on the rug.

Yownie glanced into his green-purple eyes, which were almost hidden under his over-grown hair. "Sorry I called you that. I know you hate …"

Rob MacAulay moved his head back and forth on his long neck. "I'm not as particular about things as I used to be."

Thomas snickered. "S'true. He even puts his coins in his pocket at random. But I was telling her about the Nobel."

"Even that." He was looking closely at Yownie, her jacket, her wellies, her tablet. "This is the first time you traveled alone."

"I didn't even mean to. I was just …"

"Upset?" offered Thomas.

"Feeling strongly, some way, or another," added Rob. "That's how it begins."

"And where does it lead then?"

The tall man sighed and bent his head forward, looking at Yownie through the screen of his hair. "To me. So far it's always led to me."

And then Yownie did start to cry. In anger at she didn't even know what.

SHE RETURNED to Edinburgh the same way she had left, although with more experienced help. She was much embarrassed about her ego and its breakdown, but was not without resources. She had an interview with Breton Kaye, and an idea for her own personal memoir of isolation. The interview would have to be considered a podcast instead of the face-to-face it had been, which meant any sketches accompanying it would be described as imaginary. Yownie was good with imaginary. Tony had become fond of the sound of her own voice, after Sweden. It all worked out. And Rob shepherded her home to her father's door. So Yownie had one more to and fro in the world of magic. She called it magic now.

To herself.

25

A Summoning

"and I … am a spirit, a word, a thing of air and darkness, and I can no more help what I am doing than a reed can help the wind of God blowing through it."
—Mary Stewart

The trees were vivid along the trail one day just a few weeks later when Thomas and MacBride followed Rob and Kinsman up to the ridge. There had been cold dry days and the birch was yellow and the maples all the colors possible to maples. It was what was called an "old-fashioned" New England Autumn.

Rob wasn't leading by choice. Thomas had a strong desire to keep his binary in sight today, and Kinsman did not need coaxing to lead. Their light helmets had communication devices now, so they had no need to shout.

"Did you dream last night?" Thomas asked Rob casually as they cantered uphill.

"I did. I usually do. And yourself?"

"Not that I recall. But I have a reason for asking."

Kinsman slowed to a trot. "Because you care about me?"

"Because you disappeared again. Not just from the bed. From the house."

Thomas saw Rob's head droop forward. "That again. Just what do you want me to say about it? I have dreams. Not conspiracies."

They crossed a sharp left bend in the trail and Kinsman's sleek coat shone in sunlight.

"And what did you dream last night?"

Rob sighed. "It was no pleasant dream. I dreamed about nuclear warheads again. About Russia. But then, aren't we all, now?"

It was on the tip of Thomas's tongue to say that they didn't all dream about such things and disappear from the bed, but he was too aware he was in danger of becoming a scold. "And you dreamed about—about them going off?" He felt MacBride sidle under him and took a deep, slow breath.

"Not at all. That would have been some sort of nightmare, wouldn't it have been? It was one of those dreary, repetitive dreams where one has a task to do but can't get it done. Do you know what I mean?"

Thomas thought about his own dream-history, which was a mangled mess of things done and not better done, extending for thirty years and across matters ranging from saving human lives to ruining his own. "Dreary is the word for it, Rob. Sometimes I think those dreams exist simply to keep us from waking up. For the body's own reasons. Whatever."

Thomas passed under a leafy branch, which caused him to clear his eyes with his left hand. MacBride tilted to the side, noticed, and gave a small, apologetic snort.

Ahead, it seemed that the dark horse and man had gone into the sun, for as Thomas's eyes blinked repeatedly, the black expanded into all the colors of an oil slick. They were now moving slowly forward. "What I dreamed is that I was holding the powders of plutonium in the Russian warheads. In my hands …"

"God!"

"It was only a dream, Thomas. I was holding this heavy, but small mass of powder in my hands, and I was aware of the existence of the other part of it—the part that must never be brought into contact with it, just below me."

Now they were both in sunlight, and approaching the top of a ridge. "And you were how? In a space suit? With the pieces of the shielding unscrewed or unbolted all around you? How ..."

"I was in a dream, not a space-suit. Don't make more of this than what I've said, love. And holding the stuff in my hand I understood that it was just stuff. Not the ingredients of nightmare, but just a physical element. Much simpler, actually, than the leaves of this bush, here."

Thomas had his vision back now so he could see Rob's long fingers snapping against leaves of some encroaching bush: probably a blackberry or another thing with complex, serrated leaves. The water liberated into the air went into the brief colors of a rainbow, but Rob was still talking. "And as I understood the simplicity of the thing's make-up, I also understood how the lepton and baryon fields could be so simply changed. It was only a matter—I shouldn't use that word in this context—it was an issue of changing the pattern."

They rode on into opening of the trail into the meadow. Neither horse seemed eager to break into a faster gait. Kinsman's ears were backwards and MacBride's stiffly forward, as though both horses were listening to Rob's dream.

"I did tremendous damage to Kinsman trying to use him for the source of energy for transformation. I learned, from that moment of shifting direction in travel, that there are more and better ways of gaining energy for transformation." Rob lifted one hand from its resting place on the horse's withers. "Call it Hawking radiation. Call it anything. And besides, I must remind myself that this was all a dream."

Thomas felt that every hair on his body was standing

straight up. But he kept his mouth closed, and MacBride continued to clop forward.

"And so, in the dream, I altered the construction of the plutonium into something more stable. All the way into lead, actually. And when I was done, from a sense of … of balance, I suppose, I altered that of the other half of the warhead also. Although that really meant nothing towards disabling the horrible thing.

"And here is where the dream entered the part where such dreams become wearisome. The same situation, with small changes, kept recurring to me for what seemed like all night. The warhead, in different placements, fittings, orientation, kept presenting itself to me and I had to repeat the same simple actions each time. There was a sense it would never end.

"And actually," Rob said, and without the helmet speakers, Thomas could have never heard him, "I am tired today. All over, tired."

Rob proved the reality of his statement by falling asleep on the back of his horse, who carried him carefully back down the easiest of the trails leading homewards, through the glorious autumn woods.

THOMAS WASN'T LOOKING FORWARD to an argument on the subject of dreams and their nature. Not with Rob. Instead he placed an emergency request to one of the closest of the technical people in the area, who might possess a primitive Geiger counter. To his intense relief, he found no more than background radiation coming from Rob's body as he slept like a log in their bed. No radiation, even from his hands.

So a dream was really a dream then. Whatever that meant. It didn't mean Thomas ceased to worry.

THE NEXT DAY was busy for Thomas, as he was trying to catch up on all he'd missed on his private news sources, as well as pay those bills that weren't on automatic. He heard Rob clicking on the piano keyboard at the other end of the house, being quiet and considerate. Yet Thomas would have liked to hear everything that Rob came out with in his musical studies. Especially now that he could tolerate equal temperament. He approached music so much like math that Thomas found it amusing. And on the piano, unlike the banjo, he showed possibilities.

But, no, that was not his business today. Work. Read the damn depressing news. And breathe.

Later he walked into the kitchen to get a bite to eat, and spotted there a note on the table, on a sticky-pad in Rob's careful, square block print. BACK SOON.

Thomas hadn't heard the car. Then he snickered at his own thought. Of course he hadn't heard the car. And the rain was spattering the windows. The brilliant colors were filtered through a grey sky.

Thomas needed a workout. He had become spoiled, having a workout partner at his beck and call. He would leave a call for old Kyan Sensei. He changed and entered the mat-room, and looked out through the smear of rain at the same red tree under which they'd first met Tony Kaye. He lifted his arms out in a careful stretch and brought them together as he bowed. Exhaled.

26

Father Antonio Scala, F.C.C

F ather Tonio Scala had just performed the sacrament of baptism on one Isabella McGrath, ten days old. She had been a healthy, darling creature, and had wiggled rather than cried at the drops on her head and the sight of the bright colors on the ceiling over the old piscine. Everyone was happy. Of all the sacraments, baptism was the sunniest and least complicated. Families tended to want their baptisms conservatively done, with lots of lace. The wee mite could scarcely complain about the style of the thing. Unlike a marriage.

He saw everyone out, took off the ceremonial garb, and sat himself at the kitchen table with his old tablet to read the news.

And that just took the jollity right out of his heart. Little Isabella was being sent out into a world where today's news was that of the furor of the week, which was the mutual threat of warfare down the Siberian coast, between Russia and China. All the loving parents and godparents of Isabella could not stand between her and the world's insanity.

Tonio remembered when he had just been about to take

his vows, and the Middle East was exploding, both into itself and outward into the other nations of the world. That had ended, if acts of feuding revenge ever do end, with the black joke spreading that overpopulation would not be the problem they had so long thought. Tonio himself had been then lit with a confidence that both prayer and good works could make a difference. That his path was clear in this matter.

Twenty years later now, why did it seem so different to him? Was it simply age on his part, or was the situation, with him locked in Scotland, and Sophia? Was the unstated but real civil war in China, and Russia—well, simply being Russia once again—really as frightening as it seemed to him?

And what did he have now? Prayer, most certainly, but his capacity for good works had been reduced to asking for alms from a poor parish.

And now, he had a friend.

He shut off such thoughts. Rob MacAulay was not a bag to be squeezed until it was empty. Of all people Tonio knew, Rob could easiest be squeezed past the point of survival. And he was not going to be the one to call him, even to discuss his fears.

"Why not?" said Rob, scraping a chair back from the other side of the table. "What are friends for, if not to talk to?"

Tonio sprang half out of his chair. "You can read my mind?"

Rob's smile was broad. "Not at all. You were mumbling to yourself."

Tonio pressed back his thinning hair with both hands. "Ach. It's living alone that does it." Then he looked up at his friend again. Rob looked more peculiar than ever with his hair grown out in all directions. In a way, though, that drooping veil seemed to fit his new identity better than the academic cut. "So, then, Rob. Why are you here?"

Rob tilted his head and shrugged. "I didn't say I can't

sometimes feel you. If your own feelings are strong enough. And it seems it was my mistake …"

"Nah." Tonio tapped the tablet forcefully, which did nothing but cause the screen to reset. "It's the news. The world news."

Rob reached out one long arm and touched that single tapping finger with one of his own. In that instant of touch Tonio was aware in some sense that Rob did also know about the world news, and the dread.

Rob did still, slightly, glow. A momentary wild thought ran through the priest's head. It must be easier for Thomas Sullivan to keep track of his spouse in the dark.

"The news, from day to day, will drive you to despair. If you let it."

"Now that's the sort of thing I'm supposed to be saying to my parishioners."

Rob reached back and laced his hands behind his neck, stretching left and right. Sighing. The kitchen was brightly lit with the late light of the day. Every bit of dust in the air was visible between the two men. Tonio could see the line of the North Sea behind Rob's back. "And then to whom do *you* say it? Surely a priest is supposed to have his own confessor. It can't just end in a boiling in your own head."

"That gets harder and harder. There are so few of us here. Why? Have you come to take my confession?"

All the boxy white teeth shone. "I wouldn't dream of it. But that doesn't mean you can't talk. Who would I repeat it to, if I wanted?"

Tonio shoved the irritating tablet to the center of the table and laced his hand together in front of him. He paused for a good long while, and the two just sat there.

"Rob. Do you ever wonder for what purpose you were created?"

Rob's head, still locked in his hands, bounced in amusement. "I've spent too much of my life looking outwards at things to be good at navel-gazing now. Or did you mean the 'you' as in people in general?"

"No. I meant you. And 'navel-gazing' is really a pejorative dismissal of a necessary ..."

"I know it. And meant it to sound so. Because I can't get anywhere thinking about that now. Put yourself in my place. How would you categorize yourself if you were me? Taxonomically? I've got no one to compare myself against. No biological ancestors. No ... descendants.

"But what about you, Tonio? You have both a calling and a great respect for introspection. Why are you here?"

The priest sleeked his hair back again. "When I was young I did this sort of thinking a lot. I didn't intend to be a priest attending a congregation in Scotland made up mostly of my own countrymen. I had great and passionate ideas about social justice. Now I just do what is appropriate from day to day."

Rob's eyes widened hugely from behind the dark fringe. "Perfectly put. From day to day. From night to night."

Tonio looked for hope, or even inspiration in that gaze, and found something. "And you don't worry about the state of the world? The threats from Old China to Russia and back again. The nasty talk of both of them against the rest of us?"

Rob lowered his head and smiled. "I spent years in some version of that pain. As you well know. Now I have this feeling —hard to explain—that maybe I am doing something about it. As much as one fellow can do."

Tonio thought briefly. "Well your theory changes everything. And that is certainly all any man can be expected to do for humanity. It's the time before the politics of the world adjust to it that—that scares me."

Rob leaned forward. He could lean across more than half the table. "The politics of the world will *never* adjust to the theory. I'm not sure politics has even adjusted to Isaac

Newton, let alone … Never mind. I was talking about my dreams."

"Your what?"

"Dreams, I said, and I didn't mean aspirations. I meant the things your head does to you whilst you're asleep."

And slowly, gathering his thoughts, Rob described the series of dreams he had been having, beginning with his memories of flying above the streets of London, and knowing of Thomas's flight to England, and ending with the endless, wearisome dream of holding plutonium in his hand and changing its structure.

Tonio listened, slowly shaking his head, but not in denial.

"And though he thought I was asleep, I know that I so frightened Thomas by telling of these that he came into our room with a Geiger counter and made certain I wasn't radioactive. I think I'm worrying the poor man too much. I ought to have kept my trap shut."

"But a body can't do that. You were telling me as much a minute ago. And you're not worrying me, so go on."

And Rob did, describing how in his latest dream it occurred to him somehow that it made no sense to stop with Russia but had slipped over to other countries. How it had occurred to him that changing the substance of the trans-uranic elements, as though he were cleaning sponges in his hand, was stupidly inefficient, like spinning yarn with the fingers. Rob tried to explain his "spinning wheel," in which he was busily turning gold into straw, but gave it up as a bad job.

"And you plan to cancel every nuclear warhead in the world?" Tonio didn't intend for his words to go up at the end as they did, but it didn't seem Rob noticed.

"I don't 'plan' anything, old friend. I just have dreams."

"I like your dreams," said Tonio. "I wish I had similar dreams, however boring they are at the time. But I'm wondering whether they will have to stop with plutonium warheads, when there are so many other ways in which man seems to be tormenting man, and indeed all of nature. Poison gas, land mines. If you can dream away one Armageddon, then ..."

There came a knock on the door and Tonio looked away for a moment. When he looked back there was no one sitting in the chair.

Come back soon, he said, but this time, not aloud.

———

YOWNIE BEGAN her blog on the day of the first verdicts with the headline: *Now that THAT is over*. She paid no more attention to her role as a combination Woodward and Bernstein. She had come to understand that any public role was like that of the queen in *Alice*: you had to run fast to stay in place, and the more important you had been to the public eye, the faster you became obsolete. So her article was all about the future. About economics and the financial benefit reaped for Scots in staying with, or leaving Britain alone. It was a mild article, compared with a lot of what she had written a year before. And the accompanying sketch showed only herself, from the back, sitting on a hillside looking down on Hadrian's Wall—one of the famous bits that hadn't crumbled. She cribbed a lot of what she said from what Rob MacAulay had told her, and it had little of Scottish Nationalism about it.

But the sketch was grand. It was an off-take of the famous map of the US, done from the view of New York City, with the rest of the country being only the tail wagged by the New York Dog. (Only hers would have to be, of course, the Scotty.)

She tracked down Fred, at his flat. She thrust a wee-drive into his hand. He wasn't happy about taking it. "Fran gave orders," he began, and she countered.

"No one on Splint gives orders. That's the way I remember it. If it has so changed to the bone, then I'll be starting my own competing 'zine. Think, Fred, on which side of that you want to be." Then she left the door, for she had never exactly been invited in—just her hand with the drive. And she waited.

Eleven hours later the new edition was available to the public.

━━━

THE DAY FERRIS was found guilty of manslaughter, conspiracy to attempt murder, and various other crimes, Thomas Sullivan read the news with other things on his mind. The British news was not even easy to find amid the headlines.

He wondered if once he would have been full of energy to involve himself in the catastrophes occurring in the Western Pacific. Not in the basic standoff between the remains of the old Red Guard and the country that was increasingly called, in the US, "The Children of Putin." He had never been such a Don Quixote as that. But once he might have thought of dashing in somehow to rescue someone. He wasn't even sure how, or if he was reading his past self correctly.

But now he was more concerned with affairs at home. Not his country's isolationism, but his own. His role as the binary of Rob MacAulay. Hell. Binary. These days he felt more like an orbiting satellite.

These days Rob slept so long. And when he slept sometimes he was there and sometimes he wasn't. Thomas spent those hours in meditation and in workout, and still did not feel centered.

It was Rob, who woke at ten in the morning, bright and bushy-tailed for once, who suggested they go for an arena ride. It had been a long time since the white horse and the black had done their dance. And the white head and the dark.

The horses were certainly up for it. MacBride had never minded the close work of arena jumping or even the dressage that drove some of the horses nuts. And Kinsman, since his brush with death, was even more responsive to Rob.

"Let's start them slowly, Rob. They're out of shape. Especially for this." It was so easy now to communicate with the intelligent helmets. They didn't have to wait for a time to pass together and shout out telegraphed messages.

"Kinsman certainly is," answered Rob. "No offence to Mr. O'Brien in his exercising him whilst I was away. But I think you'll find MacBride hasn't lost his edge."

Thomas snorted and went over a series of cavaletti. "You're the one who keeps saying he's such an old geezer."

Kinsman went over a small jump, and, as always, over-jumped it through sheer arrogance. "I said old, Tommy. Not geriatric."

Rob knew that calling him Tommy sometimes was a poke in the ribs to Thomas. So he must be in a rare old mood today. "So how old is old?" He asked MacBride for some flying lead changes. "As old as me, maybe?"

"Older, I imagine," Rob said placidly, and Thomas called his horse to a halt.

"Okay. Enough of this."

Rob pulled Kinsman in beside him. The black horse was reluctant to stop.

"So then, how old is Kinsman?" asked Thomas, as calmly as he could manage. "Old enough to run for President?"

Rob smiled broadly. He still grinned like a horse. "No, though I doubt he'd do worse than some who have. The records have him at seventeen, which is old enough to drive, at least."

"So what are you saying about my horse?"

Rob dropped his head forward, and the bush of his hair concealed much of his face. He fiddled with the reins. "I'm saying that MacBride is something like me. There. I've said it." He pushed Kinsman forward. Thomas followed.

"You mean he's not actually human? I'm sorry, that's not what I meant to say...."

Rob was giggling. "About MacBride or about me? It doesn't matter anymore, Thomas. I'm not offended. I just thought you might want to know. He's your partner and you care for him. I thought you would like to know he's not likely to fall apart beneath you." Rob let Kinsman out into a canter that became a gallop around the ring. MacBride stretched out and kept with him. Moved up beside him.

"Say more," said Thomas, in the old voice he could still use to scare people. Rob grinned wider.

"I don't know more, Thomas. Except that I think he's always a horse. I wasn't certain for a while. But if he can change shape I have seen no sign of it."

Thomas looked at the familiar broad withers under his hands, which were slightly freckled with black spots. "Why would you think he could change shape?"

"Well, he can jump. I mean, flinch. Translocate, or whatever you call it. And he didn't learn it from me. I've searched my mind carefully. I never touched him during the process. Nor has he even been in contact with Kinsman. He could probably always do it."

Thomas Sullivan looked at the ears of his horse, which were pointed back at him, the way a good horse's should be when listening to his rider. Listening to his rider. On impulse Thomas said, "Hello?"

MacBride whickered.

Shortly after that, Thomas called an end to the exercise. They let the horses out in the biggest pasture, where stallions usually weren't allowed. Let O'Brien make something of that. If he dared. Besides, it was autumn, and MacBride had always been a gentleman.

When Thomas was watching, of course.

"SO WHO *IS* ordinary around here, then? Besides me."
Thomas came out of the shower drying his hair.

"You are most certainly not ordinary," answered Rob, who
was already clean and dressed. "But if you mean who can do
these—things—who was found under a bush, let's say; well,
how in God's good name should I know?"

Thomas sat on the bed next to Rob and asked the day's
big question. "So what did you dream last night?"

And Rob told him.

___

YOWNIE'S COLUMN went down a treat, and in a week she
was back in harness at Splint. But before there could be any
probe into Scottish opinion on separatism, it all became back-
screen news, as the Chinese Hard-liners (Old-liners? No one
had settled on what to call them) went head to head against
Russian claims to the Pacific Coast. And the world watched to
see what the US, with its own faltering economy, would do.

What it did was dither, of course, being of such a size, and
with a House and Senate that hated each other and a president who spoke unheard. But dithering for thirty-six hours
was not such a long span of time. And Russia sent its first loft
of missiles southward even before the dithering was analyzed.

According to satellite scans, none of the missiles were
nuclear in nature, but the message was received all the same
by China. More missiles were exchanged, and if the warheads
weren't nuclear, the people behind them were.

Yownie sat in her loft in Edinburgh and could only wonder
where Geoffrey was at the moment. Where was her son? It
was the sort of moment when she had to know where her
son was.

___

FATHER TONIO SCALA was sitting in his dusty kitchen with the wind blowing against his window. He knew he shouldn't keep following the satellite feeds, but he seemed to be helpless to stop. He wondered where Sophia Benneli was.

His first posting after taking final vows had been Korea, on the coast. The people had been then just starting to repair their sad united country, and where he was posted was not exactly a Franciscan Catholic Chapel. It had not been any sort of chapel, really. Just a scattering of efforts against starvation, and helping folks to find relations so long lost. It had been not too different from his current position, next to wild water and poor countryside. But he had been so young. Burning with energy.

He used his Geo skills, which he hadn't kept up to date. (But then whose were, really, when the technology slid by so fast now?) And there it was, in the little bay, which he remembered more by shape than name. His Korean had never been more than rudimentary. And his fingers began to shake so that the touch screen kept bouncing in and out of scale.

There was the same old building, and there were people in it. And torn up land on both sides and scurrying figures with long weapons. No voice-over accompanied the visuals. This was simply a satellite feed, and so no time delay either. On one of his trembling touches to the screen he backed out enough to see two huge ships pointed toward the place. US? He couldn't know. Tonio disciplined his fingers and pressed in, and in, and he could see the doorway of the place, which hadn't changed in almost twenty years. And there was an old, bald man in the door, holding his hands to each side of the door to keep people from leaving the room. And by sweet Jesus, he knew the old man.

He thought about Rob, who had been there so recently, and who seemed to have so much power to help. And about the exchange of missiles. All dud missiles, so the journalists said. He thought about calling to Rob, and then remembered the last thing Rob had said before the knock at the door. Warheads being simple. Everything else, however ...

The heart of man was not simple. So Tonio called on God instead.

ROB AND THOMAS were also watching the news, although for them it was the middle of the night. As always, when machines were involved, Rob let Thomas do the driving. They bounced from image to image, print font to print font, almost faster than Rob could follow. Occasionally Thomas gave commentary.

Rob spared a glance at Thomas and saw again the cold and contained man he had first met. Hardly more than a year ago. White and icy.

White and icy seemed so appropriate at the moment that Rob didn't attempt to touch, to interfere.

"I can't predict what the ships are going to do anyway," Thomas was mumbling. "Can't even tell who is giving them orders." He spared a glance at Rob. "And they have small scale nuclear weapons, of course."

Rob didn't have time to answer, because Thomas answered himself. "But no reason to think they'd use them. And you didn't dream anything about conventional weapons, did you?"

"I don't even know how they work," Rob answered, lacing and unlacing his hands and feeling vaguely ashamed of himself.

Thomas's stone face cracked a bit. Almost smiled. "Don't worry, Rob. Not mistaking you for the Almighty. If there is one." The expression on his face faded. "There had better *not* be," he added in a tone of peculiar vengefulness, as though ready to take Jehovah to task.

Rob felt pulled. Not by Thomas's words. Not even by the

images, or the sleeplessness. Just pulled somehow. He followed his binary's advice and just breathed.

"Please put us back, Thomas. Back on the coast."

Thomas looked sharply at him. "You want direct feed?"

"Whatever. Just please do it."

Muttering that there was a lot of coast in the Western Pacific, Thomas did so.

———

TONIO NEVER SPOKE to his personal concept of God without feeling answered. He was lucky that way, although almost always the answers were of the sort that implies, *That's what I've given you a brain for.*

This time his answer seemed more direct. He remembered being carried from pillar to post by his strange friend. Being used as a conduit to help a few people survive their imprisonment. And having been told that once he had "travelled" with Rob he was somehow now able to do it himself. It had not even occurred to him to try.

Everything had a reason, although Tonio Scala was neither so stupid nor self-important to think the reasons revolved around himself. Certainly he believed there had been a reason he had happened to be there when Rob needed him, as a fugitive in his own country. All that had happened between them since, while chaotic, was not random.

Rob could evidently disarm nuclear warheads. Tonio couldn't. Rob had been "found under a bush." Tonio wasn't. But still, they were more similar than dissimilar. They had hearts.

Tonio scraped his kitchen chair back over the floorboards so quickly it fell on its back. And he stood there, hearing the wind from the North Sea knock against his window and prayed hard. Without words. He prayed for the old man in the doorway. He prayed for the whole suffering world.

And there came a feeling of movement and the air was different and the wind was different and his ears were battered by people chattering and weeping in a language he no longer remembered. His balance was off, and in order to keep standing, he found himself holding on to a wooden wall with one hand, and the arm of someone or other with his other hand. He shouted at the old man, "Do you remember me?" Damn it, what had they called the man? "Ryan. Do you remember me?"

The old Korean man looked at Tonio and looked through him with such an understandable expression of overwhelm that no words need have been said. In any language. Carefully, while still holding on to the arm of the woman he had grabbed, he asked slowly, in English. "Where is the nearest safe place?"

He thought in another moment he'd be shouting at the poor fellow, as people do when they can't be understood and hope to eliminate the problem through decibels. But old Ryan said, in clear English. "The nearest refugee camp is fifty kilometers away. Too far. Too far."

Tonio let go the wall and used his right hand to touch the man he once had known. And as he touched him, he suddenly knew the camp: the look of it, the position, the history. For a short moment he thought *this is what it must be to be Rob*, but he hadn't time for more of that. The woman was holding a child in her other hand, and both were weeping.

Tonio closed his eyes and opened his arms. In the next moment they were in that camp. His ears popped. The woman kept weeping. He let go of them, called for strength, and returned to the old man.

ROB WAS STANDING by the sofa. The machines on the coffee table had fallen over. "I'm not being pulled," he announced without explanation. "I'm being channeled. I *am* a channel. Empty as a flute."

Thomas stood up beside him. He had felt something like a movement of air, and at the moment Rob's overgrown hair was blowing in some unknowable wind. "Someone is using you?" He reached out for Rob's arm, but missed somehow.

"That's not the problem. It's ... who? Who? I should know!"

And it may have been an illusion, but it seemed to Thomas that he could see through Rob, even as he stood there, wearing jeans and a sweatshirt.

"It's happening again," said Rob, and now his voice was too calm. His attitude was more curious than alarmed. He was listening. "And now. Again."

TONIO NEXT JUMPED MORE PEOPLE. He didn't attempt to ask them to touch hands. He made a circle of his intent and he prayed and he jumped them into the camp. No one seemed to land on top of anyone else and he was somehow not afraid they would. He came back to the side of the old man, who now had his hand over his heart and was wheezing. Tonio included the old man in his next flock of intent. It went as before.

There were shots from outside the building. It was automatic fire, and incredibly loud. Tonio raised his arms and included everyone he could see inside the building.

Now screaming rang inside the refugee camp also. Tonio didn't have time to sort it out. He went back.

"GOT IT!" sang Rob with complete conviction and Thomas

reached for him, knowing he was about to disappear. He reached right through him.

Thomas Sullivan could think on his feet like few other human beings. Before his arm had finished its useless grab he was moving. Running. Out of the house and toward the horse stables.

———

TONIO STOOD by the doorway now, as the old man had been, looking wildly into the room. Looking for anyone missed. His ears were singing, singing. He found he was breathing in tight, hard gasps. There was only the dim light from a corner of the steel roof which had recently been bent up. Behind him the chatter and the thunder of guns made it impossible to think.

Then something else moved in front of his eyes, which were stinging with sweat. He wiped them with his hands, which were dirty, and that made things worse. But the disturbance resolved itself into a form he recognized, and a different air was passing in front of his face.

Tonio found he was looking at the face of Rob MacAulay, only Rob was not quite all there, which made some sense, because Tonio didn't feel he was altogether "there" either. Tonio reached out but felt nothing and he heard himself saying, "Was it you, then? I thought it was God behind me."

He was talking to himself again. On the coast of Korea, or the coast of Scotland, he was talking to himself.

"It wasn't me who did all this," Rob's voice sang back, softly, but easily heard over all the whine and blasts. "Not at all."

"Ach, then," said Tonio Scala, and it was the last thing he said.

Rob's eyes looked up and beyond Tonio, out the door, and there was a figure with an automatic rifle in its hands running at them. Firing. A blast cut straight across the doorway and cut through Tonio's body at chest level, leaving a row of holes like those in a piece of paper meant to be torn in two. Rob knew nothing about the uniform or the nation of the shooter.

Rob MacAulay came fully into the place and into the moment in time to catch his friend's body as it fell. A response of pure rejection exploded forwards from him, and the figure with the gun sailed away high in the air, tumbling. A number of trees and a shed went down also.

Rob felt Tonio and then felt Tonio's body. They were separate. He dropped the body and dropped his own body and sailed upward after his friend.

And he hit a wall so hard he bounced back into his own form before he had had time to fall.

Rob wailed. He stood in the doorway and rocked left and right and wailed. The ground around the small oratory rolled like a blanket shaken hard.

Everything went down. As in a massive earthquake, the ground liquefied and all the plants and all the little coastal buildings crumbled. The soldiers of two countries were buried up to their knees in an earth finer than sand. The wheels of all the armored vehicles disappeared and then the earth rejected them all again, with a visceral anger. Everything bounced upward and the sea itself retreated as though in fright.

In the little shack, now empty except for Rob and one body, nothing moved. Not even the rising red dust entered.

In that complete scene of horror appeared behind Rob a white man holding on to the neck of a white horse. The horse stood with legs spread stiff and black eyes perfectly round. The man looked about him and his face of stone opened. "Rob!" Thomas shouted.

No answer. The wailing was deafening. Thomas leaped forward and grabbed onto the dark shape in the doorway like a monkey on a man's back, clinging.

"Rob," he whispered, face touching face. "It's over. Let's go home."

Rob MacAulay turned to Thomas and the wailing stopped. He breathed out and out and out as though a set of bagpipes were emptying. He turned and looked around the room. Saw MacBride.

"We take him home," he said to Thomas, reaching down for the body on the floor. He put the remains of Father Antonio Scala on MacBride's back and then they all winked out.

Forgetting Korea. Forgetting two armies. Forgetting all that was unimportant.

———

IT WAS Rob's idea to take them back to where he had last met Tonio: the kitchen of the rectory. MacBride, however, had his own ideas, which were stronger and more sensible. They came to rest in front of the church doors of St. Francis of Assisi, where the horse needn't be bothered by wooden floors and doorways. It was Thomas who took the body from off the horse's back, while Rob tested the church doors.

They opened to him. He had a moment to reflect how little time had actually passed since Father Scala had prayed for help. Minutes. The two of them walked down the aisle of the small church.

Thomas was looking for a respectful place to put Tonio's body, and he chose the flat table at the front, behind the wooden rail.

"Not there!" said Rob, in the remains of his voice. "Don't you dare put him on the altar."

"But it seemed only ..."

"He wouldn't like it one bit," said Rob, his voice breaking twice in the short sentence. "Put him on a pew. No. On the tile floor. That can be more easily washed." Seeing Thomas's eyes look dubiously at him, he added, "It's only a body. Surely as a Buddhist you can see ..."

"I can, yes," answered Thomas, putting the small, lean corpse on the tiles in front of the stairs leading to the altar. "I wasn't sure that you would."

Rob looked down at the somehow meaningless shape, stapled, from the front, with a neat row of holes. He looked up at Thomas's pale grey sweats, ruddy in front and already browning. His face, too, was stained. And his white hair. Rob, who had somehow escaped the blood, sat himself in the foremost pew.

"I never thought about him. Not as I should have done. He spent two years saving me from people who would kill me, wangled new hands for me, hid me in his cellar, and then had the incredible nerve to force me to confront my own nature. And I never thought of him, except as a simple friend." He had to clear his throat a few times to finish this statement.

Thomas thought of a half-dozen things to say in response, but said none of them. They sat in silence for neither of them knew how long until the air in the church aisle sparked and Jack Benneli was standing there, holding the sleeve of his mother Sophia in his hand. Young Jack seemed to have grown a good deal in the few months since they had seen him last. "I told you, Mama. I told you," he was shouting.

Sophia looked down at the mistreated body of her priest and she began to weep. This set Rob off, and soon all of them, even Thomas, were crying soundlessly in the church. Rob never knew who finally told Sophia what had happened, if anybody.

"What do we do with him?" Sophia asked. "Does Antonio, of all of us, not even get a funeral mass?"

Rob cleared his throat again. "Amongst my own people. Islanders. Funeral masses sometimes had nothing to do with the bodies. My own parents, for example. The question is—

how many people do we want to trust, or to burden, with a secret of this size?"

She thought about it. "But how can we bury him? The techniques of the police these days ..."

"Oh, I can bury him," said Rob quietly.

This time it was Rob who carried the body out. Out to the churchyard. MacBride, his back still stained with brown, scraped a spot with his front right hoof. And Rob stood there and asked of the earth to open.

He had never asked such a thing before, but the earth did open. Not in the way the earth had responded to a different Rob in Korea, but decorously it split open, making a deep grave between old headstones. Sophia had spent the time washing the body; she insisted it be her to do it. She wrapped it in his single, spare bedsheet. Rob lowered the body without touching it—one more small skill he had never known he possessed.

And as Jack had been an altar boy in past years, he knew where to find the book that contained the burial service. His mother spoke the words. After, she said, "First, he thought that the rules of the priesthood would be changed. Quickly. When that didn't happen, he planned to leave it. But one thing happened, and then another, and we both grew older. And this was it. This was worth the whole wait. At least it was for him."

Then Rob allowed the earth to fill in the deep grave. Even the scrub grass from before was replaced, undisturbed.

As they walked away, Sophia said, "I'll have to wash the floor in there."

"I've taken care of that," said Rob in a murmur.

"How? Oh, never mind," she said.

Jack wanted strongly to ring the bell. Only one aged bell hung in the small belfry, inherited from a much older church, but he thought it only right to ring it now.

"Tomorrow, Jacomo. Tomorrow, when people notice the priest is missing, you can ring the bell."

"And how will anyone ever know what he did for those people in Korea? How he died?"

"Do you think he'd care?" It was Thomas who spoke.

As the sun's light was fading the two men and one horse left for Massachusetts, leaving the little church, the new grave, and this small congregation—or family—behind. The sea wind had faded and the land breeze of the night was beginning over the North Sea.

BEFORE EIGHTEEN HOURS HAD PASSED, the world news-streams were dubbing the strong and highly localized trembler on the central Korean coast as "The Fortunate Catastrophe." Or, in the US, "The Lucky Break-Up." Two squadrons of armies had been rendered unable to fight, or even to move. One US aircraft carrier and a battleship had been rocked by the tsunami and, more importantly, their communication systems had broken down. All communication systems had broken down at the same time except the satellite feeds, and they were, at first scan, unreliable in what they showed. Experts on the major news droned on about possible wave-length interference, but they were not given much time on air, considering the human effects of the event.

No one could establish a death toll from the earthquake, because neither the Russian Government nor the rogue Chinese would give out their own numbers. And the death toll of the progress of the two forces was so easy to slide into that of the natural disaster, that it was a given that neither army had killed an innocent soul. The earth had done it all.

27

Interlude

T he "earth" sat on the piano stool in the Sullivan
house and invented simple songs for his own amusement, experimenting with the flavor of the bass
harmonies it was now easy for him to invent. He still liked
open fifths over complete chords, but wasn't strong about it
anymore.

The "earth" seemed to feel no guilt for what he had done
in Korea. Thomas Sullivan, who had burnt his grey sweats in
the fireplace, watched the "earth" for any symptoms of breakdown. Of PTSD, at least. But Rob seemed to exhibit none.
He did weep frequently, and silently, but did not seem to be
what Thomas thought of as depressed.

Thomas nudged himself onto the piano bench next to
Rob. He took over the left-hand side of some of the simple
pieces, which made them much more complex. And the two
spoke to each other with some eloquence in that manner for at
least an hour.

Then Thomas said, "What now, Rob?" He didn't know
what sort of answer he would get to the question: physics,
alchemy, magic, dinner?

Rob put his hands in his lap and smiled at Thomas. It was the first real smile out of Rob in a long time.

"Now," he whispered. "Now we teach the children, of course."

28

Shimmer

" the leaves are filled with children ..."
—T.S. Eliot

Professor Robert MacAulay discussed, one more time, his "marks," the camera direction, and background with his consultant.

This was supposed to be the first of a series of talks called The Nature of Reality, addressed to children. His idea that it would therefore be simple had been quickly shaken out of him. "You've gotta remember, Rob, that you're not talking to people like yourself, or even like me. You're talking to kids."

He brought down his dark arched eyebrows. "I've always tried not to talk down to anyone. How can I know what a person, of any age ...?"

"I know. I do know, Rob. You like to include everyone and that usually works for you." She patted his arm soothingly. "But this is a video and you have only one shot to make yourself understood.

"And what I'm saying has nothing to do with your

message. Just the background. You can't just sit in a chair—
like now—and expect kids to keep following what you say."

Like now consisted of the two of them sitting on a *chaise
lounge* in the east hallway of the Sullivan house, with the outer
wall a row of arched windows looking out onto the garden,
where the leaves of the trees were half-gone and the sculpture
of the branches made such a dramatic backdrop that it
seemed to Rob that this hall, itself, might be such a huge
image that his little bit of teaching might get lost.

"What, exactly, do you want me to do? I am just talking
about atomic structure. Or I hope to be."

The consultant shifted against the upholstery of the chair,
sighed, and looked over at the older woman with the notebook. "I know. I know. It doesn't have to do with your words.
It's the twelve-second rule."

As Rob opened his mouth to inquire, she continued, "Oh,
I know it used to be the thirty-second rule, but things are
moving faster these days."

He just shook his head, blankly.

"If you don't have something different to focus on, the eye
stops seeing things."

Despite his long training not to loom over people smaller
than he was, Rob found he was looming over her. She didn't
seem to mind. "I do know something about that. Perception,
though. It's about the eye's perception. Not simply paying
attention."

She shrugged. Rolled her eyes. It was a familiar gesture to
Rob. "Can't you even use a green-screen?"

Rob looked out the window again. "I've never liked the
appearance of those. Besides, they are expensive, and we're
doing six of these videos at once, just to minimize expense."

"But you've *got* the money. I know it!"

The woman on the other side of the hallway stood. "Breton! That's enough. That was beyond enough! You apologize
to Rob."

Rob put up both of his hands to placate Athena Kaye. The autumn sun seemed to glow through his pale fingers. "No, 'Thena. No. Tony's doing exactly what I asked of her. I needed the viewpoint of someone closer in age to my audience, and I got it."

Athena slammed shut her notebook. "Well, I hope you're not going to take it!"

He smiled and rubbed one hand through Tony Kaye's hair. "Not in every detail. No."

And he didn't mention to the mother that, at that time, anyone named Tony might have been as rude to Rob MacAulay as they liked.

THE NEXT DAY was colder and bore occasional driving rain. Thomas watched and listened as Rob chatted with his script consultant, who was considerably older than Breton Kaye. It amused Thomas to watch Rob in this role. It was so much as he had first seen him—in a video—and Rob seemed so experienced at it. And so patient. Thomas sat on the piano bench and tried to follow the conversation. As the videos were being done in bits, the first through the sixth being intermixed, there seemed to be much confusion—at least to Thomas. Rob was saying carefully, bending down to the neat young fellow in the sport jacket "Yes, I want that bit: 'Physics, mathematics, music, and magic. I have been able to find no clear distinction in the fields.' I am not adding a bit of inappropriate humor here. It will make sense in the end. People who have followed my arguments will understand what I mean."

The young fellow was obviously not convinced. But then, it was not his job to be convinced. It was his job to make the script flow, and it wasn't so much of a job, because Rob could make his words flow without any help whatsoever. Thomas found it all wonderfully amusing, and he needed amusement badly right now. He needed to see his own Rob looking so composed—so competent. Much as he had first seen him. And first loved him. He only hoped the weather would make some outdoor scenes possible. Rob was always at his best outdoors.

———

AS IT TURNED OUT, the first day of filming was brilliantly clear. A breeze blew from the west, and those leaves that still remained on the trees sailed through the air in the same direction. This seemed to bother the chief cameraman, but it did not bother Rob, nor Thomas. There were some neighborhood children sailing over the fence also, and when Thomas paced over to see what was happening, he found them being disciplined in almost martial fashion by Tony Kaye. He picked her out from the crowd of them by her red knit cap. Thomas, on impulse, opened the wrought-iron gate.

"Don't get in the way," he said, in a whisper. The response to his words was a complete, obedient silence. Even Tony shut up. But the children moved in, one by one, like so many birds approaching a newly-filled feeder. And as he walked away he felt he had done something right, like a cook adding the perfect spice to a dish in preparation. Children were necessary, here.

A battery of lights were being placed, some of them on quiet drones. These, the wind knocked out of place. The tall ones also fell over in the occasional gust. A woman with a light meter was turning in a complete circle, shrugging. And Thomas saw the lights turned off. It seemed the sunlight was perfect, at least for the moment.

And here came Rob himself, dressed in the grey sport-jacket Thomas had had made for him. It looked stretched out of shape already, but any other look would have not been Rob

MacAulay. And he was wearing blue jeans. That had been Thomas's idea.

The haircut had also been Thomas's idea. He had merely mentioned to Rob that it would be better for him to get the hair out of his eyes, so that he could see. And he had brought in an expensive stylist from the West Coast, to create out of the overgrown mop a more stylish overgrown mop. The man had done it in the kitchen.

The guy said—to Thomas, not to Rob—that it was a good idea to let the hair try to conceal Rob's outstanding ears, and also the uncommon shape of them, so that it wouldn't distract from the fact that he was doing a documentary.

"A tutorial," Thomas had corrected him.

"Whatever." Then the expensive stylist sighed. "I just wish you'd let me *use* those eyes. That face."

"For what?"

The fellow scratched his nose. Then chuckled. "I could make him such a good—a good elf, or something. Wouldn't even need to use make-up."

"Don't," said Thomas. "Don't think of it."

Rob had never even asked for a mirror, to see the result of all the work. And the expensive stylist had refused to be paid, except for his travel. Wouldn't think of it.

The entire film crew had approached the project with the same overly respectful attitude. As though working for a man with the peculiar history of Rob MacAulay was an honor. Thomas wondered just how long that attitude would last, once confronted by Rob's certain and unconventional ideas of filming.

ROB KNEW a bench that seemed good. An old park bench which had been lifted and put down over the open path that led to the north end of the property. It was that same path

Rob MacAulay had once ridden Kinsman along on a night in the spring. A path that had not led to the north end of the property at all. Not on that night.

But when Rob placed himself on the bench his knees stuck up distractingly. It was simply too low a bench. While the staff buzzed around, cursing the delay, Rob stood again and ambled into the shrubbery.

"Here," he sang out from behind a hazel bush. And they found him sitting on one of the boulders that marked the retreat of the last ice age, and which Thomas's aunt had refused to allow to be dug out so many years ago. It was of surprisingly perfect height and shape to fit Rob's long, bony legs. It also looked totally right. Around it was enough cleared ground that they could carry or hover the equipment in.

It was a perfect little bower, covered by an oak on one side and a red maple on the other. The woman with the light meter did her little dance and mumbled again.

"There are still leaves falling? What do you expect us to do on the second take?" asked the lead cameraman, who was beginning to feel both irritated and unappreciated. "Or on the tenth, if we need a tenth?"

Rob smiled at him, as an oak leaf fell by his shoulder. Someone in the crew felt impelled to take a photo of that. Thomas heard the click. "Ah! I don't expect miracles of you, sir. Just do what you can with what you've got here."

So they began. By Rob's insistence, the first shot was to be the first line of the first script. He had asked for that much sanity in the procedure. He leaned forward and focused on the nose of the camera, as though it were a person.

"Children," he said softly, heard both by the surrounding people and by the concealed mic in his jacket. "Girls and boys. All of us.

"I want to talk to you today about the thing you hear about called Physics. The thing I like to call the nature of reality. Of what is real."

He rested his elbows on his knees and drew his large hands together, making a loose cup. "I've always found, myself, that what I know to be real changes from day to day. As we grow up, we all find that to be true. We learn things, but we never learn the last thing. There is always something new.

"So," and he bent his head forward, regarding his own empty hands for a moment. "Let's start with something simple. Something simpler than ... oh, than this leaf falling now."

And there was a leaf falling now. A bright red maple leaf. This was not according to the script, but Rob had paid no attention to the glowing script-reader beside the camera.

"And much simpler than the eyes we have, that are looking at the leaf."

Thomas, standing to one side, wondered what the cameras were doing with those huge eyes half hidden now behind the hair that had fallen forward with the dip of Rob's head. Better not to think of that at all.

"Your teachers might have told you that an atom is a simple thing. They weren't quite right in that, but it wasn't their fault. A teacher has to start somewhere. So we can start with an atom."

In Rob's cupped hands was now a small glowing thing like a sun. And around it was a wave of light that moved in and out as it circled the sun. And then another joined it. They were not all sunny yellow. There were all sorts of colors in that little shape. And they shimmered.

The camera kept running, and the crew members looked from one to another, each wondering what memo they themselves hadn't received. Rob's face was glowing softly from the reflected light in his hands. At least, Rob's face was glowing.

They didn't need a tenth take of the scene. Nor a second. In fact, they went farther than expected on the first day of filming.

There were children in the bushes, but no one was aware

of them until much later in the edit process. And Rob did have the final say in what was released.

⊏==⊐

THE FIRST VIDEO was released without cost to the viewer, as soon as could be practically done. Long before the first snowfall.

Some groused that a Nobel Prize winner should be using so much CGI in a teaching video, but not many. It was so obviously for children.

The video did not go viral, as was hoped. It went everywhere.

About the Authors

R.A. MacAvoy published her first novel in 1983. All others she has published since then can be found online, along with awards she has won or for which she was nominated.

She studied various martial arts, starting at the age of eleven, but is no longer any sort of lethal weapon.

She has raised and educated ponies and horses and been educated by them.

She dived the waters of the Pacific Ocean, which was an experience as close to being in outer space as she is likely ever to know.

She has been married to Ron Cain longer than she has been publishing books.

She is uncomfortable speaking of herself in the third-person.

Nancy L. Palmer tells stories in words and pictures, and has done so as long as she can remember. She has looked carefully at small things and carelessly at large things until she's quite certain there's no difference really, and no space between them either.